Many thanks to Dick Halbert and Linda Ahlswede-Cox for their help and support

More titles by Ann Ahlswede

Day of the Hunter
Hunting Wolf
The Savage Land

What readers say about the work of author
Ann Ahlswede

A most enjoyable read...A compelling tale of villainy, revenge, and redemption set in the American West following the Civil War, this is a beautifully written story of a man's struggle with loss and outrage and paid – "one man's feeble testament for justice." It is also a tale of delightfully crafted characters of the West and their adventures through the gold fields of Colorado and beyond – and beautiful descriptive passages of the stark, unspoiled beauty of the post-Civil War West. A book to enjoy and a book to challenge one's notions of injustice and revenge.

Hunting Wolf... Hey! This is NOT a book about hunting for wolves. On publication it was well reviewed and went into several editions, including school-use additions. It's a tale of average people and gross injustice set in historic times. It's a good, solid read.

Hunting Wolf... This novel of the gold country West by Ann Ahlswede, as in her other novels, is a gripping example of how character and story development should be done in the writing of fiction. We are given, in beautifully sculpted descriptions, a violent injustice and the subsequent raw emotions of rage and hatred and a driving compulsion for revenge – with a challenging resolution. We are also given compassion and the beauty of the American West. Ms. Ahlswede's *Day of the Hunter* and *The Savage Land* will please as well.

THE LAST ENEMY

Texas– 1843

Ann Ahlswede

❧❧

PART I

SOMEWHERE IN THE COMANCHERIA

ঔৼৢ৵

The boy pressed down into the hot ground, tasting the dust in his mouth. He hoped they couldn't see him this time. The small half-cup of water he had taken from the spring, drip-by-drip, left a taste of moss and earth; and now he was waiting for the cup to fill again. He would take it to the woman.

He pressed down harder and shut his eyes; though he knew they were out there somewhere. He heard little sounds, a crackle of breaking brush, a soft faraway grunt, then stillness, not even the sound of a bird.

Stillness. He almost slept. He was tired. He was starving.

In drifting reverie, he thought of the woman. The words she spoke so softly from the books, night after night, until there was no more oil for the lamp.

Remember. Remember.

He thought of her dress, pale worn flowers, thin, so thin and threadbare he could see her arm, her shoulder. But the remembered words, the magic, the unraveling magic of words, taking him away, away. He thought of the questions he could never answer.

Where? Where are we? How can we go away? Why can't she walk?

He remembered that night when the big panther cat prowled on the roof, scratching, scratching to get in, hungry; he remembered the cat's screaming and growling; the woman's terror, his own. Then silence. He remembered she crawled up there the next morning. What could she fix? Old dry torn shingles full of blown sand? He remembered she'd slipped away, off and down to the hard earth.

He worried about the panther cat. He worried that she'd hurt something in the fall.

She couldn't walk.

Two days later, she'd touched his face, as though measuring, as though her fingers might remember.

You are a canny boy, she'd told him with a smile, but he wasn't sure what that meant.

You are like a good plough horse, you'll do, you'll do well, she'd said, and smiled again even as he almost laughed because it was a joke. They both knew he wanted to think of racing horses and soaring birds.

Then she'd said; *now you must go. You must tell them.*

How far away was the Colony? The nearest farm? Why had his father left taking the wagon and the horse, but so long ago? Never came back.

They waited. *Maybe an accident, maybe the Indians. Nothing.*

You must tell them.

He knew the woman called him Jack and Son. He knew he was around nine or ten years old, maybe younger, but he didn't care. And he didn't care about his other name. He had other urgent concerns. All the frogs were gone. The spring had dried. There were no corn cobs left in the dry field, no squash, no pumpkins; they had eaten the last sweet potatoes. The man, his father, had left. When? Long, long. There was no food now, after summer. A long time. Nothing for the woman to preserve for winter, she'd said. He'd killed all the small things he could find. He couldn't catch the birds.

The silence of the birds told him.

They were nearby.

Those. The faces that sometimes looked at him these past days. The faces that blended into the dry brush, watching, watching. Then gone. He was unimportant.

Then back. Sometimes he heard the distant ringing of a bell, far away, carried on the wind for a breath; sometimes he smelled smoke, just for a moment. He would need to go tomorrow, when he had enough spare water; walk for a day back to the first farm on the trace road, overgrown now, back to the Colony. Help, help for the woman.

He smelled the smoke again, stronger. Bitter.

He lifted his head. Wake up. Go on. He pushed the tin cup against the drippings of the spring, against a bit of drying moss that gave him its dank smell. A bit of relief from heat and dust. Not enough.

Drought, his father had once said.

Then he heard the strong breaking of brush, careless breaking, no stealth. Careless noise. He lifted his head further and saw the face; round, ugly, scarred from a recent pestilence, intent, painted, dark as old leather. Curious intent eyes, staring, staring. His heart pounded, raced suddenly into his throat.

Now it was over, he thought. Hiding was over.

He had no weapon but a dry stick. It would break. Maybe a stone. In dull panic he thought of the water, the woman. But he had nothing. He stood slowly, sandy hair like a mane, his gray eyes blinking and scowling; a spark of fierce resolve rising. He was thin and slow. He was very deliberate. He turned his back to the staring face. He pulled down his baggy pants and leaned over, showing his boy's buttocks. All he had.

The laughter broke across the bird silence. The man's laughter, joined with others.

And it was over.

They took him away, only him. Behind him, the roil of smoke moved with manic energy, turning the sky suddenly black. Wind and the column of smoke where the cabin stood.

His mother.

Where the woman waited for her cup of water.

He fought, his fierce resolve spending itself in the grip of hard arms; thick animal smells; and words he heard, but had never heard before; like animal sounds. Then a hard discipline of pain, hard, and nothing left.

It was over.

They played with her quilt, tossing it, wrapping themselves in it, laughing. They drank from her old tin cup, they made jokes, he knew, but he couldn't understand. They played with the books and he watched; watched to see who carried them; who tore pages to make cigarettes; who laughed at the pictures. They coveted her fork, her knife. They draped their horses with her old dresses. They had found almost no food; just scraps they threw away. They had taken her kitchen knife. They took everything easily carried and seemed in no hurry, without fear of the Colony down that long trace road where the smoke billowed far away.

They will come. Help us. They will know---.

But by the smoke, by the easy leisure of these wild men, he knew that no one would follow. There would be no rescue, no fight. These dark men just laughed, and looked ahead in anticipation. Soon others came; other dark men joined them from the far-away smoke; raising their old muzzle-loading weapons; their painted shields and lances, with rough shouts of triumph. They were mostly young, except for one old man who was painted and adorned with feathers and booty. He had two severed, white, hands attached to his saddle and his horse wore paint in white circles and stars, jagged lightning lines. Another tied a rag around his arm; twisting the rag to stop blood from pouring in pretty red spurts. Two wild men had wet hanks of hair hanging from sticks; another had a wet bundle of pale hair attached to his horse's jaw bridle.

4

And then, Jack saw the captives, the other captives; two children with round, white, blank, and dirty faces, lost in shock. One boy, maybe older than Jack, soft looking, a town boy, his clothes filthy and torn; one girl, in a blowing rag of a dress, yellow hair tangled, younger than Jack. He saw all the horses, some heavy, for the plough and the wagon; and the mules, kicking, biting; men yelling, laughing, with their new riches, in a bedlam of happy thievery from the Colony. This was just a simple raid for horses and captives, but Jack didn't know that. He didn't know how such things worked among these kinds of terrible people. His heart raced, beating so hard that he might fall beneath the churning hoofs. He thought they would hurt him in some way, kill him; but, the man who laughed let him go. He jumped up, onto his painted pony's back, and seemed to melt into the crude saddle, padded with buffalo-hide. He reached down and jerked at Jack, dragging him up before him with grunts of ugly word sounds. Jack tried to get away as the horse bolted and turned in tight circles, but then he just hung on. The man's body was slippery with sweat and grease and paint, and Jack hung on to the horse's mane, his fingers in a tangle. He thought of struggling, more fighting; His eyes were wet with grief, angry that the woman was dead. Surely, she was dead and he was leaving her there in that smoke and burning fire. He yelled because he saw it was hopeless. He wept hiddenly in his rage. But this dark man, the man who laughed at him, just tightened his grip. He wore a bonnet with feathers of red and gray. He called out and raised his shield and the others stared, their dark faces changed. Then they turned, all of them gathering and herding horses and mules ahead, toward the trees without leaves, along the dry creek and the old animal trails, heading south, away from the settlement, away from the smoke and ringing bells. Away from the Colony where others like Jack might still be alive to follow, to help, to know.

But soon, as the day turned to dusk and the sky grew gray and heavy with the smell of rain, they went fast into the darkness, a long way from the smoke and the colony.

Before dawn they came to an encampment where other dark wild people greeted them with what sounded like happy grunts and shouts of welcome. There were young boys herding horses; camp dogs barking. Women hurried forward to take the shields of the returning men, carrying them high above the ground, never letting them touch the earth, to display them by brush shelters. Jack, pushed off the laughing man's pony, fell. He stood, wobbling, not knowing what to do, where to go, what would happen next. He might have slept for scant moments during the long night ride; or the laughing man might have held him on the horse. Now he just stared as the daylight came, the hard shock of the night in his face. The women gathered around him with angry faces, but the laughing man chased them away and pushed him to the shelter where his shield hung. He slumped down and tried not to sleep, but hunger and thirst and fear made sleep a deep refuge. Then when the sun was half-high he awoke to the smell of smoke and meat. These wild people had butchered one of the slow farm horses, and now were feasting on the burnt red flesh and drinking from buffalo paunch water skins. A woman wearing layers of animal skins, with fringes, came to him and threw down a piece of the meat and a water skin. She stood staring down at him, clutching a blanket around her shoulders in the cool morning; her face hard and watchful. Jack gulped the strange tasting water; and then the wonderful rich smells and the cramping of his stomach took him and he ate the half-raw meat.

He knew now, with water, with food that awakened his mind, with the hope that he would live a day, another day that these people must be the wild Comanche or the Kiowa people, or maybe the Apache, wild people he had heard the men in the Colony talk about sometimes in the past. They were also called savages, and damned Indians and filthy heathens and fucking red devils and other names. The Colony men spoke with anger, but with caution, and what sounded like a reverent dread. They spoke of the hardships of starting farms with crude tools, free land, the weather. They told terrible stories about captives, terrible deaths, horrible mutilations, what to do, how to fight, save and protect their people, their livestock, their crops and their new place in the wild open land where everything was still half built, half ploughed, half planted and withering in a drought. The corn crop dried, dead, the kitchen cabbages and turnips, pumpkins, root crops gone to varmints. No rain. The cabin, his mother's place just salvaged wood and logs but still unfinished, a barn started but undone, the promised spring water that dried up, the cow long since killed by prairie wolves, no game nearby, too far away from the Colony, or any colony. Farmers. Promises.

He understood now why he'd seen all the smoke, of course; and heard that very faint knelling of a bell; and how the children had been stolen away so easily.

Now the rain came, softly at first, months late for the people left back in the Colony. If there were any people left. Here, Jack watched the man who had stolen his mother's books tear the magic pages and crumple them, to stuff inside his shield. Here, the women gathered up the camp, packing away blankets, meat, dried fruit, whatever they prized.

A group of men broke away to the west, with horses and loot; and the little girl captive tied on top of a packed mule, her pale hair wild and her dress torn. Jack watched her go and thought he would never see her again. Jack and the town boy stayed with the laughing man's band, tied to restive mules. The wild boys with dirty faces and jeering cries herded the horses and mules. Women led the pack animals. They rode in the rain, always south. The town boy wept.

Jack, surrounded with human beings, ugly wild human creatures lost in a vast unknown, unknowable wilderness, knew he was alone.

Days passed, with sun and then heat. Green grass blades pushed from the earth in little spears, and small wildflowers began to bloom, even so late in the season. They would wilt and die soon as the big cottonwood trees in the gullies and canyons turned a dusty yellow. But the brief grass shoots nourished the animals with new strength. Jack sometimes thought about his mother, about what he had to remember, urgent pictures in his head, sounds of her voice, words from the books, and where he would keep the memories, away from the frantic scramble of new, dire information that, when he made a mistake, earned him a blow. He sometimes helped the wild boys with the horses, he jumped to obey the laughing man's hard-faced woman with cooking or packing or anything she fancied. He was not allowed to talk to the town boy. He was not allowed to go alone to gather wood.

The wild men sometimes stared at the child captives. They would ride by on their shaggy paint ponies and stare, and sometimes sounds like words passed between them and the laughing man. Sometimes the women stared and then quickly looked away. Jack came to understand that he and the town boy must appear ugly and strange, their bodies pale as the bellies of the dead fish in the bad water they had passed that day. Burned by the sun, they were still different. They sniffed to see if the captives smelled, they made faces and mimicked the town boy's whimpering.

But Jack, by some alchemy of shock and shrewdness, did not whimper.

Then, on a blustery morning with the fall moon fading in a pale sky and cottonwood leaves blowing through the camp, Jack heard the camp dogs snarling and barking behind them. He saw that the town boy had gone.

Another band joined them, coming from the south, wild men, more and more coming together with greetings and ritual gestures, their hands covering their faces. Some of these dark men had a different look. Many had sickness scars on their faces. They led packhorses and mules laden with plunder from the villages south of the big river, packs of chilies and corn and dried fruits and sheep carcasses wrapped in hides, and other meats, woven blankets, calico, books and copper pots, everything, and they carried seven young girls and children, unhurt, guarded, taken away as easily as the food looted from those far *ranchos* and Mexican schools in the south. They drove mules and horses, not like the Colony horses but smaller shaggy ponies. And they carried a youth, maybe a shepherd, and an older man with soft hands. They looked like the Mexican people Jack had once seen working the Colony fields of the few prosperous farmers. They looked beaten, starved, afraid.

Jack watched and did the work the woman ordered, with her harsh words and gestures. She wanted more buffalo chips, more wood gathered by women and girls of the band, the others always watching him. Jack wondered why the two men were kept separate. But that night, camped by a stream under old cottonwoods and pecans, he watched the dark visitors sink a great thick stake into the ground, dry wood that would burn easily. The two captive men fell to their knees. They were dragged to the stake and tied, the women piled wood all around them and then threw burning branches into the dry old wood.

Everyone sang. Drummers beat a steady drumming. They danced. The men called out stories of their deeds, their raids, their heroism, their grievances. The two burning men screamed but were quickly silent, gone far away from the fire.

Jack shuddered. His heart thumped like the heavy drumbeats. Life seemed to rush away from him at the sight. Then, he looked at the burning wood only, at the trees along the stream, at the leaves falling and then flying up in the hot night wind of the fire, as though seeking escape. Everywhere the night was black, except for that pillar of fire, and filled with lurking death. He understood the lesson here very well.

He learned much later, after he had begun to understand the harsh words he heard all around him, that Comanche men had raided the Colony, angry at the ploughed earth, the buffalo grass destroyed, and looking for horses and captives in payment.

Now the Kiowas came, comrades, brothers to these Comanches, but these wild men covered their faces in greeting. So cruel and cunning, they rode the raiding trails in the Comancheria only with permission.

They traveled on, a large number now travelling a worn, well known trail. The hunters brought back antelope and deer butchered into wet hides. The nights grew colder. They came to a trail that opened into a deep canyon with rocky escarpments; below the cliffs were many bare trees and running water reflecting the sky. The dark people smiled and made happy sounds. They paused, while the men painted their faces black to show that they came victoriously into the canyon, with captives and packs of bounty and many horses. Then they rode down into the canyon as a chill wind blew above the escarpment, but down into this canyon, this winter home place where no cold wind blew and where the coming snows would pass over them.

Jack saw peaked tents made of animal skins, brush arbors, walking trails, long flats of green grass for the herds, fires and thin pillars of smoke. There were more skin lodges than he could count, hundreds more than he could imagine. More living places and people than he had ever seen, all along the meandering river and sheltered under the escarpment. He saw no strife, only order, in this huge encampment. He saw children with dogs, chasing each other. Again, he felt the sudden emptiness of loss, he was lost forever from his own people and buried here among this wild multitude.

The mad Kiowa woman, Ekopadl, had a prophetic dream and tried to kill Jack with a skinning knife, as he slept that first night. The police warriors carried her away to her own family, according to their mysterious laws. His rags of clothing were taken from him; and now he wore only a breechcloth, belted at his waist and a torn, poorly cured, skin shirt. He had a scrap of old blanket for the snow, and hardy moccasins with rawhide soles. He obeyed and was allowed to sleep, huddled by the lodge opening where the cold seeped through. Slowly he learned that he was a slave now, he must work hard until he became a bother, to throw away; or a boy worthy enough to be adopted by his owner; or an object to trade. He was sometimes the butt of rages against him, his kind.

Tejano! Tejano!

But the smiling man held him safe from serious harm. Now and then, the mad woman fouled his food or woke him with hot coals in the night.

After a time, the smiling man took him to a big skin lodge with painted drawings around the entrance. A war shield hung on a rack near the door, a war lance had hair dangling from its shaft, a good bay pony grazed nearby at the end of a long hide rope. An older woman with unbraided hair that fell down her back and a small tattoo near her left eye, knelt as she worked to scrape an antelope hide of all its fat and flesh. Her face was round, dark, angry, when she looked up at Jack. She spat a word he didn't understand.

An elder man sat against a backrest on a blanket in the sun, enjoying the thin winter heat. He set aside a fringed leather scabbard decorated with drawings and beads. The scabbard held a long bone-handled metal knife. He handled the knife with a certain respect, even reverence. His hair was black, parted in the center, with the part painted red. Long and unbraided, his hair shined with oils and held ornaments of charms and feathers. The scalp lock at the top of his head had been carefully braided and bore a long black eagle's feather. He was older, but not old. His eyes burned with intelligence, with calculation, as the smiling man approached. He wore a soft antelope skin, finely beaded shirt, so long that it would fall below his knees when he stood. Patches of long hair were sewn into the fringes, hair of many colors, pale yellow, red, but mostly black. His face was dark, finely lined, bronzed, untroubled, very watchful. He smoked a gray stone pipe and talked quietly with a youth sitting at his side.

The smiling man spoke to the elder man with great respect and waited for a greeting. Finally it came, a mild sounding word, and the smiling man pushed Jack forward. A flurry of words and gestures followed, all sounding ordinary to Jack, voices of men conversing, maybe bargaining, agreeing. The elder man nodded, then smiled at a shared bit of story, as though sharing a joke. The youth beside the elder man, who seemed to Jack to be some sort of leader, stood and looked a greeting glance at Jack. But there was something wrong. This youth, taller than Jack, older, was badly made, a shoulder twisted, an arm bent, a leg that hardly held his weight. Yet he smiled. His face was smooth, unblemished, exotically handsome, his slanted black eyes friendly, his nose thin, his mouth shy and mobile with the smile.

The smiling man spoke sternly to Jack. Jack could not understand a word, although he knew exactly what the words meant.

Now you are his property. You must obey. You must forget everything else. Your people are gone. We are your people.

I am Pony Boy, the youth told Jack. He looked down at his broken body, *but I call myself Ghost Boy.*

Two seasons passed, almost without notice, and the boy sometimes now called *Tejano*, lived on and grew. He knew the language now. He knew many of the rules of behavior, the everyday customs, even the custom of eating raw animal flesh that made his stomach heave; but his face reminded the Comanche people of their most hated enemies.

Tejano.

He became the companion of Owl Stands' frail, gentle-spirited youngest son by his favorite Comanche wife, who had recently gone, taken by the Supernaturals with a coughing sickness and whose name could never be spoken again. The youth called Pony Boy, and sometimes Ghost Boy, had been broken in a horse accident when his racing pony stumbled in a prairie dog hole. The healers and old men and women with strong medicine had done their best to put him right. But he walked badly and his arm could not draw a bow. He loved music and poetry more than he loved the bow and the lance, and he made fine arrow points from flint and obsidian in the old way the village craftsmen had taught him. He liked the music made when he twisted bits of metal and little bells in his moccasin fringes and took his halting steps. All the people could hear the soft clatter of his walking, hear Ghost Boy's laugh at this always-music. He was useful and loved by Owl Stands and his relatives; but scorned by his father's elder Kiowa wife.

This woman, who spat words at Jack and ordered him to tasks whenever she could, had an older son by Owl Stands whose name was Dohat. He had his mother's anger and scorn for *Tejano* captives, but less scorn for the score of Mexican captives in the camp, young boys who had become hardened Comanche fighters and remembered nothing else, and women who were wives with children. But mostly he liked the young girls, especially the youngest ones he caught out alone without their mothers or sisters. These he took sexually, according to custom. No one seemed to care. He watched the older well-guarded girls coming into age for child bearing, and ready to be trained and taken as wives.

Akima, the elder wife, was also called Woman's Mouth. She muttered and complained of the hardness of her life with no other woman to share her burdens, even when Owl Stands traded for new copper cooking pots. As a bride of Kiowa-Apache lineage, she came into the camp and insisted on four lodge poles, in the Kiowa way, when she was lifting Owl Stands lodge at a new campground; but Owl Stands, a man of high rank, gave her his anger and a single blow. She was only a woman. They would live in a Comanche three-pole lodge.

So Akima, Woman's Mouth, began her soft complaints and resentments. But she cured hides well, and made fine tunics with elaborate beadwork for Owl Stands and for herself. She enjoyed sharing Owl Stands sleeping robes at night, and often made guttural sounds that woke everyone.

Her son, Dohat by Owl Stands, that youth with a scowling face and secret eyes, walked like he carried all of her resentment in his heart. This burden he welcomed as a mark of distinction among the other youths of his age.

The Kiowa and Comanche bands met, broke up, scattered, and came together seasonally. The People traveled to the south in the Time When Children Cried, and everyone was hungry in that hard cold and unseasonable snow. They ate the last of their pemmican, even fish baked in clay, and hunted for whatever they could find, small game, and flying creatures. They wintered with friends of the Fish-Eating band, in narrow valleys surrounded with rough hills and distant mountains over which Jack knew he could never pass alone. Not yet.

In the new moon he learned to give thanks to the Power for the changing cycles; for although the old moon died, another always took its place. He would remember, he would say words softly, he would draw words, symbols with a stick in the sand when he was alone.

The Comanches traveled north again, growing fat again with strong meat, traveled east following and herding their buffalo, an endless task to keep them fat in good grass, separate from the other herds and from border thefts by other tribes. The men set out on hunts, hiding from the buffalo behind their ponies. They clung to rawhide cinch straps and held to strong leather loops as they rode; around and around the herd, to keep it milling so that the great beasts were easily killed. Sometimes they walked to the edge of the herd from downwind, before the buffalo noticed them. They shot their arrows, and followed as the young cows faltered and died. The women followed to get chunks of fresh liver, to skin and butcher winter meat and gather hides. Children crowded around, begging for scraps of raw liver and gall and buffalo brains, laughing. They made camps in the oak groves where the children swung from the branches and played in the deep grass; and the women gathered oak bark and acorns and medicinal herbs.

The Comanche bands met for visiting, finding wives, telling stories, trading slaves and food, old pemmican, or what they did not need, for the news from the borders of the Comancheria, their vast and closely guarded sacred buffalo land. Where were the White Dog invaders now? Near what Comancheria border? Where were they tearing up the good grass where buffalo fed since time began?

The bands scattered, waged war against Tonkowa and Apache hunters wandering into the Comancheria. As night approached, captive Apache women's' voices rose sadly, as they chanted their sorrows with the sunset.

The band headed south again, across the big river, for easy captures in Mexican villages and ranchos, for food, weapons, ammunition, and more girls and children; then north against *Tejanos* driving small bunches of cattle or wagons, cutting ruts across the grass of the Comancheria; against White Dog women tending garden patches and White Dog children playing under the elms and pecans along the creeks of the open prairies.

Jack watched other captives brought into the encampment, sometimes bound to stakes, people like himself, but children who cried.

His skin turned dark as the skins of the People in the constantly shifting bands. Some noticed, as his face grew darker, that his eyes grew paler, like ashes. An ugly and unlucky color. Watchful eyes, but dry, as though they had never known everyday tears.

Ugly Tejano.

He did not think he was truly a *Tejano*. Maybe half white, or half Mexican? A White Dog or a Honeytalker? No, under the antelope-hide crotch skins, and tunics he threw aside when he bathed in the streams with other youths, and after studying his white and sun darkened skin, he didn't care what they thought, what they called him. From some deep place in his faintest memory, he believed he knew what he was.

He was used as a companion to Ghost Boy, whose father, Owl Stands, was an important civil chief of high rank, and a historian of the People; a man of great, stern power and authority, a man whom arrows and *Tejano* bullets could not harm, because of his supernatural strength. A courteous man also, generous with his scores of horses and his possessions.

With respect, no man would dare to violate his protection of the *Tejano* boy; although some were puzzled and thought the slave boy was not worth much.

Every warrior in the band sought to be as brave and successful in raids as Owl Stands, now a powerful civil leader, had been in his youth. So this *Tejano* boy, who was reaching an important age among the People, managed to survive.

He learned to relish mustang meat and mule meat when there was no strong buffalo meat, to smoke oak leaf cigarettes with Ghost Boy, to strain scum and insects from the surface of bad water by drinking through handfuls of prairie grass. He served Ghost Boy, brought chunks of obsidian or flint for arrow points when he could find them along the trails, brought fruit and pecan nuts and good water; helped him mount his gentle bay pony, where Ghost Boy seemed to become the young warrior he could never be. When Ghost Boy was busy flaking his arrow-points, Jack tended Owl Stands' herd of horses and mules, both the gentled ponies with the clipped left ears and the wild prairie mustangs. He learned to cling to the backs of the shaggy ponies, and sometimes wrestled and raced with other youths his age, the few who did not scorn him. From the boastful stories of visiting Kiowas, he heard from Dohat that all *Tejanos* would soon be killed; that he would be among the last of his ugly, thieving tribe left on earth. But Dohat was often a liar and liked to make trouble with him. Jack turned his back on Dohat and thought of the woman long ago, never ugly, always soft, but her image often faded. He struggled to remember the words, the long-ago pages of long-ago books.

He learned to draw a short bow of strong wood and sinew, and shoot quickly, to kill small game with his arrows and snares. He learned reverence for the Sun and the meaning of important prayers and legends. Fever swept through the band; but not the terrible sickness that had left the pock scars on the faces of some of the elders. A child died with the coughing fever, twins born to a woman were trampled to death in her rage at their unlucky birth. A young girl died when she went out with the other women to skin a fat buffalo cow and the great cow rose, in a death agony, and hooked her belly on its horns. No amount of prayer nor herbal doctoring nor drawing of witchcraft objects from her body could save her. The family mourned and buried her in a rock crevice, with a proper stone covering, and left her behind as the band moved on.

As the growing boys of the band reached the important age when they were taken away to the training camps, they would learn the horse skills, and the fighting skills, and the duty and fierce passion of Comanche fighters. They learned the cunning ways to steal horses, to fight trespassers into the Comancheria, to take captives for trading, to kill *Tejanos*, who were hated more than even the Mexican Spanish whites whom they often traded with along the Brazos River. At puberty, the girls of the band went away to training camps where experienced women taught them the hard rules; young girls could never walk out alone, or any man or boy in the band was free to attack them with their sex, but there were always girls who welcomed night crawling boys. The women taught them the hard every day work and skills they would have to master to be respected, and worth many horses in a good marriage. They were taught how to cook, and heal, and gentle horses, even to fight like a man, and to bear many children.

Warriors, young men, older men, sent criers through the camp calling for fighters to join them on horse stealing raids or vengeance raids. Sometimes they died far from the People on lonely ridges, in canyons where *Tejano* horse soldiers caught them, or under quiet oaks in quick, small skirmishes. Jack listened to the drumming, the prayers, the weeping of the women, as they slashed their bodies and cut off their hair in grief. More often the men returned with the blackened faces of victory and spoils. The old men gathered with pipes and told stories. Jack listened and learned of the old Dog Days before the Spanish, when only dogs pulled travois poles and the people walked. When they had to leave the old and the sick by the trailside, wrapped in blankets, with a little food and gourds of water, all they could spare. When the elders told stories that were almost lost to memories and that went back from grandfather to grandfather, Jack learned of the bad Spanish days, days when the People became the slaves of the Spanish, and then rebelled for their freedom. He learned of the land far to the north, a land of boiling waters. He learned of origins and the mysterious center of the earth.

But there was the emptiness in him, heavy and hidden. His deepest memories spoke to him in his dreams. When he saw blue soldier coats, worn like trophies, in the dancing over scalps, he knew the coats had come from his own almost forgotten people. The fighters bragged of their kills, their coups; and their women erected scalp poles by their lodges, or sewed scalps into the fringes of beaded shirts.

17

When he was as tall as the boys of thirteen summers, he walked away toward what he could not clearly remember. He ran as the geese fled winter, by instinct to survive.

"How can this be?" Owl Stands asked when the hunters brought him back. His voice was stern, with a knife edge of anger. The old man, who had never touched Jack before, ran his hands over Jack's body and found bruises and the swollen shin bump of a broken leg. "Have I fed you so that you could leave me?" Jack heard arrogance, but also a certain curiosity. "Has some trickster spirit spoken in your ear and caused this foolishness?"

Jack believed he would be thrown away, taken from the camp, as dead captives' bodies and other refuse was dragged beyond the camp, so that the fighting of the dogs and wolves would not bother the People.

"How can this be true when it is this man who saved a boy from the fire?" Owl Stands spoke, his anger suppressed but there, ready for the punishment he must pronounce. He had no trust, no tolerance, only a certain curiosity. Jack was only a *Tejano*. Then he looked at the hunters, at Dohat's scowling smile and the heavy club he held in his hand, at Owl Stands' Kiowa wife's hard face, her satisfaction. Ghost Boy's eyes grew large with respect, with an urgent petition.

He is my friend.

His father, always a fair man who loved his good son more than any other human being, understood.

In the silence that spoke, Jack survived again. The hunters stared at him, gauging his spirit, his penance, his worthiness. Was he so useful that the venerated old man had spared him? How had Owl Stands allowed this? Dohat walked away, anger in his strides.

A woman with the bone healing power tied two good straight wood sticks to Jack's leg and bound it with soft hide, singing her song to encourage healing, accepting Owl Stands' payment. For three days Jack lay under a brush arbor. By day his fingers found the dust and began to draw almost forgotten, nurturing shapes; strange rectangles within rectangles, which somehow meant shelter and safety; round

18

shapes that were not moons nor suns, but shapes that spun. By night he stared up through the openings in the brush arbor, repeating old words, watching spiders spin lofty webbed strands, airy bridges, brave architectures but each morning the webs tore and shattered in the wind.

Learn from our little brothers.

But Jack was not sure what the lesson was meant to teach. Did the spiders live only brave, but futile, lives?

A young girl, poorly dressed and shivering with fear, came to him with poultices and salve of the good black medicine that oozed from the ground. Her fingers touched over him lightly, like the flocks of small birds that moved through the chinaberry thickets. She was a captive Mexican child, at early puberty and already raped many times since her capture. Soon she would be taken as a low-ranking wife, or traded away to anyone with a handful of ammunition or a good striped blanket. She never spoke, she obeyed to survive.

Ghost Boy, so favored by his father, brought morsels of meat or liver, dried fruit, mesquite seed cakes, and flavored water. He came to Jack with the soft bell chatter of his moccasins; and told stories of old days, camp gossip, jokes and laughter. He taught him foolish gambling games to pass away the cold days. Even in his talk of long-ago times, he had not yet spoken of those hated others who looked like Jack, nor the red coated Mexican lancers. Perhaps he had not learned to hate anyone.

On the third night, in a state that was neither sleep nor wakefulness, Jack listened to the prayers, the drumming, and the sacred songs coming from the old man's lodge. Many men sang and performed the sacred peyote rituals. Others were silent. He heard Owl Stands speak of his people, good grass and good hunts. The old men told stories of the past, told over and over from the long ago, wonderful myths, success against countless enemies, anecdotes from before the Spanish days. They marveled again at the story of the great burning rock that fell from the sky. Jack lay very still in the darkness as Owl Stands spoke of the sacred burning rock. Surely it was a powerful sign. Always practical, the wisest among the People still sought the insight of the Supernaturals, the hard-won spiritual wisdom and understanding of their universe, the stars, the earth. Peyote Woman offered visions, perhaps a place of beauty and happiness. Perhaps it was time to send a runner south to bring back a new supply of the little buds.

Jack wondered if he would be left behind when the camp moved on; he could no longer keep up.

A shadow passed across the night and filled his vision. The old man crouched over him and Jack could no longer see the stars nor the drifting webs.

"Are you willing to live?" the old man asked softly against the background harmony of songs and happy stories. His breath carried the perfume of tobacco, new smoke and something else. "Only those men die who are willing to die." The old man's hand reached out and settled on Jack's head, Jack looked up, uncertain of what to expect.

"Drink." The old man's hand stirred on Jack's head.

Jack drank the bitter black drink. The old man rose and returned to the singing chants.

Pain floated away in the night. The spider's web grew larger, spangled with colored light. Then the spider seemed to drift upward, and its shape changed into that of a wonderful flying horse, white against blackness; colored sparks flew from its magically racing hoofs. And then, he was the horse, and in it, and free of the earth with strange winds in his face and sweet sounds in his mind. Then the astral horse changed shape once more and he left it; and watched from the earth as the shape became huge, smothering, and seemed to come down on him. He awakened and remembered rectangles within rectangles which became wooden cabins with a door and windows; round shapes which meant motion, wheels spinning, wheels of wagons; and a voice speaking words of comfort which he spoke now to himself.

The band moved on, tending their herds and following the season. Jack rode the back of an old war pony and hobbled like a buffalo cripple, each day his leg a little less painful. Soon, he rode a half-wild mustang and walked with the slightest limp. And then, with none at all. The bands met for their yearly gathering where men of high rank elected new war chieftains and civil leaders. The people heard news and rumors. Apache hunters, sometimes friends of the bands, now came into the Comancheria, again from the west, after buffalo and without permission. They had to be driven back. Men of the *Tejano* leaders came with talk of treaties. Honeytalkers? What were these treaties? Useless scraps of paper? Empty talk? Lies that killed so many leaders of the People at the big Council House fight? Now the People claimed over ten times ten white-skinned people were captives, and soon to be traded for high prices: new long guns, ammunition, vermillion, flannel, good striped blankets. Men of the Buffalo Hunters band boasted to the listening People that they were so feared they sometimes rode into small *Tejano* settlements demanding talk, demanding war against certain *Tejano* chiefs who angered them, demanding the return of Comanche prisoners in exchange for the starved, damaged white captives whom they held. Sometimes they laughed when they told of the *Tejano* honeytalkers who sought to pit the People against the Mexican traders, who then wanted to turn the People back against the *Tejanos*, who were cunning and greedy, without respect. They wanted everything that belonged to the People: the good grass, the four-leggeds and the winged animals. Their food. Their life.

Ghost Boy made a ribald, scornful song about these crazy treacheries. Were the People so foolish? Without good sense? Had they forgotten the bad experiences all the way from the long-ago past? All those scraps of meaningless paper no one paid any attention to? The Council House treaty killings, all the other treacheries? Many laughed, but the men of rank listened with bitter, serious faces. There were fewer buffalo grazing on the prairie grasses; there were fewer people in their bands as raiding youths and warriors died.

Jack learned to rope and gentle the shaggy prairie mustangs in the gentle way of the women, with his firm hands and his breath in their nostrils. They too must obey. He learned to make straight arrows and he tried to catch eagles, but never succeeded; perhaps he had to be one of the hard youths from the training camps. Big councils of the Kiowas, the Kiowa Apaches, the southern Cheyenne, and the Arapahoes met to visit and talk of peace among themselves; and of the fighting and war and death of their good fighters in Mexico raids. There was more talk against the *Tejanos*, and the Pawnees in the north. He saw the gatherings for the great trade rendezvous, in the Sierra Guadalupes, and along the Pecos River, among the cottonwood groves of the Bosque Redondo. Comanches, Kiowas, Lipan Apaches, and Mescalero trade parties came from the south; Mogollon Apaches came from the west to meet at the New Mexican settlement called Santa Fe.

Traders from the north, from the old Spanish times, sometimes called Comancheros, sometime called *Tabbahos*, were white men, and half-white men, yet of a different breed from the *Tejanos* or the Mexicans. They came in their many ox driven wagons, and spoke a mixture of Spanish and *Tejano*. They spoke secret words to each other in a language none of the People understood, and they talked the hand language everyone knew. They sat on buffalo robes and smoked pipes; they gave gifts of trinkets and whiskey to the leaders of the tribes. They talked of future trades and of the movement of white troops and militias, and of places called reservations, places reserved for wild Indians, places far away from their prairie homes, their buffalo. Places where Indians ate bad meat and died. The *Tabbahos* spread their wealth all around them on robes and blankets, and promised that there was more, much more, for the free People of the prairies. They bartered fine, striped blankets from the pueblos, wooden combs, blue cotton drill and calico, red strouding, copper kettles, looking glasses, hatchets, pots and containers made of yellow tin for the women. They traded long guns, plugs of tobacco, knives, bullets, packages of gun powder, more looking glasses and whiskey for the men. In return, the People brought hundreds of horses and mules, taken from *ranchos* in Sonora, Chihuahua, Durango and Sinaloa. They brought finely cured buffalo robes and pounded meat. But the most profitable trade of all came from the selling of the scores of captives brought by the different bands; young boys for the

Mexican salt mines and silver mines, for tending the huge Comanche horse herds. Most valuable of all, were the young females, many made good by rape by their captors. These females were worth double the trade value of young boys.

In the great milling, noisy camp of the rendezvous there was, nevertheless, a rigid order. A man might kill his disobedient or sickly slave; but he could not fight with a rival, nor steal from a stranger. He could not refuse a horseracing debt, or any gambling debt, without restitution, or steal another man's wife without penalty. If a man committed murder over a woman, or a gambling debt, the family of the murder victim bore a stigma of shame and scorn until a brother, or an uncle, caught and killed the murderer, or received a heavy restitution.

The men of the police societies swung their sticks against women who crowded too close to the traders, or against anyone who drank too much of the trader's crazy water, or who broke the civil order with quarreling.

Jack watched the procession of brutalized captives and saw again with what little regard troublesome captives were thrown away. He watched the *Tabbahos* because they were almost like him, but free. Under their clothes their skins were almost white and the eyes of some were almost as light as his eyes. But they were free to come and go from this place, to leave behind them all the cruelty of life.

Free. Remember, he thought, hardly knowing what. *I must remember*.

The last day of the great gathering, Jack walked too close to the trader's encampment, his heart pounding. The deep, dusty shade of the cottonwood trees along the river seemed like a darkness of his mind. Sunlight and sound faded, his steps wavered, then steadied once more. The traders sat on good blankets and soft hides, talking earnestly with Apache elders, doing business, sharing news. Talking among themselves in their own Spanish and *Tejano* secret words. They gave him no interest, or perhaps they glanced with a moment of curiosity, then lost interest again when Jack tried to speak, rudely interrupting the rituals of trading. The police society drove him back, and Owl Stands' half son, Dohat, came in a rush.

Deep in the night Owl Stands came back to his camp, under the cottonwoods. He rode his best gentled roan horse, and Dohat, on his showy paint horse, led a pack pony laden with new wealth from the traders. Akima, Owl Stands 'hard-faced Kiowa wife, watched eagerly to see Dohat unpack; to see what presents she would receive from Owl Stands' generosity, more than cooking pots and combs. She watched for the pretty vanity items she could brag about to her friends and relatives. She draped red strouding over her shoulders, scarves of calico, and big beaded necklaces of many colors; her hard face happy at the packages of little colored glass beads, the trinkets. Dohat wore a new blue calico shirt and he, too, was draped with necklaces and trinkets, carrying a new tomahawk and an old musket, with packages of ammunition.

Owl Stands walked slowly over to the brush arbor where Jack waited; his face set, his steps weary from many days in talks, and from the long words of trading. Ghost Boy sat beside Jack, showing his friendship. Jack attempted to rise, but Owl Stands' foot pushed him down and held him. For a long time, he stood staring down at Jack, as though listening in the night, to voices only he could hear. He appeared very calm, standing powerfully above Jack in all his finest ceremonial beaded doeskins, with long graceful hair fringes. He wore shell breastplates and pendants, and his long hair was wrapped in strips of otter skin. The firelight glanced across the burnished planes of his face, across the surface of his eyes. His mouth scarcely moved.

"Stand." The pressure of Owl Stands' foot left Jack's body. Both boys arose. They waited respectfully.

In the flickering firelight Owl Stands saw Jack's bruised face, the places where blood had run.

Dohat had a club. Now he had a hatchet, and a musket.

Owl Stands shook his head. "You have disobeyed me,"

"I know the words," Jack answered carefully. His lips were swollen.

"I warned you of the spiders!" Owl Stands spoke quietly, angrily, without trust. "They spin and spin, but their webs come to nothing!"

Jack's breathing grew labored. His heart raced. "Trader words. I hear them."

"You shame me!"

"Many words."

Owl Stands stared, listening at last, thinking, his eyes suddenly narrowed, intense. Ghost Boy smiled.

"Trader words?"

Jack nodded. He lied, for he understood only a few, memory mixed with mystery, old practiced sounds, guessing. Words that were like lifelines, saving him from the slow creeping darkness, day by day, in the midst of bitterness and cruelty, the darkness of growing a Comanche heart.

He knew that Owl Stands, like all Comanches, scorned any thought of learning another language. Let those other kinds of inferior people learn his words, and then he would talk. Now Jack had to say what made him of value to Owl Stands. What made him worth saving.

"*Tejano* words?"

Jack nodded again, trying for more of the truth that he knew Owl Stands honored. "Some words," he said. "Yes."

They walked away from the camp, through darkness. Jack knew this darkness. Somewhere in the night behind them, Dohat took the horses back to Owl Stands' grazing herd, making distant drunken sounds, laughing. Ghost Boy sat on a buffalo robe, under the encampment arbor, with the gifts his father had brought him, singing softly, a new story song.

The cave was like the caves and crevices in which the People buried their dead. Although it was in the steep bank above the river, it smelled of dry dust and old decay. Piles of rocks and debris covered the entrance. Animal bones lay scattered across the rocky floor. Bats circled in the night above the bluff.

"I will find you here when I come back," Owl Stands said. Jack understood this was an order. Perhaps a final order. *Why here?* And who could know this old man's mind? Owl Stands piled rocks and debris in the entrance, a casual effort, then walked away in the darkness, his shoulders bent, his steps slow.

Gradually, the silence and the darkness of the cave sank into Jack. He was not uncomfortable, only a prisoner who would obey. There was no Dohat here, no stick blows from the woman when he was slow, or for no reason.

Words.

As he grew used to the thick stone silence, he thought of the Supernaturals, those beings who came to prayers, who listened, who sometimes laughed. His heart raced for a moment, then slowly hardened. Then he composed his mind and slept.

Light hurt his eyes. Concussions of sound broke against his ears. He smelled the deep, hot smell of sunlight against stone. He breathed dust and coughed. He heard a voice singing some kind of ritual song.

"Have I disposed of a troublesome slave?" Owl Stands asked. He stood outside the cave dressed for travel. Jack drank from a water skin the old man had dropped in the dust. He saw two youths waiting below the bluff, idly squatting in the shade cast against the rocks by four ponies. One horse was Dohat's fractious paint, throwing his head, impatient, another was the pony gentled for Ghost Boy.

Owl Stands searched Jack's face. Why did this stern man, who was loved and honored among his people, bother with a low, reckless White Dog youth? Why did he bother to walk two paths, one of a merciless anger and one of lofty tolerance that seemed to have a scrap of his heart?

But Jack had seen Owl Stands' little moments with Ghost Boy, who was not a young man hoping to be a fierce fighter, a warrior like the other youths in the band. He remembered Owl Stands listening to songs and poetry, listening to the boy's dreams.

"Perhaps someone else is in his place." Owl Stands spoke in a way that clearly made his intentions come to resolution in some way and seem almost unimportant. He told Jack, in this way, that soon he would not care. Soon he would lose his last patience. Except for

Ghost Boy, the welfare of this rude youth would soon be below the notice of a man of his rank and responsibilities. Yes. Soon he would not care.

Jack watched a hawk drifting in the sky. He waited.

Owl Stands looked down at the two youths squatting in the shade, Dohat scratching and dozing, the broken Ghost Boy looking up at the cave anxiously.

Owl Stands' expression changed, as though his heart turned to water.

This gentle boy.

But Jack knew, as much as he ever could know, this man's cunning mind; that his *Tejano* trader words, also, were of great value in Owl Stands' mind. Their secret words cheated the People. Their secret words promised hidden information, hidden lies.

And Jack knew, as well, that somewhere in Owl Stands' mind there was a scratching of Comanche rage against him, Comanche bitter mistrust. Against the *Tejanos*, all the *Tejanos*. All White Dogs.

Now the rivers and bluffs were no longer nameless, the mountains and war roads, the canyons and valleys carried designations burned into Jack's mind as he learned more, as he remembered captive fires. He learned of Chinaberry Tree Springs, Double Mountain, Big Rock canyon where Owl Stands sometimes left history pictures in the face of the great rock. He learned of Red River, Wind Gap. He learned of wagon roads, scarred into the *Llano* by *Tejano* settlers and traders daring to cross the land where the People lived.

The mad Kiowa woman Ekopadl, a relative of Dohat's cousin, fell behind on an ordinary day's journey and no one saw her again, nor spoke her name. A score of men left on a long raid, after horses and captives deep into Mexico, near Tamaulipas and did not return. After a season of waiting, the women cried and slashed their breasts in mourning. The smiling man did not return. A woman gave birth to a boy child whose face was deformed; and the child was taken to a high place and left to the sun and wind. A quarrel broke out when a young man eloped with old His Shield's new Mexican girl-wife, and the youth gave a horse and two ears of corn in restitution.

Three times, Jack listened to trader words, before he began to truly understand. His life hung on these words. Only a few; those that he had hoarded and practiced so long, or faintly remembered, those he had written secretly in the dust, and only a few numbers, spoken at the Pecos River rendezvous. Then more and more. True *Tabbaho* lies, tucked into the trading talk and the whiskey, but the secret words that spoke of news: twisted words rousing Owl Stands' most intense interest; what they had heard the *Tejano* chiefs say to each other up in the Spanish village, Santa Fe, or at one of the new forts rising like boils across Comanche land: rumors, new treaty talks with the Pawnees or Utes, or how many blue coat soldiers rode at the borders of the Comancheria. Sometimes the *Tejano* words, urgent to Jack, meant nothing to Owl Stands. They had no value, because they spoke of another world, unknown and unimagined by the People; and sometimes Jack thought he had failed, that he was useless to the old man

But some of the secret words were like precious gifts, giving Owl Stands the power of wisdom, in his civil leadership. He sometimes went away from the People, with other council elders and chiefs. He came back, often silent and troubled. He painted symbols and figures on his calendar robe, recording day-by-day, and season-by-season, happenings, his face set with memory and concern. Jack never knew what these journeys meant, nor where they went, unless Owl Stands spoke in council. He and the other boys were busy running races or practicing with the bow; or watching the pretty young girls, carefully chaperoned, learning women's tasks.

Groups of seasoned fighters gathered in small bands and went east, against *Tejano* settlements; vengeance raids against *Tejano* horse thieves who liked to steal great herds of their horses and mules, or who chased Ute buffalo hunters out onto the Comanche plains. The identities of famous enemy fighters often remained lost in quick skirmishes; in the vastness of the *Llano;* or hidden in the wooded edges of *Tejano* settlements. Now and then, if an enemy fighter were known, perhaps a high Pawnee war chief, and high vengeance carried out by intention, such men earned great admiration. They were of the highest moral order, for few showed such perseverance and patience.

"So," Owl Stands told Jack. "You are ready."

His Kiowa wife spat angry words and made shooing gestures with her arms.

Go away! Go away!

"You will go to the training camp."

Jack felt a jolt of excitement. He had thought to be ignored, an unworthy slave. Perhaps his halting *Tejano* words had gained him this miracle.

Dohat, with his ax and his old musket, liked to strut and boast of his skills learned at the training encampment last season. Since then, he had gone away on one raid that gained him only one poor pony and little booty, but he had captured an old Spanish flintlock *pistole,* with elaborate silver scroll work decorations, gold inlay and patches of rust. He had no ammunition, no way to make it belch fire and kill, but this weapon was strong medicine to Dohat, the source of a powerful spirit-dream he couldn't quite remember. He allowed no one to touch this trophy. It was a bragging ornament, as well, and he wore it at his waist, for the prestige it brought to his hungry spirit.

He claimed loudly that the leader of the raid had failed his followers, or they would have won more booty. Now he talked of fighting, of leading a group of raiders, of herds of fat horses, of killing *Tejanos* and capturing women and children.

"When you come back," he said to Jack. He waved his ax in an almost expert arc in the air near Jack's face, and smiled.

Akima, his mother, laughed.

Strong Comanche women, older wives, warrior women who had ridden against enemies, ruled the training camp, helped by strong Comanche men of good reputation. The boys began weeks of hard training, measured by the waxing and the waning of the moon; hard riding on wild ponies; learning to shoot a long bow at moving targets; learning to ride easily, with only the rawhide surcingle, leather loops holding him; then hiding and shooting arrows from under the pony's neck. They learned difficult horse skills: leaning far down to rescue a fallen comrade; hard falls; hard fighting with shields and lances and knives and any weapon; hard games with lances; wrestling; running hard foot races; the lore of hunting and trailing, learning the land; the language of secret animal sounds and smoke talking; the secret messages left along the trail for warriors to meet, to find each other, to find water, or their way back to the home camp; going on long lonely missions they dared not fail; going hungry and thirsty. They were taught of the heraldry of warfare; all the rules and rituals of manhood and the many ways to defend the People and keep them safe and well fed.

At night they sat by big fires and heard stories from the long ago past, all stories that would pass on practical knowledge and hard, personal strength. Stories of supernatural heroes and of bad men who brought terrible harm. They heard of the many thousands of People, fat with buffalo grazing beyond the rim of the earth. They heard of their wealth in buffalo and slaves, their strength and their success against other envious tribes. Even the Spanish people, when they came, gave their great respect to the Comanche People. Then the changes: the terrible sickness that killed the People beyond counting, the treachery, the storyteller lies, the honeytalkers, the greed of the new people, the White Dogs, and how the fierce Comanches took the vast Comancheria lands for their own to save themselves.

The women watched the boys who won the lance games; won the wrestling matches; won hand battles; won well and with generosity. These youths fought each other to attain rank and show honorable dispositions, for they would surely be the leaders of the future. The women watched Jack. He tracked well; he grew skilled with a knife; he won every foot race with generosity; for he understood they might all become like fighting dogs if they did not own this important civility. But his arrows were slow; his riding a little less than the best riders; his war cries less harsh than the Comanche screams, meant to terrorize enemies.

Ghost Boy welcomed him back to the home camp, his moccasins chiming with pretty bell sounds. Now Jack had a scrap of acceptance, a small bit of approval. The people were willing to look at his face, they no longer looked away as though he were nothing.

Ghost Boy showed Jack the fine flint and obsidian arrow points. He had made both good hunting points fastened to the shafts in vertical positions, for piercing buffalo ribs; and fighting points tied horizontally, loosely, for piercing the horizontal ribs of men.

"These points will come off and stay inside and they will die slowly," he bragged, not without merit. His arrow shafts were always straight, hardened wood that men of the band sought in trade. In the near-time, most fighters wanted pieces of the white man's metal, stolen in raids; barrel stave; small knives; any good metal sharpened into points, but the old, far-time ways kept Ghost Boy busy. He said he had no time for the training camp. But his broken body spoke silently when he tried to strut around like his half-brother, Dohat.

"Walk like my famous relative!" he said. He danced an awkward little dance and laughed with Jack.

Jack learned to kill fat buffalo bulls, with a single arrow, following them until they died. He learned to hunt antelope at water holes; or by hiding in tall grass and mimicking the plaintive cries of lost fawns until anxious mothers came close to his bow. He hunted eagles with Ghost Boy, for their ceremonial feathers, and listened to his friend's turkey wing flute playing love songs at night. He felt his own growth pressing everywhere in his body. He discovered that the hardness and strength of his sex had wonderful attributes of its own.

A girl with bright, slanted eyes passed him with her sisters at midday, carrying water from the creek. She smiled, and Jack knew he could sleep-crawl into her robes, after the old people had fallen asleep that night. He would lie face to face with this one or that one, often silent, sometimes laughing and whispering, while the old people snored. His hands would caress her body, learning every cleft and softness and hidden place, while her hands found him and guided him, and brought him to pleasure deep in her warmth. He sometimes forgot where he was, who he was, when a pretty girl smiled and he knew he could crawl past the sleeping dogs to lie with her in the secret night; and there he could tease or please with roughness, or coax little groans and shudders, which made the old people toss irritably, or throw sticks at the fire, and the young people laughed hiddenly. Sometimes he crawled away at midnight and met other sleep-crawlers returning in the darkness. Sometimes he spent hours with the girl, lured again to pleasure, lying half awake and whispering; but it was always of trivia they spoke, whispering of idle nonsense easily forgotten. He cared for nothing more, and the girls cared only for pleasure and small gifts. They would brew sage tea in the morning and drink to prevent conception.

Yes, let the old people under their buffalo robes grumbled and complained of sleeplessness. They said Owl Stands' favored *Tejano* slave, while showing some practical value in other areas, would no doubt crawl into every dwelling in the village if it held a pretty, willing daughter; and thereby cause every parent to throw sticks at the fire and growl at the innocent dogs. Some told ribald jokes and stories, they loved to laugh at natural obscenities, and recalled other famous sleep-crawlers, often themselves. But there were others whose respect for Owl Stands kept them from killing this hated *Tejano* slave youth. Dohat, whose sex had few attributes, and therefore little success at sleep-crawling, watched at night and listened to the secret talk and laughter with envy. Although he was brave, he did not possess the honored regard he craved from the People. He broke the civil peace with minor quarrels and suspicions of affronts, and, sometimes, disrupted games with petty jealousies; but he always stopped short of banishment from the village, however short such discipline might be.

A visiting Kiowa youth, Kuito, distantly related and who left his band after a dispute, became Dohat's friend and taught him the clever ways of the Kiowas, who were known for their brutality, for the way they liked to wave a white flag of friendship outside a *Tejano* settlement and, then, ride in and kill all the people. They liked to throw *Tejano* babies in the air and catch them on their lances. Kuito had been on his first raid, with modest success, against Mexican sheepherders. He was allotted one new horse as his share, though he never mentioned any act of bravery. When he returned to his people, he quickly stole old Esaki's nubile young third wife. Esaki, supported by his strong and respected family, demanded Kuito's best hunting horse as payment to his honor, and bragged that he had made the better bargain, considering his age. Kuito was left to ponder how he had lost in this exchange, and soon began to beat his new wife, for being the cause of his troubles, until she ran away from Kuito, finding refuge with her family. Now his reputation became that of the poorest commoner, because of his violence to a woman who had neither been an adulterous, nor disobeyed nor caused him injury. He rode out on a second raid to regain status and acquire wealth; but grew so miserly with his new possessions that his companions set upon him because Kuito hoarded food and tobacco after the other men in the party had gone without food and tobacco for two days. But no one thought Kuito had learned much from this basic lesson in generosity.

So, he left his band for a while and visited with the Antelope band, and while he was related only distantly by blood to Dohat, the Kiowas and Comanches had smoked peace pipes long ago, they intermarried to strengthen that peace, and sometimes they took the war road together. The People knew of the bad rumors about Kuito, but they watched him strut around mimicking warriors from his band, braiding horsehair into his own hair and making long, trailing braids adorned with pretty feathers and charms. He liked to walk around the village looking at the girls combing their hair or gathering wood, looking for young girls he could catch alone and unprotected, but even in this petty violence he was often inept and did not have Dohat's skills nor bravery. He liked to join the many dances and sing and eat like a hungry bear at feasts.

Food gave him a belly and a measure of scorn. He was tolerated because he was a relative of Owl Stands.

The People moved on over the old trace roads, the men, youths and warriors alike, driving their herds ahead, while the women packed bedding and cooking pots on travois, dragged by gentle ponies. Their wealth was such that the women rode fine horses and carried their babies on their backs or, occasionally strapped them to the travois packs. These old roads were from the long-ago time, dug by thousands of travois poles and unshod horses' hoofs from before anyone could remember. They crawled across the Comancheria leading to the best river crossings; the best campgrounds, with plentiful wood and water; the hidden places, like the canyon of the great rock where Owl Stands carved the passage of the seasons, in eloquent, ritual pictures.

Owl Stands rode at the front of the band, talking with friends, gesturing, laughing. The travois carrying his possessions, only one travois for he often gave his possessions away, close behind. Old Akima followed, complaining of all her work, Ghost Boy followed, with Jack riding in the dusty wake of the huge herds, always watching, searching out the wonders of their beautiful land.

The seasons passed. Jack grew taller than the Comanche boys of sixteen summers.

Then Dohat called a horse raid against the *Tejanos*.

Eight young men answered Dohat's invitation. He paid a crier to walk through the village twice, calling out Dohat's name, his brave raiding plans and experiences, exaggerated but always with a grain of truth. The People busied themselves with their work and looked away. Only eight youths, all of them novices and eager to win respect and wealth, pledged to join him. Dohat was the leader, the oldest among them. Kuito, who wanted to steal any sort of horse and any sort of woman, or anything that would help him regain status, eagerly made his pledge. The others were among the inexperienced young men who had served apprenticeships on horse raids, holding horses and cooking the food for the fighters, always obeying. They boasted and prayed for success and acted fearless in front of each other.

Jack listened to the boasting and the prayers. He wondered how long he could stand away from Dohat. His friend with the singing moccasins, who often earned Dohat's scorn, would never go on such a raid. But Jack had learned his hard lessons and earned that scrap of respect.

"Come" Dohat said with a smile. "You are nothing but an ugly White Dog slave, but I will teach you to be a man."

Three nights later dancing and singing went far into the night, with families and sweethearts there to support this brave little band. Then the youths faded away from the fire and the singing and went into the night to gather their weapons and shields and personal possessions. They met again at dawn and quietly rode away.

They rode east, into the dawn, looking for *Tejanos*, some of the youths, from their boasts, too eager for fame, too certain of their success. Their faces now were serious, intent.

One among them, after so many seasons, felt both dread and a strange excitement. His own people, Jack thought. Those *Tabbaho* traders at the rendezvous were not his people, but he wasn't quite sure what that meant, what this raid meant. He rode a good paint pony given to him by his friend, who had also given him a supply of his best straight arrows with the finest carved flint fighting points. He carried pemmican and dried fruit, everything else he would need in a leather bag as he had learned to do at the training camp. In a smaller bag he carried his medicine, his good luck, something he scarcely believed in but wasn't sure about. It was only a stone with a curious pattern, found when he finally caught an eagle.

Only a stone.

He rode behind a leader who must be obeyed, a leader who was jealous of any youth more favored than he.

On the sixth day, rain swept across the edge of the prairie. That night, with high clouds drifting across the stars, they came to a *Tejano* camp by the side of an old trace road, guarded by Mexicans wrapped in canvas blankets and dozing under oak trees. They stopped to paint their faces for war and to leave their bundled possessions away from the *Tejano* camp. Jack left his shield, taking only his bow and his long knife. Then they approached downwind and lay in the darkness under the trees. They saw horses, many horses all haltered and tied to a rope strung between oak trees, fat bays and sorrels and painted ponies all in star shadow, tails twitching, half asleep, bigger, sleeker horses than the shaggy mustangs the raiders rode, and their hearts began to pound with excitement and with visions of swift and incredible success. They saw wagons drawn close under the trees, one wagon tilted at an angle. Something had broken and spilled mounds of trade goods. They saw a low fire. They saw lumps and bundles on the ground, only a few men sleeping, and smelled wet fire coals and other smells that told of foreign people, strange stale foods, burned tobacco and sour body odors.

White Dogs.

They heard the soft clatter of water, an unseen stream freshened by the rain.

How careless the white men were, Jack thought with dismay, how foolish to camp by the hurrying water which covered the sound of any stealthy enemy, or by a travelled trail.

Leave the bad wagon, hide, camp away under the trees.

How unlucky, how foolish, to doze away their fat horses or, perhaps, their lives.

"They are stupid and lazy," Kuito whispered, adjusting his shield. "They don't even have dogs."

"All *Tejanos* are stupid and lazy," Dohat said softly.

Jack heard the words, but only looked toward the wagon wheels, remembering.

Circles and squares.

"We will kill them all and take everything," Kuito whispered eagerly, "everything will be easy---."

"Maybe there are more men in the wagons," Jack whispered.

"Maybe someone is afraid of stupid *Tejanos*," Dohat answered. "He can go home, and we will do the work here. We are not afraid of---."

"Maybe someone's mouth is full of lies, like the shit the buffalo make," Jack said, "and he's a bad leader on a sore-backed horse, if he forgets these fools have guns---."

Dohat glared at Jack, but it was no secret that Dohat gave his ponies poor attention.

"Guns?" Kuito muttered. "Yes, guns." His ventures against enemies had been against remote Mexican villages and sheepherders who had no guns because they had been taken away long ago by the Mexican Red Coats, for fear of an uprising against their government officials, which made the Comanches laugh as they raided.

"Shut your mouth, cousin" Dohat said in disgust. "White Dogs always have guns."

"This is only a horse raid," Jack said stubbornly.

"I have a gun," one of the others said, but they all knew it was a poor old musket given to him by his uncle.

"It's better to steal their ponies without a fight---." They all knew this was a high honor, this kind of clever, silent theft while the *Tejanos* slept.

Dohat longed for a good long gun; the new kind that the *Tabbahos* sold at the yearly rendezvous to the important men of the villages who had the high price. He had not even brought his musket, for he could shoot arrows faster than the *Tejanos* could reload their muskets. But he understood that he would lose the little band of warriors if he appeared too rash or lacking in common sense. They would refuse to follow and speak badly of him in the village. He studied Jack for a moment, a little smile on his face. The others waited to hear what he would say, listening to the soft clatter of the stream that covered the sounds of their whisperings and rustlings, in the damp grass and leaves.

"Then we'll hide our horses and sneak back and take those horses and go home. We will tell the story at the dance," Dohat said, and the others agreed.

"We'll leave them afoot." Kuito whispered. "Perhaps they'll just go away. Maybe they'll starve. We can sneak back and take the trade goods. No one will get hurt with guns."

The band drew back quietly into the deeper darkness, watching the stars, waiting for cloud cover. A chunky youth, nicknamed Bee, because of his love of honey, quietly led all the Comanche ponies away to a hidden place well back on the trail, where he and the ponies could wait safely, with packs of food and dry clothes, for the raiders to return.

In the *Tejano* camp, the fat horses began to move and shift, tossing their heads uneasily as the wind shifted at dawn, and they caught the scent of the Comanche raiders. The Mexican guards slept on.

Only horses, only horses.

When the clouds covered the stars, the youths crawled forward and rose up among the horses; stroking them; moving softly; whispering softly; untying their bridles carefully; giving the horses time to get used to their scent, before they led them away. Then something happened.

Jack heard a sound, like a sneeze. The raiders froze. One of the sleeping *Tejanos* called out a name and a Mexican guard answered sleepily. The youths held immobile a moment longer. Then a horse rose high in the darkness with a squeal of alarm. Jack saw Kuito pulled up, hanging on the headstall of his prize. The *Tejano* men scrambled out of their blankets and out of the wagons, yelling the alarm and shooting their guns at the sky. Jack grabbed for the fat bay horse he had cut loose, then felt a silent burn of pain through his upper arm, coming from behind him. His fingers tore loose from the tangle of mane as the bay horse lunged away screaming, an arrow in its neck.

Jack saw the *Tejanos* and the Mexicans scrambling, running; he saw Dohat crouched behind him, his bow raised; then lost the sight of Dohat, as the frantic horses pulled and lunged, most of them still tied to the ropes. But the *Tejanos* were afraid to shoot into the wild tangle of Comanches and horses; with yells that put winter into Jack's blood, the *Tejanos* ran at the raiders, swinging their rifle butts and their long knives, shooting at close range.

Jack grabbed a paint pony with glassy eyes, and pulled it free; then one of the *Tejanos* tried to shoot him with his long gun, but he had come too close. In panic, Jack dropped his bow and caught the long gun to shove it aside while he brought his knife up in his right hand. In the gray, growing light Jack saw the man's grimace, his wild sandy hair, his pale skin, and the man hesitated when he saw Jack, bewildered, as if he had made a mistake.

Jack hesitated, but the Comanche youths were screaming treble war cries, trying to drive the tied horses away from the ropes, and the *Tejanos* were yelling and shooting. Everything had gone wrong. Jack yanked at the long gun and felt the man's solid power against him; he felt the gun pulling away from his frantic grasp and he leaned forward, close to the man's body, guiding the knife. Somewhere, he heard the high singing of a song, a broken voice, Comanche words. Jack pulled back from the man with the wild sandy hair, as a gush of dark blood bloomed on his *Tejano*'s belly. Jack backed away from the falling body, standing stunned for just an instant, while he understood what had happened. Nothing touched him, no *Tejano* bullet came near him.

Then he felt a great colliding blow from behind, tumbling him in the dirt under horses' hoofs. He rolled and scrambled to his feet, spitting dirt and blood. He saw Dohat riding past on the back of a tall horse, swinging his shield and yelling as the tall horse galloped into the oaks.

Jack scrambled for his bow, lying in the dirt, then ran for the paint horse with the glassy eyes. The horse stood snorting and rearing away from Jack, smelling blood. His halter rope loose, but tangled, in a deadfall. Jack slashed at the tangle of rope and mounted with a jump. The horse was already bolting away after the others, with Comanches on their backs, and who were using their bows to whip their new horses into the cover of the trees. One youth ran afoot, his legs a blur of desperate speed, his arrow case flapping against his back. Jack yelled at him, then bent low and pulled him up behind. The youth held tight and the paint horse carried them away.

"Now they'll follow us with their guns," Kuito complained between hard breaths. They raced between the oaks. "Everything went wrong---." The others heard nothing but their horses running through the trees, breaking small branches, and breathing with snorts of fear. The side of Kuito's face bled from a fall during the fight, and he had lost his bow. The horse he'd stolen, a heavy boned wagon horse, labored to keep up with the others. He looked with envy at Dohat's tall sorrel, at Jack's painted horse with glassy eyes. "Now they will come after us with guns!" Kuito called loudly.

One of them had been left behind, singing his death song.

"Maybe you've forgotten, one man is not riding away with us!" Jack yelled, anger churning in his belly.

But confusion raced through his mind, as fast as his new pony raced away from the *Tejanos*. He had killed a *Tejano*, in a bungled, inept raid.

They rode hard, watching for those *Tejanos*, who had many horses, to follow. There had been many men, many guns. Jack glared ahead at Dohat's back, remembering the moments of the raid, the fear, all those *Tejanos* so close, a Comanche youth beginning to sing his death song in all the chaos and darkness. *How could they go back? How could they save him? Drag him away, save his body from the Tejanos?* They were all bruised and sobered by the loss.

They had left a comrade behind. No one would wear the black paint of victory going home.

He was confused, and he was angry. No one wanted to think of his own death, with the morning sun now shining brightly. They hurried toward the hidden place where they would find Bee holding their horses.

The rage boiled in Jack's belly. Twice Dohat had tried to kill him, to shoot him with an arrow that only killed a horse, and to run him down, leave him trampled, leave him behind, a prize for the enemies.

And in the confused moments of the fight who could say Dohat's arrow, or his galloping horse, were anything but common accidents that happened when men fought? Jack felt the small pain in his arm. All the boys were bruised, scraped, shamed by their own mistakes and poor planning, their boasts had died into an empty place of silence in which they could never speak the name of the dead youth again.

He is gone. He is gone. And I have killed that Tejano.

"A horse stepped on my foot," Kuito said plaintively when they stopped to rest their heaving horses. "This was not a very good idea."

"Shut your mouth, cousin," Dohat said. "You have a new horse. If you hadn't made so much noise with that other horse---."

"I heard one of those *Tejanos* sneeze, that's what---."

"We don't all have new horses," the youth riding at Jack's back called out angrily. "Will someone give me one of his many new horses?"

"A good leader doesn't shoot his own men," Jack said.

Dohat stared at Jack and the others fell silent, watching. Then Dohat smiled. Even in the face of so much bad luck, accusations and general misfortune, he was the leader and held the leader's powers. "Maybe I should give that good paint pony to someone else."

"Maybe you should try," Jack said quickly.

"Wait, I saw this man fight with a *Tejano*," the youth at Jack's back called loudly. "I saw him kill that man with his knife!"

"Where is proof? Did he count coup? Where is that scalp?" Dohat asked.

"He picked me up! Am I alive now? I saw all this!"

"I am a witness too!" cried the youngest of the band whose nickname was Bird Walks. He had lost his bow case and all his arrows. He waved an arm that trembled with the aftermath of fear and excitement. His eyes ran with tears for his lost friend. "I will testify."

The Comanche youths looked nervously back over the way they had fled. They had left so many horses behind that the *Tejanos* could easily follow them. They looked at Dohat, waiting.

Dohat understood, once again, that the others stood against him. Clearly, they favored Owl Stands' spoiled White Dog slave who hadn't even attained adoption, but had managed to steal a fine paint horse and count coup by killing an enemy.

"Some people are lucky for themselves and all bad luck for everyone else---."

"Not for me," the youth at Jack's back said.

One of the youths whose new pony wore only a short halter rope, jumped down and fashioned a quick jaw bridle with his *reata*, then remounted.

"Bad luck," Bird Walking said. He rubbed, angrily, at his eyes. "Now he is gone."

Kuito touched the side of his face where a trickle of blood still ran, smearing the paint he had applied before the raid. "No women, and my new horse is no good---."

Dohat glared at his cousin, his clever smile forgotten, for he couldn't lead without consent, even after their pledges to follow him. He turned away and made a show of searching back the way they had fled, looking for enemies, showing concern and leadership, which was somehow slipping away from him. Again, that spoiled White Dog slave.

"Come on, stop this complaining and let's go before the stupid *Tejanos* decide to follow us into open country."

They whipped their horses with less panic, watching the back trail, hoping the *Tejanos*, who were not so stupid after all, would fear the open country. They began to think of the stories they would tell; searching for scraps of truth; searching for the careful words of brave acts and terrible dangers.

Kuito grunted unhappily. He had no bow he could use to beat his wagon horse's flanks, so he had to kick hard to make it keep up with the others. "I've had enough of this bad luck. I want to go home."

They did not ride into the village wearing black paint thirteen days later. They signaled their loss from a distance, and the family of the one who didn't come home began to cry and mourn. Of the ten youths who had left, nine returned and seven led new horses. They told their stories that night, while the people listened with occasional cries of approval, and they gave witness to each other's acts against such a strong *Tejano* enemy.

Owl Stands stood by Jack as the people feasted, dressed in his finest soft antelope shirt with the blue and green bead designs, and long fringes in the sleeves. His hair was braided and wound with red cloth. He wore chains and beads at his neck. There was almost a smile on his face, as he listened to the young raiders talking of the raid; of the many dangers they had overcome, the good acts they had performed, embellished as they were but always spoken with fragments of truth. The youth Jack had picked up told his story.

"We learned that skill at the camp," Jack said with a gesture of dismissal. Of course, Owl Stands knew this.

"His family will be grateful with gifts," Owl Stands said. "I dreamed of many running horses one night. Was that you?" In a guarded moment, rare, not quite whole with any true approval, he touched Jack, "The other."

Jack watched the people talking, laughing, getting ready for the dance.

Owl Stands finally said, "Well, I will ask a friend to give you a strong new name."

But Jack, too, saw things in his dreams. He saw dying captives; he felt the terror of a ten-year-old boy; he saw blood and wounds; heard dead children screaming; and he sometimes felt tears when he awoke. He found no joy, no success now, except that he had survived Dohat's raid.

He had survived.

Torches lit the night of celebration for those who were alive; while the dead youth's family mourned at the edge of the village, rending their arms and legs with slashes of grief, as they prepared to give his possessions away.

Owl Stands held a gift in his hand. The gift was carefully wrapped in soft doeskin. He folded back the doeskin and Jack looked down at the big steel knife with an ornamented antler handle. A fine showy knife, with a huge sharp blade. It lay in the beaded buckskin sheath with hanging fringes. A *Tejano* knife. A rare gift, a treasure of great value that he knew had been captured into Owl Stands' possession for many seasons. He knew it was coveted by Dohat, whose antics and effort for honor most often ended badly, and never merited such a gift. He knew any youth in the band would covet such a gift from this important man.

"You have done well with the enemy," Owl Stands said, as though speaking to a son.

But Jack saw the seasons ahead unfolding endlessly, filled with the same smoke and drumming and songs and dancing, the same smiles from this girl or that girl. The same dreams. The same confusions. Nothing would change for him except as he gained respect and perhaps hardened in his heart. But for now Owl Stands' adopted son, soon to be given a strong name in a respected ceremony, nothing would change, the People would wander free across their prairies and groves and deserts, following good grass and buffalo, except as they raided and fought in the endless bitter heraldry of warfare which brought them foreign wealth, trinkets and guns, even as their numbers fell away.

Another season passed and Jack guessed from the counting of winters on Owl Stands' calendar robe that now he had come to his ten plus seven years. He thought often of the many things that were unknowable to him. If the white people were such cowards, so afraid of open country, how could they make so many wagon tracks through the buffalo grass? They were looking for gold, he had heard, that yellow metal from far away; and they crossed the Comancheria anywhere, cutting through the grazing grass and killing Comanche game. Why was gold so important? And why had the *Tejanos* not chased the boys after they had bungled the horse raid? Yes, those wagon men wanted to protect the wagons and trade goods. But why had they been so careless, so asleep? And they had seen him, that man and Jack both with sandy-colored hair. That *Tejano* had hesitated, startled.

He had hesitated.

No one had come looking for him at the last trade rendezvous because of the dead *Tejano*. The *Tabbahos* sometimes came searching for white captives, with certain names and descriptions; for the rewards the White Dogs sometimes offered. But no one searched for Jack.

Now he had killed one of the white people. Would they know?

Would they give him a name?

Would they look for him?

Mexican captives who were warriors among the Comanche bands grew to hate their own people, and killed them in raids. They had embraced Comanche hearts. They would never change; never regret nor wonder; but Jack did not have a Comanche heart. And the People talked, they loved to tell stories, and those *Tabbahos* looked at him in a different way at the rendezvous and only whispered their secret words when he came too near.

Dohat had gained new status from another raid against *Tejano* horse thieves; still he had no friends among the People, in spite of his growing status.

And how was it that Jack's friend, Ghost Boy, could be so loved and respected by the People when he had no war honors, only ribald humor and songs and good straight arrows?

"He Walks Away," Ghost Boy said. He made a fierce, empty-handed gesture, as though he confronted a terrible enemy, and laughed. "Man Who Walks Away! I am afraid!"

This new name meant nothing to Jack. Owl Stands had given the choice to a respected elder, an old friend who shared the peyote ritual, who had found this name after serious meditation and singing. *But where was its strength? Its meaning?* Jack thought it was only an empty name.

The day's heat had faded away with a gentle breeze and left the promise of a soft night. A good night for courting.

They sprawled in the afternoon shade, on a little rise. At the base of the rise, a score of hidden peach trees flourished, fed by the trickle from a small spring. Soon the women would find this peaceful little orchard and carry away all the ripe fruit

Ghost Boy fussed with the tear in his moccasin. He glanced secretively at Jack. "She has eyes for you."

Jack shook his head.

"Pretty Crow Wing has a good family."

"No," Jack said. He couldn't say why. But whenever such talk came between them his mind always slid back to the horse raid of months ago. Again, he felt a sear stab of confusion. But this good friend who walked with singing moccasins, thought as most of his people thought, day by day, good food to eat, simple acceptance of every day, jokes, hunger, anger, stories, practical matters.

But Jack had heard that death song, and they had left that nameless youth behind.

What am I?

"Look! Look!" Suddenly Ghost Boy pointed. Below them in the ravine the brush moved, the branch of a peach tree bent down. A young girl, alone, no more than twelve or thirteen winters, reached for a peach, her brown face alight with anticipation.

"She's alone! You can go get her! You can have her!"

Jack stared, knowing that old tribal law allowed him or any man to take that girl, caught out alone and unprotected in the brush or by a stream. He could force this girl-child, he could beat her and discard her, her family might frown but by the laws, no one would care.

"Hurry! I am too slow---."

But Jack only stared, and then they heard a voice calling, and the girl-child quickly withdrew, slipping down and away like a phantom.

"Well." Ghost Boy said. He savored a bite of his juicy peach. He remembered something and smiled. "My relative wants your knife.

He has always had eyes for that big knife and now he grows more hatred for you."

"Let him," Jack answered.

Ghost Boy's smile broadened. He always smiled at the memory of a recent dance, because Dohat had made all the People laugh.

"Dohat. Yes, all that long hair!"

Jack lifted his head and looked into space, into the sky. "That night. When we came back from that wagon raid." He thought of the mother who had chopped away her hair in grief for the nameless youth they had left behind.

He spoke softly, recalling an angry, even puzzling, grievance. "He took away the mourning hair from that woman."

Why can't I be like my good friend? Why can't I be a Comanche?

"He made his hair so long for the girls, but it fell off in the dance later." Ghost boy laughed. "It all fell off! He should have used horse hair." Ghost Boy loved telling the stories of his half-Kiowa brother's follies. "He wove it into his own hair! He danced in front of the girls, but it all fell off! The people laughed. Everybody laughed at him!"

"I laughed," Jack said.

"Remember when he tried to shoot that old pistol he stole on the last raid? The one with all the pictures in the metal? He said it was big medicine, the Supernaturals loved him. But nothing works. Nothing! If he has gunpowder it blows up and turns his face black!" Ghost Boy laughed again. "Maybe I will make a new song."

"No. He will find a way."

"Maybe he will go. Maybe to a place far away."

He'll find a way to hurt you, Jack thought.

Ghost Boy sighed. "Well, now I am thinking of Old Otter's youngest daughter. I think her family will take three horses and they know I can provide well for her now. My arrows are good, and I can keep her in meat now. She sews well, she has a pretty face. Maybe she'll make me new moccasins." Ghost Boy looked down at his torn moccasin. "And sometimes she looks at me. She has a good family too."

"She looks at you because you killed only that one lame old buffalo?" Jack teased with a smile. He thought about Ghost Boy's new pride. "Perhaps you killed that buffalo by accident?"

But he knew that he had given his friend a handful of this new pride. "Everything is better for you," he said.

Ghost Boy looked at Jack with a stillness that often-meant approval. He bit from the ripe early peach again, licking at the juices. He had a great weakness for such sweets and often foraged ahead for such treats when the band travelled. His father had recently given him a new long gun and a package of ammunition with powder and caps. Not an old musket that someone had already used and broken. This wonderful weapon made hunting possible for him, and he would learn soon to be a great hunter. His face showed that certainty.

Jack bit into a peach, watching the village below as people settled into the evening tasks and general family visiting whenever they made a new camp. Fat horses stood tethered by each lodge, alarm horses in case of trouble in the night. Two small boys chased a dog through the camp and a woman called after them.

"Who will teach you that long gun?" he asked.

"Perhaps you."

Jack laughed. "I will have to learn first. Who will teach me?"

Kiowas came visiting that night, their faces covered in greeting. They had many relatives and friends in the encampment. They brought looking glasses and copper kettles to trade for Mexican ponies, even the wild ones that hadn't been gentled. They brought news and gossip about their latest fight with soldiers, and they brought three white captives.

Jack watched as the Kiowa visitors and the People, shouting and laughing, cut heavy post from the cottonwoods at the edge of the encampment. He watched as they buried them in the ground like stakes. Darkness fell before they had finished. Maybe only two of the soldiers would die after the dancing and boasting by the warriors, and maybe the other would watch tied to a post, believing his own end was near. Maybe when the Kiowas left, they would carry him along with a skin bag over his head so he could see nothing; and they'd stop at the next friendly village to trade, and they would make another dance and another burning.

The captives were young men, a little older than Jack. They appeared stupefied, as though some merciful priest or elder had already given them the black drink, and sent them to a faraway place. One soldier had round blue eyes in his pale white skinned face, and hair like straw growing on his head and his upper lip. He stirred a shadow of memory in Jack's mind, but only laughter and taunts from the women who waited to goad, to light the fire. The second soldier had a small, tough looking body, with darker skin. His hair was black and his hands and feet were narrow. The third soldier had hair the color of copper kettles, copper tools, and ornaments. His white skin had peeled in flakes across his nose and shoulders and left raw red patches all over his body. He had a wound in his chest, ugly and gaping. His head hung and turned from side to side. The women laughed at him because they said he had tried to kill himself when the men caught him; better that then face the long cruelty of captivity.

They were all naked, sunburned, scratched, bloody and bruised, wounded by arrows or war clubs, so that one had dried blood in his hair, another an arrow puncture in his hip. But these wounds appeared minor. The soldiers promised to live a long time in the fires; they were still strong enough, still alive, and, afterwards, the camp dogs and crows would find them.

Jack turned and walked away.

The grass lay deep and dark on the ridge above the encampment. He knew yellow summer flowers bloomed in the darkness at his feet. He saw the moon, low in the west, a true Kiowa moon giving little light. Owl Stands' pony heard grazed along the ridge, moving softly and quietly searching out the richest tufts of grass. They were guarded by young herd boys who wanted to be down among the cottonwoods, joining the celebration. Jack's horses grazed in Owl Stands' herd but his best horse, the paint with the glassy eyes, stood on a tether by Owl

Stands' lodge in the encampment, kept close in case of any alarm, and beyond his reach now.

Jack heard the first cries of celebration and felt a shudder go through him, shaking his hands. He knew how the hearts of the children watching would grow strong against White Dog enemies, who cried out and died so easily. Yet he knew the young men tried to die well.

He carried his bow, his shield, his arrow case, his big knife, his saddle and pad. A packet of mesquite seed cakes and dried fruit, a little pemmican, his water skin and extra moccasins were wrapped and tied in his blanket roll. His catching rope circled around his waist. He walked quietly among the horses and they took no alarm, they knew him well from when he had been a herd boy, a keeper of Owl Stands' wealth. He found a tall bay which had once belonged to a white soldier courier, given to him by the family of the man he had caught up in the raid. He found another horse, a tough, wiry buckskin gelding that could run all day on a mouthful of grass. But before he could finish knotting his rope into a jaw bridle, he heard a sound behind him, and he crouched fast and turned, his knife swinging wide in an upward arc.

The body fell away from him in a soft clatter of bone breastplates and shell amulets and a turkey wing flute, all rattling as the body struck the ground on its back and lay as though paralyzed with surprise in the deep grass. No breath escaped, no sound. Jack's knife had passed through the soft substance of the fallen man and found the deep pouring artery.

A night bird called below the ridge. Jack's breath caught in a strangled cry. Then at his feet Jack heard a terrible sound of indrawn breath, dragging, dragging. But not enough breath for a death song. Not enough. He stared down through the darkness and saw his friend who walked with singing moccasins. But now he wore silent moccasins. New moccasins. As Jack watched, the straining went out of Ghost Boy's body, as though his good spirit were fleeing, fading away into the deep, sweet grass.

Jack wandered north and east while the moon waxed and waned to a crescent once more. The bay horse pulled up lame with a crack in its hoof and a sore back; he left it behind and threw rocks when it tried to follow. Now he rode the tough mustang gelding and went on, wandering.

My friend. I didn't know.

Grieving. *How? How?*

And then, *find your brothers.*

He watched the moon in the morning sky over his head, and tried to think of all the ways he had learned to cover his tracks; to be as though never born, perhaps just a story told on a cold winter night. Each day became his last, each night reprieved him. He watched his back trail, crouched on high bluffs, careful not to be seen against the sky; he drank stinking water, he couldn't find good waterholes, others were dry. He went thirsty and hungry. He followed landmarks and thought of his friend whose name could not be repeated.

Your moccasins---.

He knew there could be no punishment great enough.

Once, in the second month he thought he saw riders following and he caught his grazing pony and hurried north into a canyon. Another time he awoke in the night and heard laughter, the sounds of men talking in the darkness. He crept away and caught his horse and hurried west toward the buffalo plains.

He saw hunters in the distance and rode away before they saw him. Great storms turned the sky black with torrents of rain and swirling winds. In the weeks that followed he came to old camping places and found discarded awls, a file, a lost stone knife. He killed a lame buffalo calf, and with the awl and sinew, made new sets of moccasins with the crudely tanned leather. He dried the good meat to carry. At night he kindled small, smokeless fires and moved away after dark, staying to rough ground. At streams he sometimes found watercress and ate the peppery leaves with relish. He stopped to boil bear grass and love vine into a thick liquid he used to wash his body and his long hair.

At the end of the third month he began to grow deeply hungry, forced out onto the plains beyond water and food by large parties of Comanches riding southwest toward the war road into Mexico. He thought of the bay horse he had left behind. He ate cactus fruit, anything, and grew weaker as the days passed without strong meat. He led his buckskin pony most of the time, searching for grass and water, rubbing him down at night with handfuls of coarse grass. He found buffalo wallows shimmering with stagnant water and green grass growing up through the old bones of hundreds of buffalo carcasses scattered across the prairie.

He went on, alone and lonely. He did not know how to reach his people.

His brothers, my people.

Who were they?

He thought about the great shame that followed any man of the People who did not avenge the murder of a relative.

He thought about the death of his friend.

At night, in his short sleeping, he dreamed of his friend, who smiled and played his turkey wing flute, or danced his awkward dance with his moccasins singing. He woke at dawn, his face wet with the salt of tears.

He kept on, but each time he turned east he was driven back by bands of Indian raiders, or by buffalo hunters, or parties of *Tejanos* with wagons and guns traveling old trace roads. He watched buzzards circling in the sky. Soon he would grow too weak to kill meat or make new arrows. By now he had counted four full moons since he'd left the Comanches, and he knew by the yellowing of cottonwood leaves and the sharp winds, that winter was near, that he could not survive winter alone on the plains.

He cut his good pony's throat, making his apologies and giving his thanks, and took meat from its loin, smoking all that he could carry. Wolves followed him and came close at night for the meat he carried, and he shot them with his arrows, and cured a rough fur night robe with the animal brains and hard scraping to soften the hides. He went on, changing camps two or three times in the darkness because he thought he heard the howling of a wolf that was not a real wolf, or an owl that was not an owl. He went on doggedly eastward through fall storms that pummeled him with huge ice stones; and hid from great gusting winds that funneled down from the sky. Winter rode his thin shoulders and crept into his bones. Now, if he saw wild mustangs, he was too weak to crawl near and catch one. Now, if he saw riders in the distance he crouched down in hollows or deep in high sere grass, waiting for the riders to pass by, and once he found Indian sign everywhere, surrounding him, but he grew less and less concerned. He was weaker, his strong food gone, his last arrow used. When the moon grew full again, he began to starve.

He knew this starving time, he had been to this hungry place before, long ago as a boy. He lay on his back at night and watched the serene white moon gliding over him. He thought how the land, the night appeared very peaceful in this vast dark silence in which he was entirely alone. He thought of the Power which made everything, Owl Stands' words, of all that was unknowable, all the unanswered questions. He thought of his friend, of poetry and songs, of turkey wing flutes. He thought of his friend whose name he could speak only in his heart.

He heard no more wolves. But his mind wandered, and he was lonely, and when he heard the rushing of wings in his sleep he dreamed again of a boy's terror, of fires, of captives at the stake. He dreamed Owl Stands had found him.

He came to a wagon road and stopped and stared at the road for a long time, not sure of what he was seeing. His hunger had given him visions and his tattered moccasins had begun to leave a careless trail through the frosty grass. He began to follow the road, trying to keep out of sight, watching the white men coming and going on ponies and in wagons as if their village were nearby and they were busy with everyday tasks. They were men like himself whose skin was as light as his own under its shabby coverings, but now that he had found the *Tejanos* he grew afraid again.

He came to more roads, trees, oak groves, low hills, orchards, distant square lodges made of wood. He remembered such lodges, and then cows that gave milk for children, and then fat animals which rooted through oak leaves with long wet snouts. He remembered.

He saw how easily he could steal horses here, how easy to take women and children. He saw fences, the tracks of many cattle and smelled dung and wood smoke.

He saw a man mounted on a dun mare driving cows ahead of him. The man carried a long gun in his saddle holster. Jack stopped at the edge of the oaks bordering the clearing. The man was old, heavy in his body, and his breath made a cloud around his face in the cold air. He wore a blanket coat and a wide hat pulled down on his forehead and his jaw bristled with ugly gray hair.

The man saw Jack and stopped abruptly, then scrambled for his long gun. Jack knew he could not run very far or very fast because he had been hungry too long. He hoped the man saw him throw his bow aside.

The man shot his gun wildly. High above Jack's head an oak leaf dropped down, cut away by the ball. Jack flinched at the sound of the gun, then bolted for the trees at his back. Behind him the man beat his horse in a frantic dash across the field away from Jack, yelling one sound over and over. His cows scattered into the grass and began to graze.

Jack crawled back to the edge of the clearing and watched for a long time, but in fact it was only a few minutes, the cows had scarcely moved. He tried to think clearly, to know what he was doing. He could never find his people by running away from them, and he had come so far. He got to his feet. He had not found a stream to bathe away the grime of his journey, his hair was long, held by a band, darker than sand. One moccasin hung so tattered that it flapped around his ankle and he pulled it loose and discarded the other. He walked out into the clearing, leaving his bow and empty arrow case in the grass behind. He would like to have killed one of the cows to satisfy his hunger, but he had nothing to give in payment, and he guessed this would anger that man who must be the owner. He followed the dun mare, hoping the encampment of the *Tejanos* was not too far. He resolved that he would also throw his knife away when he came to his people as a gesture of his good will, and that he came as a stranger, alone, weaponless and troubled by hunger and fatigue. Even the Comanches respected such shows of peace from strangers. Surely the *Tejanos* would see he had come from far away by his condition, they would understand that he meant them no harm.

He prayed as he walked, to entreat the Supernaturals to surround him and protect him, but he was not a priest, maybe prayers were just words, songs, and he had no strong spiritual helpers to whisper in his ear and tell him which way to go. He felt his heart beating with fear, with excitement. He had seen this kind of excitement in the eyes of desperate animals. He walked on, singing his prayer softly, his body very thin and burned dark by the months of sun, his long hair blowing in a stir of wind.

Presently he heard more than the drumming of his heart. The sound came up from the earth through the soles of his feet into his body and he knew horsemen were near, many horsemen, more than he could escape if he tried to run now. But he hesitated and closed his eyes, and grew calm again, and walked on looking for another clearing. This was a good bright afternoon, cold and clear. The weak sun lay over in the west, throwing long shadows though the oaks. The frosty grass brushed around his feet.

Such good grazing grass---.

And if the *Tejanos* were going to shoot him he would rather be in the open, than under the trees.

He stopped in the next clearing. Now the sound of the horsemen grew, drowning the sound of his song but not the wild pounding of his heart. He heard shouts which he couldn't understand, one gunshot, all behind him. He stood unhurt, his legs braced. Perhaps they meant to ride him down.

The horsemen surged around him. He smelled their sweat, their fear, the sweat of their horses. Something bumped him, a hard, sharp bump of metal and he saw their long guns all pointed down toward him. He heard yells and shouts, but it was all a great confusion to him, all dust and fading light, all bewilderment. He thought the day had grown too dark, they would never notice the color of his hair, his eyes, his empty hands. He thought they would kill him as the Comanches might kill on a whim. He looked up expectantly.

There was just enough light to show one man the gray of Jack's eyes.

Since one white youth, gone wild, did not portend another redskin uprising which the settlement constantly guarded against, and since it was clear enough that the youth arrived unarmed, underfed and alone, most of the settlers managed to overcome their certainty that any Indian of any age, white or red, was dangerous and never to be trusted. They took Jack in and tried to tame him.

He was not the first. No one wept for joy over another captive saved from the savages, although Jack had saved himself. There were so many others unsaved. A few of the settlers still swore that the wild youth must have raped and killed, along with his Indian captors, in order to survive so long. They had never seen male captives of such an age, and only heard of two who had not been traded but escaped on their own. Who knew if they could ever be trusted? But by now the emigrants from Missouri and Louisiana and Pennsylvania and Germany and Georgia, who had come ill-prepared, in creaking ox drawn wagons; who had fled from debt, and what they called difficulties, and worn out soil, and low wages, and no hope of bettering themselves, and; who had survived floods and cholera and prairie fires this far, to make a settlement out of common need and fear, and the availability of wood and water and decent soil; faced the wild youth as further evidence of the cruel land and the Red Man's mundane brutality, always threatening at the edge of the civilized world. They looked on Jack with both wariness and a stolid sort of Christian pity, and determined to put things right.

They began by shearing his hair, scrubbing him, and covering his body. The last seemed a foolish effort to Jack who doubted that their women were ignorant of men's bodies. Nevertheless, he allowed everything, in his gratitude, his relief. He obeyed every gesture and attempted to understand the unmusical speech that became a little more familiar every day.

Families came to look at him, sometimes coming from far away, names like San Antonio de Bexar and Austin and Fort Davis. They came searching for lost relatives, children from long ago or perhaps only a few months ago. He tried always to be careful, to show only the truth of his own expectation. The guilty truth of the *Tejano* he had killed remained locked away, almost beyond reach; but because he lacked a small birthmark or a scar or some other remembered mark or eye color, he fulfilled no one's hopes, and his secret remained hidden.

The clothes they gave him were stiff and uncomfortable, but he wore them without complaint. He tried hard to wear a pair of cast-off boots. The food disagreed with him, but he ate almost everything to replenish his body and to please them. He couldn't swallow pig's meat nor cow's milk. The slippery gray lumps they called soap melted in his hands when he washed, as he did often with so much good water available and he thought of boiled bear grass and love vine, but their soap had a bitter, ashy, faintly remembered smell.

He had no name. As he came to understand more of them, they asked him, with their own words, what he remembered, but there were just a few words tenaciously held from long ago and from the Comanchero traders, a jumble of Comanche, Spanish and white man's talk. The rest he could tell them only with gestures and pictures drawn in the dust. Now and then his memory opened suddenly, sometimes faintly as with the soap, sometimes in a bright kaleidoscope of pictures and strange sounds; a bell ringing to call in men at the edge of the field, or a dishpan bumped against a porch rail. Sometimes he recalled a vivid image of color, flannel or wool, and knew that he knew the shape of a garment without knowing how. But these things from the past did not trouble him anymore, as they once had when he was far from his own people; for now, he had no time for the past when the present required his strongest interest and effort in trying to learn the new customs and words of the whites.

The pastor of the settlement, a childless man, who had once been a printer in a place called New York, but finding little demand for his skills on the frontier, where men could not eat words, nor fight the Red Man, with printer's ink, turned to raising apples and preaching. He wrote letters for his illiterate neighbors, he married sinners on his regular routes among the far-flung settlements, and took care of his orchard in order to keep himself and his wife in victuals. The collection plate was his only cash crop, augmented by twenty dollars a year raised by his congregation when he agreed to take the wild youth into his house.

Gradually Jack became a calling, a genuine mission. He had observed, with some surprise, a mind not hopelessly damaged and befuddled by his violent past. When the pastor was not out riding circuit, baptizing babies and marrying sinners, in that order, or comforting the dying and carrying letters and news, he came to consider Jack his true work on earth. He set out to teach the ways of the Lord and the white man. He taught Jack New York English. As a reward for Jack's effort, if not excellence, he wrote letters to the army, to Indian agents, to the Department of the Interior, to any authorities he could think of. Because he was an educated man, who took good measure of Jack's age and his teeth, not unlike he judged the age of horses, he could place Jack's birth in the early '30s. On his travels riding circuit, he talked to settlers and searched back through old records and newspapers and came at last to the Kiowa and Comanche revenge raids along the gulf coast in the '30s and early '40s, especially after the bitter Council House fight in San Antonio de Bexar. Eight months after Jack had found the settlers, a letter came to the pastor, and Jack knew who he was.

He didn't remember a place called Brushy Creek. Maybe there were many places called Brushy Creek. He remembered drought. The name Rainie was a word in a foreign tongue placed in his mind. There were no Rainies living along Brushy Creek now, only burned out farms, empty fields, remnants of an old land grant village with an old trading post and one grizzled trader.

There was no great tract of land since the old Galveston Bay and Texas Land Company's fancy script had proven worthless, only an impresario's unfulfilled contract. The trader held on by little more than his hope of a new day, a new village now that this country was a part of Texas, and not Mexico, after the war. He hung on in the hope of no more heathen savages, whom he as a Texian, hated for their random depredations. But he was stubborn, as determined as the persistent frontier people. Just wait, he said. Good times were ahead. And he remembered the hard days, the raids, the killings, all those settlers leaving at about the same time; they realized they didn't own the land, after all. Some dug in anyway. But they hadn't yet lifted their roof trees for a decent cabin before the Comanches came up the creek early one morning.

So much had happened since then, in the way of struggle and hard luck, to dull anyone's memory. But the trader remembered a few names. Thompson, Smith, McGiver, or McGivern, Rainie.

Jack didn't understand everything about this news, but he understood that he had no people after all. Perhaps he was the boy who had once been called Jack Rainie, perhaps he wasn't. Had there ever been a father, gulled by the Galveston Bay and Texas Land Company? Had there ever been others, a woman? The letter did not recall a woman's name. If she existed, she existed in a shadow bending over a washtub or a loom, sitting by a spinning wheel, drinking from a tin cup of water; never remembered by the trader, unnoticed.

Jack Rainie.

Like the stories the old Comanche men loved to tell, here was a being born one autumn morning staring up into the faces of the true People.

He went to school and learned to read quickly, since he had already learned to read signs in the dust, symbol carved into rocks or oak trees, or painted on calendar robes, or the language of the skies. And he remembered more each day, books, pictures.

Run, run thou tiny rill,
Round the rocks and down the hill;
Sing in every child like me;
The birds will join you full of glee---

But soon he threw the reader away in disgust. He was too old for nonsense. The reader told him nothing of what he needed to know, it gave him no insight into the hearts of his new people. Even as the words of his first language came more easily, he knew he had no time to waste with impractical things.

He ran errands for the parson's plump wife and ate, with relish, her occasional offering of honeyed sweets. He tended the parson's growing apple orchard in the hard winter of 1850, and often found his only sanctuary there among the sleeping trees, trying to sort out the contradictions in his days. He thought about the great knife Owl Stands had given him, a terrible gift for killing that *Tejano* trader; he thought about his friend; and he went to the place at the edge of the trees in that pasture where the settlers had found him months before. He found the knife, tangled in snow and dead grass.

He tended the parson's carriage horse and his handful of strays, old horses, mustangs, taken in trade, one horse the parson considered a poor trade; but Jack knew he was the kind of mustang the Comanches favored, a shaggy pony both fast and tough. He ran foot races and pony races with other youths, and jeered when he won, and he lost poorly, and he taunted them with their softness. They were only farmers' sons, merchants' sons, and Jack Rainie had fought, had killed to be free. He sat glowering in a church pew beside the parson's wife, a captive listening to words that made little sense to him. Could this God do anything? Was he related to the Power, to the Supernaturals? He stared around at the church, only a small square building of raw wood smelling of rosin, crammed with earnest people who sang and listened to long speeches and prayed. He stared at the backs of heads, innocent people, terrified of Kiowas and Comanches or any Indian, of tornados, of locust and plague and God's wrath. But they were here; they worked; they stayed. He attempted to occupy his mind with all these trivial things, but he thought most about the red shimmer of the tinsmith's daughter's hair.

He learned that among the whites he couldn't belch loudly after a meal to show his appreciation, nor relieve himself behind the church after the service. He learned he must not fight with his knife, but only with his hands. He learned he couldn't court white girls with a reed flute, nor sleep-crawl at night.

He learned that he had little value in the White Dog world.

But, by the power of the white man's Jesus, the tinsmith's daughter had wonderful russet hair the color of maple leaves in the winter frost outside the chapel door. He knew the texture, the weight of her hair, from sitting behind her in the church pew. He thought of poetry and songs. His own hair had the dull, rough color of sand beside hers, his eyes a wintery gray, compared to hers which were the blue of the finest blue day. He spent much time thinking of her; of, by some benevolence of the Supernaturals themselves, finding her alone someday, secluded in a green shaded thicket. He imagined she had wandered far away from the settlement gathering sumac bark and herbs, and sometimes flowers, since he'd observed Comanche and white women all liked flowers. In his mind he imagined lying with her, safe from whites and Comanches, from priests and parsons, meeting often, talking and laying together.

But when he approached the girl, wearing a new shirt and bearing a small gift, the tinsmith drove Jack away with shouts and short words he already knew were curses.

As the months passed, he fought more often with boys, older and younger; with anyone who laughed at his mistakes; his many blunders; his earnest efforts to explain Comanche lore and customs, his only knowledge. He fought for other reasons he seldom understood, other than that he had approached the red-haired girl.

He spent more time in the seclusion and peace of the apple orchard, watching the deer creep from the oak thickets to eat the fallen fall apples, pondering all that troubled him, his own vast ignorance, his questions. He harvested baskets of apples for the parson's cellar, for trading. He ran more errands for the parson's wife, who sometimes frowned at him now. He learned more of the Mexican troubles in the past, old land grants, endless disputes, a war the People had talked about in the villages, rumors and terrible stories and much killing between the whites, and now Texas was a state. He learned about law.

What did all that mean, except that the new people came in droves?

Now, when he practiced writing in the leather-bound workbook with all the empty pages, his letters became sentences and the sentences spoke haltingly of his day, his thoughts. He read every issue of the Texas Gazette, even the old ones. He learned to shoe horses and other practical blacksmith skills because the parson spoke often of how each settler must know many trades in order to prosper. He spoke of money, though real money was scarce on the frontier. Jack would surely be rewarded for his skills with coins or script, the parson told him. He learned to repair harness, to plough and plant corn, he remembered corn, empty cobs.

Drought. The ache of hunger by a dry seep. Not enough.

He let his hair grow long again and refused to crop it. He said hell and Jesus and Goddamn and shit, American words, he heard fucking Indian. He threw away his cast-off boots and made moccasins for himself. By now, the settlement boys came looking for fights, in the same way they found, and stoned, unwary dogs. Jack lost more often because no boy now confronted him alone. The sight of his own face at night made him smile into the looking glass in the parson's little parlor. His heart grew harder, more confused. It was as though the confusion he'd known for so long kept on and on.

He found other books in the parson's camelback trunk, not school readers, but books which spoke powerfully of other men's lives, and gave him insights into other men's struggles. Toward what? Sometimes he read aloud, practicing the language until it sounded fine to him, with only a hint of rough accent. He learned of the greatness of the world, which reached far beyond his power to imagine, great waters, great mountains, mysterious and hostile lands and people. But perhaps these were only fanciful stories the whites liked to tell their children, not unlike the myths and stories old Comanche men liked to tell on cold winter nights.

He learned that he had stolen the books from the parson's camelback trunk. The parson gave him slate work, to be copied one hundred times.

Beautiful faces are they that wear
The light of pleasant spirits there;
Beautiful hands are they that do
Deeds that are noble, good and true—

By this, Jack knew it was time to leave the settlement. He was not meant for endless slate work and other absurdities.

He dressed himself in clothes similar to those he had worn when he came to the settlement, wanting to be fair, his old antelope hide shirt, cleaned again, but brown wool trousers like all the white men wore. The parson gave him a blanket, a canteen, food, a six-dollar horse from his small herd of strays. The parson's wife gave him a bit of brass, in the form of a cross.

In the best days, they had given him everything. Now they helped him to leave. They spoke few words. Jack had nothing to give for their kindness, except what he had given all along, which had been the restraint of his strong nature, the control of his Comanche ways, and his true effort to please. Yet, he read in the parson's face, how Jack's sharp, starved mind, his combative spirit, his long silences, had come to alarm this God-man. In the woman's face he saw that he was wrong in most ways, hell-bent, perhaps beyond all hope. In her face he had always seen hidden embarrassment for his blunders, his coarseness. Plainly she thought he'd reached the settlement too late.

He wasn't suited for much of anything. He owned fragments of skills here and there, enough to keep him in victuals most of the time, and sometimes shelter. Mostly he was curious, and he came to think often in the next two years that the parson's woman had been wiser than he'd known.

He knew what the Comanches and the parson had taught him of practical things, but he still didn't know much about the ways of the whites. He rode his six-dollar horse, that shaggy mustang the parson thought worthless, into villages and settlements, working for food, and saw how these frontier people helped each other do almost anything, helped raising a new barn, helped with a grass fire, tended injuries, helped with the ploughing, often fed strangers, helped search for lost livestock, lost children, helped guard against the Indians they hated hiding among the thickets. But he was sometimes cheated of his wages after hard days clearing land or digging wells because he didn't know money well enough but learned quickly. Clearing land, digging out stumps, digging privies, hauling trash, he threw his journal in the trash, angry at the work, but knew no other.

He didn't know white girls or friendships or whiskey or cattle, and learned these things more gradually, always careful to say little about himself, never his full name. He had learned more about the powerful word known as law. In one settlement he traded for a long gun, a packet of ammunition and a good Green River knife with a steel blade to add to his weapons, and heard stories about militia, volunteers, Texas Rangers, those fighters who tried to protect the settlers, but sometimes there were muttered stories of their secret killings, mostly Mexicans, or they were often fighting and chasing somewhere else. And there were never enough soldiers at the scattered forts, never enough.

He heard about new forts being built, and more soldiers, and men locked up in small cages where they stayed all their lives.

Law.

He saw two dark skinned men left hanging from oak trees by the side of the road and never knew why.

He learned how to drive freight wagons, how to swamp taverns and dance halls. Once, with others, he went after a herd of wild mustangs and drove them to market, and he saw other captured bands of mustangs driven through the town, all with the clipped ears of Comanche ownership. Stolen. He heard of a dispatch rider, found dead and scalped by the side of the road; he heard of just plain foreign fools sport hunting shaggies out on prairies, huge lumbering buffalo herds wintering along the Brazos River.

In the town called San Antonio de Bexar, he rode through the dusty plaza and stared with wonder at all the people walking, riding; all the fine carriages and wagons; dragoons from Fort Sam; children running; dogs everywhere; fine ladies shopping; others who looked like whores, in fancy clothes; and, some who looked just poor and shabby and hungry. He saw *padre* schools, churches, saloons, a theatre with faint sounds of singing drifting from a doorway, stores with big signs advertising apothecary goods, working gear, harness repair, new saddles, tobacco shops, dry goods, weapons, custom boots and shoemaking.

He went into the dry goods store marveling at all he saw. He read news posters about Indian captives lost, and he wondered. He bought another journal and a blue flannel shirt, just over from New Orleans, he was told. Merchants ordered supplies for a year, two years, to save on cartage and just hoped to hell the Indians didn't raid the wagons and carry away the new flannel shirts and cookware and umbrellas and bolts of red calico. They complained that friendly Indian bands, looking for trade, liked to tie that bright calico to their horse's tails and run with wild shouts of revelry through the streets of San Antonio de Bexar.

Along the street he heard hammering and heavy saws dragged across rough wood, new shops and houses going up, some wooden houses with peaked roofs and pretty porches in front, foreign looking houses built as if in defiance of the harsh natural land, and others of mud brick with flat roofs and arbors with grapevines and stone thresholds with brightly painted wooden doors. Across the plaza where chickens foraged through clumps of weeds, he saw a tall, fine building in disrepair, pocked with holes and gouges in its dirty plaster, carved columns around its tall tightly closed doors. The Alamo fort, he remembered from the pastor's stories. A bad fight the Mexicans won when they captured San Antonio de Bexar.

Soldiers wandered the plaza from the fort nearby, some with Mexican girls on their arms, others bent on errands. A livery with good corrals advertised feed and care. Another shop had hanging cuts of beef and deer meat and offered game butchering services, next to it a shop with baskets of apples and turnips and cabbages, root cellar offerings, pecan nuts from last year's crop. Flowers spilled from a noisy Mexican two wheeled cart nearby, where a woman offered seeds and greens and bundles of herbs. Wonderful smells of spiced foods came from a blue colored cart where a Mexican man called out his wares, and Jack stopped and ate with relish, only a few coins left. An old Mexican woman wrapped in a striped serape passed by, leading a cow from door to door, selling fresh milk.

This village had the feel of an old place, worn but enduring, with outlying irrigated fields, old Spanish and Mexican buildings and old customs all attempting to grow new with immigrant energy. He stopped a man to ask about work, and the man smiled a welcome and replied with a foreign sounding accent, very guttural. Jack heard the pride in the man's voice, a pride he'd heard from new settlers before any Indians and horse thieves and droughts found them. He learned that this town boasted ten thousand residents, mostly old *Tejano*

Spanish-Mexican families and Canary Islanders along with Poles and Germans and Basque. The man in front of Jack answered his questions and bowed to acknowledge his own origin. He mentioned that there were also Spanish *hidalgos*, *charros*, thieves, and shooters of all variety, and a few Americans, mostly from Kansas and New Orleans, bringing all manner of merchandise and new ways along the dirt traces from Galveston and other ports. Good workers were scarce and eagerly sought but many who came just lived in the saloons until their money ran out, or they got into fights. He told Jack about pounding nails, hauling and splitting wood for fireplaces, building chimneys, working in the irrigated fields, chasing settlers' cattle that had wandered away, riding shotgun or driving one of the endless numbers of freight wagons. One big ox train was leaving in three days for a fort being built far west. Looking for crazy men to carry the wagons there, he said, through Comanche country.

Damn Indians, yah! He heard the comment and foreign words he couldn't understand.

Jack rode on, looking at everything, marveling. He found the river with the bridge and caution signs posted in three languages. He watched the redbirds flying in the high trees and smelled what he thought must be the rich smell of spring water that became river water. Further up he saw Mexican girls washing clothes in the river, laughing, washing their long black hair and bathing at the edge of the river with little concern for modesty, their colorful clothes and *rebozos* laid out on the bank to dry. He watched for a while with appreciation then turned back and stopped and stared at a storefront advertising all kinds of legal services.

Law.

The word always jolted him, made him pause and remember.

A second sign advertised good land for sale, 10c to 25c for an acre.

He found the place where scores of oxen lowed and milled in a corral, and big wooden wagons sat idle in the sun, a few with men loading and cursing as they adjusted weights.

He joined a line of men moving forward slowly, most of them rough, with the look of drifters, some drinking from flasks and bottles. They moved gradually toward the place where a heavily bearded man sat at a table made of sawn boards leaking rosin. He sat with pen and paper, asking questions. He spoke with an accent, impatient, no time to waste. Maybe another German man; busy with his optimism, and his work. Oxen. Indians. Weapons. Money. Hurry.

The line moved forward step by step in the dust. Jack came to the table and waited. The man stared at him for a time, with a keen eye and ponderous consideration, clearly questioning if Jack could be useful. He did not see a burly, sweating teamster or a half-drunk drifter. He examined Jack's worn antelope skin shirt, his weapons, the faded scarf tied at his neck, his moccasins, his old hat, his long hair, his face.

His six-dollar horse.

Then back to Jack.

"Young," the man said.

"What's old?" Jack answered.

The man barked a laugh. "A philosopher! You some kind of Indian?"

"No sir."

"Half breed? *Mestizo?*"

Jack saw no reason to answer.

The man studied him for another moment. "You don't look like no cook. You hunt?"

Jack said, "Anything."

The man narrowed his eyes, searching.

"Scout?"

Jack shrugged, then nodded. Why not?

"You fight? Them Indians who come? Them bad ones?"

Jack looked at the man, "Sure."

"Wrangler?"

"Sure."

"Blacksmith?"

"Some."

"No brawling. No whiskey. We got scouts. We got no hunters yet, them we had gone off up Chisholm's road---." He stopped, reconsidered his words. "You do what you're told. You get paid when we get there. You quit, you lose, no money. You got a better horse?"

"He's good."

He's fast. He's tough. That's what counts.

"You know about them Indians?"

"Some," Jack answered again.

"Put your mark here."

Jack saw that most of the other men had made their crude signs and crosses, but he signed his first name only, with a practiced flourish. "How long?"

"Weeks. Three months, maybe longer. The weather, them damn heathen Comanches. Maybe Apaches. We get there soon enough. It's early. Grass is still pretty good! Bring your own gear."

"How much?"

"Maybe $30.00 by the month when we get there, no trouble." He handed Jack a provision list to look at, then snatched it back. "Five o'clock sharp, three days, in the morning. We leave." He looked doubtful for a moment as he looked at Jack, he saw thin saddlebags, a vintage saddle with a holstered Sharp's rifle and old blankets on Jack's six-dollar horse. Maybe just a young braggart. But he was impatient for the next man in line. "Three days, here. Next!"

Jack rode back to the dry goods store. He bought a good coat, wool pants and socks and a soft felt hat, ammunition. His last coins went for a painted canvas waterproof tarp, a bar of Castile soap and an extravagant box of waxed Lucifer matches. All the while he was wondering about what he had done, this random urge to sign up, to go on. San Antonio town offered great temptations, perhaps the kind of opportunity any green settler grabbed, but he thought about the far places he'd read about at the parson's house, he thought about the town, easy work, taverns, women, those pretty Mexican girls by the river, and then he thought again about all those far places and the constant, elegant invitation to risk. Everywhere he felt the urge to risk on this hustling frontier, once here and then on to mountains, rivers, free government land, past all good sense. On, looking for a mountain or a river he'd read about, or the Big Ocean Water to the west. There were other roads and traces across the wild prairies, taken by the early men looking for good trails, good river crossings. He thought about who he was, about crossing the Comancheria, out there again.

Comanches.

Taking chances. His recurring nightmares, his deepest fears, Overcome, or maybe just buried.

He shook his head in wonderment, because, fear or not, he was ready to go on.

This sounded a hell of a lot better than mending fences and digging privies. The parson had sent him out of the parsonage door with tales of frontier folks and their need for many skills. Every skill they could muster.

Now he'd signed up for everything; now he would hunt and wrangle the *remuda* and fix wagons; anything for this long plodding oxen train of eleven high wooden wagons, each drawn by four teams of oxen, and all heavy with military supplies for the new fort yonder, across the prairie. A cook wagon would drive out in front of the dust carrying barrels of flour and sugar, beans and bacon, yeast, baking powder, salt and spices, clarified butter, and anything the cook demanded for his skills, as well as the teamsters' bedding and packs. Enough of everything to last for three months, maybe 600 miles or more. Another wagon followed at the rear carrying barrel hoops, spare metal wheel parts, tools for repairs, a small forge, horse shoes and wheel tires, barrels of grain for the stock, anything that might be needed along the way. The wagons banded together by custom and necessity, offering opportunity to work or to pay for passage and protection from wandering hostiles across the wild prairie lands beyond the forts.

A few strays signed on, farmers paying in coin or barter in return for the protection of the train's numbers, on their way back to outlying newly claimed farms and ranches, and if they went all the way to the open prairies and the Comanche hunting lands, they were bound to go all the way for building the new fort on the Rio Grande, called the Post at the Pass, or for just going across to Mexico, or to take the long southern trail to California through Chihuahua, that invitation to risk all the way up to all that fabled California gold.

The German wagon master, whose name was Otto Ahls, sometimes called Boss, told Jack that he had a United States Government military contract to deliver the goods, come Comanches or Kiowas or twister storms. He had trailed before, and never yet been bothered by hostiles.

Lucky man, Jack thought.

Otto Ahls had no taste for adventure, only for success and payment for his labors. He had left Germany, and bad luck, behind and now he was here to prosper in this new country.

Two scouts signed on with the train. Old Billy Fustus claimed to have set out west from Missouri at fourteen because he was the oldest of his family. The younger ones needed his food at home, and because he'd heard tall tales of the Shining Mountains and he damn well had to see them for himself.

He stayed in the mountains once he got there, learned the ways of the Sioux and the Crow, trapped fur, did well enough at the yearly rendezvous, left a scatter of little half breeds among wives he claimed were happy women, and then, when his hands twisted up with the rheumatiz, and all those government surveyors started traveling west, chopping up the country, he finally just gave up complaining and scouted for them for a while and then grew tired of snow, the mountains, and the cold that made his rheumatiz a misery.

"Used to get $100.00 a hide for them beaver, now it's $3.00. Shit, too many people, not enough beaver. Its them new steel traps, I say."

But he could still ride and pull a trigger, he was a good trailer and his eyes were hawk-sharp. He wore three pistols at his waist, without explanation or apology. He had heard that Texas was warm. Well, plain hot was a better description. Maybe the women too. He had a wry sense of humor, and a clever mind, and he had been over parts of this road before.

The second man, a Delaware Indian scout named Tomaso had experience with the military around the forts to the north. Delawares made the best scouts, he told Jack. His English stumbled along when he spoke, but he was mostly a big quiet man looking for a way to find his woman and son, stolen, and carried off by Kiowas, somewhere down across the Rio Grande, near the Mexican El Paso. Maybe sold to a *hidalgo* family for servants in Chihuahua, maybe just dead. He had to search, but if he couldn't find them soon, he would give up, find another wife and start a new family.

A man named Sinfarano hired on as another meat hunter. He looked like a withered, long-haired Indian of mixed blood. He gave no information about himself, but his looks and his Indian ways, and the few words he grunted now and then, made Jack certain that he was from the Tonkawa people, who sometimes acted as guides to the military. These men were the eaters of human flesh and hated by the Comanches.

The drovers and their helpers, who signed on as hustlers, came from Germany and France and Louisiana and the Canary Islands, and some places Jack never heard of. The cook with the chuckwagon was a free black man who brought his half-grown son to hustle the pots and pans, and gather wood. They were all hardy, tough men, acting fearless and glad for the work, a few laughing about this adventure into hostile country, others scowling with grievances. Some who scowled, spoke quiet words of anger aimed at the Negro cook; Southern men with generations of grudges. But on the whole, they planned to savor the rewards of good wages in hard money, and a romp in the Mexican villages and brothels they'd heard about south of the new fort. They liked to call themselves bullwhackers, and that's about what they did best. They talked about gold, and California and woman. They carried all varieties of weapons and showed little concern that troopers were not guarding this wagon train. Those pretty blue boys were no doubt busy guarding wagon trains full of settlers, or chasing Kiowas and Comanches somewhere else. After all, this was no new road. They had heard this was an old Indian trace, like the many that crossed the prairies. They had heard that back in 1848, or so, a military supply train with hundreds of wagon and thousands of cattle had traveled three months to start a new fort on the American side of the Rio Grande at El Paso del Norte. Now they were headed there again. More building, more restoring after years of abandonment, more protection for all the new settlers pushing west.

The teamsters and their men yelled, and spit tobacco juice, and kissed their women goodbye, cracking their long whips, as the oxen train slowly left the town of Bexar in the dark of early dawn, plodding on to the San Antonio Trail. They were followed by packs of dogs, two young dandies on fancy horses and dressed for the dance halls, and skipping children, all quickly turned back from the cumbersome dusty train, as the day warmed.

They nooned, at hot midday, to rest the oxen and let them graze. They ate beans and bacon and fresh baked bread. They stopped at darkness for more beans and bacon and tough beefsteak from their commissary herd of steers. Guards watched in shifts, as the oxen and *remuda* of horses and mules grazed and rested, sometimes singing and talking to stay awake.

Day by day, the train headed northwest for the distant location of the fort at the Pass, at the place now called El Paso del Norte, more weeks away across the Comancheria, following the wagon road with deep ruts and muddy hog-wallow bogs after rain, where the heavy wagons foundered and had to be dragged to firm roadbed. The oxen plodded a few miles further each day, and the wagon wheels screeched and groaned until Jack showed the drovers how to crush pear cactus as a lubricant after they ran out of black grease.

They stopped at ranches and farms along the way, three of the stray travelers dropping off, the black cook bargaining for fresh onions and corn and whatever the settlers could spare. They passed two burned out farms where wild cattle browsed through long dead kitchen gardens. At another ranch Jack saw a wooden cross in the front yard and a half-burned house and barn. They passed old abandoned groups of buildings in the distance, maybe old forts or trading posts. Then they came to more open land, beyond all the abandoned forts, a prairie empty of any signs of settlement.

Now game ran in the shallow canyons and over the rolling hills. Jack brought back antelope and deer rousted out of thickets where they sheltered by day. The scouts rode out ahead and at dusk guided the wagons to good campgrounds, some old and littered with discarded trash. The wagons circled near good water and trees, or sometimes in open grass land. The oxen and *remuda* grazed under heavy watch as the drovers built high fires, eating, complaining, telling stories, clear signals to any Kiowa or Comanche eyes miles away. Jack mentioned old Indian sign, travois tracks of Comanche families moving after buffalo, and the fires sank down to cautious coals. He rode out before sunrise, before the oxen were yoked and the fires buried, and returned with the sun overhead, packing antelope and deer on a pack horse for Reuben, the cook, to butcher. Sinfarano, the Tonkowa hunter, often came back from his hunts with little or no game.

It suited Jack to do his job well as he mended wagon wheels and shod horses and mules that had thrown their shoes. He didn't care much about the rest. He sometimes dug wild onions and other tubers he knew Comanche women favored and gave them to the cook. He found small herds of buffalo, now and then an elk for the chuckwagon and taught the cook's son, young Ely, how to help him field butcher for the chuckwagon. He followed herds of wild horses, some with the slit ears of Comanche ownership, and cattle with long horns hiding in mesquite thickets, more dangerous to hunt than old rogue buffalo bulls. Wild Spanish cattle grazed everywhere, more numerous than the buffalo, always wild beef for the cook pots if their traveling commissary of steers ran off or ran out.

As the weeks passed and they moved deeper into the Comancheria Jack felt the uneasiness begin.

He knew.

The prairies and thickets seemed empty, but he felt the eyes. They were being watched, he knew.

The scouts knew.

He could not be surprised, after all, because he knew their ways, their stealth. Their love of theft and cunning. Unless they were south, following the herds, or the chiefs had called for councils or raids far away, they would be here, they would know. Indian runners would spread the word of these wagons, these many *Tejano* White Dogs with their oxen and horse herd and steers.

All this insult to be challenged, all this plunder to be captured because this was sacred hunting grounds. He couldn't name which bands they were, whose eyes were watching until days later. Sometimes at night he heard night birds or the bark of a fox, sounds he knew were not animal sounds. The Tonkowa Indian meat hunter, Sinfarano, after boasting of his prowess at hunting, became surly and began to complain and watch the hilltops and thickets. Slowly, over time, the dogs that followed the train disappeared.

Jack wondered, with a distant sense of wonder, if any of those who were watching were Comanche men he knew, known to him and he to them as the Comanche peace chief Owl Stands' favored White Dog captive, a son, and often mentioned among the People in idle rumors, but no one important until that night with his friend, whose name he couldn't speak.

He knew there were bitter grievances, shame, far-away anger. Sometimes as the days passed he couldn't think why he had returned to all this, here on the Comancheria, but then his own heart would harden against the constant memory, the constant threat.

One among many. No one important.

But they were Comanches and their memories were long.

On a blue day as they travelled, Jack and the guides saw the smoke rising in puffs from a hill far south, reading the signal. The wind quickly carried its meaning into nothing, just smoke from a dry lightning fire. Tomaso, the Delaware guide, nodded to Jack as he read the sign, Then Sinfarano went out hunting at dawn and never came back. The wagon master cursed and called a serious gathering, hashing over what had occurred that made some good men, even those acquainted with Indian trouble, now uneasy.

Them damn Indians, somewhere around watching, maybe ready for a fight. Pull the wagons in a tight circle, get the oxen and stock inside the circle, look to your water and your ammunition, get ready to shoot.

"They want the horses---."

"They'll shoot the oxen---."

"They've gone," Jack said.

"No, they are---," a drover yelled his fear.

"They've gone."

"Who speaks? You know this?" Otto's guttural voice barked at Jack. He frowned his doubt.

"Well they ain't here. You still got your stock," the scout named Billy Fustus with a wry look at Jack.

"They are only a few. They won't fight against so many guns here." Jack saw the Delaware scout Tomaso make a small nod of agreement.

"You know this?" the wagon master demanded of Jack again for every man to hear. They all stood in a circle around Captain Ahls, waiting for his orders, ways to protect themselves and their animals, how to fight the hostiles. A few knew something of minor fights with Indians, a few kept silent with what they knew, but mostly they had just been so confidant.

"Who are they?" Otto Ahls demanded, staring hard at Tomaso, at Billy Fustus, then at Jack. How would this person on his six-dollar horse, how would he know anything important? He was only a meat hunter.

"Comanches," Jack said. "Maybe some Kiowas."

There was another lifting of voices.

Fucking damned savages. The worst.

"When they come back they'll be after the horses and mules, they'll try to stampede your *remuda*, split it, drive off what they can," Billy Fustus said with an expression that always seemed to marvel at these ignorant travelers. He paused to rub his hands with bear oil against the rheumatiz that plagued him "You boys need more guards. No gunshots in a fight, no wavin' blankets or y'all just stampede the herd yourselves."

Jack said, "They are not fools."

"You've found signs?"

Jack's mouth almost smiled at this. "Yep. Everywhere."

This was only the first alarm. He knew there would be others now. They were deep in the Comancheria now. They plodded on, more guards at night, pickets stationed on the hills, watching. Like the military boys, Billy said.

An oxen now and then pulled up lame, wagons fell behind and hurried to catch up by dusk, wheels broke. There were stops for rest and repairs under cottonwoods and pecans, by wandering streams and willow thickets where rattlesnakes abounded. This journey dragged on and on, slow weeks of hunting, everyday discomfort, injuries, dirt without wash water, growing tired of hard work, more dirt, stupid damn oxen, sometimes bad water, rain and heat.

Jack listened to stories and lies around campfires that were kept low at night. Somewhere in the camp a wagon driver played a soft melody on his concertina and another joined in with his harmonica.

He began to write in his journal again, spare lines by firelight, he wasn't sure why. But those lines somehow validated true events and thoughts. When he read back weeks of lines he'd made on the early days of the journey, short as the sentences were, he knew who Jack Rainie was, with moments of surprise.

His name is Reuben. Not Cookie, not boy. Not nigger, won't answer. His face is black, some hate him. Good cinnamon rolls. He brings a boy. Wants to be a cow boy.

Reuben was a tall, thin man of great dignity among the rough teamsters. He often wore a red skullcap with one long turkey feather that blew in the wind. His skin was night black, his teeth large and white. He moved with grace and purpose and, always polite, barely suffered the many fools in the wagon train, especially those who scorned him for his color. Nigger Reuben, they sometimes said. His owner long ago had raised him with hard work and genuine caring, and showed it by permitting Reuben, then a gangling youth, the rare gift of a little schooling, Reuben worked on the rundown old farm, for the old man who sometimes forgot his name, doing everything but mostly working in the tobacco fields. Hot sun and hard work did not bother him for he knew he was meant for more. He had a lofty regard for the old man because of his good treatment, his good heart.

The place was too small and now too poor to be called anything but a poor farm and his owner, a man of books, was never suited for such a hard scrabble life. But Reuben never went hungry. He married a pretty girl from another farm, who showed her father's mix of Seminole and black, but Reuben didn't care. She had long flowing hair, Indian hair that he admired, not like his own tightly thatched hair. She bore a boy child and then in the bad sickness winter two years later she died of chills and coughing and left Reuben with the boy.

The old man, too old, too sick with age, brought them into the house. There was little work on the farm with the last tobacco cheap at the market, where they heard bad rumors of random violence across the land. Then a crop full of disease, worthless.

The old man began to fail in his mind. He talked to his wife, Miss Letty, long gone. The slave field hand, a surely boy full of anger, had kept the land producing with ploughing and planting and drying the tobacco. The plough horse died of a colic, the turkeys and most of the chickens gone to the kitchen or to weasels. Now Reuben worked tending a kitchen garden full of pumpkins and cabbage and a small peach orchard with old, dying trees. All the outbuildings had fallen into rotten wood, leaking slave quarters, roofs and gaping barn doorways. The field hand slipped away, and the old man didn't notice. But that simple black fool would have a hard time of it, caught soon, Reuben knew, maybe reported or just absorbed into another gang of field hands in another parish, no one left to claim him and the law, or an overseer, just looking the other way with bribe coins in their hands.

Reuben had his young boy, Ely, and stayed. But the black house-cook, Marvel, a woman of generous girth and cooking enthusiasm---look at how fat I am, she liked to boast to prove it---stayed for the old man. She remembered the old man's favorite dishes, saving a bit of this or that for him, she remembered the good days and a measure of prosperity, good crops, a kindly mistress with a dowry of slaves and this poor land for a husband she loved, her little Miss Hettie, and a daughter who married away and never came back. Those were fat times, she said. Now the good old man was just shuffling along to his grave and she'd just pray to Jesus for him and wait.

This was how Reuben learned about cooking. Not much to do, no angry grievances in his heart like he found in the hearts of others, no running away like that fool boy, nowhere to go, waiting. Hoeing in the vegetable garden, washing the old man, listening to his conversations with Miss Letty. Marvel told him she had the papers that made her a free woman, signed long ago by the old man. Free. Together they coaxed the old man to sign Reuben and the boy's freedom papers. He understood what they asked of him for a moment, he smiled a happy smile and ate a bite of Marvel's elegant pumpkin duff.

When he died Reuben made a good box out of cypress wood, washed him, wrapped him in a swaddling of old curtain and laid him to rest next to his Miss Letty in a land that had given him little in return for his hard work and kindness. Marvel said words and wept honest tears. She walked away, wearing her best purple dress with a petticoat made from the last frayed curtain. She was careful to leave everything in place that belonged with the old house just in case those legal folks, or maybe the daughter, ever came looking before the thieves and beggars came. She walked away to find a place where a free black lady of generous proportions could find a kitchen worthy of her skills.

Reuben, who had no other name, became Reuben Freeman, and his boy became Ely Freeman. They walked away together, headed west.

"He wants to be a cow boy," Reuben said to Jack one night. The summer air drifted in balmy puffs across the prairie, a fine night with stars and the lowing of oxen grazing over the ridge. The teamsters sat around fires mending gear, telling stories, grumbling. Someone among them strummed on a banjo, making a soft music. They were ready for El Paso after weeks of travel and minor hardships, they were ready for their beans and bacon and whatever else landed in the pots

Beans and bacon, Jack thought wryly, meat from the shunned mud animals he had learned to tolerate.

Reuben butchered deer meat into fat chunks and threw them into the bean pots bubbling on his fires. He added herbs, chili, salt, chunks of deer fat, and two young butchered rabbits. He smiled. "He likes to hunt, that Ely. Rather hunt than wash pots."

Jack breathed the savory fragrances of the pots, the baking bread, a hint of sugar and cinnamon and dried apples coming from Reuben's ovens.

"It's a poor life chasing cattle," he said. He'd heard of a few ranchers driving small herds of wild cattle to towns along the gulf, maybe selling them for two or three dollars a head.

"Better than washing them pots and hunting wood."

"Cattle." Jack shook his head. Mostly he liked just riding ahead of the train on scouts for game, all the land to see, but you had to watch out for those old wild mossyhorns that charged a man on horseback like old rogue buffalo bulls. "The Indians favor buffalo."

"Yes sir, but them shaggies getting scarce."

"They are." Jack studied Reuben for a moment. They had spoken, exchanged a few words when Jack brought in meat from his hunts, talked a little on quiet nights. Now he leaned against the wagon and watched Reuben go about his work with simple, efficient gestures, all calm, all unhurried and carefully planned. The long feather in Reuben's red cap blew in the puffs of wind. He raised his head now and then, sniffing the wind, looking about. He seemed well pleased with the pleasant night and his pots of food.

Jack wondered again if Reuben sensed what they might have in common. No. Jack's past belonged to him. But words, stories, rumors circulated through the camp, gossip became a form of recreation on a night such as this. Talk about wars, fighting. Talk about the slavery issues and maybe what the South would do. About the Yankees. Was slavery any different for Reuben than it had been for Jack? He wondered. He noticed that Reuben spoke his words carefully, not many words except when he spoke of cooking; the merits of buffalo and venison, sugar sweets, spices, now and then a name. Maybe some schooling in his past. But Reuben couldn't hide, Reuben was black.

"Them old shaggies anywhere hereabouts?" Reuben asked.

Jack shook his head. He thought about the other things he heard the teamsters talk about over their fires most nights, idle banter and speculation, commonplace things, whores, blacks and whites, fighting, poverty, rye whiskey.

"I'll take him hunting with me."

Reuben nodded, sliced a thick piece of fresh hot bread, slathered it with butter and handed it to Jack.

He knew they were nearing the shallow Pecos river still some days ahead. He had been there, somewhere along the river when the People met for trading. Somewhere, he wasn't sure what thicket or copse of big old cottonwood trees, what good crossing, what distant familiar sign. They were crossing barren land with no trees here and little water. The coyotes that followed the wagons looking for scraps were thin, their fur ragged. He saw fewer birds.

He rode out at dawn without a packhorse, always careful, scouting for sign, for Indians. He flushed a young buck out of a gulch full of dry brush and half dead trees, a dry place wet when the rains came in a deluge, with an occasional small seep of water. He dressed out the meat, wrapped it in the hide and left the rest for the hungry four-leggeds to find.

He found the woman.

The wind shifted. His six-dollar horse stopped abruptly, head up, ears flicking forward. Jack looked at the woman, yards away. He had seen no sign. She was kneeling, bent over her knees at the edge of the scrubby gulch thicket with a patch of green where a small seep was hidden and where the animals came to scratch at the wet dirt and drink. She was digging, digging in the hard dirt with a long knife. She talked to herself in a singsong voice. Now and then she stopped and looked around warily, as though she had heard something frightening, perhaps his gunshot when he shot the buck two miles back up the tangled gulch. Her furtive face was round, dusty dark, her black hair long and loose and tangled. She was barefoot, her feet streaked with brown blood. She wore antelope skins with fine patterns of beading and strips of red strouding, and her breasts were heavy, as though she nursed a child.

She saw Jack and stood with a sound like a gasp. She swayed for a moment, then her body became rigid. She was tall and surely once very strong, with broad shoulders and firmly set legs. She looked well fed in the past, well dressed now but showing signs of terror. She grasped the bone handled long knife, staring at him, firm in her angry stance. Her eyes were obsidian black, narrowed, her mouth a thin dry line. He saw on her good clothing the small tribal signs that she was not Comanche nor Kiowa, but maybe once a woman of the Cheyenne people. Now, by her dress and by her look she may have spent time among white traders or trappers, maybe as a squaw wife. He searched around, looking for others but he saw no one, heard no one, sensed no one, and he had seen no horse sign. Nothing. She was alone.

I am without harm, he said with hand signs.

She stared. She had seen. She glanced around in hurried, hard glances.

I am alone, he said.

Who? She signed.

Jack couldn't say to her who he was, except to say,

Friend.

Her expression hardened with disbelief. Anger. She was not a young girl but a woman with small lines in her face. She had heard his gunshot and now she'd been caught in the open, digging for tubers, careless, frantic. She stood tall, rigid, the knife ready, combative, like one of the warrior women of the People.

Your child? Jack signed.

She shook her head. Her face did not change.

You are going?

She pointed vaguely north. She did not trust him. She stared at his horse, then at the deerskin pack of fresh meat behind his saddle.

Help? Jack asked.

She shook her head violently. She made a harsh word sound. She stepped back and raised her knife toward him, toward herself.

Help? He repeated.

She thrust the knife toward him, toward herself.

He watched her for a time, He looked around for a small child's grave bundle tied in a tree but saw nothing. A hawk circled above and made a sharp, keening cry. The woman's eyes flickered to the pack of meat, back to Jack. He gave her time, waiting. She stood as the Dog warriors stood in a fight when they were ready to die.

A chorus of distant coyote yaps and barks came from where they had found the deer offal. Soon the scavenger birds would begin to come, following the scent of meat. Crows already danced through the dead branches behind her, talking to each other.

Jack untied the pack of meat and let it fall to the ground. She watched. He dropped his canteen, the bit of tobacco he sometimes carried, and waited. She saw all of it but would not be tempted.

Take, he said with his hands.

She gave no sign that she understood, but he knew she did. The crows screeched and fluttered.

Jack turned his six-dollar horse and rode away.

He knew what she would do, what a woman of the People would do. She would eat raw meat for her hunger, and drink sparingly. If no one found her and took her to slavery or to sell, or for a wife, then over the next few days she would hide and watch and carefully smoke as much of the meat as she could carry. She would scrape and cure the hide with smoke over small hidden fires, so the smoke wandered through dead branches above and disappeared in the twilight sky. She would make new sets of moccasins from the hide and challenge the coyotes and wolves and any other four-leggeds drawn by the smells. She would make a pack with the rest of the deer hide, maybe patched with the red strouding to make it large, as much as she could carry. The crows had already fluttered away in boredom. She would walk away to find her people, leaving no trace behind.

But her people might reject her, consider her spoiled, an enemy. The squaws might fight to tear her good clothes away and take everything, leaving her naked and alone. He would never know.

He had no canteen, but he didn't care. There were spare items the wagon master carried in his wagons, or he could make a water skin. He could make anything, he could survive like the woman. He leaned down and scooped up a long black crow feather and put it in his hat, feeling for a moment as light hearted as thistle seeds blowing in the wind. But shortly, he took the feather from his hat and threw it away.

Today we crossed the Pecos. Water hub-high after storm. Problems. Water moccasin bit a horse. One mule drowned. Fool accident. Reuben cooked the meat, good dark meat. Wagons poor. I am glad to leave llano, no trees not much water or grazing, no military escort yet. No game today.

He began to wonder again about the fort ahead, about the law. But he was just a meat hunter for this wagon train. Someone no one would notice.

Hills ahead. Apaches ahead. Always Comanches.

The Indians came in the night, creeping past the sleepy *remuda* guards. The horses and mules began to mill with snorts and squeals of alarm.

Jack woke with a start, ran to the herd. No moon, only faint star shine. The Indians tried to divide the *remuda* and stampede the animals, some toward the camp and the others out into the night where they would scatter and steal them away, along with any steers left in the train's traveling commissary. They were shadows hiding among the horses, clever shadows. Jack yelled at them, at the guards, angry words the People would have shouted.

He jumped up on one of the wildly rearing horses, tried to keep the herd milling, circling, until the guards came. No rifle shots, no great explosions of noise, or waving blankets, that would stampede the *remuda*. He saw teamsters running afoot, trying to help. Old Billy Fustus appeared at Jack's side in the darkness, then vanished.

"Well, they got a horse and a mule," he said when it was over. He rubbed his aching hands. "They'll eat that mule if they're hungry. Them fellers're always hungry for mules." He looked quizzically at Jack. "Comanche?"

He didn't know if Billy meant the raiders or the words he had shouted into the night. He didn't care.

Billy held out a dirty moccasin, crumpled and old. "Looks Apache. Left it for us."

Jack almost smiled.

Billy Fustus hawked and spat dust. "Reckon they'll be back."

Another scare. Watch out. We were lucky.

They plodded through the dry lands and deserts beyond the Pecos. Drought. Poor grazing, little water, game scarce, but by now they knew they were drawing closer to their destination. Signs of shod horses, military. Timbered mountains in the far distance, scattered signs of abandoned habitation. Several days passed, just slogging along. Then they came to a rise and looked across a desert valley and saw a group of buildings in the distance. A company of troopers rode out to meet them and escort them into the fort. They had come at last to the Post at the Pass.

Not much of a fort, Jack thought, not yet anyway, but still building. Mud bricks, a few trees and other signs of greenery and water, parade grounds, a picket stockade around the buildings, activity everywhere. He saw a building with a cross on the steeple. Elsewhere he saw an American flag whipping in the breeze. Riders came and went through the gates, a huddle of Indians camped outside, maybe drunk, begging for food.

They were not Comanches, but some other tribe he did not recognize. Then he saw another group of Indians, strong looking men, women wrapped in striped blankets, all watching the newcomers as the wagon train passed through the gates. The troopers inside stopped their work to stare.

The post at El Paso del Norte began as a settlement in 1839 or thereabouts, Jack learned later. Originally called Franklin, he saw just three poor scattered ranch houses on the north side of the Rio Grande. The United States government, after winning the Mexican war, decided that travelers on their way to Yumaon the Gila trail over in Arizona territory, probably needed protection from the hostile Apaches who had raided into Chihuahua regularly for decades and then vanished into their strongholds in the Guadalupe Mountains and all the way up into Arizona. On leased land, the government sent troops to build a fort of mud bricks as fast as they could. In spite of hot, dry, dusty days and nights, and endless monotony, it was known as the Post at the Pass, and the town of Franklin began to grow a mile from the fort. Then the government transferred the troops to other locations considered more important, always scrambling to stay ahead of the settlers and the hostiles. ThePost at the Pass lay abandoned to rats and rattlesnakes. The Apaches resumed their raids into Mexico and Texas, for food, weapons, horses, mules, women and pretty children, whom they carried deep into Mexico to wealthy *hidalgos*, mostly of old Castilian decent, or churches where they would be baptized with new names and become servants and field hands, or up the trails to Santa Fe for trading, where new settlements were springing up along the way. They would sell their captives and stolen horses to Comancheros at rendezvous or carry them up to Santa Fe and buy more American weapons. Such sales were forbidden by the new American government but universally ignored.

Everything was new, a chaos of new American laws, new uncontrollable settlement, new customs. Then word of gold in California spread like fire across the land. The government reconsidered. To those who followed available news or rumors, and turned cynical by past experience, it seemed the government couldn't make up its mind.

The surveyors came along and decided the location of the fort would be in Texas, not New Mexico. The Fort at the Pass became known as the Fort opposite El Paso. The soldiers returned in 1851, this time to stay. The building went on as more travelers and settlers came into the area. Independent foreign traders carried goods from Mexico to any settlement that paid well for their risks. Favorite trails and trace roads which were becoming well-traveled roads, led to Yuma in Arizona, to San Diego in Lower California, and north to San Francisco and the gold fields.

The southern trails were rough and risky. More easily traveled but with acknowledged risks of breakdowns, loss of merchandise and life and marauding Indians, the traders and merchant travelers just went north through the Rio Grande valley, through hills and mountains and on to Santa Fe in New Mexico, avoiding snows and Mescalero Apaches whenever they could.

Now a Butterfield overland stage came through, without much of a regular schedule, often just open wagons bouncing and bumping along a poorly cut and still unfinished new road carrying hardy passengers, news and mail from anywhere. The rough town settlement that sprang up outside the stockades grew, with now and then a shooting at a *fandango* or a *fiesta* or a cockfight there and across the river. There were saloons, gambling houses, dance halls and all kinds of hot

Mexican food served from dark little *jacals*, Mexican fruit girls with baskets of exotic fruits, apricots, mangos, grapes, a few stores and rooming houses and other opportunistic enterprises complete with bordellos and swindlers and shooters that came and went, depending on the willingness of soldiers and travelers to part with their coins.

For many this was the end of the road. They stayed, wandered down into Mexico to the little villages where they were welcomed with *fandangos* because they were willing to fight the constant Apache raids. Many never returned or got into fights or died of sickness from drinking bad water or from malaria and other fevers.

Jack wrote in his journal, *went to a bull fight across the river. Bull lost. Reuben working at a saloon, more of a tavern. Old Fustus went on south. Men from the train drinking, trouble. Fights. Some sick with fever. Talk about yellow fever and something called leprosy down in Mexico.*

"My land," Reuben said in his mild voice. "This a place for trouble. I say stay away from them swampy mud places by the river. Bad air make those boys sick. Bad water. We got to buy our spring water for this kitchen." He had found himself a good place, a small kitchen in a tavern that offered crude rooms and, until Reuben came, rough camp food. He handed Jack a plate full of new wonders, *tortillas*, corn *tamales* full of spicy meat and goat cheese, hot chili peppers, beef, limes, pineapple, mangos, oranges, many foods he had never tasted and now relished.

"You staying on here?" he asked Reuben.

Ely, Reuben's half-grown boy, ran into the little kitchen, his arms full of fresh cobs of corn. He saw Jack and stopped, his cinnamon face breaking into a smile. "Hey," he said.

"You helping?"

"Better than dragging old fire wood and washing pots." He dumped the corn and turned to go.

"Not a cow boy yet?"

"Will be," he said and ran out on some urgent errand.

Reuben shrugged. "That boy Ely need some roots. Some education. You heard, still say he wants to be a cow boy someday chasing cows around. No cooking like his Pa. Lot happening around here." Reuben shook his head. "You?"

"I got a room in a boarding house, good pasture for the horse."

"You staying I guess." Reuben spooned green *tomatillo* sauce over Jack's plate.

Now Jack had to think of a good answer, for himself, a good one to offer Reuben.

"They got a long ways to go with building that fort over there."

If he stayed, he would have to stand before some military man at the fort, give his name, answer questions. Looking for a job. He had managed to put aside most of this reality in his travel across Texas. Like some pure fool, just looking around and hunting game. Now the gnawing seed of concern that hid in every thought he had of the future crept back

Law.

That man I killed. That white man.

He felt the beginning of the old uneasiness. Now he had to be known and counted in a legal way.

Law he thought.

"Hell, I spent three months getting here. I expect I'll stay a while."

"Name?"

He stood reluctantly before the man who sat behind a desk cluttered with papers, quill pens, spilled tobacco, a dish of discarded pipes and the name, J.J. Hunter, on a small metal plaque. The man wore a blue uniform coat open at the neck. The room was stone cold despite the heat outside. He took some moments studying Jack. He looked harried, tired and he took his time as though there was no end to it, no hurry, no importance. Jack saw shelves heavy with books on the wall behind him. Jack saw weapons, noting the make and caliber of the long guns, the hand guns, saddle bags, a poorly made reata, a shelf with blue bottles and small glasses. A jar with an inch of brown liquid sat on the desk

Crazy water, Jack thought.

His jaw tightened at the mistake in his mind. His Comanche thinking.

The sound of horses moving, troopers shouting and talking, came through the open doorway. Jack felt a rising of unease again. His name would be known by the record keepers, the law people, and here he stood in his old antelope hide shirt, his hair long, with moccasins on his feet. He'd meant to change into the new blue shirt brought from San Antonio de Bexar, maybe even cut his hair shorter. Maybe he had made another mistake.

"Name?"

He looked back at the man, more uncertain. He had thought himself almost secure in his silences, in the passage of time and distance. But the present, as he stood there, became a sort of sudden unfathomable chaos. The earth floor under him seemed to crumble, falling away in all directions. The man seemed not to notice as he looked down at his papers, shifting them here and there.

"Do you understand English? Are you Mexican? From the German settlements?"

Jack recognized that the man's voice was very calm, patient, matter of fact discussing simple things on a commonplace day. He believed the man had not seen any sign of ordeal nor sensed any chaos in this stone-cold room. He stared down at the confusion on the man's desk, at the man himself, trying to make a decision. His own sense of confusion slowly drained away. The man looked up, waiting, waiting, and then Jack knew he had asked the question three times and that he knew all about the chaos in the room.

The man asked in a quiet voice, "Was it the Lipan Apaches? Comanches?"

Jack hesitated, then answered. "Comanche." He imagined he heard a hint of rough accent still in his voice and was dismayed.

"Comanche," the man repeated, as though he had been through this conversation before. "When?"

Jack had no certain answer.

Law, he kept thinking *Law*!

"Where?"

"Maybe Brushy Creek."

The man took a deep breath and let it out slowly. "There are a number of Brushy Creeks in Texas. You are one of hundreds." He shook his head. "Hundreds. You were traded?"

"No."

The man stared at Jack. "I have heard of only two other captives who escaped."

Jack nodded. He believed it.

"Most captives want to stay with the Indians after they've been with them as children"

Jack looked at the books on the shelves behind this man.

"I've heard many captives became worse than the savages. More cruel," the man said.

Jack's heart thudded heavily. There was nothing he could say.

The man in the blue uniform jacket gathered some papers on his desk, his pen dipped and poised.

"Name?"

"Jack."

"Do you know your full name?"

Jack thought of lying. He could go on with just one name, as much a mystery to others as to himself.

"Jack Rainie, maybe," he said, and repeated, "Jack Rainie."

He had hidden for so long among the People and among the whites, the wagon train and his wanderings, that he'd lived a sleeping life, as the grasses of the prairie lived sleeping lives. Now it was over, now perhaps they would know of him and he would know of himself. He felt perspiration slide down his jaw, he felt a huge sense of relief, and a lingering fear.

"How old?"

Jack shrugged.

"Family?" The man had written his name.

Jack shook his head again. He looked at the books on the shelves again, at the book on the man's desk.

"Narrative of the Texas Santa Fe Expedition---."

He wanted to touch it.

"Can you read? Can you do sums?"

Sums had once been the season count on a calendar robe, the marks on the parson's wafers of papers. Now they were the coins from the wagon train that he had in his money belt.

Jack nodded. "The parson."

"The parson." The man almost smiled, understanding. "You were fortunate. There were thousands like you in the old Spanish days," the man said quietly.

So many.

"Just a way of life," the man said factually, but with a twist in his voice. "It is against the American law now. We are trying to help, to find the captives. Also, you should know it is against American law to sell whisky to the tribes, or weapons. Guns."

Jack nodded again.

"Are you interested in scouting?" The man, plainly educated and interested, asked with courtesy.

"No sir." Such men were scorned and thought to be half breeds or renegades, always under suspicion, never trustworthy.

"It pays thirty dollars a month."

Jack shook his head.

J.J. Hunter nodded. He understood.

Those other rare captives who had escaped their Indian captivity and many who had been recovered, now were sometimes military scouts but they were never respected. Jack knew from drovers' stories around the campfires.

"Experience?"

"Mostly hunting. Hammers, nails." He stopped, thinking about the words. "Wagons. Horses." He paused again. "I can dig latrines," he said, and smiled.

The man laughed, a sharp sound that seemed foreign to this cramped room with the books. He scrawled a note.

"Take this. They will hire you. They are enlarging the stables and the hospital." He looked up at Jack, then away. "The surgeons are asking about peyote. They say it is good for pain and such when they don't have opium."

Jack studied J.J. Hunter. "Yep."

"Where?"

Jack shook his head. "South. Mexico."

"Well then, take this. Good luck."

Jack took the note and turned away. At the door he turned back and caught the man staring after him, pondering something.

Jack said, "They will go."

"Who?"

Jack made the hand sign. "Comanche."

"Go where?"

"After the buffalo. The shaggies. In the season. Anywhere."

"They smoked the pipe. They will go to the reservation."

Jack gestured in scorn. "That old chief by the gate thinks he speaks for all the People. Only for his own band. They go anywhere after buffalo, guns. Captives."

Jack turned back to the door.

"Wait." The man held out the book from his desk. "Bring it back."

A year passed. The fort grew, with quarried stone and pine logs dragged by mules from distant mountains, all long hard work for troopers and laborers, but the last poor leaky brush lean-to shelters with crude staked walls full of insects gave way. Barracks for the soldiers took shape and enlarged as did the officer's quarters, the armory and the sutler's quarters.

Jack's English became less accented, a little slurred, sometimes as rough as the troopers spoke. In time he learned to drink jars of whiskey with almost no sign, a discipline he imposed on himself while watching troopers and travelers carouse with single minded devotion to the rotgut whiskey and *tequila* and home brew they found in taverns that had sprung up like mushrooms in the town outside the fort. He learned pretty Mexican whores across the river. He learned brawling and more whiskey and guardhouse, where he stood alone one night in the black cell, his heart pounding wildly, not sure how he had gotten there. He wanted to batter stone and wood with his body, anything to be free of this astonishing, sudden, tomb. His mind flung against doors and walls, it probed ceiling, corners. In the wild thrashing of his motionless panic he wanted the smells of clean dust, hot sun, crushed grass. He only smelled whiskey and old excrement.

His panic passed. He learned calm. He learned a different kind of survival. He sat with his back to the wall, unmoving by the hour, while ricocheting fear slowly subsided. It would never control him in this way again. And he learned patience, and a strange kind of kindness that grew like an orphan in the tangle of his groping character. Kindness was not practical in this hard life. It would not give him food when he was hungry, nor help him survive. But it remained, it was just there.

Over time, he realized finally that there was no record of the man he had killed in that Comanche raid.

He worked at the fort and in the village, where raw mud brick and wooden buildings rose up everywhere like some ragtag boom town, Visitors came and went. Men built roads, the Overland mail arrived and left with a fresh team for Yuma and up into California. He learned more of civilization. He read every book he could find. In time he came to trust the officer named J.J Hunter, even others, with small revelations of his past.

Jacobus James Hunter, sometimes called J.J by the troopers under his command, but never in his presence, considered the fort a wilderness outpost, of renewed importance but also of numbing boredom to a man of his curious mind. He was well liked, respected because of his love of fairness and whiskey. The frequent tedium of his days became opportunities for him to indulge a favorite interest which drew him into old El Paso and into the new town of Franklynor over the border or anywhere, to wander the streets whenever he could, talking with old settlers, visiting *jacals*, searching.

J.J. Hunter collected maps, old documents and letters, memories, lore and legend and anything that pertained to New Spain and the old Spanish days. Once when Jack went to his office to return a book, he had maps spread across his desk studying one, and then another, old maps on sheepskin, stained, vague brown lines and drawings; newer maps on fragile rolls of paper, and good recent military maps. Jack saw that Mexico claimed vast lands on the old maps after the Spanish fled, massacred by the Indians, who called these vast lands *Nuevo Mexico*, showing a few notations of springs and roads, the old *Chihuahua* road to Santa Fe called *El Camino Real* on the maps, a few villages and mountains, a few notations of the wild tribes.

"The Spanish and then Mexico claimed all this territory---all of it, California---."

Jack studied the map. "Who'd they claim it from?"

J.J. Hunter shook his head. His lips moved cynically. "You have asked a big question." He went back to his map. "See here, this is the road the American captives walked barefoot from Santa Fe to Mexico City. They died along the way from starvation and cold. They were left in the snow by the side of the trail. My God, over a thousand miles."

Hunter drew a deep breath, as though such a truth was unbelievable. "Well, the Mexican people were friendly along the way. They tried to help with food, but that damned bastard Santa Ana was president, he thought they were spies. He ordered the captives jailed in the old Spanish convents. He is a despot." He paused, drew another deep breath. "Well, before our time, before our time."

But the new maps showed a different world of territories, survey lines, rivers, roads, mountains, forts, trails, names; Texas, New

Mexico, Colorado, Arizona, California. New lands, new states, new territories.

Hunter, who seemed to be pleased by Jack's audience to his passion, spoke a simple phrase. "Indeed. You see before you the chaos of change."

Settlers came through and went on, heading for California by the southern road or across the border into Mexico, or up the old *Chihuahua* Trail. Now and then Comanches and Apaches shot arrows from the bluffs, and then faded away. Troopers rode out chasing the Indians and sometimes came back with arrow wounds or broken bones and spent time in the post's hospital where soldiers were most often treated for malaria, accidents and gonorrhea. Wagons filled with provisions came through, freighters from Mexico, from Texas, bringing news, letters, oddities like the man who called himself a photographer and sought to take images of everything, even the idle, hungry straggle of Indians begging at the fort, who feared this strange soul-snatcher man.

Jack wrote in his journal as he could, trying to perfect his skills and understand his thoughts. He wanted to think of himself as inconspicuous; as those things which no one sees after a glance; nor remembers later.

Who were those wagon men so long ago, who was that man he had killed, with hair as sandy-colored as his own? They all had names. Did anyone know? And what were the names of all those captives from the big yearly Comanchero trading encampments?

But wandering photographer's sepia photographs where troopers in wrinkled uniforms and others wearing ill-fitting clothes stood self-conscious in brown half-tones, Jack Rainie stood out. Not laughing, not scowling, not joking with his companions, he did not look away, as fondly thinking of home. He was just himself, as though the photographer had drawn dark lines around him. He was not obscure, but emphatically there.

Then an Eastern man from a newspaper, in a place called Massachusetts, came by stage to the fort. He wanted to talk to the officers, the troopers, anyone who could tell him about the wild Indians, about broken treaties, starving reservation Indians, all words that, already, he knew and expected to hear. When he found Jack, he stopped in his tracks: here was this rough half wild looking frontier youth who probably couldn't read or write his name, certainly not a trooper, and dressed in rough clothing, working with the troopers hauling logs from the hills.

He smiled. Here was his source.

The man interested Jack, for a moment. Here was a man who lived by what he wrote, sharing his thoughts on paper. A journalist, he called himself. But after Jack had paused in his work to speak his name, he turned away. The man knew nothing. He wanted Jack's life story, but there was little Jack wanted to give away.

Maybe it's time to head out; see more of the country.

Then one hot fall day he saw Sallie Flynn.

He didn't remember the actual date when he first saw Sallie Flynn. She came from Santa Fe, in a train with two wagons and a fine carriage, showing red wheels and wear from a long journey. A portly, bearded man rode beside the carriage on a fine bay horse that Jack could admire. He was well-dressed, sporting new-looking coat and vest, with a fresh new broad-brimmed hat. He smiled at everything he saw, as if well-pleased with the rag-tag settlement, at the base of the garrison walls. The heavy carriage carried two women, the older woman driving two mules and speaking rapidly, her face stern. She was strong looking, with black hair in a tight bun and a bonnet tied loose around her neck. The other was a wisp of a girl, with long wavy golden hair stirring in the wind.

Oh, Sallie Flynn!

Had any being, so graced with natural beauty and animation, ever arrived at this hot, dusty, isolated wilderness fort? Every eye watched her passage. She rode with ease and seemed hardly to be listening to the stream of words coming from the older woman's busy mouth. She seemed to smile at some thought of her own, and angel wings might have sprouted from her shoulders, no one would be surprised. But that was only one of Jack's rampant fantasies as he watched her, and every other man laboring, sweating, had his own fantasy. She wore a blue dress and Jack swore to himself that she surely had sky-blue eyes, and that he would find a way to go to Sallie Flynn.

Reuben's kitchen had grown too small for his culinary creations. By now the tavern had been remodeled, gentrified for a higher class of guest, or so the owner boasted. Now the tavern bore a large sign above the door.

THE RITZ-- LODGING AND FINE FOOD

When he determined to meet Sallie Flynn, because she and her people were living in the small, rustic rooms above, Jack gathered his tools and went back to work enlarging Reuben's little kitchen. Troopers came to the tavern dining room for good food and for Sallie Flynn. Officers, tradesmen, any man who could afford a meal came to see Sallie Flynn. They tipped their hats, mumbled mild words, unable to say more in the presence of such a lady. But Jack saw her every day.

Every day! He made sure that he saw Sallie Flynn every day and she saw him.

He carried packages for her, he ran errands, described Reuben's growing menu. He told her stories. He told her of the area, the sights, its dubious charms, its dangers.

Sallie Flynn blinked her beautiful blue eyes at all this. She looked at his rough sandy colored hair, his intent gray eyes. She examined his slimness, his height, the shoulder bulk his hard work at the fort had given him. She looked into his eyes again. Sallie Flynn had noticed him.

He smiled and gave her his name.

"My," she said, her voice a little breathless, as though his name were a gift. "Thank you. I do appreciate your help, Mr. Rainie."

Jack's heart moved strangely in his chest. He nodded. Was there more to come from this vision of a girl?

"I expect there are sights to see," she said to him three days later. He thought that her eyes had a special blue sparkle whenever she looked at him.

"Yes ma'am," Jack said hopefully. He was dusted with sawdust from his work in the kitchen. "Tonight---."

"No," the older woman spoke. She and Sallie Flynn sat at a table, dining unhurriedly. She stared at Jack, a message in her expression. "There's a dinner at the fort tonight. It is for the visitors, everyone will be there. The new Catholic bishop will be there. From France I hear." She paused, she was a Baptist. "We have been invited. We must get our rest and look to our attire. We must attend."

Visitors from Washington or Kansas or France or anywhere in this wilderness, had fine clothes, fine manners, far more than he had to offer.

"We cannot be rude," the woman added, watching Jack.

The older man who had arrived with the women, with his fine clothes and a new hat and his good-looking bay horse, called himself McGregor. Just that. There was a bit of a showman about him in his expansive, happy look. He had a deep resonating voice and a ready smile. When they left Missouri for the free government land in Texas he promised Mariah Matilda and little Sallie Flynn a new home, a farm with trees and gardens and all sorts of better possibilities. They could not afford anything more, everything else lost to poor crops, Mariah Matilda's schoolroom growing emptier by the day, bad choices, and then the debt. So, he gave Mariah Matilda this fine dream and showed her all the good land, much of it already taken. He had little for payment, so he took to trading. A year at a time he prospered, and he came to believe in what Mariah Matilda named *McGregor's Dream*. He said one day he would give her a fine house, with good water and friendly neighbors, he would have a dozen wagons carrying every kind of trade goods everywhere, from cough drops to cartridges, and his name would be written very large on each wagon. McGregor. He would be known all across the land.

He talked loudly, and often. He was a chronic optimist in spite of years of hard times, full of ideas, eager to recount his experiences and always ready for the gambling tables at the end of a profitable trip. He never lost much, he never won much, so by his method of reckoning he had nothing to complain about.

He called the girl "Missy" and the older woman "My dear," or "My dear woman," depending on his mood. He often looked at her with a mixture of fondness and puzzlement, as though wondering how this woman had happened to him, and for such a long time.

The woman's name was Mariah Matilda, a good mouthful of a name but always complete, never shortened. Jack judged her to be Sallie Flynn's tenacious *duena*, her stern guardian from all the ills of the world. Ills like rough young men with nothing much to offer. She was a woman bent on different varieties of worth and purity. She saw to it that their little party always left on time, arrived on time. She knew names. She knew where they were going. Where they would lodge. Sallie Flynn called her Auntie.

"Do you dance, Mr. Rainie?" Sallie Flynn asked on a Saturday after Jack had thrown buckets of water over himself and dressed in his best shirt and good wool trousers, something hopeful in mind with Sallie Flynn.

"No ma'am." He had remembered to say a polite "ma'am," "I mean yes, at the *fandangos*. Sometimes."

"I was thinking how nice it would be to attend a *fiesta,*" she said, again with that blue sparkle.

"With me," Jack said.

Sallie Flynn looked around the dining room. It was empty. Mariah Matilda was off at the privy.

"Yes," Sallie Flynn said.

McGregor announced that his business in El Paso and across the border in Juarez would be completed soon. Only a few days, then back to Santa Fe before the snows.

"Praise the Lord," he said, in all innocence never meaning to take the Lord's name in vain. "My wagons are empty again! Time to fill up across the border." The new merchandise, he said, would bring a welcome profit.

Mariah Matilda frowned. She knew what was coming, her face said. *Always. Without fail.*

McGregor would spend a few days down across the border buying goods and visiting the gambling tables.

"I'm feeling ill, Auntie," Sally Flynn said. "I'm going to my room, please don't wake me. I'm going to sleep all day."

But she did not sleep all day.

They rode together on the back of his six-dollar horse and that mustang pony managed through patience and age not to throw them. They rode away from the village, the people, looking for a private place, and found a small leafy cave of branches not far from the river where the leafy shade saved them from the sun.

"Tell me," she said later. By now they knew each other in every way and yet he still felt a starvation for her and would have died on the spot to keep her. Well, to know more of her at the least. Much more. Everything. All of her.

"Oh Sallie," he said.

"Tell me," she smiled. "You have a little accent. You are not like the others. There are so many others," she teased, but only a little. "But I know so little about you." In the shadows he thought she blushed. "You are my only lover, Mr. Rainie. I want to know."

So, he told her he'd been taken, about ten years old, his mother killed, Indians. He left them when he was about seventeen, he wasn't sure, he had spent all the recent time trying to learn where he belonged, who he was.

She kissed him again. The fresh green grasses near their faces smelled sweet, so full of life, though they would soon wither. The green leaves stirred overhead.

"Yes. I know of such travail." There were tears in her voice. "So many died. It was an epidemic. My mother and father died, I was just a baby. The cholera. Auntie nursed so many, but she couldn't help them. I don't know why. They just died. I was so young. I never did feel sad then, I never knew them. But now---." She sniffled and grew thoughtful and his arms firmed around her. They made love again, slowly, and marveled at the beautiful day.

"Marry me," she said.

He was dumbfounded. "Marry you?" She spoke as though such simple words were the natural result of their lovemaking. This child, so much younger---.

"Yes, marry me."

She was just a girl, perhaps just a farm girl before McGregor took to the road. A girl that men from his rough world seldom spoke of, except with something close to reverence, if they ever spoke of them at all. They were used to easy women, comfortable with whores and bordellos.

But maybe life was catching up with young Sallie Flynn, maybe she was tired of wandering, riding around in a wagon. Maybe she was tired of Mariah Matilda's constant cautions. Maybe she was in a hurry.

His mind emptied of all good sense, all caution.

"Yes! Marry me Sallie Flynn!"

They laughed. They kissed. They made plans to meet in Santa Fe at the chapel, or at one of the old *fondas*, at the big inn called La Fonda, she remembered.

"We always stay there," she said. Or they could meet at the chapels she knew, maybe one of the private chapels. "No one was there when we last passed by, the one with the bell, but I am sure we can find a *Padre*."

"I'll come as soon as I can,"

"McGregor will be there for weeks trading in the *pueblos*. He is always there in the spring and the fall."

"I'll finish Reuben's kitchen and catch the next wagon train."

"Promise me you'll not ride alone," she said "No, it's too dangerous alone with all those Indians, Mr. Rainie. I've heard so many terrible stories."

"I promise." But he wasn't sure. "Promise me you'll wait."

She sat up, fussing with her clothes. "I have to tell Auntie I am sick for two or three more days, so I can come here---."

"More than three---."

She laughed. "More than three if I can. I do love you, my only Mr. Rainie."

But she couldn't.

After the second day, Mariah Matilda sat waiting in the dining room.

"Shame!" she hissed, so that others dining nearby would not hear her wrath.

Sallie Flynn flushed. Then she smiled, full of confidence. "Too late, sweet Auntie. We will marry."

"Never! A---one of those people? One of those---he was one of those Indian captives. Those people?" She was almost speechless with outrage for a moment. "Ruffians! Common dirty half breeds. Their own families don't want them back, they are ruined, they---."

"We will marry in Santa Fe."

"Never! He is crude, he is dangerous---."

"Who has told you all this?"

"It is no secret!   Now you listen---haven't I raised you to be a lady---?"

Sallie Flynn smiled. "But there's more. More than being a lady---."

McGregor burst through the door, interrupting the angry reply on Maria Matilda's stern lips. McGregor was laughing, waving a handful of papers. "We have a home! We have a home!"

All the diners paused in their eating and turned from watching Sallie Flynn, to watching McGregor's flamboyant entrance.

Sallie Flynn stared at McGregor, wondering if this were true, or just another of his many wishful plans. She thought that everything important just seemed to happen all at once sometimes. She would marry Mr. Rainie, and now, maybe, she would have a home instead of the jolting wagons and carriages of the last few years.

McGregor's Dream, Mariah Matilda called it.

Mariah Matilda hardly believed him from her expression as she looked at McGregor. Sallie Flynn's awful dilemma was momentarily put aside, but only momentarily.

"You have a home, my dear," he urged the wonderful information on her again. He looked at Sallie Flynn. "And you too, Missy. We have a home." He looked back to Mariah Matilda expectantly.

"What are you talking about?" she asked, still struggling with Sallie Flynn's terrible disgrace, that ruffian---. "What---a place? What kind of a place?" she asked finally.

But McGregor was still full of his recent adventure. "Ah, the poker tables! Yes, I did well, never better, never, never better! I will never play at the Monte tables again!"

"What are you talking about?" Mariah Matilda repeated.

"Leagues of land, my dear. Leagues! A house of stone and wood. A good roof. A good barn and well. He said wild cattle are everywhere, game everywhere, a creek, good water, neighbors---."

"Indians," Mariah Matilda said in a dark voice.

McGregor looked at her. "My dear woman, life is a risk everywhere out here."

She drew a long breath, coming back to the present. "Why would any sensible person risk his land at the tables in *Juarez*, speaking of risks?" She was clearly full of doubt, thinking that such a man could only be a fool. She sniffed and sipped at her lemonade. She scowled at Sallie Flynn, then at McGregor, on the verge of a fluster with so much happening.

"Why, why indeed---there must be something wrong---."

McGregor struggled with his affability. "Because he damn well hates it, woman. He hates the place, the farm. He's from Virginia. It's not Virginia! He got it in a poker game himself, for a bad debt, it was an accident! He's only seen it once, too much work. He has no slaves, he says. Hah! He travels around on a river boat mostly. He's a gambler. He is no rancher---."

Mariah Matilda laughed. "As you are no rancher."

McGregor drew a deep breath for the sake of patience. "We shall see, we shall see."

"Where?"

"It's settled, with neighbors and a good track for wagons---."

"Where?"

"It is in Texas. In Young County. It is called Elm Creek ---."

"Is it legal? Are the boundaries properly described? Are there any disputes over old grants? Are the papers properly signed and---?"

"Enough! My dear God, you have complained for six years---."

"Five."

McGregor clenched his jaw, ground his teeth a bit. "You have a new home if you want it! I will lose it in another poker game if you don't!"

Mariah Matilda just looked at him. It had been such a long-ago promise, so wonderfully envisioned, so often hoped for---. But now, entangled with Sallie Flynn's shame---.

Finally, she sighed. "You say a house of stone?" she answered, a scrap of interest in her voice.

They left El Paso del Norte three days later, with a train of wagons and pack horses and one heavy carriage with red wheels, headed north to Santa Fe ahead of winter.

Jack did not see Sallie Flynn again after a brief goodbye, secreted in Reuben's kitchen. But she left a scrap of paper in his hand.

"Promise," they said to each other, and then Sallie Flynn was gone.

Elm Creek.

She'd told him about a chapel in Santa Fe, an old inn there, but he didn't know about a place called Elm Creek.

Three weeks later, he finished his work in Reuben's kitchen, not a bad job but hasty. All he could think about was Sallie Flynn.

"You in a big hurry," Reuben said, his way of making a joke.

"Winter's coming." Jack answered.

"It come every year. This year special?"

Jack gathered his tools in silence.

"That a bad trail you going on?"

"Some. The *Jornada* part. Ninety miles, no water."

"Them Indians?"

"Mescaleros. Chiricahua. I hear there's a fort, maybe a few old settlements."

Reuben nodded. "Them settlers. They keep the blue boys busy." He began assembling packages of food, *tortillas*, corn, dried fruit, grapes from the local vines, extra spring water. "Long way, I expect."

"Three, four hundred miles, the old Spanish trail up from *Chihuahua.*"

"Old Indian trail too. Now get on. Ely finish with them last shelves. He needs something to do or he get in trouble. You get paid?"

Jack nodded, took Reuben's pack of food, shook his hand and left. His tools, three books, his journal, blankets, everything else he wanted to own in saddlebags and a saddle holster for his rifle, a pack tied to the back of his saddle with saddle strings and his money belt strapped around his waist. He rode into the fort, returned a book to Captain J.J. Hunter with true thanks, and left the fort at El Paso del Norte, for the Rio Grande Valley north to Santa Fe, wanting to shout his elation, thinking he was on his way again, that he would never return.

Good days, Cold nights.

The six settlers' wagons, in one of the last trains to Santa Fe before winter, were tough, good hardwood wagons with good wheels, not too heavy, wagons that were smaller than the big Conestogas, but they would hold up well, with no weak cottonwood patches or axels to cause breakdowns.   Jack hunted for the settlers in exchange for whatever they offered, corn cakes, stewed up root vegetables with game meat, apples and, after the first frost, trees heavy with pecans. He learned these travelers had little experience on a wilderness trail, although this trail was more like a road well-travelled from the Spanish days.   They were in a hurry, headed for California and the gold fields before all the gold ran out, they'd heard stories of the streams still yielding nuggets, and they were determined to stay ahead of winter even though they were bent on a northern route because it was faster.   They had an assortment of provisions but not enough sugar and flour; maybe not enough barrels for water when they came to the *Jornada.*   Six wagons and a dozen pack horses made a small group and a clear temptation to the Mescaleros when they reached the southern end of the *Jornada,* where the Indians raided so often that the United States government had just built another wilderness fort. Horse thieves and shooters preyed on travelers, but with troopers at the fort he reckoned they would make it safely. Every man and some of the women in the train carried muskets or rifles and a big supply of ammunition, as though Indians and shooters were their only danger.

They kept a good watch over the train at night and tended their stock with occasional buckets of grain. Jack figured they had more than three hundred miles or so ahead, but even with poor grass for the stock left along the way from earlier travelers, they would still make better time every day driving horses and mules instead of oxen.

Maybe less than a month!

But not good enough time for Jack. He would have flown if he could. Sallie Flynn was waiting in Santa Fe.

They passed trails leading off to distant struggling settlements, old camps well used along the way. Most of the troopers were away chasing Apaches when they came to Fort Fillmore, set on the escarpment east of the river. Jack and two men from the train rode across the river for any news, any warnings of Indians and raids, and came back with tea for the women and a little tobacco for the men, wilderness gifts from the blue boys who hadn't seen women in months; just wishful gifts.

The settlers moved on to the *Jornada,* their stock well-watered and their barrels full for the hard journey. The river looped away from the trail but ninety miles ahead the river looped back at the end of the waterless *Jornada.* The settlers moved across the harsh land called the Journey of Death. One horse died, an old potbellied mare the settler' children sometimes rode. Men and women rationed water to the stock and to themselves, they walked, then rode, then walked again on their way to California.

When they came to the end of the *Jornada,* some of the children began to cough. They liked to walk beside the wagons, playing games and gathering treasures of rocks and sticks and now and then a button or a tin cup lost from an earlier passage or campsites. The track followed the rising land, the river, following the easiest way to Santa Fe through barren hills, through pungent pines and sage. The train paused only briefly every day to let the stock graze for whatever dry grass they could find. But fewer of the settlers' children walked or ran playing through the sage and the junipers.

They passed old ruins, mud bricks melted away, sandstone ravines, old Spanish missions and ruins that looked like military posts from long ago. Occasionally they passed a crude burial cross or stone, old stations and camps near springs and water holes. Other pack trains came up the trail from the south and passed them, in a hurry to move ahead of the lumbering wagons.

Twelve days after leaving El Paso, two of the coughing children lagged, falling so ill and feverish that the women begged to stop, just for a day, so they could brew their herbal tonics. But Santa Fe lay enticingly up the trail, just another two or three weeks ahead, and winter already blew snow clouds overhead at night.

Then, a dozen of the settlers began to cough, and the spots appeared, ugly red pustules. The two feverish children died, then one of the women. Jack never knew their names.

The train stopped beside the trail to bury the woman with her young boy, and one eight-year-old girl with long braids, buried alone. No time to build proper boxes. Just shrouds for them and rough crosses, hastily fashioned from whatever wood they could find, using precious, square-headed nails, brought from Indiana or Missouri.

---forgotten soon.

He remembered the children running by the wagons.

---some say it's the measles, not the pox. Everyone coughing. They talk about complications, brain sickness---.

The wagons rolled on. The settlers sang hymns at night, and sometimes sat in the smoke of their fires burning pungent herbs to drive away the dangerous humors of bad air. They prayed, the women wept and brewed remedies that seemed to have no effect. They had never prepared themselves for this kind of danger.

These hard journeys for settlers, coming from a softer land of green fields and grassy meadows, killed off children and old folks first, a sobering commonplace fact everyone knew. But, when the cholera, or the pox, or the numerous mysterious fevers found them there was little to stop the ugly pestilences. The sickness sometimes came on slowly, sometimes like a blow. The children just followed along, forgetting, playing when they could, gathering stones and flowers, while the tough, old people worked, and walked, and took their chances. They did not want to be left behind, alone, their families gone.

He thought of the old mountain man Billy Fustus, down in Mexico now, a boy who left his people at fourteen and never saw them again. Another everyday story.

Stay warm and well, Billy, he thought.

They passed a recently dead mule by the side of the trail a day later, its ribs like rails, and sores on its back. The wagon dogs sniffed at it, but the big scavenger animals had not come yet, although something had nibbled. The settlers watched the vultures circling, waiting, and went on.

Sallie Flynn, are you well? Are you safe?

He wanted to race ahead of the plodding wagons. He thought of her waiting there for him, that blue sparkle in her eyes.

Instead, he went on long scouts for willow bark when the settlers ran out of fever tonics and hunted through the sandstone gullies and brush for game.

The wagons moved on, making their best plodding time. Three others died, an old man and two women. He heard the rest of the women crying, wailing, and praying like they were at a camp meeting.

---complications, they say. Maybe still ten or fifteen days to Santa Fe---real slow now---.

They saw small farms and distant settlements, where the river broadened in little valleys, but they looked old and poor--maybe from Spanish days, just hanging on. They passed turnoffs, tempting to some of the wagon people who prayed for medicines, doctors, but the old villages looked too poor, without crops.

Then the river narrowed again, and they were pushing through dry land. They came to the turnoff that led to a larger settlement, maybe Albuquerque. Two wagons followed the turnoff, taking the chance they'd not be driven away because of the sickness they brought, but they kept on with the hope of finding medicines, tonics, a doctor, anything for the blight that spread among them.

Jack stayed on the Santa Fe road, maybe sixty slow miles more by now, maybe less. At times he knew they were being watched but no one came near. There were pueblos all around, people everywhere, far away and nearby, but he saw no one. The land, the junipers, the sage, the hills and arroyos all lay in what seemed to Jack to be a profound silence.

The second day beyond the settlement turnoff dawned bright and quiet with the promise of rain in the clouds far ahead. He went on a scout, watching for sign, unshod horse prints, deer, any kind of game. Riding through hills, empty of game, a half day north of the train, He rode west, with the sun, until he rousted a buck, in fall rut, chasing a doe. He dressed the buck, but as he lifted the heavy pack, he stumbled and fell.

Shit, wake up, he told himself.

Then he felt a blow of confusion, pain in his head, heat in his limbs. He began to cough.

He lost the daylight after that, looking for the wagons. They were still far away, east. Or west.

Maybe south.

He had wandered into the night, his head throbbing, coughing, growing sicker. He expected his six-dollar horse would just take him back to the wagons, wanting the company of other horses.

He let his horse drift out of the night into sunlight, through thickets and ravines. Now he thought the wagon train must be close ahead. He recognized nothing, everything looked wrong. Heat and pain spread through his chest. Shadow-clad mountains filled his eyes and he made some attempt to reach them, guiding the horse, without much hope. Searching for the sun to guide him.

Too much confusion. Too far away.

The sky darkened to the color of smoke, wind blew in hard gusts. Dust and sand blew into his eyes, against his teeth, great drops of water spattered against his face. He opened his mouth to drink. The brimstone smell of the rain against the ground rose around him, he smelled spruce and pine across the miles, as the sky darkened and lightning flashed far away. His pony, his six-dollar horse, drifted downward and came to a stop in the lee of a cutbank. Jack clung, he coughed and slept fitfully through the rain. He imagined he saw strange carvings in the rock of the cutbank, dancing figures, rising suns, strange writings in a language he didn't understand. When he woke, he realized that if he fell from the horse he might not mount again.

He found himself in bright sunlight again, his horse drifting between red cliffs, stopping to browse, to drink at a spring where bees gathered, and little Inca doves flung themselves away from him on whistling wings. He decided he dared not dismount, not even to drink. Later, as the horse climbed sandstone hills, its passage stirring pungent odors from the sage, he thought he had made a mistake in leaving the water and wondered if his efforts were as aimless as the horse's wandering.

Little things can kill you---stupid little mistakes.

He laughed aloud at his dilemma.

---lost.

But the laugh came from his fever, much more of a cough.

---fool---, he thought.

He couldn't follow the thought any further.

He had lost the reins, so he tightened his fingers in his horse's mane, hanging on, but his hands slipped more easily, and his body throbbed with pain.

His horse ambled through dry stream beds recently dampened by rain, over low bluffs, across plateaus, stopping to graze, in no hurry to find the wagons, while Jack felt a growing need for haste. Fever had burned him to the bone, so quickly.

Two, three days? More---?

He had lost the sun. He felt old beyond generations, bewildered by a sense of loss for something that had passed him by.

---complications, they said.

How will I find you?

Sallie Flynn.

He opened his eyes and saw the ground moving beneath him.

Jesus, he had just never been so sick.

Then he was conscious of stillness, of his face in the horse's mane, of his rattling breath. He coughed, the pain searing his chest, bringing tears to his eyes. The smells of heat and ash pierced the nearer smells of leather and horse sweat, and his own sickness. He frowned as a weak sweat broke from his body.

His six-dollar horse nickered and started forward, his ears alert.

Juniper smoke.

Jack pushed against his horse's neck, sitting a little higher. He thought he saw a shape unlike the hills, the bluffs, the winding arroyos, the sage. The shape swung out of his vision, then back.

His horse stopped, waiting. Jack saw a mud *jacal*, awkwardly rectangular, adapting to the sandstone earth. The walls were made of adobe and old dry brush, the roof of cottonwood poles and grass, the arbor thatched neatly with branches, and under the arbor the shape of a seated man.

He stared for a long time, not certain of what he was seeing. Then his six-dollar horse began to throw his head, and paw at the soft patch of sand. Jack felt the shifting of his weight, and he began to slip. He pitched sideways as his horse dropped and rolled in the soft sand, saddle and all, grunting in relish.

In the days that followed, he believed the faces he saw were the faces from his recurring nightmare, the howling noises the cries from men burning at the stakes. But it was only the burning of fever. He slept and awakened, trying to breath, breathing juniper smoke, drinking a bitter drink that increased the distortions of his mind; but leaving him, at last, senseless and without pain.

Someone moved beyond the smoke when he opened his eyes. Someone ministered on the other side of his sleep, never speaking, yet always there. He tasted broths. Bits of meat--*goat meat, sheep, horse?* Sometimes he heard singing. He dreamed he was on the back of his horse, his face painted for war, riding back and forth in front of the *jacal,* firing his rifle over and over, not just to empty it, but to draw fire to himself, like a good Dog Warrior.

Sallie. Sallie.

The faces were always there when he awakened. They hung on the mud wall, at the foot of his pallet, waiting for him with grimaces, their skeletal travail and stiff sorrow. They wept sparkling tears and their grotesque, elongated, bodies twisted on rood beams bleeding downward from piercing wounds.

Finally, he recognized the steeped herbs, maybe the *peyote* drink. Maybe he had known this before. He coughed less, and with less pain. His body felt clean, his breathing easier, his mind growing clearer. He became familiar with the face of the old man who spooned food into his mouth. He drank less of the black drink; his nightmares drew away. From outside the *jacal's* open door he heard the silence of wilderness, the silence of winter snow.

He spoke a few words, scraps, whatever came to mind. The old man answered in Spanish. He saw the interior of the *jacal,* low smoke-blackened *vigas* hung with bundles of herbs, cobs of corn, red chilies, small animal skins, smoked meat. The room had mud walls, with bits of straw showing, ledges, a small conical fireplace in one corner, and a wooden doorway filled with blinding light. He smelled juniper smoke, and resin, and wood chips, and roasting chilies, in rich meaty stews. He looked up at the wall, at the foot of his pallet, staring for long periods at the elongated figures and faces, lovingly carved from cottonwood root and painted in expressions of ritual suffering. The goblins of his feverish brain. He watched the old man sharpening his knives, his chisels, carving, working slowly and with infinite care, to find the pull of sinew, the plane of vulnerable bone, which would give the inert wood that divine anguish he sought with such patience.

Sometimes he studied Jack, his eyes squinting and gently probing, as though searching for a line, an expression that had eluded him.

---*this face must be worse than that one you're carving,* Jack thought in fragments. He felt his thinness, the beard on his cheeks.

But he never minded the old man's probing eyes. He was too tired to mind much of anything.

The old man chuckled, as though he heard Jack's thought, and smiled a sweet, tooth-sunken smile, spoke an idle word, then bent his head over his carving again.

Jack came to realize that weeks had passed. *Weeks.* Winter had come to these mountains, wherever he was.

Where was the wagon track?

He'd almost died. Damn near. He felt it, even as he felt his slow healing.

---complications.

He heard the deep silence of snow. Now and then he heard the scolding of a distant jay, or the old man splitting wood. But something was over.

Sallie Flynn was over.

She couldn't wait so long. How could she wait alone? He knew she couldn't. She'd gone with McGregor and the woman, wherever they went next. How could he find them?

He had to let her go, at least for now. *At least for now.*

Strength came back slowly. It came with the plainness and simplicity of passing days during which he ate, and drank, and listened to small noises--the calling of jays and doves, then the silence.

He listened to the old man, Estebanico's, infrequent words, his soft language, attempting to imprint their sound and meaning in his mind. He watched the old man faithfully go about his tasks. Sometimes, he felt as though he had never known another life. As he began to approach comprehension of the old man's great patience, his accepting and unquestioning presence beyond the smoke, Jack thought about his own youth, his apprenticeship, in all those things that enhanced this old man's life and caused, perhaps, even the least of his kind to thrive.

Estebanico was a *santero,* a priest of *Santeria*. He made periodic short journeys away from the *jacal*. He journeyed each year in February, at the beginning of the Lenten rituals in Santa Fe. Later, in March, for the Holy Week processions. He went for the feast day of San Antonio de Padua, who was the patron of the village, and to gather cottonwood roots along the river for his *santos* and *bultos*. He purchased pigments and dyes he couldn't make himself. He went for wool; and for *pulque*, hens' eggs or a bit of sugary sweets. In late June he carried his *santos* to the village for the big trading days. He had once made a longer pilgrimage, south to trade for *peyote*, taking with him the fine *reatas* and bridles he fashioned of hide and horsehair. But he had grown too old to travel to the gathering places himself, and now he wanted only to carve and paint and tend his summer garden patch. His life, Jack saw, had distilled to this simplicity.

Everything Estebanico required grew with his scrupulous care. Every stone, gleaned from the endless desert, formed a wandering border that followed the growth of new vines that emerged as the snow melted. Every drop of spring water fell from his old bucket exactly where it was needed to give the vines new life and nourishment, as the sun brought more heat. Now the soft sand in front of the *jacal*, where his horse had dropped to roll, had a cleanly swept smoothness.

New corn had begun to sprout in clustered hills. By summer, the leaves would sway like bright green banners. Beans, squash vines and peppers showed a bit of green, pumpkin seedlings rose above the soil.

The horse, that amiable six-dollar horse, once a shaggy wild mustang, once fast, but always willing, had disappeared. Bundles of carefully dried meat hung from the rafters by the fireplace, among the herbs, coiled *reatas* and bridles the old man made by winter fires. In the corner lay another roll of hide, for more bridles and *reatas*, and maybe good horse-hide gloves.

Estebanico, the *santero*, understood balance. A poor *peon* such as him, who wore only yucca fiber sandals, and coarse, homespun, woolen tunics and britches; and who had no fine *sabanas* for his bed, only loosely woven sack cloth, could not feed a great hungry horse. Jack's money belt, the rifle and the bandolier, too, had disappeared, as though such promise of violence and greed had no place in Estebanico's saint-filled *jacal*. In every way, he provided richly for himself in an existence of narrow, but profoundly deep dimension that freed him to express his love for the holy Passion of the Cross.

Jack learned to make Estebanico's *reatas*. He had made them before, as a young boy among the Comanche, but now he learned to make *reatas* of elegance, of beauty. He breathed easily now, the sickness had almost left him. The scars of the pestilent rash had faded away. He was thin, but growing stronger. When he thought about the settlers, the dying children, his feelings rose to the surface and he blinked away tears.

He fashioned the fine *reatas*, with Estebanico's guidance, and pondered his situation. He had nothing now. His pack horse and few tools, his clothes, his journal, everything, left back with the settlers. Gone, he was sure, with the practicality of poor folk burying their children and looking for gold.

He did what he could for Estebanico. He brought in great piles of dead juniper wood, strengthened the old roof, threw handfuls of new adobe plaster to patch cracks in the walls, turned the soil in the garden, snared small game for the pot and painted Estebanico's old wooden door a bright blue.

"I will have to go to the village for more pigment," the old man said with a smile.

"Santa Fe?"

"Not far. Only three day's walk for a young man."

"I will go. Bring you more blue."

"You must go," The old man's voice was soft. He let the silence stretch, as he often did, because his words were enough.

Jack waited, he knew there was more to come when the old man was ready.

"To the village. The one beyond. You must go to see an honest man." Estebanico smiled again.

Jack set aside the water jug he had brought from the spring. "When?"

"It is almost June. The vines tell me. Soon. You must go."

Estebanico gathered his wooden saints into a pack. He added Jack's bandolier and his rifle. He tied a thong holding a charm around Jack's neck.

"For protection from the devil. He is always near."

Jack didn't know which devil Estebanico meant, he thought there were many.

"You will walk for me, I will come later," he said to Jack, but his face grew troubled. He studied the pack, the *santos*, the weapons.

"Everything has changed," he said, yet his face grew untroubled again as he looked at Jack, who stood like a *peon* in white shirt and britches, one of Estebanico's old straw hats, his worn yucca fiber sandals and with hair that had grown long again. His smile returned. "Follow the small river. You will find my brother between the villages."

Estebanico's pack held his many saints, carefully wrapped in dried corn husks, four fine new *reatas*, the weapons, a wool blanket, a packet of corn cakes and dried meat and a gourd of water. The pack was heavy for Jack, after the hard winter, but this journey was his gift to Estebanico. This could never be enough, just carrying his saints to the market three days away. Never enough.

The old man held out Jack's money belt, still weighted with coins, all he had owned.

"His name is Joaquin. He will know you."

He gave Jack more directions, details of how to find the wagon road and how to find Joaquin's *jacal* in the hills between the villages.

"He puts crosses up on the hills. He defies the new order. You will find him."

Then he turned away and Jack left him bending over his young vines, softly speaking words of encouragement.

He would go, only go. The old man, in his serenity, in his wisdom, did not ask him to return. By the time he reached the wagon road, he had settled the pack with a degree of comfort and fallen into a good stride. The air was cool, and he breathed it with appreciation. When the sun stood high he stopped for rest, for a swallow of water.

He had left half his coins behind where the old man would find them when he hunted again among his pigments, but he knew Estebanico scorned coins. Kindness and good deeds were his coins, his wealth. He thought ahead, about the road he travelled now.

Santa Fe.

Perhaps a way to find her. Sallie. That marvel of a girl.

He saw her face, the wholeness of her as they loved each other. He let her into his mind again, fully, and with almost forgotten pleasure.

Sallie Flynn

He walked on, watching the land, the hills; watching the prints in the road, sandals like his own; small flocks of sheep; shod and unshod horses, donkeys. Here and there he saw smoke, *jacals*, off in the hills and paths that left the road, disappearing into the sage. A river. But he stopped before sunset, worn, the pack heavy, the hard winter still in his bones.

He found Santa Fe on the fourth day. He lowered the pack and breathed deep, weary breaths.

Was she here?

She could not be here. Not after so long.

He entered the village, step by step, past low adobe houses among old trees, budding with delicate green, narrow paths and roadways, outdoor ovens made of mud bricks, goats, a few flowers like strays in the weeds, dust, a wandering dog, quiet. Travelers passed him, two old women, with heads covered and faces hidden, a man riding a thin, shaggy horse and leading a burro.

Horse, he thought.

One like his six-dollar horse, and new britches, and maybe boots if he could find any that fit. Another journal.

He came to the square, surrounded by adobe dwellings and shops. There were burros carrying huge loads of sticks and wood, two-wheeled carts, noisy, with big ungreased wooden wheels, a few horses and mules and people hurrying. There were big freight wagons, with red-painted wheels, backed up to warehouses; commerce in the square, and on side streets; men who looked like *Norteamericanos*, carrying supplies to their wagons; women in shawls carrying bundles and pulling children along, talking; a sound of distant music; two dragoons from Fort Union; and a fine *hidalgo* riding an elegant high-stepping horse, crossing the village square. The smell of spicy food came like a sudden dizziness. He found the vendor and ate hungrily. The vendor, a stocky dark-faced man, who spoke rapid Spanish words about Indians, scoundrels, and danger, gave Jack a tin cup of *pulque* and a sweet roll, when he finished eating.

"What danger?" Jack asked.

"They have fights on the roads with the soldiers, with anyone. The Mescaleros, the Kiowas, the Comanches sometimes. They come here to trade; they get whiskey; they lie about everything; they are bad. Very bad."

"Where are the soldiers?" Jack asked.

The man shrugged and shook his head and would not speak again.

Jack finished the meal and stood watching the street and the people of this village, old, from the Spanish days. He thought of J.J Hunter's maps, the changing lines. Spain. Then the Mexicans rose up and drove the Spanish out, and the lines on the maps changed again. Then the American Yankees came along and made a war, made New Mexico a territory. He thought of the years of big freight wagons rolling across the flat prairie from Kansas and Missouri; and of the wild tribes still raiding around the forts and villages. He thought of the soldiers building ramshackle outposts, the best they could do, trying to stay ahead of the settlers and hold back the hostiles.

But McGregor traded here. McGregor the trader, the gambler, who owned a rock house and a patch of land somewhere in Texas.

Thinking about it, he felt a growing sense of relief, almost excitement. Now, he suddenly felt closer to Sallie Flynn. There had to be a dry goods store or a trading post nearby, some place where McGregor traded, where he was known. And a good, safe rooming house, or an inn--hadn't she mentioned an inn? Where genteel Eastern visitors stayed when they came out to sport-hunt, and to see the Wild West; where Sallie Flynn stayed. And where was the chapel with a bell? Maybe there was an office for posting letters, the Overland Mail, a stage office. Something, somewhere, a message.

A message from Sallie Flynn.

But he was mindful of his debt to Estebanico first, he would return to this place. He would ask his questions and look everywhere.

He lifted the pack again, lifted his rifle and started through the village, onto the road toward the town called Taos. A day's walk with the pack would take him first to the brother, Joaquin, the honest man, who lived on a hill with crosses, and then another day back to Santa Fe to find what he could find.

Sallie. Where?

At the far edge of town, he passed a large, sprawling campground, under towering cottonwood trees; some of them tall, gray ghosts, while leafed out with pale green leaves. A narrow stream wandered under the trees, crowded here and there with willows. He saw wagons and watched the bustle of men and women. There was a tall, closed, wooden wagon, with bright paintings and signs, camped a distance apart, lanterns hanging from brackets and barrels strapped to both sides. There were two fat mules hobbled and grazing the sparse grass. No wagons with *McGregor* painted on the side. He walked on, past a grassy graveyard, old leaning stones and crosses, larger buildings, old crumbling adobes and others that were half-built or half-demolished, he couldn't tell which. Then he changed course to follow the worn, traveled road and the little river, out into the sage and the hills, passing an Indian man herding seven sheep. He spoke a word, but got no answer. Then on again, with the sense of distant people everywhere, the *pueblo* people, often hostile, he had heard--quietly unseen.

Joaquin Cruz, the honest man, stood waiting for Jack by the path to his *jacal*, as though the wind or the birds had told of Jack's coming. Jack marveled at the mysteries of traveling news, here in this land that looked so empty. Joaquin Cruz just waited, showing no surprise, only an acceptance of Jack's arrival and the burden he carried. He did not seem to know how to smile a greeting. His hair was long, black, well cared for, bound with a bandanna. He wore the white garments of a *peon*, yet his *jacal* looked strong, enduring, and his bare yard had the scratch marks of frequent sweeping. The heavy woman standing solidly in the blue doorway, held a broom of tightly wrapped twigs. Clearly, she took pleasure in her efforts to impose order on the vast *pinon* and sage wilderness with a sturdy broom made of twigs. The door, the framework, and a small window had been painted with Estebanico's favorite elegant blue, a little faded. A small corral for sheep, or goats, stood empty near a spring under cottonwood trees.

Green vines, with tight clusters of unripe green grapes, covered the brush arbor sheltering one side of the *jacal*. A table and two chairs stood in the late afternoon shade.

"He sends greetings," Jack said, trying to form the proper simple words in Spanish. "He is well." He lifted the pack onto the table and set his rifle to the side.

Joaquin Cruz only nodded. He worked at the pack, setting aside the fine *reatas*, the bridles, the blanket, then lifted the carefully wrapped *santos* setting them on the table with something close to reverence. He looked at Jack, as though searching for some sort of understanding of this moment. He saw only a tired face, *a Norteamericano* face, brown from the sun but unlike his own.

Jack started back to Santa Fe late the next morning. He had slept on a clean pallet on the pounded dirt floor of the *casa*. The woman had made him new yucca sandals. She had brought him washing water, a small jar of cool *pulque*. She had fed him generously with hot spicy food and sweet spring water with the taste of honey at the end. She had given him a little pouch of tobacco. Despite her strength, her immaculate, clean *casa*, her determination with her fierce twig broom, she only smiled shyly when he thanked her

"Everything has changed," Joaquin Cruz told him quietly. "Be cautious."

He left them, carrying his weapon and bandolier, a small pack on his back and with the *reatas* and bridles slung over his shoulder-- Joaquin Cruz's words unexplained.

Darkness had fallen when he reached the outskirts of Santa Fe. He had traveled faster without the pack, thoughts of Sallie Flynn pulling him on.

Where in Santa Fe had she stayed? Was there an inn she had spoken of? Where? And that scrap of paper, Elm Creek, he thought he remembered, where was that? Texas? New Mexico Territory?

He stopped by the old buildings, looking for a chapel, a *padre*. She might have left a note, a message. But the old adobes were dark, even in the early moonlight closed, empty. The whole of this part of the village, with its old mud bricks and brush arbors, its busy commerce and wandering roads, seemed, for a moment, overwhelming in its night silence, its subtle resistance, its mystery.

He heard voices, men's muffled laughter coming from the darkness off the road past the cemetery and the big wagon campground.

Time to ask questions.

Maybe just teamsters' or settlers' drunken laughter, but someone here might remember McGregor. Someone would surely remember Mariah Matilda and Sallie Flynn.

He moved forward slowly to the edge of light coming from the large campfire, and saw men standing in the shadows, town men, wagon men. A tall man in a long, brown, hooded habit stood watching the score of revelers who squatted in the darkness around the fire. Some had their arms raised, holding weapons, some rose to do little shuffling dances, all drank from jars, bottles and tin cups, shouting, laughing.

He stopped abruptly. He knew, suddenly, what was wrong. They were shouting words he understood.

Comanches. Maybe some Kiowas---.

He walked forward slowly and saw a commotion at the far edge of the fire. He thought it was a fight, or a contest of some sort, perhaps a wrestling match between two youths. Then he saw through the darkness. The body on top was one of the Comanche men, thick and short, and the one beneath was much smaller, a child or a young girl. The Comanche had already pushed himself between her legs.

The girl was so deep in shock that she made no move to defend herself. She allowed everything, her arms out flung, her knees bent awkwardly, moving in the darkened trough of dirt only as the Comanche moved her under his violent attack. She was like a moth caught in the web and quivering at the poison, like a rag doll with eyes sewn wide.

The Comanche man convulsed between her legs. His comrades yelled and cheered. A scuffle broke out somewhere in the darkness.

The brown-robed man, who had watched with no expression on his face, moved back through the crowd and disappeared.

The Comanche jumped to his feet and dragged the girl upright. Her dirty skirt hems dropped down around her ankles. Her ragged, torn blouse hung open, her half-formed breasts ignored. Where she had been thrown and pressed against the ground, her hair, her hips, her long dragging skirt, everything, was covered with bits of broken leaves and grass, horse dung and trash, the rank powder of the trampled campground.

"Now she is good!" the Comanche called loudly, and all those who understood hooted and jeered, laughing with him. The girl stared fixedly at the ground, her cheeks dirty and streaked, her black hair wildly tangled. "Now I have made her good! Who wants to buy her?"

Jack slipped back through the crowd and walked into the darkness. The willows and cottonwoods cast dense moon shadows. His feet felt the downward slope of the ground. Roots and twining branches grew into the darkness to entrap him, and flood-hewn pits yawned at the edges of the small game-paths and trails. He fought through the black tangle coming to the edge of the stream where he sat down.

He watched the stream, the light of the moon glittering on its moving surface. The smell of wet earth, and stone, and vegetation, a heavy fertile smell, enclosed him. The yells from the campfire faded for a time and all he heard was the singing of night insects. For a time, he could believe he was among the young vines again, pouring water from his bucket to wet the roots of the maze, the bean vines, the sprawling squash. For a time, he wanted to think that when the sun stood high again at midday he would walk to the shade of the arbor and eat roasted pumpkin seeds and corn, grilled over Estebanico's root fire. He would watch insects hovering in the sunlight, then, perhaps he would doze, or work for a while on a new *reata,* as the old man had taught him. The old man would whittle and paint endless pantomimes of ritual suffering on the wooden faces of his *santos,* and nothing would change, nothing would ever change.

Moisture burned his eyes. He rubbed them roughly. A convulsive pressure of anger began in his chest. But he stopped himself, quickly sheltered by an old, engulfing numbness learned long ago. Maybe reckless, maybe saving, a numbness that never quite prevailed.

Somewhere in the night he heard laughter again, and a child's forlorn crying.

He bent and palmed cold water onto his face. He hid his rifle, his knife, and his bandolier of shells under a cutbank, covering them with brush. Then, he gathered his pack, slung his *reatas* and bridles over his shoulder, and started up the bank, passing through the branches and roots and flood pits, toward the sounds of the trading.

Jack sat cross-legged on the buffalo robe, the Comanche man, Soltero, opposite him with two companions lounging on either side. They came together without weapons, the custom of the trade. Beyond the fire he saw a score of other men, Comanches and Kiowas, a few town men moving about, idly watching. One old Kiowa woman tended the fire where long strips of meat charred at the ends of pointed sticks. The girl was only a stricken shadow. After a glance, Jack did not look toward the girl again.

He smoked an oak leaf cigarette slowly, drawing out the ritual, giving himself time to think. The sounds and smells of the camp, the nearness of the Comanches, the subtle excrement dead animal stench lying almost below his senses, began to summon all the old, oppressive feelings of fear, of dread.

He drew on the cigarette, a fine tremor hovering in the center of his body. He knew he looked like any *Tejano*. He was dressed like a *peon* and appeared to have little property of value except for the bridles and *reatas,* the sort of common person the Comanches often killed, without thought, when it suited them. But here, he thought, the peace of the trading prevailed in this camp.

Soltero, himself, did not appear to be a man of any wealth or rank. He was clearly a member of the band known as The Wanderers Who Make Bad Camps, who moved often and were filthy and slovenly in their camp habits. His hair fell long and loose, his skin had a dark copper shine, his eyes were narrow in a brooding, heavy face. The eyes of Comanche children were bright and clear, but Soltero's eyes had grown hazed, the whites yellow-brown. He was short and deep-chested, very powerful. Ear discs dangled down on either side of his face, and he wore, around his neck, a large American peace medal given in some forgotten travesty of a white man's peace council.

But this sort of market-place smoking had no ritual meaning and sealed no bargains. It might not carry the pledge to honor the trading peace. The cigarette burned down to Jack's thumb and forefinger. He took a last drag and crushed it out in the dirt.

"How much for that female?" Jack spoke casually in his limited Spanish, as though the question was of little importance to him.

Soltero laughed loudly. "Which female? This old woman who cooks the meat?"

"The other. There." He gestured with his head.

"The one I mounted? She is new and not very comfortable for a man yet." He drank trade whiskey, crazy water from a tin cup but he was not as drunk as he seemed, for now and then the firelight showed a shrewd agate glitter in his eyes. He was in no hurry now, even though he smelled a pinch of profit and was bound, like many Comanches, by a will to drive a bargain at all costs, even his own. From such cunning ignorance, the New Mexican Comanchero traders grew wealthy, Jack knew. He smiled with scorn, an expression that Soltero, deep into his crazy water, did not recognize.

Soltero chuckled. "Maybe you mean one of my old wives, eh?"

"The young female," Jack said.

"You don't look like a rich man to me," Soltero said in a booming voice, his manners apparently grown careless and addle-witted with whiskey. "What do you want with such a fine, strong female?" He laughed again, as though he could guess.

"She looks weak and sick to me," Jack said. He switched to words in Comanche, he knew this was dangerous, but he couldn't say all he wanted to say in Spanish, or in hand talk. "She is not worth much. I suppose she will die soon."

Now, because of Jack's clear speech in his own tongue, Soltero's glance grew suddenly sharper. He looked quickly at Jack's feet, his clothes, looking for band identity, but all he saw was what he had seen earlier, a man, a youth who looked like any *Tejano*, and dressed like a Mexican sheep herder or a wool gatherer and who spoke like a Comanche, who had no pretty amulets nor stone beads, only two horsehair bridles and four good *reatas*.

Suddenly Soltero scratched his groin and shrugged, but his eyes, which appeared so indifferent, carefully examined the *reatas*. He drank from the cup again, then passed it to Jack, who drank and passed the cup along to Soltero's companions.

Now it seemed to Jack that Soltero's brain groped with another problem that caused him to look away uneasily, scratch his head, belch, all gestures which made him appear loutish and stupid.

"Cousin," Soltero said loudly.

A call---*Cousin?*
Cousin.
But no one answered. No one spoke. It was time for another smoke but Soltero offered no tobacco or pipe, and Jack had nothing left.

All around in the darkness he saw horses grazing on long tethers, other fires under the trees, heard talking, laughing, an occasional sound of anger. A woman's voice rose querulously. The miasmic dung and carcass stenches of grease and bone and charring flesh hovered close to the ground, the old stenches strong in this filthy camp.

Jack watched the fire, thinking of the settler's wagons across the campground. Far, beyond the old cemetery, too far. Because something had changed.

He waited against Soltero's silence, aware of women moving under the trees but not looking at them. The sharp smell of steeping herbs cut through the other thick smells. Comanche women drank desert tea to kill the mystery of conception, but he didn't think they would give this balm to the raped girl. His glance moved back to Soltero. An appalling hatred shifted like a landslide inside him.

Soltero laughed abruptly, "Eh, *Tejan*," he said.

Jack remained as he was, his hands loose on his knees, his face unchanged.

"I am called Jack," he said.

"I have heard of someone called He Walks Away."

Jack didn't answer.

"Have you heard of this person?" The look of cunning narrowed Soltero's eyes.

"I am called Jack."

Soltero shrugged again. "Jack. Juan. He Walks Away. Perhaps he has many names. You talk like one of the People, but you look like a *Tejano*. Maybe my eyes are tricking me." He rubbed his eyes with exaggerated gestures. His companions laughed and drank crazy water from the tin cup, then passed it back to Soltero.

Jack watched Soltero's sinister buffoonery and knew the talk, the path had turned away from his intentions that he had reached some subtle, dangerous moment with Soltero.

Now Soltero shifted ground again, growing serious, even earnest, a merchant selling his wares. "This girl works hard. She is young, just right for bearing."

"She looks sick and starved."

"I've fed her well ever since I caught her in Mexico."

Soltero's companions laughed at the mention of Mexico, that place where captives abounded so easily.

"She's starved and damaged with neglect."

"My women have taken care of her and trained her and now I have made her good. You saw."

"I saw," Jack answered.

"Well then, for you she is worth the price of four good mules. Yes, yes, that much."

The price was beyond anything Jack could afford from the coins left in his belt. Then he understood they were not bargaining for the girl, but for something else. He drew a long breath. His heart began to beat heavily. Yet he knew by long custom, even by law among them, that the Comanches dared not break the peace of the trading here in Santa Fe.

"The price is too high. We are finished."

Soltero's smile grew fixed. "From you, the price is not too high. From you the price will grow higher. Yes, yes, my heart tells me this."

Jack got to his feet slowly, with care, the *reata* bundle hanging from his shoulder.

Soltero laughed, the buffoon again. "Eh, Tejan, for the price of those miserable *reatas* I will tell you something as one brother to another."

Jack waited, looking down at Soltero who still lounged on his buffalo robe between his companions. A stirring of watchers at the edge of the firelight left one man standing apart, staring, but Jack saw only Soltero and his leering grin. He dropped one *reata* on the robe in front of Soltero.

"Eh, Tejan, then I will tell you only a little for one *reata*. Are you listening?"

Jack waited.

"He, whose name is unspoken between us, *he* is searching." Soltero's face settled into somber lines, all buffoonery forgotten. He blinked his eyes several times. His voice grew heavier. "He leads a paint pony whose only task is to carry bones."

The noise of the encampment went on in the darkness, swelling and receding around him. Soltero and his companions stared up at him, uneasy, suddenly wary and restless. Slowly Soltero's face grew settled and full of hate.

"Who will stop me?" Jack asked, so softly that only with concentration could his meaning be understood by anyone near him. "Who will stand in my way? You, thief?"

The Comanches did not move, nor speak. Jack glanced around at the watchers, the faces, as he could see them beyond the fire. One or two village traders, Comanche men, Kiowas. His eyes lingered for a moment, he saw one face, one stance, then he turned and walked away from the light.

The old cemetery loomed like a refuge in the darkness, a refuge for those who lay under the stones. This weedy, neglected ground, swarming with spirits, warned the Comanches away to safety. None would ever come into the graveyard, he knew, because of all the witches, and bad spirits, and the laughing pranks of the Supernaturals, but he watched, thinking of how to double back, to retrieve his hidden weapons and bandolier.

Too far away. Later, when the Comanches left with their plunder.

Or some would pretend to leave and wait, watching for prey, using one of their fondest tricks.

He lay for a time on his belly, hidden by the darkness, by the stones and old wooden crosses.

I can't save her---.

A wind came up, shaking the brush and weeds. He turned and crawled back toward the old adobe buildings, over a low wall. He saw a door half open, in darkness, walls and other openings, crude foundations, this abandoned God-place empty and quiet with night.

Cousin? He wondered.

Soltero's voice, his word? Speaking to the Comanches crowding around, watching.

That face, that man's stance at the edge of the crowd as he walked away.

I couldn't help her.

Then he heard a soft sound from beyond the adobe openings, and saw a soft light ignite, faint as a single candle. He waited, watching, and saw something pass back and forth across the light, as though a man paced back and forth between Jack and the light. Jack crawled closer, and watched, and saw the tall man who wore the long brown robe, its hood thrown back, pacing back and forth in front of the little candle set on a stone wall.

Jack stood and stepped forward softly in the leaf debris and gravel. "You must help the girl," he said.

The man started and stared. A moment of paralyzed fear passed. He frowned. "Who are you?"

Jack shook his head. "You must help the girl."

Another silence dragged on.

"What girl?"

Jack believed the man had not heard, he had not understood.

"Soltero's girl."

"There are hundreds of girls."

Jack thought he had not spoken plainly. "The girl---in Soltero's camp---. That girl."

He was a *padre*, Jack saw from his robe, his hood, his belt with the hanging wooden cross. This was surely one of the men whom Sallie Flynn had called a *padre,* a priest, and now he looked out into the darkness without answering Jack. The light from the candle showed that his mouth had become a severe, compressed line.

Jack said, "You were there."

The man looked at Jack. "Who are you?" he asked again.

"I came from Estebanico, the *santero.*"

"Ah. Yes. You are certainly not of this village."

"I came looking for McGregor's trade wagons."

But this man, this priest, didn't hear.

"A new apprentice for Estebanico's *Penetente Cristos*?" His accent was a blend of English and Spanish, carefully spoken. His mouth twisted suddenly. "Has he forgotten that public penance has been forbidden?"

Jack didn't understand the *padre's* meaning, or how to answer.

The *padre* looked out into the night again. His thoughts seemed to drift away. "Tell Estebanico, the *santero,* that there is no longer a market for Christ in the attitude of his Passion. He must take his *bultos* and *santos* to the renegade sects hiding in the mountains. They are outlaws now. Tell him public penance exists no more. Tell him the new French bishop takes away our native priests and replaces them with his European friends. He rebuilds our native churches with the help of the *Norteamericanos*---."

The *padre* drew a long breath. "Tell him our barbarous native *santos* will soon be replaced by plaster saints that all look alike." The *padre* turned his head to examine Jack's hair, his skin color, his eyes. "You are one of the *Norteamericanos?*"

"Texas."

"A Texian, a *Tejano*. You have an accent, I hear it. I have heard it before---." The *padre* stared.

"I was held with the Comanches until---," Jack stopped.

"Ah," the *padre* said again. "One of those. You are signed into the Church registry. When were you exchanged?"

Jack shook his head.

The *Padre's* voice changed. "My son, you were abandoned then? You have no faith?"

The *padre* waited expectantly, but Jack had no words for him.

The *padre* straightened, his voice grew firm "Have you been baptized?"

Jack frowned, confused by such a question.

"Do you want to lead a virtuous life devoted to serving God's will?"

Jack looked his frowning question. *How had they come to this place? These words? This ugly night?*

"Now you must repent." At Jack's silence, the *padre* went on, "It means goodness, forgiveness. Obedience to God's Will, which is evidence in all things." The *padre* paused, explaining his wisdom. "You must repent, you must do this for the sake of your soul."

"Forgive?" Jack asked. "All things?"

"Yes, all. Even those heathens. Even their salvation. Even yours."

Jack looked away from the man, seeing the darkness, the shapes of abandoned gravestones, the false peace of night, of slumber, the single candle flame.

"There are many girls," the man in the long brown robe said bitterly. "There are many children."

"You must help the girl," Jack repeated, again. Suddenly, without knowing how it happened, he felt the tears rolling down his cheeks. He was shamed by such weakness. He lifted his arm and wiped his sleeve across his face and lowered his arm again, waiting.

The *padre* spoke in a low, intense voice. "I *cannot* help the girl. Don't you understand?"

Jack shook his head.

"You were there too. You saw those beasts. You saw that abomination."

"The girl---."

"There are hundreds of girls. Hundreds of children. Hundreds of souls to save. Two hundred years of children!" The priest paused. "You did not try to stop that abomination!"

"There were too many---," Even as he spoke Jack understood that he had fallen into some sort of certain folly, maybe the folly of his months of sickness and all the anguished wooden faces he saw every day and every night. Probably he had thrown himself away to the Comanches already.

But someone in that filthy camp of Comanches and Kiowas knew of him. Someone knew that he was one of the bad stories they loved to recount around campfires, keeping the shame and the anger alive.

"I tried to buy her."

"You?" The *padre*'s eyes traveled over Jack, searching for a miracle. "Tell me," he said, drawing the words out with sarcasm, "where does the apprentice woodcarver find so much wealth?"

"Not enough---."

"Not enough. Perhaps you will tell me for what purpose you tried to buy the girl? Did you want her for yourself? God forgive you! Did you want her only for that reason?"

Jack's anger rose suddenly, easily. The *padre* had no idea of its power, its readiness to strike at him.

The *padre* stepped suddenly closer, lifting his candle towards Jack's face, looking for something small, hidden, when everything else seemed more important this night.

The girl.

Cousin.

The familiar Comanche, in the circle of watchers, who knew who he was.

A breeze tugged at the *padre*'s robes with a dark, agitated motion. It caught at his lank hair and caused his eyes to narrow and plucked at the candle flame.

"I cannot." he said. "I cannot help her. Or the others. I am poorer than you."

"You are a priest---."

"Yes. A *padre*. A priest. So, I will sprinkle them with holy water. I will give them new names and I will write these names in the Book of Baptisms, but only if they live long enough to enter the households and beds of the *hidalgos* and *rancheros* in New Spain," His tongue fumbled for a moment. "In America."

"This is still permitted?" Jack asked softly, turning his head to look at the black silhouette of the half-finished mud church, the village beyond in the darkness, the old cemetery, the low wall, the heart of this crude, tenacious civilization in which, he had thought, the priest surely stood at the center.

"Yes, permitted. Condoned. For profit, for commerce. The new government forbids, but the Americans look away until the tribes are subdued. They talk about territories, more reservations." He drew a deep breath. "The tribes run wild. There is no end." He paused. "Well. Many adapt. Most adapt."

The sadness found Jack again. He thought he had to get away into the darkness, quickly. To be alone.

"My young friend," the priest said, "did you really believe that people flocking together into their civilizations equals salvation? No.

No, you are wrong. It is not enough. You must try to comprehend. There is nothing more I can do. Nothing more. Soon I shall leave."

Jack struggled with his anger, his confusion.

"They will excommunicate me. It means that I have opposed the new French bishop. That I continue to teach in the old way. I am only a native priest, I can teach only as Bishop Zubiria taught us after the Franciscans---," he waved his hand. "Well, no matter. It means also that I fight to preserve the old churches, the old *bulto*s and *santos,* like those Estebanico carves out of his love for Christ's Passion."

He stopped speaking again, as though thinking. "It means I must become an outlaw in the mountains. I can do nothing else. And those who follow must suffer. But soon they will return to their villages, to what is familiar. To what is comfortable. They will forget."

A dog barked in a frenzy, back near the Comanche encampment. Jack turned his head, searching, listening. But the night gave him nothing. He thought of the girl again, moving cruelly in the dark trough of dirt beneath Soltero.

The *padre* stepped forward, lifting the candle. "What is this?" he asked in a quiet voice. His fingers reached out to enclose Estebanico's charm on the thong around Jack's neck.

"A charm---."

"Against what?"

Jack saw the new anger, the new outrage in the *padre*'s face.

"Against what?"

Jack took a step back.

"Against heathenish spirits?" The *padre*'s sudden wrath poured out toward him.

"No," Jack said, sensing the *padre*'s intent.

"Who gave you this charm? Estebanico gave you this? The maker of holy saints for our altars gave you this pagan charm against evil, did he not? What evil?" the priest demanded.

It seemed to Jack that, tonight, he had learned, better than this God-man, what evil neither his charm, nor the evidence of God's will in all things, could dispel. Only the priest's passionate illusions remained.

The *padre*'s face grew dark as wine. "It is a peyote charm."

Across the graveyard, the dog barked with greater frenzy, then stopped with a yelp of pain. Somewhere an owl called softly, distantly.

"Give it to me." The priest's fingers tightened. He drew a knife from his habit to cut the leather cord.

Jack's hand shot out, caught the priest's wrist, twisted hard, took the knife away. He held the *padre*'s wrist and drew the man toward him.

"Stop," he said. He wanted to strike sense into this mad foolish man, but he only spoke carefully, keeping his voice low. "Stop! I've listened to you. Now shut your mouth, be quiet if you want to live. Listen to me. The Comanches are here. They will take me if they can. They will kill you too. They don't care. They will do it for nothing. No one will know. Now get away." He pushed the *padre* from him.

The *padre* stared, in another moment of new, paralyzing, fear, the candle falling from his fingers, as he began to understand the night. He attempted to speak, perhaps to reason, to speak more holy words. Then he turned, hunching, tripping over his robe, his sandals scratching, gouging at the gravel, as he tried to run in the darkness.

Too much noise---too much noise.

The candle flame still flickered where it had fallen in the litter of leaves and gravel. Jack stepped on the flame.

Only a stiletto. The *padre*'s weapon.

He went back over the low wall and into the darkness of mesquite and weeds, which would soon overwhelm the old, leaning gravestones.

He knew they were out there, watching, waiting.

The mad priest cries abomination. The girl huddles in the stench of the Comanche camp. *I can't help her.*

He knew again he had probably thrown himself away.

He crawled into the thorns, under the mesquite. He lay still with his heart pounding while the sounds of dogs barking, now here, now there, came closer.

They knew. He marveled that he'd walked among them, that he'd dared to bargain, as mad as the priest, that he'd been the greatest of blundering fools.

They knew.

One man at the edge of the watchers knew him. Half Kiowa, half Comanche. Finally recognized. *Cousin.*

His name was Dohat, cousin to Soltero? *Cousin.*

Half-brother to Owl Stands' dead, good son.

Maybe not a fool. No. He'd just taken the chance.

His heartbeat slowed, calmed. He watched through the thorns and branches, his hands spread on the ground. He heard soft sounds punctuated by long silences, whispering sounds of movement at intervals so remote that he thought he imagined them, and knew better. Points of far lamplight blotted out, then winked on again, as shapes, branches moved in the wind.

The settlers, the big wagons, at the far edge of the campground. The ones he had seen in his search for McGregor's freight wagons, but these were only settlers. Scores of wagons. Open ground between the big old trees and the cemetery. Horses and mules staked out. Open ground, and the moon still high.

Hours passed as he waited, as they waited. He knew their patience. He gambled that the ones who sought him would never come into this spirit place, afraid of ghost sickness. They would not use noise, no muskets to alarm the ugly White Dogs and end the trading, nothing loud, no battle yells to bring trouble to themselves, from this village where they had traded for decades. No soldiers from the fort nearby and beyond Taos, no dragoons chasing after them. They were, after all, a practical people, ruled by hard necessity, and most would not even bother coming after him. Most just liked their trade whiskey, their weapons, their slave sales and the trivial booty they took back to their women. Those few, probably just Dohat and his followers, would just come in silence and cunning.

He dozed, and dreamed he felt their hands grappling, holding him despite his wildest efforts.

He woke to the change, the softened light, the deeper shadows. The moon's brilliance had darkened behind a veil of drifting clouds. Long before daylight a wind came up from the south, moving in gusts, rattling the brush and the clumps of dry weeds. The church door behind him opened suddenly. He started with a jolt, but the door just began a dull banging, as the gusts of wind caught it. He lay straining against the ground, listening. The banging of the door went on and on, a muffled, unimportant, pounding against the quiet. A dog nearby set up a sudden new frenzy of barking, a wild yapping. Jack got to his feet and ran, through the graveyard, past the old buildings, and out across open ground that had grown darker with the clouded moon. Ran hard toward the settler's encampment. Half way, he heard the whisper of arrows. He ran among the old trees gambling, gambling.

The arrow that found him passed through his side, above his hip. He stumbled, ran on, ran until he was close to the big wagons, the settlers with guns. The barrage of arrows stopped. He ran on, and stumbled to a stop near the tall, painted wagon. Pain from the arrow suddenly hit his brain past all barriers. The arrowhead stuck out from the flesh above his hip.

An iron arrowhead made from some old stolen scrap---.

He broke the arrow behind the iron point, quickly, then pulled the rest back and out from behind.

He bent to the wound. Bloody, painful. Painful. A blood trail for Dohat and his dogs and whoever came with him.

He stumbled on. Not a bad wound, but painful every step. Slowing.

The night was still too dark for Jack to see all the paintings on the fancy wooden wagon when he came to it. He didn't care about signs, paintings, only that this wagon offered a scrap of shelter. Two doors stood open at the back, above a short set of stairs. A lighted lantern swayed from a bracket by the doors.

This fancy wagon had been deserted when he passed, before, looking for McGregor's wagons. He limped forward a few steps, into the edge of light from a low campfire, holding his side. He saw the man and stopped.

The man lounged by his fire in a comfortable wooden folding chair, a shotgun across his lap, held in one hand. The other held a porcelain teacup with painted yellow flowers.

"You may be welcome," he said at last in a soft, theatrical voice. "But I don't know yet."

The man was in his mid-life, a little portly. His hair was wavy, graying, his eyes turned down at the outer corners. He wore a fine well-trimmed mustache. He looked with interest at Jack, at the blood trailing down his side, Jack's hand holding the wound, his other hand still holding the broken arrow.

"Well. From what I see, I believe I am a better surgeon for that wound than you are." He put the cup down and arose. "So, you are the cause of all the racket out there? The dogs have been noisy tonight."

Jack watched him.

"Do you speak English?"

Jack nodded.

"Some little scrape between you and those Indians yonder?" The man wrinkled his nose with distaste. "I believe I smelled a whiff of their camp."

"A scrape," Jack answered.

"And an arrow, I see."

Jack didn't answer.

"Ah. A silent uprising?"

"Trade. They won't use guns---. They want to keep the trading."

The man nodded. "Trade. I know what they trade." His expression changed. In no hurry, he lifted his shotgun and casually fired into the night sky. "Damn me, it went off. I've done it again!"

After a stunned moment, Jack almost laughed, more of a grunt of pain, of disbelief, in this night filled with disbelief. This fool man had blown the night's silence away, maybe blown the Comanches away. The dogs started barking again, voices from the wagon people shouted questions, alarms.

But this man was no fool, Jack knew at once.

"The wagon folk will be here soon asking questions," the man said. He looked at Jack, with a trace of curious judgment, seeing him as the *peon* youth he appeared to be, hearing the hesitation in some of his words, the slight accent in his voice. "Wait for me inside, if you wish. If you can read, you will see I have something to offer and you appear to have a pesky arrow wound. I will be back shortly."

CICERO SMITH, the painting on the sides of the wagon said in flourishes of blue and red paint.

DOCTOR OF HEALING ELIXIRS, HUMORS AND MINOR SURGERIES.

All sorts of scenes, flowers and other symbols covered the wagon.

"I told them the gun went off by accident. I am something of a flimflam man too," Cicero Smith said, with a smile, when he came back. "Be easy. This will hurt, but it will help."

He cleansed the wound with whiskey, by lantern light inside the wagon, then dug again into the arrow wound, using his finger, then a long pinching tool, searching.

"Only this way," he told Jack, "can we be sure. Ah! Here is the little culprit that could kill you." He held up threads from Jack's *peon* shirt, driven into the wound by the iron arrowhead.

"Infection, sir." He poured more whiskey into the wound, then handed the bottle to Jack. "Drink. This will help, too. In some ways, not as much as my ELIXIR, but it will help."

Jack drank and thought he had never felt such pain, and now such painful relief.

"---damned dirty arrowhead," he said, just a low mutter.

"Yes, that. But rusty and jagged. The edges caught the threads. Minnie balls do that. Minnie balls crush." He wrapped a rough bandage, tight, above Jack's money belt. "I believe your belt deflected the arrow somewhat. You may have some damaged coins."

"I'll pay---."

"Pay what?"

"Your help."

"Don't take from me what I want to give," Cicero Smith said mildly, as though he had said it many times. There was a distant note of impatience in his voice. "Now rest."

"I couldn't help her."

The man studied Jack. "Who?"

"The Mexican girl. In the Indian camp."

"I saw no girl."

"They'll hide her because of the soldiers. They'll wait for another chance to sell her."

Cicero Smith thought about that. "Will they follow you?"

"If they can." Jack's lips quirked. The whiskey was helping. "They would like to take my head in a leather sack to settle the debt, but I don't much like that idea."

"You are so important to them then?"

"No. Only to a few. Because of ---." He broke off.

Cicero Smith gathered Jack's bloody shirt, the bandages and tools. "Here, take this old shirt, its grown small for me." He smiled. "I've grown larger." He left the wagon. "Time to hitch up those God-forsaken, misbegotten mules and leave this place. We go before sunrise, I am told. I will have to leave then. Now rest."

But Jack didn't rest. He slipped out of the wagon, wincing, but firmly bandaged. Now he could gamble again, and he was ready.

He circled wide around the campground, around the Comanche encampment. He saw no scouts. He stayed in the darkness under the trees, among the scores of tethered horses, a few skittish mules, packs and parfleches, clothes carelessly dropped by the drunken Indians whose revelry, cries, and laughter came from a distance.

Dohat, the others, hid themselves among those revelers at the campground, he knew, he had gambled and now he gambled again. Dohat, maybe a little drunk on crazy water himself, would break trade laws with a silent arrow to recapture his honor and because he had not yet avenged his brother's death. Now he would not want to be caught risking the trade peace, he would not want civil anger from his own people, more shame to his father, perhaps a time of banishment from the People.

A man who knows nothing of honor,

I will kill him if I ever find him again.

Jack heard muffled sound coming from a thicket ahead, but found only a man and woman drunk, secretly coupling, aware of nothing else. He went on and came to the willows, the edge of the stream. Then moving downstream, away from the encampment, to that cutbank, he pulled away the brush. Everything he owned was still there, still hidden.

He started back the way he had come, more tired. His side ached and gnawed. He thought of Cicero Smith's whiskey. He thought of the girl, but they had her hidden, guarded, a commodity of value. He couldn't help her. He thought of the mad priest, the Comanches and Kiowas drunk, sleeping, fucking each other in the willows. Dogs sniffing, barking now and then. He looked at all the horses and mules, tethered, some thin and poor, some grazing, some resting.

One horse, a sturdy looking sorrel mustang with good withers and strong hind quarters, watched Jack with its ears forward. Curious, wary, smart, its ear Comanche-clipped. Jack spoke softly, approached, took up the tether to make a jaw bridle, checked for sores on its back, checked the horse's legs and hoofs. The horse nipped at his shoulder, nothing hard, a curious, get-acquainted gesture with his lips. It tossed its head and readily followed, as Jack led him away. He passed an old dead cottonwood and sank the priest's stiletto deep. Let them find this, let them wonder, let them make another story.

Still an hour before daylight. Jack thought about Estebanico, about Joaquin Cruz and his woman.

No sign of McGregor's wagon. No sign, no questions in the village.

No sign of Sallie Flynn.

I will have to give you up again, he said to her in his thoughts. But only for now. Only for now.

Back at the settlers' wagons there was a great subtle hustle, talking, the beginning of movement, then cheers and laughter, a few random exuberant gunshots into the dawning sky.

Jack sat the sorrel horse and watched Cicero Smith securing barrels of ELIXIR more firmly to the sides of the wagon.

"I'll tend your God-forsaken mules," Jack said.

Cicero Smith stared at Jack, at his gear, sitting bareback on the sorrel horse, favoring his side, but easy. He stared at the sorrel horse with the clipped ear. His smile of appreciation, mixed with a little skepticism, clearly told Jack he knew exactly what had transpired

"Well. And I will continue to heal you from that unpleasant wound, so that you do not die of rampant infections and humors?"

"Why not?"

Cicero Smith laughed aloud. "Why not. Excellent! I hate those mules. Fair enough." He shook his head, perhaps wondering who the flimflam man was here.

A horn sounded, a signal to the wagons.

"Fair enough!" In his best theatrical voice Cicero Smith added, "Now we must get ready, sir. We can't be late. We go to the edge of the earth. Now we must be ready to go find California!"

PART II

THE EDGE OF THE EARTH
ৡৄৄৄ

Too long. Almost four years, too long.

Jack sat on the wagon steps, the journal on his knee, as he wrote with the stub of a pencil. The lantern gave him just enough light. He looked out into the darkness, checking on the two mules and the horses, his Comanche sorrel with the clipped ear, and the two pack horses. No alarms, just grazing animals in a soft September night. He looked over at Cicero Smith, who sat in his folding chair by a small fire. He watched Smith rub his shoulder and wince. A moment later he lifted his new teacup with the blue flowers to his lips and drank the last of the ELIXIR it contained.

The night was quiet, with just muted sounds from owls, the rustle of a nearby dog, grazing animals, and occasional soft voices from the wagon people they'd travelled with from California.

Jack paged back through his journal, wondering why he bothered with it, as he often did on the rare nights when Smith fell quiet. Maybe to keep writing words he had learned again, words from back at the parson's, magic words from the woman's long-ago picture books. The shadow woman he could hardly remember.

Maybe he wrote in his journal only when Cicero Smith had no new thoughts to share about the mysteries of the universe, or the purpose of man, a new formula for the ELIXIR, a medical procedure, or a new, theatrical rendition from some bit of literature.

But, here and there, Jack found an entry in his journal that reminded him of his life, and sometimes surprised him, as an entry often did.

Walks Away.

Just a name. Nothing.

Smith says I talk in sentences longer than three words now. Getting civilized. Not even like a born Texian or whatever I am. Doesn't matter. He claims the credit. Claims he's taming me. Same for teaching me how to mix the ELIXIR, hold a fork, open doors for women. Never swearing in their presence. No shit---almost never.

He added a current notation:

He's better. It's taken most of this past summer. This trail has been damned slow but still faster than the Gila trail, fewer thieving Indians from what I hear. But he's well enough to handle the mules if I leave for Santa Fe tomorrow. I'm going. Still two days out. I need another journal and some lead pencils if I'm going to keep this up.

But something's on his mind. He hasn't said. He reads the newspapers when we get them and talks about the troubles ahead.

In the beginning Jack thought he'd stay on with Cicero Smith for a short time, after his trouble in Santa Fe. He'd let his side heal, get himself a saddle, when he could find a vaquero willing to trade. He'd just travel along until he was far enough from the trouble, and strong again to go his own way. Pay his debt to Smith. But he was weary. He was dog-tired of sickness and wounds, problems, Indians, fool ranting *padres*, slave girls he couldn't help, ugly memories that roused his impatience, and his ever-ready anger. He was tired of his own anxiety, his long nights when memories crept into his mind and became living dreams.

Tired of the haunting stench of the Comanche Soltero's filthy camp, his words.

He leads a paint pony, just carries bones.

Tired in his mind.

As time passed, he thought more often about leaving Smith, his accidental companion, who sometimes seemed like a simple fool.

Shit, leave him to his ELIXIR, his grandiose ideas, his ways to save the world from the thugs and thieves who abounded and casually killed; from medicines that invaded the lungs and swept away consumption; and childbirth without death. When Jack asked an idle question, Smith answered, or went to his precious books and found a big answer. All these threads of knowledge, this font of information as well as nonsense, and the nagging reality of his debt to Smith, drew Jack on to the next settlement, more ELIXIR, more of Smith's flowery speeches to his customers, words laced with his own elegant brew.

He set up camps, tended the mules, hunted, finally traded a fresh buck kill for an old saddle, added some protection from wandering brigands, listened to Smith's stories, and wondered about where the hell to go, what to do next. He thought about Sallie Flynn, long gone from Santa Fe. Where? But he kept wondering, and he could feel the determination growing in his mind.

Sallie Flynn.

And the scrap of paper she had left in his hand. Lost. Sometimes he couldn't even remember the words.

He drifted, and the first year passed. In California, he found the great blue water and stood in awe. He found drunken miners and Indians fighting each other, all still crazy for gold. He traveled a crooked road, in his mind; in California, as well wherever they went; crude tent towns; new half-built towns; mining camps; Chinese folks smoking opium and scrambling to stay alive among the miners who hated them.

And finally, gradually, he found that Cicero Smith was no flimflam man.

Cicero Smith regularly mixed up batches of whiskey, of any quality he could find, with brown sugar, cinnamon, nutmeg, fruit juice, rotgut whiskey, ginger, tobacco, tea and, whatever else seemed appropriate, depending on what village, what miner's camp, what farm hamlet, his wanderings took him to. He put up with boisterous miners and travelers; he avoided the rowdy riots of drunken miners, by testing the news along the way.

"Damn me, at least they're fighting for some form of real law now. Ha! Better than when I was here before in '50."

He gave his colorful lectures by torchlight, wherever he could draw a friendly crowd. He was seldom asked to leave town, for he never did harm. He sold his ELIXIR for fifty cents a bottle to those who could pay; and his customers went away happy, if not cured of their malaise. But he tended the farmers' children when they were sick; and set bones after fights, and accidents, and tavern shootings. He took payment in gold; but seldom took payment from farm families, unless the payment came as a bag of wild blackberries, root vegetables, a snared jackrabbit, a chicken, or a treasure of hen's eggs.

"See how well we fare, young Jack? Good food, good deeds!"

"Smith's way," Jack answered wryly. He was tired of drifting, too. Almost tired of Cicero Smith.

But Cicero Smith laughed. His eyes, so often cynical, often sad, lit with fond approval.

"Smith's way. Well said, young Jack. Smith's way."

Cicero Smith often thought of himself as a man, great in small ways.

He had long seen the larger picture; whereas this rough youth saw only the strife of his own life and the chaos around him. So, he had adopted an interesting mission. He liked to read aloud at night by lantern light, books or newspapers; and he made Jack read aloud. He imparted all kinds of scraps of information; sometimes made old jokes; or discussed old bookish ideas. But Smith had another mission in mind now as they traveled together, aimed at Jack, activated by his discovery of a ready and watchful mind, lurking behind Jack's gray eyes and the number of teacups full of the ELIXIR Cicero Smith drank in an evening.

He likened young Jack to a lump of ore, freshly pounded from the earth; or the ounces and chunks harvested in the streams and rivers of

Sonora, Tuolumne, Sutter's place and thereabouts back in '49 or '50. Smith found young Jack to be worthy of his interest, with a keen mind; yet still bearing rough edges in need of attention. Jack, still mindful of his debt and tangled in a troubled mindset, endured.

Smith's way.

The second year, they took the road back to Santa Fe; their route timed to avoid mountain snows. A big flock of woolies caught up to them; the sheep-herder hustled them along, with busy dogs and curses, when the sheep wandered, or stopped to pull at the remaining dry grass by the trail.

"A thousand sheep, young Jack," Cicero Smith commented as they waited by the trail for the sheep to pass. "Woolies. They eat anything. I'll wager they are destined for the Texas deserts where cattle don't thrive. Poor stupid creatures, but delicious! And the wool---."

Then the cougar, the big tawny wild cat settlers called lions or panthers, crossed the dusty road ahead of the wagon, following the sheep stragglers. The mules spooked and the left front wheel on the wagon, as well as the wagon tongue, cracked against a rock. The wagon swayed onto its side.

Shit! Goddamn panthers. Wheels too dry. We need new wheels if we can find them. By the time we fix this mess we'll hit the snow. Should've soaked the wheels.

Jack paused, looking into the night, remembering his frustration.

"Fate has found us," Cicero Smith had said, with a wave of his hand and without much regret. "And now we must find a profitable hamlet; perhaps one of the tent towns full of gold-miners, with heavy pockets. A place where we can spend the winter in relative safety. But fate hadn't found Jack. He thought of Sallie Flynn, all passing time. Where else to go? What else could he do, but go onto Santa Fe; to look for McGregor's wagon.

And sometimes he wondered, why go back? She was surely gone.

But I'm going anyway.

He thought about how she was always on his mind, even when he'd spent mindless time with California girls in the second winter; Mexican girls in dim *cantinas* and *jacals*, *putas* in the sleepy little villages, who found themselves listed now as Americans citizens of the new state of California in one of the recent roving censuses. But now it was three years away from Sallie Flynn, too long, or almost four years if his time with Estebanico counted.

Four years. You've gone, Sallie Flynn.

But his habit of thinking told him he was bound to go back, he was bound to look for McGregor's wagon, ask all the hard questions.

Where are you, Sallie Flynn?

In the place you called Elm Creek?

How many Elm Creeks in Texas? How many---?

For now, maybe think more about what he'd seen in California, a new state, and to marvel at such a rich country full of new advantages, vast lands that used to be old Mexican grants going back to the early Spanish, thousands of rancheros, thousands of cattle and horses on the hills.

Why not stay? Forget Santa Fe and his troubles there. Forget Sallie Flynn.

They travelled south again, into mild weather, where many of the *ranchos* were owned by American men who'd married California women before the Mexican War.

Mostly daughters of the old rancheros, Smith says.

Met some of the American rancheros, gave us shelter in a storm, got news, friendly. During the Mexican war the native *Californios* tried to burn them out. Mexican people here stole their horses and ran off for Mexico after the war, came back later, sold same horses to the Americans coming north on the Gila Trail. Crazy. Hard trail, mean Indians, live in thatch huts, steal everything, carry clubs to peace talks, kill travelers, drown settler's mules at rivers so they can eat them, fight each other. Poor land. Long way to Santa Fe.

Where are you Sallie Flynn?

Smith calls the old Spanish ranchers here just lazy hidalgos, they've let the cattle breed, they pay no attention, they don't work. They make good wine. They have dances and festivals. Fancy weddings. The *peons* are mostly Paiute slaves bought from the New Mexican traders as kids. If they pay them a few pesos, they are *peons* always in debt, if they don't pay them, they are slaves. The farmers do everything else. Same as Texas.

The herds of horses and the big California mules he saw on the hills and in the great valleys were casually neglected by the old Spanish *hidalgos*. Horse thieves flourished, both Mexicans and Utes, who drove stolen herds down across the border into Mexico. Road bandits abounded, men notorious for their violence, some shouting bitter grievances against the rich *hidalgos* who ignored their anger at the Anglo invaders and the swarms of newcomer Americano ruffians and miners, just before they were shot or hanged.

Beware of notoriety, young Jack, they cut heads off. They must be preserved in alcohol. It is an ugly practice but necessary, Jack read in his journal. Smith says they do this to identify the dead outlaws, for the town rewards.

The *hidalgos* complained about all the thievery, the weakness of the new laws. They sent riders out, shot a few thieves and Indians, hanged others and saw their deeds both praised and condemned in the local newspapers. And when they wanted money to pay for their big fandangos or their sailing trips to visit families in Spain, they butchered cattle and sold their hides. But the newspapers persistently wrote of skirmishes between angry native *Californios* and the newcomers everywhere.

Richest state in the U.S.A. the papers say. It's full of Southerners now who want to make it a separate country with slaves, all that. Shit, it's a free state, slavery's illegal. Maybe someone should tell the *peons*.

The gold rush had passed from bonanza where a miner could scrape up a thousand dollars a day for plain hard work. Opportunities still abounded but claims were still registered and quickly stolen.

Miners still fought with the Indians and the Chinese, but mostly now they were just dirt farmers full of gold dust dreams.

"We let the others mine for gold and do all that hard work, young Jack. We mine their pockets."

Smith's way.

They left Los Angeles, a poor town of maybe a thousand people in mud brick houses with thatch roofs made waterproof with tar from the nearby tar pits.

The roads were bad, heading north again, just thin animal trails that grew as men from the scattered settlements worked to build them. Further north, they passed piles of rocks at crude log ocean landings and coves were sailing ships unloaded their ballast rock and took on cargoes of logs for San Francisco's rampant building boom. They passed big churches made of mud bricks and plaster in the old Spanish style back in the 1700s with fields of green foods, corn, beans, orchards, vineyards tended by Indians and *peons*. He remembered a foggy cove with a sandy beach and watching a band of ragged Indians huddled over clumps of seaweed, gathering food. In another cove he remembered looking down in the rocky sea where a sailing ship with its cargo of huge logs had foundered, the ship, just another bound south for San Francisco, lost like others in rough waters because there were no passable roads.

He remembered a forgotten little gold town at the foot of the mountains they called the Sierras, where diggers and laborers laying pipes in a town roadway found a great gold nugget, already a legend, buried in the street under their feet. He remembered restless, surly *Californios*, young men with big hats and bandoliers gathering in groups watching the hated *Americanos*, frowning their grievances.

Trouble, Smith says. Met the railroad today, he read in his journal. *Big ugly iron engine, black smoke, cinders in everybody's eyes. Indians around here mostly poor, hungry, they call it the iron snake. Just local tracks but Smith says the Pacific railroad will change everything when it gets here. Finding work easy, built seven pine coffins for a place calls itself a hospital. Good pay. It's right next to a pest house where they take folks to die.*

He remembered his payment for the coffins, gold dust, chunky nuggets, one nugget in a pretty shape, like a little flying bird with a hole in its wing just large enough for a thin chain or a cord. He chose it among others, thinking of Sallie Flynn.

There's building everywhere, finding good tools again. Paid in gold. Not enough roads. Too many people. San Francisco's a big town. Smith says it's much bigger than when he was here before, big buildings, warehouses, cargo ships in the harbor, sailors jumping ship for the mines. Abandoned ships rotting, sinking. Prices high, sugar, tobacco, spices. Smith raised the price of ELIXIR.

But he thought most often about the valleys, the thriving young vineyards' and orchards, remembering the parson's apple orchard from years before. These peaceful places were far from the strife of ordinary frontier hustle. He remembered them with an almost forgotten pleasure. Now and then when they passed through the big valleys, he listened to the farmers' lore from Missouri, Arkansas, Louisiana, all newcomers as they drank ELIXIR, telling of seeds, grafting, plantings, soils, new varieties, new crops, more water, and always the weather.

Cicero Smith thirsted for a drink of brandy one night in the town of Sonora, flamboyant after customers had drained his barrels of ELIXIR and left him without his evening libation. They wandered through the streets until they found a tavern set under a cluster of sprawling oaks. The Mexican bartender's round face gleamed with sweat, his black mustache twisted as he spoke silent words and seemed beset with secretive frowns.

"The brandy is poor," Smith observed, "the room is dark and smells of chili and dirt, and the bartender frowns and does not want to look at us."

They took their drinks to a table. "We're *Norteamericanos*," Jack said. He drank from his glass of beer, looking over the room with its dark, low beamed ceiling and the hover of smoke in the air.

"There is bad news here," Cicero Smith said softly.   His flamboyance had died away. The saloon was noisy, with low talk and muted laughter, more Spanish then English.   Smith took a sip of brandy, watching the front entrance as three men stepped through, young *Californios*, roughly dressed, big hats, rifles, bandoliers. They looked around before stepping forward carefully into the dark busy noise which grew gradually quieter.

"Trouble," Smith muttered. "Let us hope not."

"Them?" Jack stared, taking their measure. Smith's way often included an abundance of worries and warnings. Jack's eyebrows lifted in doubt. "Those kids?"

"Do not dismiss them."

"They're kids."

"Those boys shoot people," Cicero Smith said. He sipped his brandy slowly. "They kill people, often they get away into the hills. Their friends protect them. They are seldom punished.   They steal horses, they hate *Anglos*. They believe the *Anglos* stole this country from them, they believe this is their country."

Jack's eyebrows lifted again in a mocking question.

Smith muttered, "That old question you continue to belabor." Smith's voice held a dark sound of impatience. "Damn me, not now, not now."

Jack stared at the three youths again, then took a slow drink. Now the three *Californios* noticed Cicero Smith in his come-to-meeting salesman clothes. Jack drank from his beer glass again, almost smiling at Smith's fluster.

Smith finished his brandy. "The good barkeeper mentioned news. He was reluctant, but I knew something was amiss. The justice of the peace, an *Anglo* whose name he did not bother to mention, hanged one of them recently. A youth. Like these. Here. For murder I believe, or theft, never proven, maybe he was just handy. You may have noticed the oaks outside. There was something of a riot afterwards. More killings." Smith gave Jack a hard glance. "They are still angry. They would probably like to shoot us tonight."

Jack drank again, in no hurry yet, but he felt the tension, the growing quiet. He smiled at the three *Californios.*

"Do you want to die here tonight?" Cicero Smith asked quietly at Jack's careless smile.

"What?"

"At the hands of angry boys and their comrades in this dirty saloon, boys who don't know your name or care, who probably don't speak your language? Who hate you? Who will spit on your body and bury you in a shallow grave where no one will ever find you? This is your epitaph?"

They watched the three *Californios* walk casually to the bar and almost disappear among their comrades.

Jack finished his beer and set the jar down carefully. "Shit."

"Exactly. Now I suggest we saunter out of here and go quietly on our way."

The memory still stung, a lesson learned. Jack read on, remembering.

Now rumors in the papers about troubles back in Texas and Oklahoma, Kiowas, others, taken off the Reserves. Settlers mad, U.S., afraid they'll raid the reserves, kill off all the Indians.

They're over in Indian Territory now. Oklahoma. Newspapers say the agents cheat them, no shit. Wormy cornmeal, rotten beef. But the Comanches won't hoe corn. They'll break out, they won't go in until the buffalo are gone. Hide hunters doing the job.

And the haunting memory again, taking him back to the scene, the filthy camp, Soltero's words,

He leads a paint pony whose task is to carry bones.

And the dreams, Jack read in his journal. The dreams, killing, fighting. *Can't stop them when they come.*

Jack drew a long breath and read on in his California journal.

Fish here come up the rivers every year. Bears eat them, bears everywhere. Indians never could kill them until they got guns. They come at you, not afraid. Good hunting.

Jack had learned that Smith had already found California five years before they encountered each other that night at the Santa Fe wagon camp. By way of a steamer and a sailing ship he had rounded the horn and arrived in San Francisco seven months after the great gold strike in '48. He thought to see the world and make his fortune, although already entering mid-life, so he made his way to the rivers to pan and prosper, but he soon found all the best claims taken and the work hard, dirty, often contentious with rowdy miners and Indians and only gray gravel showing in the pan.

He was not surprised. He was a canny man and saw quickly that the real gold was in supplying the miners and rank greenhorns and amateurs with whatever they wanted, needed, or craved. With his grub stake he bought an old wagon and two costly, half wild mules. Everything was in short supply and high in price, but he was undaunted and willing to go hungry until the first profits came in.

In the boom town of San Francisco, he quickly bought up supplies of picks, shovels, axes, tin cups, plates, ammunition, canned goods, whiskey, flour, sugar, fresh fruit, tobacco, dried meat, salt, and twice he carried a lady to her husband, or so she claimed, who was camped in a tent by the big rolling river.

Those women, Smith laughed to Jack in telling his story with four cups of ELIXIR in his belly. Bless their hearts! And those miners! They just come to stare at the women. Any women! They hadn't seen women in months. When they come out of the tents the miners throw their hats in the air and cheer. And when the ladies hang their washing on lines, damn me if the miners don't just stare at their drawers!

In his efforts to extend the supply of whiskey that always disappeared rapidly, he mixed it with sugar, spices, fruit juice, almost anything at hand, and good spring water, and called it THE ELIXIR OF LIFE. While the miners wanted straight whiskey and rum, the

ELIXIR was indeed like life to many, and even to the few farm women and wives trying to survive in the rowdy settlements who could drink this diluted brew without embarrassment because, after all, it was only flavored fruit juice, and they always went away happy. But in this way, he broadened his market. He began to think about a fine wooden wagon, a kind of traveling house, a gypsy house with a roof, fitted comfortably inside, a bed, storage space, good wheels for California's many bad roads, and storage for barrels of ELIXIR along the outsides. A wagon he could take anywhere. His canny thoughts of prosperity traveled ahead to the eventual building of his own wagon, to include a strong false bottom for the storage of his anticipated riches in gold dust and nuggets and silver coins, and any other treasure traded for his brew.

He painted the finished wagon with his name, with boisterous claims for his titles and capabilities, and the words THE ELIXIR OF LIFE in large visible letters.

The edge of the world, he often mused to Jack with a cynical twist of his mouth. You can be anybody you want. You can reinvent yourself, young Jack.

But he left the bounty of California in his fine new wagon, and left the wagon stored safely in the dry barn of an old Mexican sheep farmer back in Santa Fe, its false bottom empty, and took a relay of stages travelling east.

"The wagon did well, but I regretted leaving this bountiful country. Damn me, I regretted, but I knew I would return."

"Why'd you go back then?"

Smith thought for a moment.

"If he has any honor, I believe every man has his debts to pay, young Jack."

He never said more.

On his return to California with Jack Rainie, who was something of an enigma but also a little hell-bent stubborn now and then, but still a useful young stray with a strong back and a way with mules, Smith found that THE ELIXIR OF LIFE, combined with the extravagant

156

rumors fed by boosters and newspaper stories still coming from the various mines, and the hard work of two men instead of Smith alone, summoned a steady growing prosperity. Prices were high. By the beginning of the third spring the wagon's false bottom had grown heavier than ever with gold dust and silver coins.

I expect we'll start back this summer. Santa Fe. I'm heading back if Smith goes or not. I can get a stage or one of the Overland Mail wagons. I'm going back to look. Where the hell is Elm Creek?

But Cicero Smith found prosperity to his liking, and hard to leave behind.

"Patience, patience. Perhaps September! Before the snows."

September. Jack shook his head but couldn't quite get the words out.

He'd never told Smith about Sallie Flynn, never said a word. Couldn't bring himself to talk of her, to risk his foolish hopes. Now he kept his voice calm and his gaze steady.

"Well I'm going."

Smith frowned. This insistence reminded him that here was another facet of this formerly hapless youth he had not yet discovered. Perhaps a hidden history? Perhaps even a touch of hard determination?

Smith pondered. In his own mind he knew exactly what might draw Cicero Smith back to chaos and danger. A small smile touched his lips.

"A young lady I presume?"

Jack finally nodded, a slow acknowledgement. "Yep."

Smith considered. He stared into the campfire for a time, clearly thinking of his own love for the ladies with a smile. "You remind me. Well, we shall gather provisions for the trip and check the wagon. We'll find a group of travelers going over the mountains. Then we shall go." He paused, almost sadly. "I believe it's time."

But Jack sensed that Cicero Smith had other deeper troubles on his mind.

To hide his prosperity Smith wore fashionably cut old coats, a tall beaver hat, folded scarves at his neck, a small derringer at his waist, his belly gun he called it, but nothing that advertised his good fortune when he lectured his customers about the virtues of the ELIXIR.

But thieves were everywhere, rumors everywhere in this new frontier state, and caution prevailed. Jack bought a good serviceable handgun, a Colt.44 revolver with ammunition, added it to his rifle and bandolier and kept his weapons well oiled. Smith increased their presence by adding a painted canvas tent handy for California's occasional cold rains, for shelter when they mixed up ELIXIR, and for storage of supplies when they camped. Two pack horses carried everything else. They camped in villages and towns where Cicero Smith sometimes disappeared to revisit certain ladies he had met on his first visit, demonstrating to Jack what an excellent memory he had for such pleasures of the flesh. But times had changed here and there.

"Damn me, she's gotten herself a husband!"

Caution always prevailed. As they traveled south they scoured the incoming freight wagons and town depots for supplies, jars and bottles for the ELIXIR, precious paper for printing new handbills, tobacco, whiskey, and news of new roads. Long way, long road back before the snows, but they never left the wagon alone.

Why leave this generous new state with its orchards and opportunity, Jack often wondered, for Santa Fe, for Texas and all its bitter troubles? But he knew.

Sallie Flynn's there--- somewhere.

When the thieves came, they first rode idly by, just passing.

The wagon sat camped under a cluster of old sycamore trees near a spring. The sycamore leaves unfurled above and gave off a sense of shelter and a pleasant dusty fragrance. Horses and mules grazed nearby. The afternoon had grown darker, windier, with the smell of rain. Smith gave no lectures and sold no ELIXIR to customers who would soon be standing in the rain. He retired to the wagon with ELIXIR and a book. With rain on the way Jack saw to his bed and his gear in the tent.

The thieves were just three ordinary men passing the time of a dark day even as the rain began, looking around the camp, at the stock, maybe wanting a handout, trading idle news, then going on. Jack felt a ripple of uneasiness, he offered them nothing, neither coffee nor food nor talk, not in this wild country. He watched them leave, thinking he'd seen one of them before. He noticed their weapons, their curiosity. Smith snored peacefully in the wagon, lulled by the sound of the rain on the wagon roof.

They came back that night in the soft noise of a steady rainfall. Jack heard the mules first, their grunts and snorts of alarm from where they grazed tethered in the darkness beyond the light from the wagon lantern. He grabbed his revolver and ran from his blankets in the tent just as the first gunshot came out of the darkness, passed by him and hit the side of the wagon. He saw the milling chaos of horses and mules, shadows only. Afraid to shoot, afraid to hit one of the horses, he ran into the shadows and saw the men and fired at two of them, one bareback astride his sorrel and another grabbing at the hackamore of a balking mule.

He saw one man fall. A shotgun blasted at him. Jack shot back at the gunshot flare. The man on his sorrel went off in a slow fall, arms flung out, and Jack shot again, and again. He thought one man was down in the mud and rain, squirming, cursing, the other sprawled, face in the mud, silent. Another, there was another, had to be another. He'd seen three, he had one shot left.

He heard a commotion of voices and yells in the distance. He heard men shouting, guns firing. He heard a yell of pain, anger. Somewhere men were cursing, their noise all rushing quickly through the rain, closer in the darkness.

"You people at the wagon! Don't shoot! Don't shoot!"

Jack faded back into the darkness, watching.

"Don't shoot. Don't shoot!"

A score of horses spilled into the light of the clearing around the wagon. The horses reared and trampled, splashing mud and water everywhere.

The riders wore blanket coats and ponchos of different colors, with hats and crude scarves and hoods against the rain.

One rider dragged something through the mud on a tight lariat.

"We got one of them bastards."

"Here's the other two in the mud. Holy Christ looks like we got 'em all."

"Easy, easy."

One rider came forward leading Jack's sorrel horse.

"We got your mules and your other stock, mister. They never got far off."

"We been after them fools for a week."

"Who are you?" Jack spoke from the darkness.

"We're a posse out of Stockton. These boys are horse thieves and shooters."

"Horse thieves." A rider at the back of the group laughed. Somehow this was a good joke, as well as serious business.

"Easy, Billy."

"Shit, they tried to rob a train---."

If it was a joke, it had consequences lying face down in the mud, consequences somewhere down the road. Perhaps consequences here.

"We're here on business. These men are wanted."

Jack watched, without answering.

"You get that?" Almost a threat.

These men who called themselves a posse began to hustle as they gathered up the two horse thieves lying in the mud.

"One's dead, George."

The man called George nodded. He rubbed the rain from his faced. He spoke in a serious voice, a tired voice without laughter. He spoke to Jack.

"Come on out, mister."

Jack stepped forward, the revolver hanging at his side, a spatter of blood on his left forearm where a dusting of shotgun pellets had grazed him on the first shot, hardly a bother.

The riders in their wet rain blanket coats and ponchos stared at him for a moment.

Jack saw no sign of the law here.

"Where you from?"

"Texas."

They examined the wagon, then looked at Jack again.

"Good looking stock here. Well, welcome to California, Texas. You got a mean welcome from these boys."

They could take what they wanted. Jack had one shot left. He waited.

Another of the Vigilantes said, "Heard there was some big fights down your way, heard them Indians down there eat each other after a fight, cut 'em up and eat 'em---."

Out in the darkness someone laughed.

Jack watched silently. He hadn't heard of any battles, hadn't seen a newspaper in weeks. He had no answer.

"You hear what we're saying?"

"No."

He saw a stirring in the darkness, men moving, felt the tension rising.

"Easy. Billy, damn it!" The man called George spoke again. "We're done here."

Then the Vigilantes began to hustle with their posse business, stirring up more mud and mess, as though this was the end of a dangerous, aggravating chore and a successful few minutes of violence in the dark.

"We'll take care of these boys, Texas. You get it? They're ours. You don't hardly need to remember any of this. It's our business. Now we're going on home, and that's the end of it."

But Jack hardly heard. He suddenly ran through the rain toward the wagon steps, the silent wagon. He grabbed the lantern from its bracket and lunged inside.

Cicero Smith lay on his back in a mess of shattered china, his old teacup, his stored and folded clothes, books, glass jars, surgical tools, valises, his fine beaver hat. The left side of his body seeped blood into his nightshirt from his shoulder to his waist.

So much blood, spattered and pooling. Smith tried to sit up but couldn't. He spoke in short gasps of breath.

"---Misadventure--- has found us--- again---now you must help me---help---."

He lost his battle with consciousness and quietly passed out.

Hardly a bother.

Not for Jack, with a grazing of shotgun pellets on his arm, but a serious bother for Cicero Smith. A painful dangerous bother, a wound full of splinters and buckshot and shreds of his bloodied nightshirt. Blood seeping, blood lost.

Between periods of wakefulness and lapses into merciful darkness, Cicero Smith directed his own salvation, both physical and spiritual. His appeal to God came with salty curses. He was the only serious doctor within sixty miles, all the others who claimed the title were only dangerous pretenders.

"Quacks! Bunglers! God save us---!"

"Yep," Jack said. "Hold still."

"---You'll do--- my direction---damn me, now where's that whiskey---."

Cicero Smith passed out again.

Jack obeyed Smith's hazy directions by lantern light and later by the light of a morning that dawned dull, sunless, but without rain. He caught up the stock, then rummaged through Smith's scant medical supplies, mostly herbs and mysterious potions. He raked back through his memory for information, every bit of half-forgotten Comanche lore, every wound he had seen Cicero Smith tend and he had helped with along their way. Knife wounds, gunshot wounds, random accidents, burns, battering.

There was so damn much blood.

"---Look for buckshot---."

"I know, now keep quiet and let me work."

"---Damn me, that hurts!"

"Hold still."

"---some laudanum---."

"Shit, hold still!"

By mid-morning Jack thought he had stopped the slowly seeping blood, and he'd dug most of the splinters and buckshot and fragments of cloth from the wounds, using his probing fingers and splashes of whiskey and Cicero Smith's surgical tools wherever he could. If he didn't die, there'd be more to come out with suppuration, fevers, weeks of healing, and maybe some buckshot would stay with Smith forever.

Smith sat up suddenly and announced in a fevered voice,

"I believe my arm is broken, young Jack."

The old newspapers that Jack found in the weeks that followed as they traveled slowly south and Cicero Smith suffered and healed, carried lurid reports of battles between the Texas Rangers, with their Tonkawa scouts, and the Comanche bands camped along the Canadian River, more than seventy lodges. Some called it the Battle of Little Robe Creek, others wrote that there were three battles on the same day. Many condemned Rip Ford and his Rangers, not for fighting against the Comanche hordes, but for allowing their Tonkawa scouts and fighters to eat the dead Comanches, men, women and children. In their reports, the Rangers told of buckets of bloody human parts gathered by the fires for celebration feasts. Ford shrugged off outraged complaints at this ugly brutality, but the embattled settlers and homesteaders were mostly silent. They had their own terrible stories, and now Rip Ford had given the savages what they had given the settlers. Now they were all combatants.

Jack looked into the New Mexico darkness, sobered by the stories he'd recorded in his journal, old newspaper stories, maybe exaggerated, maybe not. Now the military had joined the settlers and the Rangers in the constant battles and he didn't know what to expect when he went searching for Sallie Flynn.

He paged ahead in his journal. Smith still sat by the fire in his wooden folding chair, now and then rubbing his shoulder, his new teacup with the blue flowers empty. He was thinner, his mustache a little grayer but still with its flourish.

Heard those three shooters were mostly horse thieves. Hard cases. They killed a man when they robbed a bank in S F, robbed a local train in the valley, and two stage coaches near San Jose. Just stupid, all the shooting.

The law again.

Saw their faces on posters in the post office when I went looking for news about the Overland Mail roads. The San Francisco Picayune called the posse '-- lawless Vigilantes.' Never did see a badge. They claimed the capture. And the reward. They never talked about us because of the reward. Law never came looking for us. I wondered. But they suspended those three boys from oak trees outside the courthouse, even the dead one. Fair enough.

Jack closed his notebook. He'd patched up the wagon and patched up Cicero Smith months ago.

What next? Fighting in Texas? Finding Sallie?

Cicero Smith? There was no debt between them anymore, long since forgotten. He couldn't name what had taken its place.

"You want more ELIXIR?"

Smith shook his head. "I believe we have drained the last drops from the barrels."

"About a quarter barrel left," Jack answered. "I'll be going ahead tomorrow."

"Yes, of course."

"We going to mix more? We're low."

"I shall consider it."

"I'll meet you there, then."

"Young Jack be gone. Damn me, I shall have to chase you away!" Smith looked into the darkness with a skeptical smile Jack couldn't see. "Go find her! Good luck to you, I fear you will need it."

Santa Fe hadn't changed all that much. It was still a dusty village with flat roofs and a quiet bustle of activity, men mending old cracked adobe walls after the summer rains and before winter set in, old shady trees beginning to lose their leaves. Feeling the beginning of an old wariness, he'd scouted around the big wagon campground and seen no Comanches, no Indians, no gathering of New Mexico traders heading out on the long, profitable raiding trail for more Piute slaves, only a scatter of settlers' wagons.

No Indians, but more people, and maybe more stores, more gambling houses, more saloons, and certainly a subtle sense of tension. More soldiers from the forts, old Mexican two wheeled *carretas* no longer rambling but moving with purpose. Wagons and carriages but nothing he recognized. No wagons with "McGregor" painted on the sides unloading at the storehouses. He rode forward slowly, torn between hope and reality. Almost certain he had lost this lady, this beautiful, sweet opportunity whose face he could see in his mind as clearly as he saw her that first day.

He rode further out, looking for a chapel and found ruins, and rebuilding. Back in town he rode past stores, gambling halls, blacksmith forges, livery stables, more storehouses, old adobe houses with wooden bars on the windows, riding the plaza and the backstreets, searching for anything that sounded familiar from her words long go. He found a post office at the stage coach office and stared for a moment. He dismounted, removed his hat and gun belt and walked slowly inside.

He had done this for Smith, who sometimes mailed letters and received occasional answers in California, but here he hesitated. He stared at posters of lost children, lost settlers. He saw wanted posters, shooters, rustlers. He saw notices of deaths, of town meetings and Baptist revivals under the trees.

"Mail for Jack Rainie?" He asked finally.

A man stood behind the counter, an *Anglo*, tall and heavy with white skin, pale eyes and thin black hair combed over a bald spot. He frowned at Jack as though he had the worst of jobs in terms of boredom and clientele, considering the obvious fact that he himself was a civilized man stuck in this wild place, although the availability of town gossip and bribes must be a serious benefit in his position.

"Who?"

"Jack Rainie."

"Spell it."

Jack spelled his name and felt his temper stir.

The man looked surprised. A literate hoodlum, he seemed to be saying silently. Old faded shirt, rough britches and a battered hat in his hand. Weapons left outside, at least, but something made the clerk pay closer attention. He paused, then went into a back room and rummaged noisily. He emerged four minutes later with two squares of paper in his hand and handed them over the counter to Jack.

"I thank you kindly for your trouble," Jack said. Smith's sort of words, his flimflam words, and no bribes offered. He managed a tight smile. The clerk didn't seem to know whether he'd been praised or insulted.

Fair enough.

But Jack's heart was racing as he stepped outside to read. Two letters, one folded and refolded, the paper brown, dusty and fragile with time and handling. On the front he saw his name written out in a delicate scroll, no other words. Just his name. He tore it open, his hands shaking a little. He read the words that tore at his heart.

Where are you? Please come. We are bound for Elm Creek. We could not wait. Sallie.

Jack grinned, he felt a great rush of relief. Years of relief. Years! He wanted to yell out, but he only hurried to read the second letter, this letter dated a little over a year in the past, again with his name in the same delicate scroll.

My Dear Friend. I am writing to express my appreciation for our past acquaintance. Now we must leave the past behind. I wish you well in all your endeavors. Sallie Browning

He wandered the town, looking into the shops, the *cantinas,* anything. He wandered to an old inn called La Fonda, tied his horse to the rack outside, went in and watched the milling people, mostly Easterners, he thought, from their dress. Touring around the west to see wild Indians. Or traveling for their health. But hadn't he heard the name of the inn before? He wandered out, hardly thinking.

He'd known, of course. He saw her in his mind, but she was gone.

He stopped at a tavern. The beer was cool, hardly cold, the *pulque* strong.

Well Sallie, you have made your own way.

He didn't know what else to say to her.

Sallie Browning.

What next? Go on with Smith, maybe Bexar, plenty of work. Maybe find Elm Creek and---no.

They had let each other go, with reasons. He supposed it was time to go on, as she said. Time to scour her image, her words, from his mind, his habits of thinking of her, seeing her.

He wandered on until the day grew darker, close to nightfall, and the people all around him seemed in a hurry to finish the business of the day.

Meet Smith tomorrow, maybe the next day. Where next?

Oh Sallie.

He found himself stopped in front of a store with dusty windows. He saw a jumble of items in the window, bolts of bright cloth, wool for spinning, gray enamel coffee pots, blue bottles of tonic, paper tablets, blankets, Pueblo baskets, hard candy in big jars. From a great distance he remembered he needed a new journal, an ordinary sort of recent memory but now foreign as he still thought of Sallie Flynn. Sallie Browning.

He stepped inside.

The store had a sort of dim disorder. End of the day disorder, he supposed, but he wasn't really interested. A few customers wandered among the aisles, women in long skirts, a few men and children. He moved along. He came to a pile of children's school supplies.

Sure, schools in Santa Fe.

The town was growing, the world was changing. But in ways he couldn't name right now, Jack Rainie felt lost in this new world.

Or just lost. Nothing else.

He saw notebooks and stared at them, then at thick lead pencils, some sort of coloring sticks, picture books and precious bundles of paper. A few wooden toys.

Where next?

He picked up one of the journals, empty, waiting for words.

Maybe his own words, sure. He had a lot of words to write.

"Yes, that will do---."

The woman's voice cut through his distraction

"---I will send him in with payment when he returns from the Pueblos."

That voice with its strident burr of sound, familiar. He looked up, across the store, and saw two women with their backs to him, and the store clerk, smiling, obsequious, eager to do anything for that firm voice. Both women were dressed in dark funeral colors, one slightly thick through her body, a bustle making everything about her look worse. The other woman was slim, standing quietly, her dress a simple fall of black fabric to the worn plank floor.

He walked forward. He stopped six feet away. He said "Sallie."

Both women turned. The clerk frowned.

Jack's breath caught. She was there.

He stared, and saw her face, all lovely astonishment, all blue eyes, all beauty. More than he remembered. Framed by her golden hair half hidden by a wisp of a black scarf.

"Sallie."

A sudden burst of happiness filled him, rising from where it had been so long hidden but always there. An explosion of happiness. All the time he'd been away in California learning about the world from that great cynic Cicero Smith, and now here. With her.

And he saw all the changes

He thought she had gained a subtle look of hardness, not unlike the ice that forms over running stream water in winter. But a fragile hardness. He sensed there were mountains of good reasons, her life, hardships, things he couldn't know about. But with her flowing golden hair and her blue, blue eyes, which once held so much trust, and now were shocked at seeing him, and wary, he saw the changes. Yet every man and boy in the dry goods store had to glance at her, or just stare and stare. She was a picture out of a picture book they might have seen as children.

He wanted to tell her in a rush all that had happened, why he had never come to their meeting, never seen her again, and a lot of reasons why he was here now. His own hopeful, hard reasons. But he could hardly think of what to say, where to begin, how to say it.

"I'm late," he said.

She stared as though she couldn't believe what he said. "Late?" she repeated, her voice rising in disbelief. "Late?"

"You're well?" he asked, his breath almost lost before her fairness, her simple presence. Maybe a foolish question, but he could think of nothing else to say.

"Yes, yes. Of course."

Again, he sensed the change, the challenge in Sallie's voice, and wondered, but his wonder was mostly just Sallie Flynn, the simple wonder of her presence before him.

The older woman stepped closer to Sallie.

He touched his hat to the older woman, cleared his throat. "Ma'am." He remembered Mariah Matilda well enough, with her stern features and her black hair in that schoolmarm bun and her heavy proper skirts always in gloomy colors, without a sign of light heartedness anywhere in her face.

"I see you have cultivated some manners," Mariah Matilda said, and certainly her voice had not changed either, just a level noise with some rasp. "You don't speak like one of those Mexican hillbillies around here or those Texas ruffians any more. I am surprised. What was your name again?" she asked, although he guessed she knew.

"Still Jack Rainie, ma'am."

The woman blinked at his answer. "Passing through, looking for mischief I expect?"

"Looking for someone," he answered.

"Here? In this town?"

"Something like that. And looking for work"

"Work? Are you a hard worker, Mr. ---Rainie?" Her voice carried a knife edge of doubt, almost a slightly humorous edge of random disinterest and skepticism.

"Yes ma'am."

"Or is that all talk---."

"I am not much of a foolish talker."

Maria Matilda blinked again and made a loud sound of disbelief.

"It's growing here in Santa Fe," he said, but he was just putting words together, not ready to share his thoughts. He was just looking at Sallie, still marveling.

Mariah Matilda frowned. Her face flushed. "There is certainly gambling aplenty, and thievery, murders and bordellos," she cleared her throat at such a distasteful reference, "---and general bounders and scoundrels everywhere---."

But Jack gave her little attention. He stared at the dress Sallie wore so well, a soft muslin with pearl buttons up the front over her breasts and a high, pretty collar that framed her face. But everything dark except for the pearl buttons. She had not quite left behind the girlish ways he remembered so well for she wore a thin ribbon in her hair.

"You look well," she said to him and added, with a little twist in her voice, "indeed."

Jack smiled at Sallie Flynn. "Yes ma'am, I am."

Then a boy ran across the dry goods store with a piece of paper and a crude pencil, he ran to Sallie's skirt and pulled on it to get her attention.

"Mama, I found it----."

The boy was four years old or so, maybe less, Jack was no judge of children's ages. The boy was eager for Sallie to look, to hear his announcement. He was slim, strong looking, intense, and with a good, persuasive smile on his face. When he turned to look at this stranger near his mother, Jack saw the boy's thatch of sandy colored hair, his steady gray eyes.

"Come with me," Jack said to Sallie.

"She will not! She is a proper widow woman now who---."

"Widow," he repeated.

Mariah Matilda put her hand over her ever-busy mouth.

"Come," he said to Sallie.

Sallie turned the thin gold band on her finger, around and around, perhaps as a reminder.

"He's dead, then" Jack said to Sallie. "He's dead."

"Yes."

"Come. I want to tell you." He waited.

Mariah Matilda tried to stop this disaster from the past, this dreadful and unfortunate encounter, but Sallie stepped forward and Mariah Matilda took a step back.

They found a tavern where they were offered whiskey and spring water. By special request for the lady they gave Sallie and the boy glasses of cool lemonade.

"McGregor carries these up from Mexico," she said nervously. "The lemons."

"There was bad sickness after El Paso," Jack said. "Some died along the way, kids, children mostly, from complication. Men and women. We buried them along the way. The rest kept going. They thought it was measles. I never knew for sure. I was out hunting meat when I got sick. An old man helped me. All winter he kept me alive. You were gone when I finally got to Santa Fe. Then the Comanches came with captives. They---I had to get out of there, I had to get away---."

She waited.

"There was a fight. There were too many. I knew some of them. They knew me. I never told you about---." he stopped, tasted the whiskey without tasting it. "I thought of you every day. Every night. I couldn't stop thinking about you. Yesterday I went to that chapel with the bell."

"Yes. I went, but---."

"I went to the post office. Your letters."

"Oh," she said.

"I thought I would never see you again. Never find you."

"Well here I am," she answered.

"Marry me," he said, echoing those words she had spoken to him all those years ago. But now more urgent.

The boy watched them. He heard the words and might have understood a little of what they said. He sat firmly by his mother's side as though protecting her.

"But where have you been so long? I don't understand."

"I---California," he said. A poor answer he knew. Not nearly enough.

"But---California? So long?"

"Oh Sallie, too long! I tried to get back, but I had a debt."

"A debt?" Just words repeated in her confusion, but her voice rose a little in a quiver of outrage. "A debt?"

"Smith. His name is Smith. He helped me get away from the Comanches. I was hurt. He was headed west---."

She stared at him, looking deeply into his anxious eyes, searching for honesty, searching for her own long hope, her stubborn belief.

"You will tell me more later?"

"Yes! Yes!"

"I knew there was a reason. I knew it," Sallie Flynn said from her new maturity. She sighed.

A frown of sadness crossed her face but did not take away her natural loveliness.

"It is a hard country, Mr. Rainie. I think sometimes it is a cruel country and I wonder why we stay. The Indians, so much fighting." She touched the boy, her boy. "Mr. Browning was a good man. My husband---." She drew a deep breath and went on. "He came by one day and fixed the chimney when it was smoking. He fixed the door. He carried a little canary bird in a cage and he gave it to me. He said he sometimes carried them for the women in frontier soddies and cabins who were lonely when their men were off. He said he liked being one of the bird men who helped people. He was so lonely too. A storm came in, a Norther---everything froze. Then he stayed the winter. He understood everything about the boy, he loved the boy. But he wanted a child of his own." She paused again. "He understood everything. A Baptist preacher came through, and I agreed, but---."

She breathed a soft exhalation of breath. "It was so bad. Only a year. He got that blister. He was a tinker man sometimes, and he worked for McGregor, fixing things. He helped at the ranch. His team ran away one day. All our horses were out on the range. He chased his team all day afoot and he got that blister. His leg turned all red and streaked and Auntie couldn't help him. He got the blood poison. Some of the neighbors tried to help. We didn't know what to do." Her eyes pooled with tears at such a trivial death. She took a deep breath. "He loved Jeth."

Jack looked at the boy. "Jeth." The boy with hair and eyes the color of his own. "Jeth."

The boy studied Jack, then picked up his pencil and made squares on the paper.

"I wanted to wait."

"Yes."

"But he was a good man." she said again. She looked into Jack's eyes, searching. "Do you understand?"

Jack nodded. "Now marry me," he said.

Sallie Flynn-Browning almost smiled but tears sprang from her eyes again. "Oh Mr. Rainie," she said. She stood. "Oh Mr. Rainie, hold me, please hold me."

"We must talk," she said. He felt her smiling in the darkness of the bedroom at La Fonda.

"Why? I like this better." He tightened his arms.

"When did you learn to talk, Mr. Rainie?"

"Those years in California. He was a doctor, Smith---." But that was a story he could tell her later.

"You are different. I remember in El Paso. You spoke so little I had to flirt."

"The words were on my tongue, Sallie. You just spoke them first."

"I was shameless."

"Yes ma'am. With me. Don't change. "

"We must talk about what to do."

"Do---about?"

"Where will we live? What will we do?" She stretched luxuriously in the soft bed of feathers. The La Fonda bed sheets were silky, soft by frontier standards, the finest linen against her skin. "I am very good at keeping the house. I make preserves, wild plums mostly, but we need new jars, I put up pickles in crocks and keep a fine big garden for the root cellar, I spin wool and weave and sew. Mostly quilts. There are two old apple trees and I dry the apples---."

"The stone house," he said, remembering.

She hesitated. "Yes."

"Elm Creek."

"Yes."

He thought about her words. He knew where they had led him.

"Is that what you want?" Everything important, every worry about the Indian fighting, battles, the Rangers, the military, every thought of the future he and Smith had talked about now and then, had faded away.

"It is a good place. It is the best ranch on the creek, or so I think. They are all so big. Do you like cattle, Mr. Rainie?"

It was his turn to hesitate. "Sure."

"Auntie is there with me when McGregor's away, but she likes to go visiting. I go visiting too, I don't stay there alone. The Indians haven't been around for a long time, sometimes they come just begging for food. Sometimes they're drunk. Most of the fighting is a long way away, but it's quiet on the creek. We have a neighbor who tends the stock and helps with the branding and all the cattle business. We don't do much. He stays in the old slave cabin when we're away. Our closest neighbor is only 6 miles away. Everybody helps. There's a lot of talk about driving cattle north to Kansas. They did it a while back but there was something about a cattle fever. I don't know, they say they can get thirty dollars a head up there."

"You got to catch 'em first, Miss Sallie. They're real wild."

"Yes. But they are everywhere. On the range, in my garden. They are a nuisance everywhere."

He thought about cattle. Ranching. All those cattle. The place where Sallie Flynn-Browning finally made a home after all those years riding around in McGregor's trading wagons. But McGregor was no rancher, he remembered from the talk back in El Paso.

He and Smith had idly speculated about many ventures of various sorts. But Smith worried about a war coming, and soon. And Jack mostly thought about Texas fighting, the Indians, Santa Fe, going back. Looking for her.

Finding her. Crazy. A gamble beyond anything at one of McGregor's Juarez poker tables. But he had found her.

Now he suddenly thought of building, carpentry, and of orchards, vast plantings like those he had seen in California, he thought of the parson's apple orchard. And Comanche women knowing the best trees and knocking down pecan branches, gathering the good nourishing nuts after the first frost in the fall.

With her words, he thought again of the wild Spanish cattle long neglected from old times, breeding and scattering everywhere like the mustangs from the old Spanish days. A start. They were all free to whoever caught them, unbranded and crazy wild. Everywhere. Open range.

He thought back to the wagon master's oxen train and crossing Texas from Bexar, the cattle more numerous than the wild game. Vermin, some said. And maybe thirty dollars a head if you could get them to a market instead of three or four dollars a head at some local village market, or worth nothing roaming wild on the prairies.

He had heard men talking about the big spreads in west Texas and southern New Mexico, thousands of acres, cheap government land, Indian land, ranchers looking for markets, joining together and herding cattle. To railheads? But where? There were no railroads in Texas yet. And talk of a big American war hovered on the horizon.

She went on, "McGregor goes trading and when he comes back he brings me wool from the Pueblos. They don't trust white traders, but they trust him, he is fair to them. He brings news and new ideas and he buys a new wagon sometimes, he has five now, but he is a poor rancher, Mr. Rainie. He says times are changing. He's thinking about building a trading store someday, maybe an inn for travelers. Oh, you would think we were living in a village sometimes when he is home, so many people come by and visit and these days there is so much talk about the war troubles and all. When McGregor came trading every year to Santa Fe, I never came back here with him. But after---but now, especially now---." She stopped.

Now that Mr. Browning had died of a blister on his heel.

"Apple trees?" he asked.

"They are old and not very good but Jeth loves them. He has made a fort up in the branches. He says he is watching for the Indians."

He whispered in her ear, "Do you like apple orchards, Sallie Rainie?"

Cicero Smith trailed into Santa Fe two days later. He had business that took him away, and then he reappeared, walking the plaza without his wagon, stopping here and there, leading Jack's pack horse. He carried a heavy satchel and puffed on a cigarillo. The September heat didn't seem to bother him. He looked like a man on a leisurely mission. He saw Jack's sorrel Comanche horse tethered to the rail in front of La Fonda, tied the pack horse and made his way unhurriedly inside.

The lobby was cooler, darker, and busy with people strolling, talking. He saw this was almost a civilized place, with tiled floors and decorations on the adobe walls. But among the properly dressed travelers he saw dusty stockmen and ranchers, a few proper looking ladies, military officers and miners and not a few who looked like they had some sort of miracle to sell to the unwary greenhorns sightseeing from the East.

He found them in the corner of a shady patio.

"Well," he said. He saw how they looked at each other. "Well."

They sat at a small table, with cool drinks that appeared untouched. Sallie looked up at Cicero Smith and smiled. "I believe I know you, sir."

The man was older, she saw, well dressed but his good clothes were worn. No matter, he had a dim elegance about him. His hair was graying, he had a carefully tended mustache and sideburns as though aware of fashion. His blue eyes looked tired, faded, but as he looked at Sallie Flynn-Browning and the small boy, his eyes took on a look of gentlemanly wonder.

"So here she is," he said. He looked with interest at the boy.

Jack rose from the table, but Sallie remained seated, Jeth asleep across her lap.

"My Sallie," Jack said, and Cicero Smith smiled at how he said it, the direct, simple way, perhaps with an expression on his face Cicero Smith had never seen before.

"Indeed."

She held out her hand to Smith in greeting. "I am so happy to see you, sir. He has spoken well of you."

She was all smiles, all joy, all her own special beauty, and Smith was momentarily without words at this sort of genteel young woman here on this rough frontier.

"I had no idea," he said. An apology of sorts, just drifting on the air. "He kept you secret, I had no idea---."

Sallie Flynn-Browning laughed a gentle laugh.

Smith pulled his eyes away from Sallie Flynn-Browning and looked again at Jack. He hesitated before he spoke, weighing his words, and then he just spoke, "Thank God for such a lovely, happy woman---."

But he saw at once that Jack's world had changed in just about every way and he wondered about the changes he had made in this youth, this raw material that he'd salvaged from ignorance four years ago.

Cicero Smith suddenly laughed aloud at his own vanity.

But he was a busy man, and he also knew enough to leave Jack and Sallie Flynn-Browning and the boy to themselves. He knew the changes he saw before him resolved many questions, and settled his mind, and gave him a certain peace.

"I am going for the war," he told Jack that night.

"There's no war yet."

"It is coming. I know it's coming, and soon."

"But I thought---."

"You know it's coming. You read the papers these days." Cicero Smith smiled when he said this, only a gentle reminder.

Jack frowned. "But you?"

"I am no secessionist, but I have people there. Perhaps I can help."

"Where?"

"The south." Smith smiled again, a sadness in his expression. "It will destroy the south, I think. But I must go, I must try. Virginia."

Jack took a moment to accept all this news from Cicero Smith. "When?"

"I have a ticket on the next stage east, then transfers. Tomorrow."

Jack nodded. The words hardly took him by surprise, he finally understood the deepness of the trouble that had dogged Cicero Smith. He felt the moment of loss.

"Shit. You'll miss the wedding."

"Ah. Congratulations!"

"She wants it all proper."

"Of course."

The black satchel Smith had left with Jack had turned out to be heavy with coins and gold dust.

"It's too much," Jack said. Years' worth of gold coins and fat leather pokes of California gold dust, "it's---."

"Ha! Mine is heavier," Smith said and touched the side of his head where the graying hair was neatly combed. "The brains, young Jack." He laughed, ever the flimflam man. "No need for the strong back!"

Smith's Way, the words familiar after four years, and now they brought a smile of appreciation. "What about the wagon?"

"I have found a home for the wagon in Mr. Gabriel Rascon's barn. I left it with him the last time I went east, he is an honest man who spends his days irrigating his fields of corn. He troubles no one. He raises sheep. He farms out of town, not far. It is a large dry barn, and I have told him he may keep other items in the barn if my wagon is not harmed. I have left some coins and the remainder of the ELIXIR with him for the health of his family while I am away," Smith smiled, almost the flimflam man again, "and I left your name. Wars have a way of going on and on. If I do not return by '66 or '67 you may keep the wagon or leave it with him." His smile turned evil. "I have sold the damn mules to him at a ridiculous price, so he is in my debt. Damn me, I hope he eats them."

Jack laughed aloud. He recalled that Smith would have relished eating them himself at times in the last four years. But he felt the tug of parting.

"Come to Elm Creek when you get back."

"It's settled, then?"

"It's what she wants. Looks like I'll be chasing cows."

Smith nodded slowly, a wise speculation in his eyes. "I sense there is a bit of steel in your lovely lady. Ah well." He sighed. "Then I will look you up when I come back, young Jack." Smith smiled. This youth whom he had guided for four years still showed rough edges, and maybe that was what had delivered him from frontier ignorance and general folly. He was almost civilized.

Smith laughed, then grew quiet for a moment.

"You have been a friend."

Jack heard the rare words in silence. Then he spoke, "I'll post word, at the stage offices. The trading posts---."

"Be cautious. Wars are ugly. Always ugly, and cruel." Smith took Jack's measure. "Whoever is in power, the secessionists or the north, they will want to conscript the young men, they will want horses and beef for the troops, gold, they will take what they want---."

"I will not be conscripted."

"No, I expect not." There again was that rough edge, that hell-bent determination he'd seen often over the past years. "But be cautious," he finished. "Cautious."

In spite of his usually bombastic words, his flimflam ways, Cicero Smith was never one to wallow in sentiment when his teacup with the blue flowers went dry. He thrust out his hand.

"Well." he said to Jack. Then, after a hard shake, he turned and walked away for the war.

Jack bought a white dress for Sallie, the prettiest they could find already made, hand sewn of thin muslin with ruching and tucks in the bodice and lace at the collar. He bought fine broadcloth shirts newly arrived for Jeth and himself. Mariah Matilda pondered attending such a misbegotten ceremony. A *padre*, she complained, the Pope and all that foreign business. She went on a search and found a proper Baptist preacher new to Santa Fe.

Oh Lordy, she fumed, to no avail.

Her Sallie marrying this wild man.

They spoke all the proper words in front of the preacher. Sallie carried a few fall wildflowers and swore to Jack she would never wear those ugly widow's weeds again, so he had better take good care. Jack had no ring, but he had the gold nugget he had saved for her, and he tied it around her neck on a silk cord. The simple celebration afterwards included a wandering spotted dog, a few strangers passing by, and a few hearty *tequila* toasts in Spanish.in a local *cantina*. Jeth watched his mother and Jack, his gray eyes thoughtful as always, and decided to shake hands with his father.

The creek branched off from its junction with the Brazos River. It wandered, winding and flowing from its headwaters, nurturing a wide swath of woods and thickets, a natural haven for the four-leggeds, and great elm trees full of redbirds and jays and wild turkeys along its banks. There were tall pecan trees, willow thickets, brambles and cut banks and occasional caves where high water had carved into the banks.

Good cover, Jack thought, his first wary thought when he saw the ranch, set a distance up the creek from the Brazos junction but not all that far from old Fort Belknap, and a long way from the bitter Comanche-Kiowa and U.S. Army fighting.

He studied the rock house and outbuildings.

Good cover.

He saw corrals with a handful of horses, two old apple trees, a corn crib, the beginning of a stockade wall left unfinished, a small slave cabin built of peeled logs attached to the barn, a well not far from the house.

The house sat on a rise above the creek to avoid mosquitoes, and a good ways from the road. The rocks on the house came waist high, up to the bottom of two windows with wavy glass. Every rock looked carefully placed, all the niches filled against drafts and scorpions. Above this solid beginning the house had been finished with peeled ax hewn logs cut and notched as carefully as the rock. The pitch of the roof indicated a loft inside, and all the roof was covered with long hand split shingles. A rock chimney rose in a strong pillar above. The door was well built but the wood had dried and now had to be reset in the frame, as did the windows. The corrals sagged, and the old apple trees nearby needed pruning. Inside he found a large stone fireplace with hanging iron cooking pots, and fresh whitewash on the walls, an extravagance few frontier settlers bothered with. The walls had shelves with bottles and jars and trinkets, a few books, small tintype photographs, portraits he saw. Sallie and the boy as a baby. A frowning older man, Will Browning. The floor was made of heavy planks, not pounded earth, and spread with softly colored and patterned woolen rugs. A spinning wheel sat in a corner. He saw a trap door at the back, probably the root cellar half covered by a rug. Bundled herbs hung from the rafters, and a ladder climbed up to a loft. And at the side he saw an alcove with a big feather bed piled with quilts.

Sallie's house, after all the years riding in McGregor's trade wagon.

Such a house on the frontier seemed like a castle to Jack, but it was also constant work against the Texas weather. But McGregor's frequent trading forays from the slave cabin where he and Mariah Matilda slept, had made the rock house the modest castle that it was with Pueblo Indian weavings and clay pots, wool blankets for hard winters. The land itself looked to be less than the vast leagues of land McGregor had boasted about back in El Paso, but a large holding like the others they had passed along the creek, most of them thousands of acres, and wild cattle hiding in the mesquite bush of the grassy open range beyond the creek.

A place to build and plant. Enlarge the corn field. Grow more wheat, hay. Fences, corrals. More apple trees.

Finish the stockade.

It's what she wants.

But by December of '60 the talk of secession became a somber tone in every conversation, at every meeting on distant city streets, in villages.

He remembered Smith's words: *Wars are ugly.*

The newspapers McGregor brought to the rock house printed calls for a new governor in Texas, a new election; get rid of old Sam Houston who was not in favor of secession.

Late in January of '61 the talk among the stockmen and farmers in Young County naturally went to the referendum on secession from the Union, the constant Indian fighting, the political squabbling and the convention that met in Austin in February. Fragments of news left many hard scrabble settlers just shaking their heads. But many went to the polls in February and voted, and the Unionists were soundly defeated.

Secession became official by March 2. The new constitution was not altogether unlike the constitution of 1845 except that it made slavery a lawful practice and forbade the freeing of any slave by any Texian in Texas.

Didn't the holy Bible itself uphold the natural condition of slavery for the lowly among otherwise civilized folk?

The men stood around under the trees in the yard by the rock house, talking quietly, sipping cool beer from the spring house McGregor had brought in kegs for the meeting.

"I believe we're in for it."

The March day had a cold bite, but no one minded. At least it wasn't raining. The women covered tables with whatever cloths they could muster and set out the hearty food they had brought. Molly Grace brought her own smoked ham from her own smokehouse and made a point of fussing, setting out pots of mustards and wild plum relishes while she looked over the strangers, folks visiting, new husbands, new babies wrapped, nursed and settled under the shade trees. Her eyes rested on the widow Sallie Browning, she corrected herself, Sallie Rainie, her new man, a puzzle to her and others, but a tough new settler, a hard-enough worker, who'd taught her oldest boy how to find the best bee trees down in the woods, trees with good dark combs hidden in old hollow trees. Maybe she could talk him into getting her some pecan wood for her smokehouse, like she used at home in Louisiana, better than that Texas mesquite she had to use here because her man was just too lazy to bother with pecan wood. And he grew lazier by the day, seemed to her, too busy with stomping after strayed cattle to help her scald and scrape down a slaughtered hog for her smokehouse. It brought to her mind how they'd landed here in Texas steps ahead of a mean family feud that had taken all her man's brothers.

Five men, and then there was just the one left and she got him, lazy but alive.

But as she glanced around at the men at this meeting she reckoned half had come to Texas ahead of the law chasing after them for debt, or theft, or shootings. Didn't matter much here in Texas, where everything she'd found was hard or dangerous. She looked long and hard at Sallie Rainie's man, wondering about him. Some said he was a mystery, not commonplace like most of the settlers. He talked like a foreigner of some sort, not like a regular Texian. There was something uncomfortable about him. Something distant and watchful. But she figured he was mostly like all the rest of the men here, an ordinary, sometimes ornery mix. He just couldn't seem to carryon like that McGregor, who just talked a lot, made friends and gave away his good beer.

Sallie Rainie's man was a puzzle to Molly Grace's fertile brain and she couldn't help wondering. Then she let it go.

Long as he weren't one of them horse thieves n'er rustlers n'er Quaker fools talking peace with the durn Indians all the time.

Peace?

She just had to smile, her plump, plain face happy again as she watched the younger children run chasing each other in the weak sunlight and playing elaborate games no one else understood.

Jack watched Jeth laughing and chasing: how fast he was, how smart he was in the games.

As he'd grown to know his son, he saw that Jeth pondered a question in his school books, worked with persistence at any small task, and often looked thoughtfully from his fort in the old apple trees, down toward the creek, at the tangle of elms and willows and old cottonwoods beginning to shed their seeds like snow.

Looking for Indians, he said.

When he asked Jack about Indians, Jack hesitated, recognizing suddenly how his feeling, his appreciation for this boy had grown and just kept on growing. So, Jack told him stories, mostly he told stories about how he'd lived among the Indians, something about lore and myths, how he'd gotten away. He never mentioned the fires at the stakes, the deaths, camp dogs snarling over bodies, his friend with the singing moccasins.

Maybe someday.

Stories.

When Sallie sat Jeth down at night with his numbers and letters for making words, Jeth frowned with concentration, even when he was tired from his chores.

He liked his house chores best, examining the mortar in the stones for cracks where water or drafts could come in. He liked examining the calking around the windows. He liked doing important chores. He liked to enlarge his tree house, to build small squares, houses from twigs and scraps of wood. He seemed to give any small problem serious consideration. He was quick to understand, slower to make a decision. And when the neighbors came to visit with their children, Jeth played hard, running and shouting and laughing with glee.

Maybe that part was what Sallie had given him. Jack wasn't sure what he had given the boy.

The bird man came down the road to the rock house. His wagon was tall, almost like a small, old Conestoga. The wheels screeched and groaned and there was a rattling sound to his progress, made by the bumping and swinging of a dozen small wooden birdcages fastened to the sides. The wagon driver raised a hand and called a greeting. Everyone knew Abe Simmons and the boy riding on the wagon seat beside him. The women hurried over to admire the captured birds, those precious songbirds, Larks, Redbirds, little wrens, anything to fill the loneliness of the women who were left behind, often for months when the men went out on the range after cattle, on long drives or long winter hunts.

"Any sign of them Indians?" Rafe Nye called. He was a small man, a veteran of the early days in Texas. He claimed to have ridden with Sam Houston in the Runaway Fight and still carried a Mexican musket ball in his backsides. Now he worried mostly about Comanche and Kiowa Indians, or panthers, or wolves, or Mexican horse thieves.

"No sir, nary a sign the way I come, boys." Abe Simons raised a jar of McGregor's beer. "Been looking to go after more birds, my stock's getting low again."

These men Jack stood with were all neighbors and friends, men of substance, ranchers, cattlemen, stockmen, plain hard scrabble farmers, some old timers, a few newcomers. They had come for the free range, the good grass and the freedom from past consequences, bringing their women and children, willing to take the constant everyday risks. They were dressed in simple shirts and britches, old and well washed, and leather vests. They all wore hats, some of rawhide greased against rainfall that never seemed to be enough, and often too much. One or two bore arrowheads and lead in their bodies from old fights, little Robe Creek and others, McGregor told him, and just seemed to linger with pain in their faces over the years, not saying much. Many carried weapons at their belts, and belly guns, ready to fight, always watchful.

Talk of Indians seemed like a welcome distraction from war talk. They were all just spectators to the war, as McGregor often said, so far away that sometimes war talk seemed like a story in a book.

"By Ganny," an old timer known for his white bush of whiskers and his tall stories, told the men standing nearby," them damn Indians're always around, taking shots and hiding out in the bush, you bet. I recall back when all them forty-niners were taking the south road through El Paso and down in Chihuahua and they found all them little villages of Mexican just wiped out, just all killed. Women gone, kids gone. Damned Apaches. Happened over and over---."

"Knut Johanson's hired hand saw Indian sign when he was out fishing the river for catfish awhile back, a passel of crows circling, led him to a dead mustang cut up and left for the varmints."

And where were the Texas Rangers? Another nuisance sighting of hostiles and complaints about the Rangers, the ugly stories always justified by the settlers but were as much a part of life as the sun rising. Then the men would set out on another futile chase to drive the Indians away.

A few of these men had come to Texas as children and remembered the Republic days before Texas went poor and joined up with the states. Their fathers grew old and sat on their galleries in hand made chairs with rawhide seats. They smoked cob pipes or rolled brown paper cigarettes or just chewed and spat. They reminisced about the time when deer and elk ran in herds like antelope on the range, winters when horses and cattle froze standing up as great Northers blew through. Their women made do in rough cabins, often without windows, sometimes with only hanging quilts for door coverings, they stirred their pots outside with long wooden spoons and fought off panthers screaming in the night, hunting after their babies. But soon enough the cabins got windows with curtains and rugs for the pounded dirt floors, and sometimes they had real wheat flour for biscuits. A few just naturally brought along their handful of slaves for field work and their slave women to help with the packs of children and kitchen work, but the north counties counted few slaves, and by now many like Nigger Britt Johnson were just thought of as hired hands.

The settlers brought with them a hard way of looking at the world, learned from everyday hardships and general acceptance of their circumstances. Some had a Southern way that favored more slave states. But they weren't like the southern counties down near the Gulf where thousands of acres of cotton plantings depended on large slave holdings and the ability to ship down the brush-clogged Texas rivers out of Galveston Bay to New Orleans or one of the other ports. More often the new steam boats grounded on sandbars or steamed into rafts of floating logs and trees. But many settlers here were Unionists and quietly considered themselves loyal to the Yankee States.

"Old Bobby Lee's bound to stay with Virginia if it comes to a fight."

"Yep, he's a Virginia man."

The settler women, all good neighbor women who bore their children, died now and then in childbirth or from the childbed fever, farmed their kitchen gardens and taught their children letters and numbers until the communities got around to starting up schools. They visited, cooked for big gatherings of neighbors, gossiped, shared quilt patterns, ran the ranches when their men died or just disappeared. Sometimes the settlers knew it was Indians that took their men, sometimes they just disappeared, maybe running away from hardship to an easier life. Rumors came and went but no one knew. If a woman was lucky, she had a little song bird in a wooden cage, a prize against loneliness, left for a trade of cornmeal or sweets by the bird man on one of his vending trips through the settlements.

The boys followed the men, chasing longhorns, cutting and branding yearlings when they got around to it and the price of beef made the work worth it. They learned to chew tobacco and swear and spit and fight and raise hell now and then. They hated the Indians, mostly because of the stories they'd heard for generations, stories of brutality, war, stories of lost children. Most were ready to grow up by the age of fifteen or sixteen, tough, a bit arrogant, and become solid men of substance and tradition like their fathers.

Jack listened to their talk and knew he was not one of them.

McGregor stood beside him, telling of the news, the latest rampant rumors picked up in his travels. Newspapers were always late with their news from the East, the war talk, but the new telegraph carried the news further and faster to settlements on the line. A few men had already left, headed south down the road before any trouble started.

Jack wondered about Cicero Smith, where?

Most here in the woods and farms would just keep on gathering up their gear to leave for both the north and the secessionist south, their holdings left to the care of old men and boys and to the women to tend in their absence. No one expected any kind of fighting to take very long, maybe a few months.

Jack knew these men had lived on this frontier long enough to develop a caution toward strangers who weren't Texians. But in most ways, it was a frontier far different from anything he knew. They were used to Irishmen and Scotts looking for green grasslands and huge acreages for their woolies, English sport hunters, German tradesmen, gullible greenhorns, wandering preachers and others. They had old stories about lost gold mines, the old Spanish days, shootouts and Mexican bandits, and the old stories often grew more florid in the telling from one generation to the next. They saw that Jack spoke well enough, but not like any traditional born Texian. He rode like an Indian buck, bareback sometimes, and had carpenter skills and other random skills unlike their own. He helped with barn raisings, knew how to use his weapons, useful in a fight with the damn hostiles if it came to that. Never got dog drunk on McGregor's beer, never said much, never anything about himself, helped like everybody else, and, by Ganny, he'd been all the way off to California and back.

But they knew McGregor, had known him since he and his womenfolk came along and settled in the rock house. He was a different sort too, a merchant who travelled the roads and brought trade goods and news. He got to know everyone, he mingled easily and proved to be an affable newcomer, not much of a rancher but generous with his advice, his jokes and his kegs of beer.

"The wild tribes will surely break out again if the Feds leave the forts," McGregor said. "You boys best be ready for that."

"The government agents give 'em free food and now they're learning 'em how to hoe corn up in the Territory." The rancher who spoke, Odis K. Wilson gave a scoffing laugh. He had fair skin badly freckled by the sun and now he pulled his hat down with a yank and shook his head at the thought.

Hoe corn, Jack thought, feeling a moment of scorn for this ignorant man.

"The young ones want to steal horses and fight," Jack spoke carefully, "they don't know much else---."

"Hoe more corn," Odis Wilson said with another bitter laugh. "Most of 'em just stay pissin' drunk stealing every damn thing ain't nailed down---."

Jack looked at the man, who seemed to have a notably thick head.

"They'll just break out," he said, speaking a simple logic. "They'll see the weakness at the forts."

"Then I will shoot every one of them bastard red heathens that crosses my path," Odis Wilson answered in a calm, hard statement, "I rode with Rip Ford back in '60. We chased them Comanches up on the Canadian River and I tell you I will give a dead Comanche to the Tonks to eat any time I can."

Many of the settlers here nodded at Odis Wilson's words, others looked away. They had suffered bitter losses hanging on to this old Indian hunting land, random losses; deaths of womenfolk from hardships, children killed or stolen or wandered off, friends disappeared, men shot in fights, disemboweled, burned, scalped, left to rot on the prairies like butchered game, and the other terrible mutilations and attacks they could never mention to their women, but their women knew. Two women settlers shuddered and turned away, but no one disagreed with these hard words.

"They'll wait," Jack spoke quietly, just a fact that seemed obvious to him.

"They are just dumb red savages. Damned animals---."

"---they want food. Buffalo---."

"I got no use for them Indian agents," Odis K Wilson interrupted, his voice rising again. "I swear they love them Kiowas and Comanches, all the rest, they don't give shit about the settlers! Them damned squaw men---." He looked at Jack. "Maybe you're a squaw man, Rainie--- you---."

Another man interrupted in a hard voice. He looked at Jack thoughtfully. "You have experience, sir? Military? Militia? Rangers? You've fought them?"

Jack looked at the man who spoke, saw the others frowning, or just waiting for an answer. This was no time for a fight with the likes of Odis K. Wilson, or any of the others. He thought for a moment, then lied. "Yep. Like you all."

Most of these men around him had chased after Indians and thieves they seldom caught, telling stories, taking shots at shadows.

McGregor broke in with a little urgency in his voice, "Hell, then there's that border trouble down south, that Cortina."

It was old news from the year before that seemed to drag on and on, but they liked to retell the stories, mulling stories they already knew, and McGregor liked to change the subject away from curious questions put to Jack.

"Yes sir, when Coronel Bobby Lee finally got rid of old Twiggs," Nate Wicks said. He liked to think of himself as a serious historian. He also like to embellish his stories like everyone else. "That Federal General, that fucking damn fool Twiggs closed up all the border forts and left Cortina free to tear up the border towns. Well, he sure as hell did that." Nate Wicks shook his head in wonder.

Cortina pillaged up toward San Antonio and back to the border. He stole cattle and horses, playing his violent game of hatred for the white Texians who had stolen so much of Mexico with a fight and a treaty the Mexican people didn't understand, but it ended the Mexican war.

But the patriot *banditos* scorned the treaty and never forgave their losses. Finally, Cortina occupied Fort Brown, already abandoned, and commenced to organize every Texas-born Mexican in a campaign to exterminate every *gringo*, every Texian.

¡Viva Cortina! ¡Viva México! ¡Maten los gringos!

Kill all the white people!

But there were bitter men in Brownsville, who took the fort back and called for soldiers and Rangers to come chase after Cortina and his murdering band, up and down the Rio Grande and back over into Mexico. They sacked Rio Grande city on the way, pillaging and burning as they fled with thousands of stolen livestock driven ahead of them into Mexico.

Fifteen Americans killed in that fight. A hundred and fifty Mexican shooters and horse thieves killed.

Facts now, old news.

But Mexican *rancheros*, many men who had been peaceful farmers for generations in what was now Texas, had been burned out in the fighting, so the newspapers clamored.

Eighty friendly Mexicans killed.

Jack thought of Estebanico.

In April of '61 Sallie stood upright where she worked in her kitchen garden. She adjusted her apron and her hat to keep the sun from her face and looked around. Her place, the home she'd hoped for while riding around in McGregor's wagon all those years. She felt a great sense of contentment.

Her place, and she liked the work, she liked the turning of the soil, the new green shoots and leaves coming through. Corn, sweet potatoes, pumpkins in plots further out from the rock house, all the rest. Early rain had favored the crops. She liked the day, the early blooms she saw everywhere. She liked the sheen of sweat on her body. She liked harboring the secret in her mind and in her belly just a little longer.

Soon Mr. Rainie would know, if he hadn't figured it out already. You never knew with him, she thought with a smile. He knew things maybe most hard scrabble ranchers didn't know, Indian things. You never knew.

Presently he would come up from the woods along the creek and she'd tell him. The old draft horse hauled more long poles and logs to patch the garden fence where some critter had broken through after the tender shoots in her garden. Most of the fence had a maze of dead brush piled up against the rails except for that break. Probably an old rogue longhorn bull from the open range yonder, leaving his tracks in the dust, not the first time. Here in this place you had to fence the animals out as much as you fenced them in, even the hen house had to be strong and tight to keep the weasels and 'possums from the chickens and the eggs.

But she was used to that. Jeth, often in his tree house watching everything, would be on the back of the old draft horse coming up from the creek, feeling important with helping his father. More and more he wanted man-chores, not child-chores. But that was something she'd take up with him later.

She stretched, pleasantly tired, then paused, hearing something from the distant road. She heard a far-off voice, coming closer. She heard the alarm, a repeated shouting. She heard the pounding of horse's hoofs as the rider dipped down toward the rock house, shouting the words, then his voice carried back to the road and he rode on with his message.

She walked out into the yard beyond the fence and waited for Jack. He hadn't heard the words, only the sound of the voice. He unhooked the logs and dropped them by the fence. He led the horse along as he walked up to her. He saw the look on her face and stopped in front of her.

"Mr.Rainie," she said, "we are at war. The war has come."

"When were you going to tell me?" he asked. He'd suspected from her subtle changes. In Comanche villages the women went to the women's lodge each moon, a place all men avoided superstitiously. Now he let his question be a gentle prod. They lay deep in the feather bed a few nights after the war news, in comfortable darkness, with a patch quilt over them and Jeth sleeping soundly in the loft above.

"The news was so bad about the war, I couldn't think of good news. I kept thinking of all the men and boys along the creek."

Jack lay silent, tired from the day. He held her a little tighter. They listened to hounds calling through the woods along the creek, near, then fading.

"Odis Wilson's blue tick hounds. Chasing 'coons."

The sounds had a lonely, distant melody.

"If it's another boy I will name him after you," she said. "And what will you name a girl, Mr. Rainie?"

He looked into the darkness for a while. He had no idea about such things. Girls' names.

"November," she said.

"Bad name."

"I mean the baby."

"We need a dog. A dog to bark warnings, scare off varmints."

"He'll chase the chickens."

"He'll learn."

"I said November, Mr. Rainie."

He smiled. "Well, we'll have us a dog by then."

"My old dog got caught by wolves. A big pack came through and took one of Molly Grace's calves and my dog before the men chased them off. We just found bones and hide in the woods."

"We'll get a smart dog."

She was quiet for a time. "There's been fighting already."

He'd seen a newspaper with an editorial drawing of a battle. All the news was old. All the news was bad.

"Molly said the man with the little wooden cages of song birds came through her place a few days ago. She put him up and fed him her ham, you know how she is. He left her with a bird, I don't know what kind. Just like everything's the same."

"It's not," he said. He thought about Cicero Smith, his words about war.

"What will happen now?" she asked.

The first troopers who came through at dusk in early summer wore dusty gray uniforms. A few wore only Confederate gray coats, and others wore no uniforms at all, only the working clothes of boys from ranches and farms along the way. Some of them had a look of importance, even excitement. Others had a hard look, searching around with secret eyes.

New war, new recruits.

The half dozen troopers drove horses and mules from the ranches along the road, swept away in the name and the need of the Confederacy.

Three of McGregor's wagons stood in the shade of the wagon yard under the old Elm trees at a distance from the house, not far from Will Browning's quiet grave and his old tinker wagon just as he'd left it. The painting on the sides of the three McGregor wagons faded into the shadows of dusk. They held partial loads of trade goods, precious now as many items would soon grow scarce.

But McGregor was away on the road with two wagons, and the rest of his teamsters had packed up and gone for the war.

Jack stood watching as they came to a stop, his rifle held in front of him across his arms.

"You," the captain in gray said to Jack, and pointed.

"No sir," Jack said, thinking of all the rumors of conscription.

The captain frowned, a glint of tired impatience in his eyes.

"Guns? Any weapons?"

Every rancher, every farmer had a stash of weapons collected over the years.

"Just what we need here," Jack said, and shifted his rifle slightly.

Not conscription then. Not yet.

The captain waved for his men to look around, look for all those extra hidden weapons, gunpowder, shot, food, stashes of coins, anything for the Confederacy. He pointed to the corral. Troopers took McGregor's wagon teams, picked up the gear in the barn and headed for McGregor's three wagons.

The wagons and teams now would go, Jack knew. Lost. The Confederacy needed any kind of sturdy and reliable transports. Horses were already getting scarce. They left Will Browning's old wagon and a buckboard. Others caught up the five mustangs in the corral, only herd broken but the troopers would find that out soon enough. A brindle yearling steer shook its head in warning as though it had already grown long dangerous horns, but the troopers dragged it away for meat.

The captain studied the rock house, the slave cabin, the barn, as two troopers dragged three goats through the open doorway.

"Leave them," the captain said, and asked Jack, "children?"

"Yep."

But they didn't see any women or children.

"Where?"

"Gone visiting."

"Well. Thank you kindly then." The captain's look at Jack said maybe he wasn't quite finished here. "You Texian?"

"Mostly," Jack answered.

But his men were hungry and tired after a hard day of foraging. He reached into his jacket and took out some script, New Confederate paper money he handed to Jack. He touched his hat, looked at Jack again, then led his men and his plunder back up to the road.

Watch out for that one, Jack thought.

"He's not sure. He thinks we're secessionists." Jack said as Sallie stepped carefully through the doorway, trying not to be seen if the soldiers looked back.

She followed their dust as they rode up to the road with their booty.

"Secessionists," she repeated.

"Or I expect they'd taken everything."

Even me, he thought.

"They know some of the ranchers hereabouts are loyal, they'll help."

Sallie said, "But the forts---?"

"Officers mostly gone east to sign up."

Sallie sighed. She too had read the old newspapers McGregor brought. She touched her belly where her child grew.

Jack stood thinking, remembering again Cicero Smith's words.

He took Sallie down through the woods and thickets along the creek. There was no obvious path, only grass and brush and mustang grape vines. A flock of wild turkeys flew up into the trees ahead of them. They came to a corral hidden in a thicket. The sorrel horse ambled up to Jack at the corral rail, along with four mustang ponies for the buckboard, the draft horse and a tall black mare, a runner with a deep chest and restless legs.

"I named her Racer. She's a beauty, she can run all day. The rest are loose on the range. Grass's still good."

He'd first seen Racer out on the range with a band of shaggy mustangs. The paint stallion of the band was after her, but she wasn't ready to breed, and she ran ahead, far ahead, she kicked up her heels, rude and sassy, and Jack watched almost breathlessly. Two months later with the help of Molly Grace's oldest boy Rod, he managed to drive most of the mustangs into a hidden brush corral. He named the black mare Racer and three months after that with a jaw bridle, he'd taught her to respond, to bear his weight, but in working with her he found she was stubborn but smart and willing because she'd been broken before. She'd been running free for five years or so, he guessed, smart, avoiding capture. From the age on her teeth she was seven years old or so, probably had two or three foals, and when Molly Grace's Delaware Indian handyman brought a wagon with cheese and other trade goods to the rock house, from the action of Racer's ears, nervous, pointing in an anxious search, and her sudden spell of agitation, he believed she could smell the man, maybe any Indian, because of hard care in her past.

Sallie let the mare sniff the back of her hand and laughed when she tossed her head and ran off, around the corral, kicking up her heels

"She's showing off," Jack said. He laughed at the mare, at her ready spirit. No Comanche warrior would ride a mare, but Jack had no doubts, she was a runner, probably a racer in tribal gambling and now she'd be a prized brood mare. Jack had long ago thrown away his Comanche ego. He rode the mare and knew her speed.

Sallie looked around at this hidden place in the woods, pleased. She saw the chewed corn cobs in the corral, scraps of hay, water, the hidden path, so well lost in the brush it wasn't even there when she looked back.

"They will not find this place, Mr. Rainie."

"Others are doing the same thing."

They turned and walked back to the rock house. His mind grew busy with the time ahead.

How best to keep Sallie and Jeth safe?

"I will not leave them alone here. Never."

Now mostly he thought it was time to enlarge the stockade fence, a wall he would build of higher upright wooden stakes sunk in the ground, sharpened to points at the top, a frontier fortress around the rock house.

McGregor looked down at the script in his hand three weeks later. Four bills marked *The Confederate States of America*. Recently new, issued by Louisiana, with pictures of happy black slaves working in cotton fields, and payable when the South won the war with the damn Yankees.

"Dozen of them," Jack said "They had new recruits. We hid the weapons and most of the stock."

McGregor looked toward the wagon yard. Two wagons he'd brought back, all that was left of his business, and the last teamsters had packed up and gone home to their families or gone for the war. "No way to stop them from taking the stock." It was a statement of the new reality.

"Sallie and the boy were here," Jack said.

McGregor's mouth took on a grim, straight line. "How did you know?"

"Molly Grace's Joeboy rode to warn us."

McGregor looked down at the bills again. "No need to save these in the root cellar with the coins," he said grimly. "My dear God, what folly! There is no gold in the new government of the Southern states to make these good. They'll be worthless if the South loses. When the South loses." McGregor's natural optimism, sorely put to the test by the news he heard on the road, and his own losses, began to rally a little as he thought about this new challenge. "But there are many gullible people out there who still believe the South will win."

Young Jeth, adding to his tree house with salvaged sticks and a good pine board, called to McGregor from his perch in the apple trees.

"Come look at my tree house."

McGregor waved to Jeth. Soon.

"I expect they'll be back," Jack said.

"Tell them you are a teacher, or a doctor. Better still, tell them you are a politician next time they come around," McGregor said with a bitter smile.

Molly Grace's middle son, who was known to the settlers as Joeboy because he was twelve years old in the body of a hulking seventeen-year-old, rode back to the rock house on a gentle old mule. He had appointed himself the voice of warning when soldiers were on the road. Now he came without firearms or weapons other than a small folding knife. He came because he liked to work, hard work was always easy for him, always a happy adventure, he liked company, and his twelve-year-old heart had fallen into school boy love with Sallie Rainie.

"She's nice," he told Jack. "Miss Sallie."

She had given him honeyed apple sweets the day after he rode with his warning about the troopers. He'd thanked her properly, looked around at the stockade fence, at Jack as he dug post holes. "Maybe I'll come back." He watched as Jeth made off with a handful of Sallie's honeyed sweets liberated from the shelf below the rock house's open window.

"Bad kid," he said without rancor, just an observation.

"Bad kid." Jack laughed when he told Sallie.

Jeth nodded and smiled a little. "Real bad. Good damn stuff."

When Joeboy came back, he took no money or trade from Jack. He worked for the other ranchers as a hired hand like old Nigger Britt, chasing cows, branding strays, cutting hay, mending fences, digging garden plots and post holes, digging new latrines. So many men had left for the war that Joeboy labored and smiled and never complained.

He enjoyed his new importance. He enjoyed doing anything that pleased Sallie Rainie, and Jack.

"Don't take pay in paper money. Take the old coins," Jack told him. They stood by a pile of fence timbers dragged up from the woods.

"I like coins," Joeboy said and jangled coins in his pocket for the pretty sound they made. He showed Jack the coins. They were mostly the old coins, only a few of the new Confederate half dollars, surely as worthless as the new script.

"Good enough. Now grab a shovel, dig the post holes deep, we're building fence."

Rose Rainie came into the world in November of 1861 with wide blue eyes and wisps of pale hair. She was instantly called Rosebud, a name that came on an impulse from Sallie as she held the swaddled baby for the first time but suited her well. Even Mariah Matilda, who offered her assistance again where little was needed, mentioned her infant beauty.

"Be careful, Missy," Mariah Matilda cautioned, with love and a familiar doomsday frown. "I heard those panthers off in the woods smell new babies, they like to sneak up and steal them."

Jeth studied his sister thoughtfully. He touched her with his hand, a spreading of his fingers on her small chest. He gave his mother a long look, searching in her eyes, then he turned away, satisfied.

Jack, who knew something about boys, just stared for a few minutes as he sorted through his tangle of feelings. Finally, he smiled and said, "You did well, Sallie Rainie."

She answered, "Yes I did."

The freedom loving Texians who voted for session and were now in a war for the right to make their own decisions about how they wanted to live, how they wanted to prosper as farmers, as shopkeepers, as cattlemen or even sheep men, or as the owners of the big cotton plantings in the southern counties where they needed the labor of thousands of slaves, had long since grown angry at the enemy Federals for blockading the ports of Galveston and New Orleans where they shipped their cotton. Now they grew angry at the prospect of the Confederate military conscription, voted for in order to fight the damn Yankees. Fewer laborers, families in conflict taking sides, crops damaged, profits lost.

The war raged on, far away. The settlers read of battles in places most had never heard of, but others knew; old family towns, old names. They read the sobering reports of casualty numbers in the thousands that were hard to believe, they saw editorial drawings in old issues of Harper's Weekly, showing huge piles of dead horses being burned after a battle, villages and crops destroyed, fields of dead soldiers, some stacked like cordwood, some sprawled in the grass.

They read of Yankee supplies cut off, rail lines torn up, running fights and battles, troopers without weapons, ammunition, food. Short rations. Nothing but rice. Yankee troopers starving. Surely the South was winning the war.

A few wounded soldiers began to trail home on furlough, trudging and limping along the roads. Visitors from the East made their precarious way past Indian depredations and burnt out stage stations, just to check on their families struggling on the far frontier. Now and then a letter arrived, carried by strangers passing through. The ranchers and farmers began to hear rumors of Reb vigilantes looking for Unionists.

The second sweep of Confederate troopers who came to the rock house after the conscription laws had finally passed in Austin, carried with them a handful of boys who looked too young. Hard times were grinding the settlers with shortages and losses. Men trailed home with terrible wounds, terrible memories in their faces. The settlers, holding on, mostly just enduring, looked for any excuse for visiting, for the welcome relief for the men, mostly old or crippled, to drink moonshine and a chance to tell stories and exchange the latest news.

Joeboy Grace grinned and waved to Jack from among the newly conscripted boys. Jack knew some of them, just recognized others. They all looked too young.

He has no idea.

Jack had to look away

The lieutenant led his troopers into the yard and stopped his tall bay mount in front of Jack. McGregor and Mariah Matilda stood in the doorway of the rock house, Sallie behind them holding Rosebud. Jeth perched in his tree house watching everything. Jack waited for the troopers as he had before, his rifle across his arm in front of him.

"Have you enlisted, sir? Are you home on a farming furlough?" the lieutenant asked without greeting, his voice like gravel underfoot. "Speak up!"

Jack started to answer but McGregor broke in. "He has not."

The lieutenant's face, brown from sun and wind, tired, determined, turned to McGregor. "There are harsh penalties for evading the draft, sir. Shit, don't you people know that yet? You are in the new country, the Confederate country of Texas!"

He paused, drawing breath, then went on as though speaking to ignorant frontier children. "This is your country. Your country. We have those damned Yankees on the run!" He paused, drew another long breath. "There are punishments for hiding from the draft, do you understand that? You are breaking the law if you---."

"He cannot speak English or understand you."

The officer glared at McGregor. Foreign troopers, even those who could hardly speak the language, were far from uncommon, and welcome to swell the ranks. "He will still---."

"No sir. He's tubercular. He is my wife's nephew and he has come from Germany traveling for his health. He is neither a citizen nor part of any current census or conscription."

The captain stared at McGregor, listening to the echo of his well-spoken speech here on this crude frontier, where, clearly, he believed he dealt with uneducated fools. Then he turned his glare to Jack. "You. Say something."

McGregor gestured. Jack understood. He said, *"Sadda."*

A trooper at the back of the group laughed aloud, then fell silent.

The lieutenant took a moment to look around, to look thoughtful, as if he knew the German language and only took the time to consider Jack's reply. According to his men all Lieutenants knew everything anyway. His men watched him carefully.

He nodded.

McGregor cleared his throat. "Yes sir."

The lieutenant looked hard at McGregor. "You?"

"Me, sir?

"He's too old," Mariah Matilda said loudly, in that voice that could scald. "He's past the age."

As they left with their harvest of boys for involuntary recruitment, one trooper whose face was walnut brown, angular, bent toward Jack, holding on to his old hide hat. He looked more like an Indian scout than one of the barefaced troopers. He spoke a quiet guttural word to Jack.

"What did you say to that trooper?"

"I gave the officer a new name."

Dog, Jack thought.

McGregor started to laugh. "Indian talk I'll wager. Nothing good. Well done. And that trooper?"

Jack nodded and smiled. "He's given me a name too."

But he felt a sharp dismay at seeing Joeboy taken away, and his own silence.

Wind howled outside the rock house. Little Rosebud, two years old the November past, began to stir from sleep in Sallie's arms. Jeth put down his fork full of roasted wild turkey and held out his arms. He liked to hold Rosebud, pick her up when she fell and howled her toddler indignation, even feed her when she was hungry, and Sallie allowed it. Now she was still sleepy, and he could wait.

203

"They'll all be free now to go anywhere, work wherever they want," Mariah Matilda commented. "Just camp in the woods, I suppose."

"More than just the slave problem, more like money and politics," McGregor added. "The folks in the north'll get behind Lincoln now. It's a bold move."

The big announcement had come in September from the U.S. of A. government in the East and arrived like wildfire on the frontier where a chaos of Southern anger and abolitionist satisfaction flared up everywhere. They'd already heard of riots, Negro shootings and hangings across the south, but no one knew for sure.

"But mostly they'll just stay on, especially the women. What else do they know?" McGregor went on. "Or the men'll go north to join up with the Union. That's what the South dreads. My dear God, it does make you wonder at that man Lincoln! The Union's doing better, winning a few fights here and there, and now this."

With the first day of the new year of our Lord, 1863, just six days ahead, President Lincoln's big proclamation would take effect and all the slaves would stand free in the U.S. of A., even in states like Texas and Arkansas and Louisiana and even in South Carolina where all the trouble started.

The reality, even the shock of all the mobs of black folks freely walking the roads, looking for work or just moving on, homeless, lingered as a worried puzzlement in everybody's mind.

"Well it's the law now." Mariah Matilda said.

McGregor shook his head. "We are Texians out here on the frontier. Or Texans now, *Tejanos*, whatever you want to call us. We are mostly spectators here. Governments do what they want. Most of us'll resist even if the rest of us stand back." He took a bite of the wild holiday turkey as they sat at the big farm table.

The Christmas celebration could only be subdued because of the hard times and how they would be affected by Mr. Lincoln's proclamation. Everyone along the creek seemed to be waiting. The war had gotten worse, then better, according to your views. People said that Lee wanted to take the fight up into the North, but rumors came and went in a confusion of conflicting news. Deserters walked the roads. McGregor traveled the roads less often, bands of thieves and vigilantes no better than brigands, seeing the advantage of faltering law enforcement, roamed everywhere. His wagon stock had all but vanished. Now there were shortages of everything and the roads were dangerous.

"Well, now I believe its time," McGregor announced.

"Time for what?" Sallie asked. She brushed a wisp of her hair back from her face.

McGregor withdrew a bundle of papers from his vest pocket. He handed them to Jack, and another bundle to Sallie. "Time for us to move along, Missy."

Jack read the papers then stared at McGregor and Mariah Matilda. "Your deed---to this property?"

"Your property. Both of you. You've earned it. All the papers are in order. You may have noticed I am no rancher!" McGregor laughed, enjoying the moment. He drank from his jar of beer. "We have made other plans."

"Yes," Mariah Matilda sighed heavily, adding a little drama. "I suppose it's time. Again." She didn't sound entirely happy. "I will miss the children."

"But---." Sallie began.

"This war will end, Missy." McGregor stated firmly. "It will end, and the Indian wars will have to end too, and I will be ready. I've found a decent place. The owners are leaving in April for Utah. Farmers, the Rooney family, Irish folks from County Tyrone. Six hundred acres for the livery, a good house that needs fixing. They gave us a good price considering the times---."

"Catholic people," Mariah Matilda mentioned, reminding everyone of her views.

"---they have three boys who'll be taken for the draft soon," McGregor went on. "Too young to leave on their own, and they have family in Utah. Land's not fertile there, too sandy, but they'll make do. They aim to stay together---." He looked from Sallie's face to Jack's. "They want to get away."

They all listened to the rain and wind outside. A shutter rattled softly, needing to be fixed against the draft. December snow on the way.

"A store," Mariah Matilda explained. "Can you imagine? In these times? He wants to build a store. Stay in one place after all these years. I rightly don't know what I'll do with him around all the time."

Jack stammered his thanks, his mind scrambling with questions, with all the changes ahead. He looked at Sallie, saw her surprise. He smiled for her. He drew a deep breath. "But there's that trading post already---."

"No, no, not a trading post." McGregor said. "A real store, more modern than the old trading posts. Think of it! A store with everything a growing community could want! Not just the staples. And not a lot of smelly furs---."

"Not if they're cured properly. Not just salted. I've always watched for those nasty smelly ones," Mariah Matilda said.

McGregor looked at her. "You watched?"

"I do. I did. When we were traveling. You don't notice everything." She spooned the root cellar food onto Jeth's plate. Turnips, preserved greens. Corn. Sweet potatoes. Roasted pumpkin with wild honey and cinnamon. Dried apple pie. She said to everyone, "He means a store like the ones back there in Santa Fe---."

"A real store?" Sallie said, with awe in her face at the gift of land, and a smile as she recalled the Santa Fe store where she had found Jack, and he had found her.

Mariah Matilda smiled for Sallie, and the family gathered at the table, having almost forgotten all her generalized rancor of that day. "With windows, and counters and hard candy. Spices, baking powder. Books. Tools. Bolts of fine fabrics for the ladies---."

"But the war---."

It was hard for anyone to even think of luxuries and ample supplies of sugar and real wheat flour, with everyone wary about taking their grain and corn all the way down the road to the mill for grinding. The Indians were running loose everywhere, stealing horses and causing random mischief. And supplies were always hard to find.

But McGregor, ever the frontier business man, saw opportunity, and the settlers persisted, driving to the mills together in trains of ox-drawn wagons for mutual protection.

"The Rooney place is closer to the road, easy to see when we get our sign up," McGregor went on.

"If we ever again find decent supplies for a real store," Mariah Matilda said.

McGregor frowned. "We'll enlarge it, we'll be comfortable there after our present accommodations, but its big enough now for the two of us to live in, it's well-built. Good traffic and we have neighbors not far away---."

"Like those stray Indians who come bothering. The drunk ones come begging at the trading posts, you know," she confided. "I remember them down in El Paso. I don't want them falling asleep by my door."

McGregor drew a deep breath. "Well, it's a decent house, a good start---."

"Another one," Mariah Matilda said wryly.

McGregor looked at her with a measure of annoyance.

"And maybe later a tavern---," McGregor went on.

"It has a good well, not too far from the house, and a good solid roof," Mariah Matilda added, now with a small, willing smile on her face. She was always practical in the face of McGregor's many dreams but now she liked this idea, a civilized store, maybe a tavern. Room for a livery. Perhaps even a small schoolhouse eventually. With property rights always in a tangle in frontier Texas because of old Spanish grants and disputes over water rights, Austin's and all the other old grants and arguable head rights, they often came to nothing but worthless maps and papers but were still contested in the courts for years.

"His property rights are all genuine, everything's in good order according to the court in Austin---."

"Austin," Mariah Matilda said with a shudder. "All those bats."

"Bats?" Jeth asked with interest.

"Rest assured, my dear. They have no taste for your blood," McGregor said to Mariah Matilda with a sly smile. "They prefer insects."

Mariah Matilda frowned, but Sallie smiled at the familiar jousting. She was still a little dazed by all the changes ahead.

Mariah Matilda grumped, "Too many people. Ruffians. But we tended to all the papers, everything's in order."

"Where?" asked Jeth, looking worried. He sat wearing a new flannel shirt, with his thatch of hair combed down flat for the occasion.

"Just down the road toward Fort Belknap. Less than a day, boy," McGregor answered with a smile. "Not too far for visits."

"If I had a horse of my own I could visit you," Jeth said.

Jack looked at the boy, patient with him. "I'm thinking on it."

I've held off. Worried. He's curious, he'll wander. But maybe it's time for a horse of his own. He fancies Racer. Not likely.

"I know the place, Rooney's place," Jack said. He forked a piece of venison through sweet honey gravy, a dish he relished. "The one where they started to build the rock wall. "

"Never finished. Gave it up when they knew they were going for Utah."

"He's going with a wagon train? Which trail? It's real dangerous now."

"He's got some plan or other, didn't say." McGregor waved his hand. "There's a lot of work there at Rooney's in the spring, if you're looking."

Jack shook his head. "I would, but there's work here." He drew a long breath.

Now this was the Rainie ranch. He looked at Sallie again, trying to take it all in. "Stockade's finished except for the gate. There's fencing. There's the stock, branding, we've got that contract with the military for beef---."

"Military," McGregor repeated.

"Reb or Yankee. They'll buy, or they'll take," Jack answered, watching McGregor's frown.

"Reb script won't be worth a damn."

"I know that---."

"Whichever. They'll think we're friendly," Sallie said. "They'll leave us alone."

"The children," Mariah Matilda added by way of ending the edgy discussion.

Jack set his fork aside. The fork often reminded him of Cicero Smith, and he wondered again where that man was in the chaos of war.

"I expect there's more trouble bound to come," Mariah Matilda said.

"The Indians," Sallie said, saying what was always nagging at every settler's mind.

The uprising, some called it. Word of fighting here and there. The hidden threat like a constant darkness in the mind, the worry.

Everyone talking about an uprising.

The Kiowas and Comanches and all their allies, almost free now of Union garrisons and Indian agents watching them because all the forts and agencies were dangerously undermanned, had taken to roaming out from the Territory regularly, raiding for horses, marauding, stealing and burning, now and then killing a settler caught alone on the prairie; small bands of young men, two or three warriors taking advantage of occasional open winter weather and random opportunities whenever they could.

They're looking for glory, Jack thought. The old way. They'll die for it.

"They're scattered now with this snow coming. Heading for winter camps."

"People are talking about forting up."

"Down near Fort Belknap. With the Rangers."

"What Rangers---?"

"Or Camp Murrah."

Rosebud gave a little yelp of hunger. She reached for her new doll and Sallie turned aside to feed her bits of turkey.

McGregor said, "I met up with three boys from Fort Belknap a few days ago. They were on a scout going after horse thieves. Horses are scarce, Indians again, Kiowas they said. Sneaking off stealing horses." He drank from his half full jar of beer. "And the rustlers, whites and Mexicans alike. My dear God, sometimes I just feel surrounded! The war and the Indians. Now the cursed rustlers." He sighed. "Vigilantes. Militias. People are getting tired of no protection."

"The Rangers. There's a few left---." Mariah Matilda said. She spoke with a slight shudder and a hint of reserve in her voice, clearing remembering the ugly stories about sieges and battles with the Comanches, those terrible Tonkawas, just cannibals. Everyone knew the Rangers had started the fight in the Antelope Hills back in '58, along with their Tonkawa and militia allies. They hit a Comanche camp inside Indian Territory in a hard siege and the military couldn't break the law and follow until later.

Mariah Matilda drew a long breath. "Lordy, we need them. Brutal men. But they've broken up, gone for the war. There's nowhere near enough."

"It's a big damn war." Jack said. "Most of the military and the Rangers gone for the war and the Indians know it. Shit, they're smart. They're just watching us, they're just waiting." His feelings were strong, he didn't apologize to the women for his language except with a look toward Sallie.

"It's a big damn war," Sallie echoed.

Mariah Matilda savored a bite of dried apple pie. She looked down at her plate as she ate.

"There's deserters walking the roads from both sides now," McGregor said by way of offering some uncontroversial news.

"Those Rangers were hard men," Mariah Matilda said again.

"They'd get whipped again if they weren't hard men. How many'd they lose before they went for the war?" Jack said. His words trailed off into silence.

Mariah Matilda's opinions often wandered between her long-past Missouri schoolroom full of pleasant stories, and the absence of the hard realities of frontier life. She struggled in her thinking, floundering but persistent.

"Brutal men," she said.

"They have to be as hard as the Indians." Jack said quietly. "Harder."

"Indeed." McGregor glanced at Jack, then fell silent as he ate. Jack never spoke of his years among the Comanches except by simple statements, simple facts.

"They are all a brutal sort," Mariah Matilda said in a voice finally without censure, just accepting the facts again and speaking a frontier truth.

"They damn well have to be harder," Jack said again.

"You ever think about forting up with the others? Down at Fort Murrah?" McGregor asked.

"It's just talk for now. Winter coming on, the Kiowas and Comanches, none of them'll travel anywhere in the snow. They're headed for their winter camps."

Jack thought about the coming blizzard, and suddenly he remembered how the Comanches huddled in their fur robes, safe and warm around their lodge fires. No one wanted to travel in this weather, nor hunt, nor raid. They never imagined such nonsense. But the weather always ruled their lives. They ate the rich bounty of their hunts, their gatherings, they made love. They told stories and bragged, they told jokes and laughed and grew fat, and the children played small games.

But there had been winters when the ponies froze, and the men went out for months in the deep snow looking for meat.

Jack said, "I'm figuring to round up more yearlings in the spring. After I finish around here.   Send them for a drive with the other stockmen."

But something stirred in him, something deeper than thieves and rustlers and far away wars.

In the summer of 1863 the Kiowas and Comanches ran loose in a spree of raids against the White Dogs, riding here and there like ghosts, yelling taunts in English words they'd learned over in the Territory; small bands stealing stock, burnings, luring the Rangers off in all directions.

In August of 1864 three more settler families moved away down the road, looking to move near old Fort Belknap until the troubles were over.

Molly Grace came by in her wagon on a late summer day, hurrying along in a bustle of news and trading.   She climbed out of her wagon, awkward, her skirts catching as she pulled them free.   She was a plump, dumpling of a woman, comfortable in a body used to child bearing and hard work.   She always dressed in neat, old calico, often faded, but now something was different.   Her face, round and soft, so prompt to mirror the concerns of others, now frowned at Sallie.   Her graying hair had come loose in wisps from the knot at the back of her head.   She seemed not to notice.

"My lark died." she said.

Sallie stared at her, sensing something amiss.

"Your lark---?"

"Well he's staying---."

Sallie frowned.   "Mr. Grace---?"

"He won't leave.   That man, bad as his brothers.   He's just stomping around the place, he's that fool stubborn!" she declared.   Her voice wavered, then died.

She brought Sallie three pots of rare sweet butter from her cows and a slab of bacon she cured in her smoke house.   Everyone knew the Rainie people didn't keep cows for milk or use hog meat for food, unclean mud animals they claimed, some old superstition Molly supposed, Molly didn't know about such things. She had her own valued superstitions, and she just carried rumors along with her. Who could survive without hogs and salt pork on the frontier? And then there was McGregor, a traveling trader, not a rancher, with his stock running wild out on the prairie until that Rainie fellow, the husband to her friend, came along and worked the place. Worked hard. Never heard a complaint.

But McGregor was no farmer either, and then there was that stern-faced Mariah Matilda, not a friendly woman in Molly's view, who was often sickly in the bowels, if she could believe the gossip, but Mariah Matilda wouldn't drink even a sip of Molly's bitter tonics.

But Sallie favored bacon now and then, and Molly had made a business in trading her wares among the settler womenfolk.

Sallie gathered up new jars of peaches and a basket of dried apples. She had a new quilt she'd sewn from patches of old dresses and worn out shirts. The quilt was stuffed with sheep's wool McGregor had brought from the Pueblos before the troubles started.

"That man," Molly blustered, before Sallie could speak. "He says he's built his own durn fort, and now he won't turn his animals loose for them Indians to carry off."

Molly Grace looked at the quilt Sallie offered, but she hardly seemed to see it. She looked at her own rough, square hands. "I don't know how you sew them tiny stitches." Then she looked at Sallie and began to weep. "Rod's gone."

"Gone?"

"He went off for the war. Says he's a Yankee through and through. Just left a month ago, but he's gone already---." She sniffed, then began to cry again. "One of the boys who went off with him, that George Hayes, he's not sixteen---." Her weeping quieted for a moment. "He came back looking starved and told us. He's hiding from the army now. He thinks the Yanks'll shoot him when they get here." She heaved a sigh and wiped at her eyes. "He said Rod went off looking for shoes. Better than them wood peg shoes, the ones that the pegs fall out and the shoes come apart---." Molly started to cry and wail softly.

"But---."

"---somebody shot him. Took them shoes he found. Just killed him! Shoes---!"

Sallie felt a wave of grim sympathy, anger, wash through her, for this woman's loss, and for all the others, the lost men and boys, and now a sharp, hidden concern of her own.

"Joeboy's gone too." Molly wept, "He must be gone. I ain't heard."

"He hasn't written?" Then Sallie bit her lip in chagrin as she remembered Joeboy.

"He can't write. He just can't write, can he?" Molly's voice was sharp, plaintive. Then she said, "He never could figure out the letters."

Molly wiped her face again and looked searchingly at Sallie as though hoping for a great answer. "I can't work it out. Rod went for the Union and Joeboy was taken off for the Rebs. I don't understand."

With hot tea and a quiet hour in the rock house, Molly Grace spoke more calmly. "Joeboy'll come back. He'll come back." She heaved a sigh of hope. "Well I'm just going. That man of mine can stay behind on the farm."

Sallie knew she spoke of Hubert J. Grace, a rustic grizzled man with a rough white beard, ox-slow and stubborn in his ways.

"He can just stay. He says he's bound to feed the chickens---the chickens!" Her voice wavered again. "Well he does have to feed my chickens, and my cows and hogs and all the other stock, no shit!" She looked surprised for a moment and put her hand over her mouth, then it just didn't matter. "But I got one boy left and I'm carrying him to Fort Belknap after I pack up." She finished her tea in an awkward swallow and studied her rough hands. She looked around, she had been in this comfortable place many times before, so much more comfortable than her own one room dirt floored cabin, her life.

"You know that old Delaware Indian feller works for us sometimes when we butcher? Name of Pete? The one who's near blind but he can still scrape a hog. Won't do women's work but he takes care of the stock, chases the cows when they get loose in the woods. Mostly helps with the hogs, Mr. Grace don't care much for that work anymore. Pete says he was a scout for that Colonel Marcy back in---." Molly stopped herself from drifting into trivia. She stared out the window, watching something. Watching Jack ride into the rock house's grassy yard bareback on the sorrel. He slid off, his moccasins easy in the patch of grass. He carried a string of squirrels shot from the big trees along the creek.

"Mr. Grace says---," she began, then drew a deep breath and turned back to Sallie. "Pete's nephew went off on a big hunt for winter meat, gone a month. Says his nephew saw a big bunch of them Indians. A big bunch, he said. Leaving the reservation. All the tribes. Maybe hundreds of Indians."

"Hundreds," Sallie repeated. But maybe this was Molly's latest exaggeration, just a current rumor.

Molly said, "Other women are leaving soon. The children. You come too."

The last cut of the hay lay in the fields, scythed flat, drying in the hot sun. Soon enough, he'd have to rake it into stacks and get it to the barn before the fall rains, just over the horizon. Racer had a split hoof, gimping and sure to go lame if he didn't file it down in the next day or two. The brush arbor he'd built by the house for summer shade needed more brush and shade to cool the water *ollas* hanging near the door. He thought a real veranda, a real gallery like some he had seen on old houses back in Bexar, might do, a good project when he had time.

Jack wiped sweat from his face. His old hat gave him scant protection from the sun. He breathed easily and wondered if this work ever ended.

This farmer work---, he had last written in his journal. *This farmer work---what?*

Sometimes he wondered what he was doing. Here. At this place. Now. He wondered about Cicero Smith. In Virginia. He thought about their casual conversations, where to go next, and what to do. San Antonio de Bexar. A busy town full of Cicero Smith's ELIXIR opportunities. But his wonderings always came back to orchards, like the orchards he'd seen in California. Apples, peaches. And here, maybe orchards of the big pecan trees and---.

But this farmer work.

He never wondered for long.

This is what Sallie wants.

Sometimes he had to get away, down into the woods, wander afoot, find a place of silence, when he knew Sallie and the children were safe, away visiting or when McGregor came to the rock house with his small hoard of goods; wheat flour, salt, cones of brown sugar, ammunition, powder, tobacco to trade. News.

He looked down toward the creek, the trees and bramble thickets where he cut old dead trees for firewood and fence poles; and hunted when he could.

Maybe it's time to teach Jeth how to set snares, small game. Salt the hides. *He tries---,* he'd written in his journal. Something he thought about often.

Good cover. His constant first concern when he looked at the bramble of Elm Creek.

Molly Grace told Sallie. Hundreds of Indians. Leaving the reservation.

Maybe true, maybe another damn rumor.

With all the talk of tribal raids, sometimes random images and sounds came back to him at night-- fires, the burnings, screams. He'd start awake and tell the lie to Sallie when she tried to calm him.

Nothing, nothing---

He never told her.

But he hadn't found any Indian sign, no moccasin footprint, no hidden message carved on a tree trunk, or sticks or stones placed in a

216

coded pattern, anything an ordinary settler would hardly notice or worry about.

But he was no ordinary settler, he knew. And by now the settlers probably knew, even though he walked among them.

Hard lines, he thought, and a shadowed past

The big stockade gate stood open and he could see the rock house on its rise.

"Keep the gate locked if I'm off hunting!" He'd warned, angry at any carelessness, "Keep it locked!"

He saw the few summer flowers blooming near the doorway of the rock house, withered now by the heat. He'd painted the door blue last year, thinking of Estebanico, the *santero,* and he was well pleased with it. Laundry hung from a line nearby. Chickens wandered. Still no dog but hound pups due from a neighbor's coon hound. Maybe then.

He studied the stockade. He'd made the pickets bigger and stronger than any he'd seen at the ranches along the creek, which were mostly just fortified sticks, just picket fences, maybe safer places for the women and children to hide when Indians came, but sometimes not safe enough.

More old stories the settlers told.

But Jack's stockade sprawled, not unlike the stockades he'd helped build for the military back in his days in El Paso del Norte. The well, the slave cabin, the house and the kitchen garden, Jeth's apple trees, the spring house, the two outbuildings, were all sheltered. He'd put out the word, any settler was welcome here in his stockade if the Indians came making a raid.

But something ruffled his senses, something felt wrong.

He looked up from splitting wood and saw a horseman approaching, with a dozen horses following on leads. Another rider followed further behind, and a lazy dog. He reached for his rifle and waited.

The horseman stopped some distance from the house, polite, unhurried. He waited, looking at Jack. He was slender, tough-looking in the saddle, with rough clothes, worn boots and a battered straw hat.

The stock of a rifle showed in a worn leather saddle scabbard. He wore a hand gun in a belted holster.

His face was the color of cinnamon.

"Yes sir," he said.

Jack stared, then laughed. "By God, Ely!"

"Yes sir," Ely said again, and smiled.

"By God, you look like a cowboy!"

Ely laughed. "Always did want to go chasing cows."

They had years to recount, stories to tell, but not yet. The second rider came up and stopped her horse next to Ely. Her face was darker than his, a rich chocolate brown, her forehead very high, and she too wore a battered hat on a cord at the back of her head against the Texas sun. She had a startling, fine-featured beauty, foreign and exotic, even haughty, something that took a little getting used to. She sat her horse wearing colorful draped clothes, with no show of weariness. Her belly was huge with child.

"I am Elizabeth" she announced clearly before Ely could speak. "Of Ely."

Ely looked at her with delight. "She speaks right out."

"So old Reuben's off on one of the drives," Jack said. They sat in the shade under the arbor and sipped at rye whiskey, a rare pleasure on a hot midday break. The spotted hound dog sprawled in the shade. "What about the hotel?"

"Why, he found himself a woman. Got himself a wife."

"A wife? By God, good for him."

"Yeah, she a big strong woman, don't take sass from anyone. But she likes him, he likes her. She cooks too. His feet got itchy. Told her he'd be back in a year. She said good riddance. Ha!" Ely laughed.

"Which road's he on?"

"They go anywhere there's grazing left these days. One big drive after another. Mostly the big ranchers, west. It's all open range." Ely drank his whiskey with slow relish, "About twelve hundred at a time.

Damn longhorns. Back up to Kansas, they don't care about that fever. Maybe the last one for him till the trouble's over."

The pleasure of seeing Ely left Jack's face. "You talking war trouble or Indian trouble?"

"Folks talking about leaving their places. Indians. They say Kiowas. When we coming here, there's all this talk, going off to someplace called Camp Murrah."

"They're turning it into a fort south of Fort Belknap." Jack looked around at his stockade fence. "We're good here. We'll leave when we have to."

"We come here easy, asking around. Some places empty already, stock running loose. We heard about them big bunch of Indians, but we never saw any."

Jack studied Ely thoughtfully. "You have your own trouble now?"

Ely dipped his head. "Yeah, sometimes. She with me now, and the babe." He thought for a moment. "The war sure ain't over. The Rebs don't give up easy."

"They don't."

"You off the road a ways. If they see you don't have no sad old wreath hanging on your door mourning after some dead Southern boy, they been coming after folks, breaking windows, stealing, burning, just causing trouble." Ely tamped tobacco into a cob pipe and lit a match. "I got freedom papers but that don't matter anymore."

"Mostly here the stockmen just step back. Leave each other alone. Most of the hotheads left a long time ago. Too many men gone away fighting. Or conscripted."

"Like the drives," Ely went on. "Not enough drovers, even for the pay." Ely's cinnamon face stirred with the question. "They didn't get you? The conscription?"

Jack shook his head and answered quietly, "No they did not. But they came looking."

"Lot of deserters these days. Heard they run off, then use another name and join up again for the signup pay." Ely laughed. He raised his glass. "Yes sir. Here's to you and yours. I been wondering about you."

They sat in silence for a moment, looking out over the corrals, the creek beyond.

"You work chasing cows?" Ely asked. At Jack's expression, Ely laughed again. "Well. You never did like that work."

"Nothing's changed." Jack said with a wry smile. "Damn longhorns'll kill a man afoot if they can. Hide out in mesquite thickets---you know."

"I do. Got hooked in the leg once. Killed my horse. But they're worth Yankee dollars up north." Ely looked around at the rock house, at the farm.

"It's what she wants," Jack answered his look.

"Yes sir, I know about that with a woman." He laughed. "I sure do."

"McGregor talks about the whole country wanting beef after the war's over. I expect he's right. We got a contract with the military supplying the fort. Hard money they said."

"Yeah. That McGregor. I remember. He still trading?"

"He's no rancher." Jack remembered too. "Won this place in a poker game in Juarez." Jack laughed with a kind of distant wonder. "It's his favorite story, he tells it whenever he gets a chance."

"You here."

"We're here. Our place now, the house and all. He just went on trading, but he had to give it up after the trouble started, couldn't get the goods, lost his wagons. He's down the road fixing a new place to make a store."

"He's smart. Cattle two, three dollars a head here now. I heard tell of a drover took his cattle all the way to the gold camps over in California back in '49, got a hundred dollars a head. Then some greenhorn feller drove a big bunch of sheep over the mountains, most died, a hell of a long way, ended up with just a handful left." Ely shook his head in wonder at such folly.

"Gold," Jack said. "Back then everybody was after the gold, camps full of greenhorns everywhere, boomtowns. Long time ago. Now they're driving sheep from California to Texas, takes two years. Better wool I hear." He drew a long breath. "California's a big damn country. Oceans, mountains, desert that'll kill you, bears everywhere, valleys and groves of apples and oranges, mustangs and horse thieves." Jack broke off. "Good country, big."

"You been?"

Jack nodded. "Four years." Jack drank some of his whiskey. "Maybe another boom here when the trouble's over. We could do better here, run more cattle, brand more. Most of the ranchers left hereabouts are thinking that way."

Ely looked across the yard. He looked down to the wooded thickets along the creek, the tall trees, the open range stretching far beyond, the blue, blue summer sky.

"How many?"

"Thousands out there in the mesquite. Call 'em mavericks now. Nobody's bothered branding strays since the trouble started. They drift, some brands coming down from Colorado---."

"Yeah they drift. Weather pushes them. Let me tell you, them big ranchers over west, and up in Colorado, branding all the strays they can catch. I seen 'em out there on the prairie sitting on blankets with bags of gold, buying yearling from the drovers going by. All just open range."

"If the government gives out free land to homesteaders after the war, there'll be fighting again."

Ely looked down at the creek, the wild trees and brambles, silent.

"Still thousands out there."

Ely nodded. "You?"

"Just a few this year. Folks around here need the money, hard money when they can get it, maybe forty head or so at a time. We help each other, look for a market. Over at the Territory for the military. New Orleans maybe. I hear the market's good there." Jack paused. "It's mostly all Confederate country."

"Maybe hard driving to N'Orleans, getting paid. Heard some stockmen shipping cattle out of Galveston for N'Orleans." They both knew that payment for the cattle in Confederate script would likely prove a worthless venture.

Ely's eyes rested again on the tall trees along the creek, the patches of grazing land, the wildness.

"This a good place. Looks safe."

Jack studied Ely's face. "Safe."

Ely frowned. "Lot of them fellers riding around in white sheets, Klan they call them. Over East, Tennessee and the like." Ely stopped, too proud to carry the ugly stories any further. "Well, maybe we stop awhile, help out. Let the babe get born."

His eyes came back to the rock house, the slave cabin, the stockade, the corrals. "I don't see no horses, man, just a rough old bunch of mustangs and a couple of brindle longhorns."

"Folks here keep their war horses hidden." Jack frowned at the reference. Comanche thinking again.

"Yeah, that Reb conscription. Horses scarce."

"There's thousands running out on the range, some branded. Mustangs."

Ely looked over the field of corn, the scythed hay. Mostly he looked back to the creek, the tall trees and far beyond.

"Lot of space out yonder," he said. "Shares?"

Jack nodded. "Chase mavericks, branding, cutting the bull calves," he answered. "A good cabin. Used to be a slave cabin."

Ely's lips quirked. "Yes sir," he said in agreement. "We help out, wait out the war here."

Jack looked over at the old spotted dog sleeping in the shade. "Can he bark?"

Now I'll build that lean-to I've been thinking about at the back of the house. More sleeping room for the folks come out of the bush to visit and sleep. Need to get a window from McGregor. Get Sallie that stove she wants.

Sallie and Elizabeth sat by the fireplace, sipping cool tea she'd flavored with sprigs of mint leaves. She'd dried her arms of washtub water where she was working and come inside with the black woman, just to visit and hear any news. She sat in a chair by the big farm table, Rosebud at her feet playing with her doll. Jeth lingered outside, listening to the men and their talk.

"You Miss Sallie," Elizabeth said.

"Yes."

"She a little one," Elizabeth said, examining Rosebud. "How old?" She sat in the best chair, sprawled a little, trying to get comfortable because of her pregnancy, adjusting pillows. But she seemed a little uneasy with this particular hospitality. As though she were a real guest.

"Almost three, in November." Sallie looked down at Rosebud with her doll, her fine little girl with her small bones, her delicate little face, her blue eyes like her mother's, her curling wisps of pale hair.

Elizabeth patted her belly. "November for this one too. He big already." She looked out the window. "The boy?"

Sallie looked out the window and saw Jeth with the men under the arbor, Jeth shaking hands with the Negro man in his own way of acceptance. The spotted dog lounged at his feet, where Jeth rubbed his ears. She smiled. "He's eight, but I think he wants to be old enough to do what the men do."

Just conversation. Sallie waited.

"Yes ma'am. This a good place. Ely say your man good folks from El Paso, back then."

Sallie's face registered a jumble of thoughts full of awkward hesitations. What could she call this haughty black woman? Who was she?

"You secessionists?"

Startled at her bluntness on a subject few Negro folks wanted to talk about because they'd been recently owned, and now they were supposed to be free. But they were still vulnerable in spite of new laws in this young independent Texas country. Everyone had heard the rumors of shootings, black lynchings.

Sallie answered. "No. Not Secessionists."

Elizabeth nodded. "Others around here? Secessionists?"

"Most left when it started."

Elizabeth pondered. "Now I say. We come looking. Looking for a safe place. When we hear about you folks, Ely want me to stay till the babe comes."

"You heard about us?" Sallie frowned. "How could you hear of us?"

Elizabeth nodded, her elegant face gone serious. "Your man a different kind. Everybody know. People just talk. You know. He not like them. Builds a big stockade like the soldiers do. Not no old fat farmer."

Sallie nodded, wanting to smile. "Yes."

"And you. When Ely hear, he know. He remember. Miss Sallie, he say."

Sallie thought about all this, this distant memory inching back from El Paso, her own faint memory of the thin, gangling Negro boy who often stared out the kitchen doorway at the tavern diners.

"He was just a boy---!"

Elizabeth smiled. "Yes ma'am. He just grow. Be a man. Now I say. I work. No charity. No fussing. My Ely teach me how to shoot. Hunt." Her smile widened. "I come here a free woman from back in Maryland State. I did indenture to get here, worked in a hotel kitchen for a year, up in Kansas. Then Ely come along. Now I am a free woman again and I am good at everything!"

Her smile changed everything, its brilliance of white teeth, red lips, and the softening in Elizabeth's sharp eyes changed everything for Sallie.

"Yes," Sallie said. She felt slightly amazed. So long ago! She smiled back, shyer than black Elizabeth, but more uncertain about any arrangement.

Arrangement? But she thought of the slave cabin, empty for months. She missed McGregor, and her aunt's busyness, her chatter, her endless opinions. She thought of this haughty woman who spoke with such self-confidence, the help with all the work she offered, the new child, and the weapons she'd seen as Ely rode in, his added protection in case of the rumored trouble. Extra guns if the Indians came raiding.

She placed her hand on her belly. A huge sense of relief from worry, one she hardly knew she carried, lifted from her.

"Yes," she said.

The fall of '64 the restless tribes, mostly Kiowas and Comanches and some Arapaho and Southern Cheyenne, finally, again, left the reservation in Indian Territory, Oklahoma. The young men broke out, warriors filled with grievances. They scorned the Territory, the reservation, the crude lives forced upon them there. They did not want to hoe corn, nor eat beef. They feared punishment for their rampant sporadic warfare and killings across the plains these past months with the military still gone. They rode west and north, recruiting friends among the Kiowa-Apache and the Northern Cheyenne, then came together in a huge gathering on the llano, near Red Bluff. More than one thousand Indians gathered and waited, listening to the chiefs and the elders talk of important business. The old men, the young men, the women and children, all listened to hear the decisions of these wise, bitter men. Finally, a few of the older chiefs withdrew with their young men, reluctant about more fighting, more killing, but most of the chiefs of the many gathered bands came to a hard agreement. They tamped tobacco into the fine red stone pipe bowl carved into the face of a fox, and then smoked the pipe, sealing their vows, one by one.

With the first frost, usually in November, a new year always began for the Comanches, but for Jack it was only late October again, and the day had warmed. In the old ways, the Comanche women and boys would be out beating the branches of big pecan trees to bring down the nuts for winter food, for making pecan bread. They would be calling back and forth and laughing. They'd be collecting the small bitter apples and the wild persimmons and plums to dry and mix with good buffalo meat and fat for their pemmican. The women would tend smoky fires, watching the weather and making whatever winter food they could of ground corn and bits of buffalo meat and fruit, they'd be tending children, working with scrapers and awls on scraps of hide for making new moccasins, new warm tunics, curing new buffalo robes for warm winter sleeping, and the men would send criers out to announce the coming journey to winter camp.

But this morning in October had soft balmy winds and a welcome quiet despite the general noise McGregor's old red-wheeled wagon made, and in spite of McGregor's frequent chatter. The brush and thickets along the road were busy with jays and higher up in the oaks and elms, redbirds fluttered.

"I expect we'll brand four, five hundred yearlings next year with Ely working," Jack said. "He'll round up a couple of hands to help."

McGregor nodded. "I plain don't remember that boy back in El Paso."

"Long time ago. You were busy hawking your goods in Juarez and gambling."

McGregor laughed. "Got the ranch and now the store. My dear God, I don't mind staying in one place for a time." He shook his head. "That black boy sure grew up. Got himself a baby coming soon."

Jack stroked Racer's neck and spoke softly to her. She danced restively and pulled at the bit, but she calmed at his touch. "You best be thinking about forting up the store. The front windows."

"It's getting late in the year for an uprising," McGregor sighed, tired of worrying about Indians, but he glanced around out of habit. It always paid to be careful, he liked to say to Jeth, by way of his frequent instructions.

Jack kept his silence, remembering Molly Grace's story.
Hundreds of Indians.

McGregor guided the team up the road, hauling a new, carefully packed and protected framed glass window for the new lean-to at the rock house, and a fine new woodstove with blue enameled panels and oven doors, and shiny brass handles; Sallie's new, heavy expensive iron cook stove ordered through a catalog and now firmly tied down in the back of McGregor's wagon. A rare gift, a pending surprise.

"Now Mariah Matilda's going to fuss at me for one of these fancy stoves," McGregor muttered. That woman had been visiting with Sallie and Rosebud, she hadn't seen the blue stove yet. McGregor braced himself with chatter, thinking about the uncomfortable reunion waiting ahead of him.

"Another blue one?" Jeth asked. He rode on a saddle pad cinched on the back of the sorrel horse with the clipped ear. He liked being with the men, carrying the stove, thinking about the look on his mother's face, but mostly he daydreamed about the sorrel horse, maybe now his own horse.

"No sir, not another blue one---," McGregor grumbled, then sat upright as one of the team mules suddenly stopped, lifted her head and brayed loudly.

"Shit," Jack said. He reined in Racer, staring around. Listening. The noise would carry for a mile, if anyone was listening, maybe the Indians---.

"Easy," McGregor said to Jack. "She's just a noisy fool mule. It's her mule personality."

Jack watched the woods, uneasy. Nothing new. Racer danced, worried the bit in her mouth, threw her head.

McGregor launched into his latest tale, carried along to his new store by a wandering man who came out of the bush with a banjo slung across his back, who called himself a troubadour and rode a burro so small that his feet almost dragged on the ground.

"Had a white beard down to his belly button, ate all our dinner, piled up his plate and drank a gallon of beer," McGregor complained, but he was never one to begrudge a hungry wanderer.

"Claimed Indians never bothered him, thought he was crazy. He sang for his supper wherever he went, but mostly he traded peyote buds and Mexican cigars, in little paper cases. Reeled off stories of stone prisons in Mexico years back, and old abandoned Spanish convents made into hospitals filled with waves of sick men, *Anglos,* from everywhere, Mexican soldiers, stricken with cholera, the *vomita* and leprosy." McGregor shook the reins and the mules stepped out. "Leprosy, my dear God. I wondered if he didn't have it himself, but we fed him anyway."

"Santa Ana still president back then, I expect" Jack said. The black mare danced along the road and wanted to run whenever she saw a clear trail or an opening in the woods. He reined her carefully, firmly, still training her.

"Provisional president," McGregor corrected. "This crazy banjo fellow said they all hated Santa Ana. He was just a mean despot of a man---."

"Yep. Killed a lot of Texians."

"He did." McGregor said. "This feller said there weren't enough doctors for those hospitals. A lot of foreigners from England and Ireland, Scotland, doing business down there. McGregor rubbed at his beard which was beginning to show a trace of gray. "Now it's the French and that Maximillian fellow from Austria. Says he's the emperor of Mexico, but Juarez has the people behind him---."

"Politics," Jack said, then laughed. "I'm sounding damn near as bad as you---."

Racer's ears started swiveling, searching. She shook her head, she groaned, then squealed. Jack felt her muscles bunch under him, tense, bunching for flight.

"Stop!" Jack said, to McGregor, to Jeth.

They stopped.

"But---."

"Listen!"

Jeth looked puzzled, then remembered his own tree house vigils.

They listened, staring, straining. They heard no more birdsong, only the scrape of Racer's churning hoofs scuffing up the road, her breathy snorts, a mule's dusty sneeze. But beyond that, suddenly they began to hear popping sounds. Far, far away they heard the distant popping of gunshots behind them, gunshots ahead of them. Random scattered sounds in a day that was still soft and bright.

"Get in the thicket!" Jack ordered McGregor. "Get your gun, hide in that thicket!"

"What---?" McGregor began.

"Hide, damn it! Get in there!"

McGregor, both portly and older, made a fumbling jump off the wagon seat and landed in the dirt. He scrambled to his feet, grabbed his rifle and looked at Jack. He saw his alarm, the hard focus, the sweeping stares everywhere into the brush and thickets by the road, back down the road, up the road ahead toward the rock house.

"Indians," McGregor said calmly as he understood. He looked at Jeth.

"He's with me," Jack said. "Stay quiet, don't shoot. Now hide! Get!"

They had to leave the heavy wagon and the mules standing in their harnesses, no time to cut away the harness of one mule to give McGregor a mount, although he considered this in a frozen moment.

"Get!" Jack yelled at him.

McGregor turned and plunged into the thickets and brambles by the side of the road. Deep, deep. Hide.

Racer began to crow hop and pull at the reins. Jack rode her over the footprints of McGregor's flight into the thickets until they were gone.

She can smell an Indian a mile away.

Ahead, Jeth sat the back of the sorrel horse, staring back at Jack.

"Run," Jack said to Jeth. He drew his rifle from his saddle holster, his heartbeat like mounting thunder in his chest. "Run!" he yelled to Jeth.

He let Racer go.

He had to hold the black mare back, she was too fast and Jeth had fallen behind, the Comanche sorrel a fast-enough horse, but no match for the mare.

No smoke. Jack saw no smoke, yet. He smelled no smoke. Saw no burning cabins, barns, hay---.

Jack remembered the mule's loud bray.

He couldn't hear any more popping gunshots with the pounding hoof noise the horses made. They flew past big trees, ranches, ranch roads, silent neighbors who were strangers, he saw stock running, chased across a field, saw dogs running, barking but he couldn't hear them, then he saw sudden movement through the brush, distant, horses and riders, paint ponies, bays and roans, and nearer he heard a yipping sound, piercing, high human voices in a wild celebration.

But those ponies and riders couldn't catch them as they raced along the road, even if they'd tried. Jack knew by the sounds of their screams and shouts that the Indians were too busy killing the settlers, counting coup, looting the farm houses and ranches, stealing stock, stealing captives.

Sallie.

He kept looking back at Jeth, who leaned forward on the sorrel, hanging on, elbows flying and boot heels pounding at the sorrel's sides, trying to goad him to greater speed. Jack saw Jeth's face stiff and white with intent.

He knows. But Ely's there. He'll have the gate closed---.

White foamy sweat gathered on Racer's neck, her flanks, on the sorrel. The sorrel stumbled but caught his pace again and they flew on.

Not fast enough.

Oh God, Jack thought. *Oh God.*

He saw the road torn up, pocked with unshod hoof prints, then nothing. He stopped for a moment to let Jeth catch up, to let the horses blow, and heard the nearer pops of gunshots, only that. Settlers were dying in a terrible silent slaughter, he heard the yells of the Indians start up again as they killed, the yips and Comanche screams of triumph as they pulled scalps from the living and the dead.

They flew on. The horses labored but ran hard. At the ranch road down to the rock house he saw the road again churned up, scores of unshod hoof prints going down as they flew, a chaos of prints, dust, and he heard one long scream.

Oh God!

He saw the big stockade gate standing open, something jammed in the gap. A wagon turned on its side, scattered boxes, a mule down in its traces, thrashing, beating its head against the dirt, riddled with arrows. The mule screamed again. Dust hung in the air and wove down to the trees and thickets of the creek.

They'd emptied the corral, everything gone. They'd swarmed over the fallen wagon, the thrashing mule, into the rock house yard, up toward the blue door.

Jack kicked the mare and she flew through the gate, over the fallen wagon, over the mule, into the yard. Jeth followed, the sorrel stumbling, falling, Jeth scraping into the dust. Jack saw two bodies on the ground, one a half-grown boy. The man's body moved but he was already dead, the boy's face was smashed into the dirt, the top of his head raw and hairless. They'd taken the time to pull both scalps. They'd been here long enough to cut the man's hands off for trophies and use knives in addition to their war arrows that were made for the ribs of human enemies. Something hung from one of the old apple trees, but the yard was empty of everything but death. Jack jumped from the mare before she'd skidded to a stop. He ran to the broken blue door.

He saw Mariah Matilda holding her head, screaming, weeping. He saw Sallie. He stumbled to the bed, he stood above her. He was stunned by her blood, her face. He just stood above her. He couldn't move. He couldn't breathe. Then, after a long time that was only moments, he sat down on the bed. He sat beside her, his legs shaking.

He put his hand on her folded hands. They were still warm, but cooling. His heart felt stunned. He stared.

She lay on the bed where they had loved each other so many times, so well. Her face was composed, as though Sallie Rainie slept with the sweetest of dreams. They had not taken her hair, perhaps in respect because of her fierce defense of her young. Her arms, the side of her head, her neck, the part of her breast he could see beyond the torn fabric of her dress, her hands, all showed wounds, cuts, battering. A war ax, a club. Her hands were folded over her belly, over the knife slashes that had ended her life.

He stared down into Sallie's face, looking deeply. Moments passed again but he didn't notice. He wiped his eyes. He felt the jolt, the quaking in his chest, the final deep realization. He wanted to cry out like Mariah Matilda, but he didn't. Not yet. He bent over Sallie and kissed her. He kissed her again. He lifted her against his chest and held her for a long time. But she had truly gone.

They would have taken her, but she fought. They would have abused her, maimed her, raped her, humiliated her, laughed at her, scorned her, spit on her. But she fought, for herself and for her young.

The gold nugget was gone, torn from her neck. He would never see it again, he would never see Sallie again, never feel her---.

Moments, only terrible moments.

Then he turned away, trying to hold all of it. He heard the woman's screaming, her cries of woe. He heard Jeth's scream, a boy's scream of anguish. He caught Jeth's wild rush, then let him go to his mother.

He looked around the room, saw the curtains torn from the windows, the great feather mattress ripped and scattered, feathers drifting in any movement of the air. He saw a pile of debris, rags, an eviscerated doll, arms and head ripped off.

"Rosebud," he said.

Mariah Matilda's cries rose again. "She's gone, they took her! She's gone---."

Jeth turned from his mother, his face a mask of grief, a smear of her blood on his hand. He looked around the room. He looked out the door. He took a scant moment, thinking, then he ran hard from the room, out the door, out into the yard.

Rosebud.

He found the dead man, the boy, all lying in twisted bloodied heaps. He found Ely, over near the apple trees beneath Jeth's tree house. The Indians had tried to hang him up, but they were in a hurry, so they cut off the bottoms of his feet and tore off a patch of his scalp. They left the arrow embedded in his chest.

Ely was tenaciously alive. He cursed when Jack came to lift him. He tried to speak the names but there was too much blood in his mouth.

Elizabeth.

Jeth watched his father carry Ely into the house. He looked around at the dead man, the boy in the yard, their wounds, their faces. He saw the strong gate his father had built but now it stood open, jammed open by the bird man's wagon, the bird cages strewn, broken. He saw the hole under the thick picket stockade, freshly dug over near the barn. He saw Pup, the old spotted dog, sprawled dead, arrows sprouting from his body. He saw nearby one of Rosebud's tiny blue shoes.

They made a pallet on the bed in the new half-finished lean-to, grabbing whatever the Indians had left behind to soften Ely's bed. Jack laid Ely down, almost rough in his haste. Ely cursed again in a whisper. Mariah Matilda, face red and wet with her grieving, her dress stained red with blood, bent over to look at Ely's wounds, her breath coming in slowing sobs.

Finally, she took a deep gasping breath and just said, "He was too heavy. I couldn't –." She shuddered with pain and began to cry again, softly, in another wave of grief.

Jack saw that she had blood high on her right shoulder, from a bullet or lance that had gone through and left a seeping wound high in her back. It looked to be a clean wound, with drying blood, but her right arm hung at her side.

"I shot one," she muttered, and drew another deep breath, another sob. "McGregor's shotgun---I shot him, he had a birdcage on his head, he---." She sobbed again, almost a crazy laugh at such an ugly memory.

"Jeth, get in here!" Jack yelled, but Jeth didn't answer. He groped around for clean rags, anything clean. To Mariah Matilda he said, "Wash his feet and his head, where's that damn whiskey jug---?"

"I don't know, I---."

"Find it! Pour it on his feet and his head! Don't touch that arrow!" He grabbed his rifle and ran outside, out into the afternoon yard past Sallie's dooryard flowers.

"Jeth!"

He saw the man and boy, dead in the churned dust, dead from arrows, cut, mutilated, blood still wet. The bird man's wagon jammed in the gateway, the mule finally dead. He knew the man. The bird man. He saw old Pup lying dead by the hole dug half under the stockade wall, Rosebud's blue shoe. The ground was a litter of sign, boots, moccasins, a broken arrow, cartridge casings but no settler's weapons left behind. He saw the bloody marks of something dragged across the yard,

I shot one, she'd said

He saw the sorrel, head down from the run, he saw Racer's hoof prints from where he'd left her, and where her iron shod hoofs had churned up the yard dirt.

She can smell an Indian a mile away.

He saw Jeth's boot prints running across the yard to the mare, where she'd reared back and stomped and churned at the smell of the Indians. He saw that was where Jeth's boot prints stopped.

He stood in the yard, turning, looking at all that had happened.

Sallie is gone.

He grabbed the reins of the sorrel and followed the sign out the gate, followed Racer's jump over the broken bird wagon, the sorrel faltering, stumbling on. He followed Racer's flying prints down through the tangles of brush and willow. Along the creek.

Sallie's gone.

Rosebud.

Thickets and brambles. Cutbanks and caves and churned mud. He lost the sign where Racer went into the water. He followed the direction, the sorrel laboring.

He heard the popping of gunshots too far away, then others much closer, then nothing. The silence of the raid sank his heart in deeper fear.

Jeth

How many? Where? How far? Four miles down the creek, five miles, then all sign lost. No sign in the mud and leaves. Nothing.

He yelled for his son. No answer.

He turned back, looking for sign where Racer had left the water.

Jeth.

No sign. Gone.

He stood in the doorway and felt the blow of discovery all over again, as though he did not already know Sallie was gone. He walked to the bed and just looked down at her. Then he walked to the new lean-to where Mariah Matilda wept and labored over Ely.

He took the arrow embedded in Ely's chest and moved it gently. No fresh blood welled out. He moved the arrow again and found it was loose, not embedded into a bone nor stopping up a bleeder, but at some deep place it had touched Ely's lung. Now it slipped out. He poured whiskey into the wound, Ely groaned. He wiped Ely's mouth free of blood. Maybe he would live, if he was tough enough, if he was lucky.

"She tried to stay," Mariah Matilda said suddenly. She wiped at her face. "Oh God, she tried---."

Jack stared at her

"---she just wanted to see you again. She---she just wanted to see you again---."

Jack shook his head. No more. He felt the jolt in his chest, the fierce pain, the grieving. He turned to her shoulder, her wound.

Sallie is gone.

"I came in. I was in the privy when---." She began to cry again. She held her arm.

"Enough now." His voice sounded coarse, raw. He hardly knew what he said.

Mariah Matilda nodded. "I shot one!"

She'd tried to stay for him. To see him again.

"---in here! I shot him! They were going to---someone blew a bugle. A bugle! Oh God. They all ran out---."

Jack thought all the blood on the floor was Sallie's. It didn't matter. He poured whiskey into Mariah Matilda's wound, then his hand fell away. He stared into the empty space of the rock house.

Jeth

Rosebud

The others.

"I have to build a box." He wiped his eyes, "---boxes."

He wrapped her in her wedding dress early the next morning, soft white muslin, the dress the Comanches and the Kiowas had not found in the trunk under the bed. They had taken her second favorite dress with the little blue flowers and the tear in the collar she had mended. Everything else.

He carried her to the box wrapped carefully in the torn bed quilt. She was so weightless, so pallid in death. He laid her into the box gently, carefully.

His wife was in a coffin. In a box.

He spread her hair. He spoke to her. The morning was sunless, and she loved sunny blue days. He apologized for the sunless day, for leaving her. For the children. For his tears, for everything.

McGregor, back in the night, with his wagon, and one mule with a slash in its flank, and Sallie's new blue stove battered on one side by a war ax, stood by the two graves he and Jack had dug near Jeth's apple trees. While Jack finished the boxes for the dead by lantern light in the barn, McGregor caught up his mule and dragged the bird man's wagon and dead mule from the gate, away from the stockade.

"Enough," he muttered, the only words for many of the settlers this morning. His heart filled with sadness and rage. "My dear God, enough."

They'd finished the graves before daylight, and the two boxes made from the wood meant to finish the rock house's new lean-to, now were filled.

One man who brought song birds to the lonely women settlers, and one half grown boy Jack scarcely remembered, sharing one grave, and Sallie Rainie in her own. They spoke words, each as he could find, while Mariah Matilda wept quietly. McGregor wiped his face with a big white handkerchief. Inside the rock house, Ely struggled to survive.

"I'll make up some markers," McGregor muttered. "Abe Simmons and his boy---what's his name? The bird man---." He shook his head. "Who will we notify? I sent word with the militia boys when they came through before daylight." His voice fell away. He shrugged.

Jack stood quietly looking down at Sallie's grave. She was there, in the earth. He hardly heard.

"They're still chasing the Indians," McGregor said, speaking of the men, the settlers and ranchers and any who had lived through the raid, some with injuries, some uninjured. "They got most of the livestock. But it's useless trying to chase them. They'll just scatter into the bush. Like they do." He looked at Jack. "Carson said he lost five men from his Border Regiment in a fight. Rifles and arrows. He said eleven settlers were killed here that they know of, maybe more. Caught out in the open, or in running fights. A few women and children hid in thickets. In caves along the river cutbanks. They haven't found everybody. He thinks seven women and children were taken." He shook his head. "My dear God. He said there had to be a thousand of them. Comanches. Kiowas, Arikara, Arapaho---a thousand savages with their camps and women. How---?" He shook his head again.

Mariah Matilda held her right arm in a crude sling. She raised her head, her cheeks slightly flushed with fever and weeping, her eyes hard. She stared at Jack. "You'll go?"

"Yes ma'am," Jack answered. His voice still sounded hoarse in his own ears, unused. His heart felt like cold stone, weighing him down to the earth. He knew it would rise soon enough, with rage for all Sallie had suffered, for all he had lost.

"Then kill them, the savages---," Mariah Matilda said.

Jack turned away, hearing her bitter voice. Now he had to catch up the winded sorrel, and go find Rosebud and the boy.

"No," said McGregor. "No, not yet."

Jack turned, glared at McGregor.

"What will they do with the captives now?" McGregor asked quietly. "If you chase them? You? You're not one of these homesteaders." He drew a long breath. "You---if you threaten them?"

Jack stared at him.

"The settlers think you are more of a threat to the captives. You are a threat."

Jack finally answered, "They'll kill them."

"Yes. They'll be in a hurry. Running. They'll kill the captives."

Jeth. Rosebud

Elizabeth, any, all.

Jack stared.

"Some of them may know you. The Comanches---if they know you---."

Now he let the truth fill him again with his rage. But it was the truth, the terrible hard truth, and he slowly knew it.

"They want time. Just some time," McGregor said. "They say just some time---."

"Who says?"

"The ones of us who are left."

They stood by the graves, silent. Mariah Matilda bowed her head. Jack stared out at the day, the new morning silence.

"They say they'll send someone to trade. To talk. Negotiate. Someone they trust. After the fighting, the Kiowas, the Comanches, all of them, they're all still fired up. But they'll get hungry. Maybe weeks. They'll want payment. They'll try to make talk."

"I'll go."

"No, not you. No."

His past, his skills---his anger.

But he understood that the settlers would not agree. He was an uncomfortable mystery among them. Not one of them. They had lost wives, children, friends. They would want a trusted man to talk to them, a calm man, a negotiator.

Honeytalk.

Not someone the Indians might recognize, rumors, a man with skills as cruel and keen as their own.

Rumors.

The settlers---they're afraid. Of me. Maybe they're right.

Now the settlers were busy out hunting for lost men and boys, the surviving women, lost children still hiding, livestock. Then they would eventually be gathering, grieving and telling their stories.

Jack saw that now there was little to do, as the day brightened, but help each other, tend wounds as best they could, search for stolen stock, count all their losses and wait.

He found his hat and started toward the sorrel, but the sorrel stood by the water tank in the corral, his head low.

"I gave him grain but he's finished from the run. Take my mule, the Indians took the other one." McGregor said

"Where are---." Mariah Matilda began,

"To Belknap. Wherever there's a doc, I'll find one."

Yes," Mariah Matilda said tiredly. "Ely, others, we need help."

Days later, he held the journal in his hands like something foreign, a bit of debris left from the raid, ugly. An oddity he didn't want to touch. Something from the terrible past.

Finally, he opened it. He had no ink or pen, only a dull, broken lead pencil left on the mantel, salvaged from the trash, the raid.

On a fresh page he began, then hesitated. He wrote slowly.

Elm Creek, Texas, October 1864.
Sallie Flynn Rainie.
She's gone.

PART III

LITTLE SISTER GIRL
৵৽

He lived in a boarding house and stabled his horse at the livery in San Antonio de Bexar weeks after the Elm Creek raid. He came to talk to merchants who remembered back to the days when the Comanches rode angrily into town in the bad time after the big Council House fight back in '57, when the military demanded all captives returned.

After the massacre, with all the chiefs and warriors shot down when they came in to smoke the pipe and talk, the Texians were hated more than the White Dog soldiers. Angry warriors came into Bexar with captives, children, women who were sometimes mutilated with tattoos and cut noses. Women who had been raped and beaten and were now spoiled and unwanted by many distraught settlers. The Comanches demanded payment because the soldiers wouldn't pay with soldier rifles, or because they weren't hungry, or because they liked to see the fear in the faces of the White Dogs.

But they had brought captives here, into Bexar.

Long time ago, he thought.

Days after he started his search in Bexar, the Comanches brought a new captive, a girl, white, dirty, not Rosebud. She was older by years, only a half-grown child. Her hair was a dingy brown, thin, her lips swollen with sores. They had cut her nose to disfigure her, but not badly. He watched as a settler family hesitated, then went to her and held her while she screamed with terror.

So, the little band of Comanches brought this child to Bexar for trading, because now they were hungry for corn. The winter and some kind of sickness had damaged them with starvation and a score of deaths. They had no mesquite seed cakes, no pemmican or corn, little poor meat, rabbits, prairie dogs. The shaggy buffalo had vanished. They talked peace, like the Fredericksburg Treaty Comanches, and claimed to have other White Dog captives, but they often lied to get what they wanted, and because the White Dogs were so foolish.

With hope, Jack smoked the pipe with them and asked about Jeth and Rosebud, about any captives, but they claimed no knowledge and no interest. They were southern Comanches, they were poor men.

"What man asks about these captives?"

"Say it is The Man Who Walks Away. Let the People know."

He wandered through the streets and taverns listening to stories, He rode out into the bush to find targets and practice with his Colt. He found jobs, shoeing horses and mules at the livery, plastering cracks in old adobe walls after the hard winter, repairing old brush arbors when they collapsed after snow. Stockmen and their hands drove herds of mustangs into San Antonio for weekly Tradedays and scrub races, he stared as the Military led three camels through town, all laden with big packs. Someone yelled out a joke at the big ugly animals, an experiment that the Military didn't want anymore. He watched the camels disappear, he watched the trading, he searched the crowds and wandered on.

Now and then something stirred in him, something hard and bitter. He didn't know what.

He had left dates and names, crude drawings and descriptions on posters and flyers at every trading post, every Indian agency, every reservation and township, every cow camp along trails out in the bush.

Lost children taken in the Elm Creek Raid, Young County, in October of 1864---.

He had posted notices in every newspaper and journal.

But they had vanished into the thousands of acres, into the vast prairie silence.

Once he found three wandering Indian boys, refugees from the reservations, breaking out in defiance of the hated treaties. They hunted for straggling buffalo, but the southern herd of shaggies had vanished. He spoke to them in Comanche or hand talk, but they knew nothing, and stared angrily and yelled insults at this Texian, who wore moccasins and talked like one of the People.

---*lost children*---.

The silence he met was like the deepest darkness of his anguished mind. But it was just the profound emptiness of the land, familiar to him; the terrible silent mysteries of the endless ancient prairies.

He'd left Elm Creek after Ely learned to hobble again, cursing at every step. Weeks after the raid, Nigger Britt Johnson brought the captives back.

They will make him pay, the hostiles will find him and kill him for that. Does he know it?

But he had to follow the stories, the news back to Bexar where captives still appeared, like the girl with the clipped nose.

He made trips by stage roads and livery mounts, depending on the weather, to see McGregor and Mariah Matilda.

"No new word?" She asked.

"No ma'am."

He checked on Ely, thinking about the spring work, rain, tornados, the flooding creek, the roundup, catching and branding mavericks.

He stopped to see all the settlers he'd known along the creek.

Molly Grace talks mostly about nothing. They lost one boy for the South, Joeboy, a good kid, and then another for the North.

Bad kid, he remembered Joeboy's idle complaint when Jeth snatched away some of Sallie's apple sweets cooling in the kitchen window.

Bad kid.

No news again.

He looked down towards the creek, remembering hunts there, showing Jeth snares, how to find the best bee trees, squirrels, stalking deer. Telling him the old stories when he pestered.

But not often enough. Maybe not enough.

Ely hobbles around pretty good, slow chasing cattle. Tough spirit, cusses a lot, got himself some wrangler help. Likes moccasins better than boots. Won't wear boots. That Elizabeth had herself a boy when Britt brought her back. She won't talk about the Comanches. They are doing a good job here.

He stood in the rock house and saw all the changes. He saw no tintype pictures on the mantel, no picture of Sallie. Keepsakes stolen in the raid. No bits of interest and memorabilia, only a stone found down by the creek, a bird's nest.

Red Birds, she always called them.

"Y'all care that---," Elizabeth asked about all the changes, hesitant, her face creased with concern.

Jack studied the new stove, its blue enameled panels, its brass handles, a gift too heavy for the Indians to steal from McGregor's abandoned wagon the day of the raid.

"No Ma'am," Jack answered Elizabeth. But the white rage rose in him suddenly as he thought of some Comanche buck wearing the tintype picture of Sallie Rainie around his neck, a trophy, like they wore old peace medals.

He saw other arrangements; other changes Elizabeth had made. He looked at the bed covered with an unfamiliar, sprawling patch quilt and knew he would never sleep there again. He walked outside and stood by her grave near the old apple trees. Jeth's apple trees, with his tree house still in its branches. He spoke to Sallie, hardly knowing what he said. Just words.

He left again, knowing that he could never live in this house but only come back for the help he could give Ely chasing down mavericks, cutting and branding the yearlings, driving them in the fall to join up with one of the big new cattle drives.

Cattle barons they call them, he thought. *Cattle barons.*

But he could only lose his grieving for his woman, his children, in the hardest work, and he sought it. He could distract his thoughts as he looked around at all that was once familiar, or by talking to neighbors, listening to their stories of the raid, their losses, and by gathering news

He wandered the reservations in Oklahoma, the Territory, the Indian Agencies, dodging the gangs of Mexican horse thieves and stray hostiles. He asked questions, searched faces, children's faces.

---*lost children*---.

Sometimes he saw brown faces that stirred his memory and he stopped and offered tobacco and spoke, but no one had an answer. The old men didn't know, wouldn't speak. The women didn't know, looked away, wouldn't speak.

---*little Millie Durgan?*

He thought about the handyman everyone called Nigger Britt, who had set out with a guide, weeks after the raid. In spite of negotiations for the Elm Creek captives, his slow hard-won success in trading for the women and children, for his own woman and children, he couldn't bring all of them back. He couldn't bring his own dead boy back after the raid. Britt, formerly a slave but mostly a man who helped everyone, got along with most of the friendlier Indians, the ones who liked to trade or just got hungry or drunk. The Indians had a wary trust of this man who wasn't like the hated White Dog Texians, with his black skin and his buffalo wool hair; so with winter upon them, they took blankets and bags of corn, and the captives eventually came back.

Little Millie Durgan didn't come back.

Baby Rose Rainie, Jeth Rainie didn't come back.

He knew those he questioned on the reservations were lost in silence, in their own profound strife and suffering, their own confusion and new lives of bleak, mismanaged captivity.

The hard news of Mr. Lincoln's death came to the remote frontier settlements weeks later, to towns by telegraph and lurid newspaper headlines a few days after Mr. Lincoln fell. Jack hardly noticed, until he found himself in the midst of the great celebrations as bitter Southern men and women celebrated Mr. Lincoln's death.

The Great Conflict ended in April of '65, with the end of the war, which never seemed to end.

But many wiser men and women in the North and South alike, wept with sorrow because so many believed Mr. Lincoln would have saved what was left of the South from the swarms of angry, looting soldiers; from politicians and corrupt officials preying on the defeated farmers, driven from their land by starvation; and city folk who buried their treasures while their homes burned to the ground, as the Yankee army marched through.

Carpetbaggers. Rapacious legal criminals.

But the Rebs fought on in gangs up in Kansas and Missouri, attacking whole towns, anywhere they found Unionist sympathizers and Jayhawkers. Men wearing the blue sometimes hung dead from old oak trees along the trails. Mobs of hoodlums roamed through the south, hungry soldiers, many with missing arms or legs, fell by the wayside trying to survive long enough to get home.

The Indian hostiles ran wild during the Conflict and its ending days, killing settlers all across the frontier, taking captives and raiding with impunity outside the reservations, in spite of treaties they had signed with their marks. They scorned the White Dogs and their big tribal war. The Minute Men, the Regulars and militias, the farmers, fought back with shootings and hangings of their own.

Finally, the Union military came back in force, tough and angry from the war they had fought so hard, and won. Now, again, the military ordered all Indian captives returned, all the wild Indians subdued, controlled or dead.

---*lost children*---.

Weeks passed, and then years.

The first time Jack noticed the lines of men and boys leading to the little shop on the plaza in San Antonio, with the modest sign, *LA LUZ*, he wondered.

But he went on to the post office he had haunted daily for months, years, reading newspapers and public notices of wandering oxen, offers of work, stockmen offering awards for stolen horses, lost relatives from the war, warnings about panthers roaming the woods, gators in the marshes and bayous to the east, missing children like his own, or little children who had just wandered off into the woods. He studied notices that grew weekly, wanted men, thieves and shooters who had stolen and murdered, bad Mexican gangs and thieves.

The next week he noticed the lines again outside the little shop *LA LUZ*, caught the enticing aroma, and went over to look.

THE BEST APPLE PIE WEST OF THE MISSISSIPPI

Blue words, added to the wooden sign in elegant Spanish and English.

He stepped to the back of the line and finally entered a little shop, hardly more than a *jacal*, and full of the aroma of baking bread, of spicy foods and sweet fruit baked into pastries and pies. Seven crude, brightly painted tables with chairs sat to the right, crowded with men eating half-pies, whole pies, pastries and *sopas* with relish. Through the open back door, under brushy grapevine arbors, he saw outdoor ovens, long tables, and hurrying boys and women. He bought a pie from a woman standing behind the counter, busy with sales. Younger than he, she was tall, slender, dressed in white, with coppery hair curling all around her face and luminous hazel eyes. She looked at him with indifference, as she looked at all the men lined up behind him.

So many men who want her to notice them, he thought, who want this pretty woman to smile. *I want her to smile.*

She took his money and turned to the next.

He noticed her on the plaza of San Antonio the next day, riding a big high-stepping black horse. She rode astride wearing white, a hat tipped on her head, and seemed to enjoy the horse's elegance and animation; but she soon disappeared into the busy crowds. After that he saw her walking, stopping at vendors' carts, looking and choosing fresh fruits and vegetables. Two small *peon* boys followed, carrying baskets.

He went back again to the *jacal* a few days later, bought a pie from the woman with the luminous hazel eyes, who looked at him without any recognition, and took his money.

He left thinking about the woman with the luminous hazel eyes and the best apple pie west of the Mississippi.

He went back a third time, with a bushel basket of tart, fragrant red apples. The woman looked at the apples, looked at Jack Rainie, and smiled.

Her smile took on a hint of amusement. "I am Luz," she said.

He stopped by often; for apple pie; for Luz. Sometimes he brought apples when he could find them. Sometimes he found her seated at one of the tables, often with men who were older or younger, family members or suitors. Sometimes she sat with her head bent, a look of sadness in her luminous eyes. He sat with her when he could, when she allowed it, when others tended the customers of the little *jacal*. Once he stood to warn off a drunk teamster who wanted Luz, her youth, her elegant beauty, her sex. His expression said that she was only a common Mexican girl, of little consequence, and clearly available; but soon he found himself sprawled in the street with the crowd of hungry men laughing and jeering.

When he returned to the table he found Luz seated quietly, her chin lifted, her lovely eyes level. Her mouth formed the softly accented words. "Have I told you about my grandmother, *senor*?"

He smiled. "No Ma'am. Not yet."

When he came to sit with her in the following days, she never stayed long, and as time passed he imagined she left him sitting there alone with reluctance, and he shook his head at such wishful vanity.

He heard a young man call her Luzita.

Luzita. But he couldn't get past calling her *Ma'am*. He invited her to walk with him by the river, but she turned away.

Two days later, when he found her at a flower vendor's cart in the plaza, he asked her again.

She stood with her russet hair blowing in a soft breeze. She looked at him for a long moment, her eyes searching his face, searching for something.

Finally, she said, "My grandmother was a famous woman, *senor*." Her voice had a soft, elegant accent, even with her startling words to Jack. "Dona Alicia Magdalena. Everyone knew her. She was wise. She was famous. She shot three Indians dead, and chased the others off, when all the men were away from the *rancho,* chasing other hostiles. She saved her children."

He stared for a moment.

Yes, Sallie had tried to save her children.

But this girl didn't know him, his past, she had no idea. Then he let go of the memory.

So much spirit! He thought of this Luzita with growing appreciation.

"Well I am no Indian, Ma'am," he answered finally.

No Indian.

But he found himself struggling with the impulse to smile because of his admiration for this elegant Luzita girl.

He learned that she came from an old *Tejano* family that, after generations, still brought forth now and then children with the old Spanish Castilian blood in the form of reddish blonde hair, clear light-colored eyes and creamy skin.

Her family trained their fine high-stepping town horses, they tended their hand-made tack and saddlery business, and their sprawling old land grant fields of irrigated crops. Her mother had passed shortly after her birth, but she had an ageing, stern grandfather, Don Ernesto, and many sisters and many brothers and cousins and uncles who spent most of their time chasing Indians, and border rustlers, with the Rangers, and now with the Minutemen.

"They are warriors," she said once as they walked under the big trees along the river. Redbirds fluttered through the branches overhead. Her English words always came with that soft fluid accent, and he wondered about the little *jacal,* the pies, and why she often had a look of sadness. Why she seemed to be alone even among her family. He wanted to know all about her, almost with a sense of urgency.

The men of her family were compact, with watchful dark eyes full of intelligence. They were hard men, but they harbored a rare appreciation for the absurd in everyday life, which appeared in their love of wry stories and jokes. Their hair was sometimes curly, showing a bit of Basque and Mediterranean history. Their speech was a different sort of Spanish. They were *rancheros, vaqueros,* with jangling spurs and magic skills with *reatas.* They were *Tejanos,* people of a culture unto itself, although the name was often misused and scorned after all the years of foreigners and troubles. At *fandangos* and other celebrations, the old men sat at brightly painted tables, drank *pulque* and *tequila* with salt and slices of lemon, and told stories of the old fights over water rights, feuds, Indians, relishing jokes as they recalled the past.

"We had to go away sometimes," she said, telling Jack her own story. "In the bad times we had to leave Bexar because the Texian army thought we should be Confederates and wanted to take us away to fight, and sometimes they thought we were the bad Mexicans like that Santa Ana everybody hated." A moment of scorn crossed her face, then vanished as she went on with her story. "But we were *Tejanos. Rancheros.* Long time. People who knew us said we were the good Mexicans. This was our home. We always came back to our land and our ways---." She broke off and stared at the river water. "My father died in the big Fort Alamo fight. Two of my uncles, Rodrigo and Thomas, died fighting in Sam Houston's fight later. They were just boys."

But her uncles and brothers and grandfather, as they came and went with their Minute Men duties, noticed this tall Texian who appeared from nowhere. What of his past? Was he a *vaquero* from one of the big *Anglo* ranches they heard of, many thousands of acres out west in the *llano*? He didn't wear the big spurs that the old *vaqueros* always wore, spurs like their own. Had he ridden with the border *banditos* who plagued the old trace roads? Was he a trader of goods from Kansas or Missouri? Did he come like the ones they called *carpetbaggers*?

Or just another Texian?

They watched the two of them together as the weeks went by.

They spoke to this Texian with polite reserve, as proud men.

But they were watchful and some of the younger cousins spoke in anger.

In time Luz and the Texian spent long nights together. No one was surprised. She was so young, so headstrong and already a widow, although that hardship was just a practical fact in this widow-making country, and hardly uncommon after the big Yankee war,

Her menfolk watched and nursed their pride, they were hard men, practical, traditional. But when her brothers and cousins angrily protested this unknown *Anglo* man and her behavior with him, her answering words had the swift fire of temper, words as strong as their own angry words.

You will do him no harm! No harm!

He was not like the new *Anglos* who were often ignorant and rude and without manners. This one, this tall Texian, was not like that other, that boy from the past. This one, she believed, did no harm to her or to them.

"*Basta,*" she said quietly to them again, and often. "No more. Enough. Leave us to ourselves."

She lived in a small building off the grassy clearing, behind the busy restaurant with its brush arbors and outdoor ovens; one of several small, old adobe buildings well lived-in over the years; and now mostly used for storage and random emergencies. Her little house had one room with one small window. The walls were covered with colorful *serapes* and hangers holding her clothes, her hats, her shawls. Her shoes collected on the floor beneath. She had a white bowl and pitcher of water on a ledge, good water from the well outside, a looking glass on the wall. Her bed looked virgin, neat with colored weavings and spreads and big pillows. But it hid a mystery, their mystery.

In the night they often spoke, she of her day, her people, the hungry men who were her patrons, but there were empty places in her words, sentences that died away into silence.

Jack spoke his few words in answer and sometimes felt he had no words at all because his mind fled back to Sallie, to Jeth and little Rose.

He rolled onto his back and lay looking up into the darkness, gone away from her. Where?

Always back there. Into some darkness, some silence.

"Tell me," she finally said.

"What?"

"Tell me. About her."

Jack pondered. *Of course, she would guess. But how to speak of Sallie Flynn? Sallie Rainie?*

"She was my wife. My woman. She's dead."

Her silence seemed to fill the darkness. "I am sorry," she said.

"They killed her. Comanches, Kiowas."

"When?"

"'64. October---."

"I remember---there was a big raid. In Young county---."

"Yes."

Luz lay silent, imagining all of it.

Finally, she asked, "There were children?"

"They took both, the boy, a little girl."

They lay in silence and darkness.

"You go away from here," she said finally. "Then you come back."

He thought about those searches, the years of frustrations.

"*Si,* you look for them," she said, as an accepted fact, something she understood,

Jack drew a deep breath. "Yes ma'am, I'm looking."

Luz was silent for a long time. He thought she slept. "You have not left them," she said, another fact she understood.

"Never will," Jack said. He turned to her, gathered her to him. "There's room for you."

"I must tell you," she said on another night. They lay together in the familiar darkness after loving each other and listened to an owl's lonely call.

"You must tell me. Tell me what?"

"My family, they say you shame me."

In her world, maybe he shamed her. He thought of the Comanches, others of the People, the bold night-crawling, the younger girls who dared not walk alone without protection.

"You are protected," he said.

"*Si*, my family---."

"By me."

"They are very traditional." He felt her stir, almost resist him. "My family is traditional. The men are free to do as they please, but they want you to say words to me." Her voice took on a tone of hardness. Toward him? Toward her family? He didn't care.

He lay silent. What words? The words he had said to Sallie Flynn?

"Words they will understand."

They lay silent for a long time. Then she sighed. "Now I must tell you. There's more. It is very bad."

She waited, and felt a subtle tension leave him, felt him coming back and begin to listen.

"When I was very young---."

"You are still very young---."

She spread her fingers softly over the rare smile on his mouth.

"My family said I was headstrong. Foolish---always foolish. *Loco*. Too much like my grandmother. They admired her, but---." She paused. Her voice changed. "His name was Epi. He had a fire in his heart. So much anger. We ran away to another village." She drew a deep breath. "The *padre* blessed us, he forgave our sins and gave us penance. He married us---." She stopped.

He stroked her hair, thinking about her story, this headstrong girl, still so young, so full of ready spirit.

"But he was just a bad one, a *bandito,* he was a bad Mexican," she said sadly, but with an echo of her own anger. "I didn't know---," she paused again. "They got caught in a fight down on the border, he was a horse thief---they had a big herd, stolen from---the *alcalde* said they were trying to push the herd across the border into Mexico---."

He thought about this headstrong girl. He knew now why she was apart in her family. He held her and heard the rest.

"The *alcalde* asked me many questions. Names. Everyone hated these horse thieves---."

"Still do."

She fell silent, and he waited.

"They were all hanged up in the trees there, where they were caught, the *alcalde* told me---. Boys, all hanged."

He gave her a moment while she thought of her hard memories.

"It isn't over. It's getting worse," he said.

After another moment of silence, she answered. "*Si*, worse. But I thought he had a good fire."

Too hot, Jack thought, and he wondered about himself. *The fire was too hot.*

After that, she was a young widow, angered by her foolishness, even by her sadness, but still a headstrong girl, and her family watched over her, especially among all those lonely foreign men, fresh from baths in the bath houses, hair slicked back, hats in hands, who came looking, maybe even courting, offering everything.

But she had changed. She had embraced a good fire of her own. A hard fire that burned away her childhood fancies. She allowed herself to be proud of her many skills, her Castilian heritage. She taught herself Texian English. She told her family respectfully that while she wanted to be a Mexican *Tejano* woman, like them in most ways, there was change everywhere, in Bexar, everywhere, and she wanted to be free.

"Yes, I wanted to be free!" She sighed. "Such a fuss. Such a scandal. Another one, they said. Like my grandmother." She paused, reflecting. "They were surprised by such an idea. It was not traditional. They forgot how strong she was, how they once admired her. But my grandfather didn't forget. He keeps a picture of her in his house, a big picture by a painter who came to Bexar before the American war. He painted her with hair like autumn leaves and eyes that were calm and certain---of what? He painted her all done up in ruffles and fancies she never wore. Grandfather didn't care, he said the painter died of yellow fever after he finished the picture. I used to stare at that picture." She paused. "I knew I wanted to be free of the old ways. Not just a wife with many babies. I wanted to make something good."

LA LUZ. Her *jacal*, her little place in the chaos of busy change, out in the teeming streets of Bexar, her *jacal* filled with tempting aromas where she made good things. With hard work and stubbornness, and of course the help of Holy Guadalupe, whom she prayed to in the dark of every night, Luzita Ramos made herself free.

He waited for more.

"My family," she finally said. "They are always away, always chasing *los Indios* or those bad men----. And you, I think you will go."

But he hadn't really answered her. He let it go, warm in this woman's bed, remembering Sallie.

They want me to say words they can understand, he wrote in his journal.

Sallie

This Luzita, she will not replace you. Never.

But if Sallie had been like the sunshine, Luzita was surely the bright autumn, an often-intense haven with her quick wise smiles, her fire, her words of endearment he didn't always understand, but welcomed. In a world that seemed to embrace tradition, her world, she was hopeful of her future, fiercely determined. She was elegant in her demeanor, thoroughly beautiful in her own way, her face, her soft creamy skin, her mobile expressions, the lushness of her body as he knew it, and his heart began to melt a little when he saw her standing in her doorway, waiting to greet him.

He came to marvel a little at this spirited Luzita. Too often in this hard frontier struggle to survive, to prevail, women died young in childbirth or random violence.

Why do they come at all? He wrote in his journal.

But he knew, as he knew from Comanche women and from his own Sallie, that women had the hearts of lions.

It's October of 1867, he wrote.

Three years. No news.

Talk of Goodnight and Loving making a new trail to Fort Sumner in New Mexico. 2,000 head. None of ours. Going around the Comancheria. Good luck to them. Maybe better luck going up Chisholm's road.

But he didn't believe in luck, neither Comanche luck nor Texian luck.

In the late summer of '68 he began to hear the rumors.

He dismounted in front of the house, now a store with a sign on the Elm Creek road, looking at all the changes.

Looks like McGregor's made himself a good place here.

Jack took the bundled fliers from his saddlebag and headed for the doorway. The walls of McGregor's store were strong split logs, well chinked to keep out drafts, and held two windows with sturdy open shutters added to the front of the old house. An older man with a long white tangle of beard and dressed in greasy fringed buckskins like the old mountain men, walked through the doorway and paused. He just scowled at Jack and passed on by to McGregor's livery corral.

Jack stood in the doorway. He saw shadowed shelves inside, dry goods, boxes still unpacked, a bundle of early winter furs on a counter. Two customers lingered in conversation near where a woman silently sorted through merchandise. Mariah Matilda. He saw McGregor' broad smile.

"Well, well, my dear God! Get in here before the beer's gone!"

"Never happen here, I expect," Jack said with a smile. He touched his hat in greeting to Mariah Matilda, "Ma'am."

She studied him quietly. "Have you heard anything, Mr. Rainie?"

Mr. Rainie. Sallie's words.

"No ma'am. The military looks the other way. They want the captives back but nobody's pushing. There's no enforcing. They're out catching gun runners and fighting Indians now."

Mariah Matilda nodded. "I believe the children are gone."

"No," Jack said, but he couldn't say more.

"Sheridan's getting mad," McGregor said a few minutes later. He wiped down the counter in his store after the last customer left, then closed and locked the door. "Moonshine? Taos Lightning?" He offered. "It'll take the paint off the barn."

"No sir." He gestured to McGregor's beer.

McGregor set out a jar and filled it, then drank deeply from his own jar. "Where to?"

"Heading for the ranch. See if Ely needs any help. Whatever he needs."

"I'll make up a pack for you to take along. The missus wants molasses and some needles. Just came in. You hear about old Britt Johnson?"

"What?"

"Found him out on the road, dead and scalped. Just driving his wagon when they jumped him."

"They got him then." Jack felt a jolt at the news, but it was no real surprise.

McGregor heaved a long sigh. "How's Ely doing?"

"Doing good last time, I was here. Walks better. Hiring some hands to help out. Settled in. Still cusses up a storm."

A faraway look came into McGregor's face. "Settled in," he repeated. "I just read about a fellow, by the name of McCoy, in a Kansas newspaper a drover left here yesterday. Came from out west. Texas steers're still quarantined in Missouri and Kansas."

Jack nodded, not much interested, thinking about Britt Johnson, who'd finally paid with his life for bringing the Elm Creek captives back. He shoved a stack of new fliers toward McGregor. Words about lost children. Old words now.

"Seems this McCoy's bent on making a new trail up to a little town in Kansas. Says it's just a dead little place now with maybe 35, 40 people, but it's near a new railhead. McCoy's been talking to the railroad people. Kansas Pacific Railway. They're building the railhead there now. Texas longhorns're still quarantined but those folks want the business, so they don't much care about that cattle fever. You know how that goes. But there's opportunity, Jack. McCoy's sending out notices to the cattlemen; he's building stock pens for their cattle. Says Chisholm's old trade road's already there. Place they call Abilene, nothing much yet," McGregor said.

Across the store, Mariah Matilda turned her head again and stared at McGregor.

"No, no." McGregor said to her, "no, my dear. Just news. Talk. We're doing well here." He looked thoughtfully at Mariah Matilda and added quietly to Jack, "She doesn't smile much these days."

"She still talk about starting that school?"

"She hasn't got the heart for it yet. Its---," McGregor's voice trailed off into silence.

Jack drank. "No other news?"

"Old McNeely died a while back, one of the neighbors used to come to meetings and drink my beer. Folks said he carried a lot of lead from a fight when he was with the Rangers." McGregor paused, turned his head to look out the window.

"What" Jack said.

"And the damn Cheyenne're off raiding again, along with the Arapaho and some Comanches and others. Kiowas."

Jack frowned. "Where?"

"Mostly Kansas, Missouri, Nebraska, Northern Texas. The Santa Fe trail; they're running off the reservations and then running back. That way they try to get double allotments from the agents. They're fighting the railroads. Railroads building on free government land, then selling it to the settlers. Military's trying to talk peace at them."

Jack just listened, knowing there was more.

McGregor drew a heavy breath. "A gang of them killed fifteen settlers up in Kansas, took off some captives. Raped some of the women, killed some, they say."

After a minute, Jack asked, "Who says?"

"The troopers who come through here. Fort Cobb. You know they have big mouths. Mostly just boys bragging. My dear God. But there's talk about Sheridan. A party of Regulars came by last week hell bent for a fight."

Regulars, Jack thought. *Farmers, merchants, boys, stockmen.* Jack said, "There's mostly just military up north, Cheyenne, Arapaho."

McGregor nodded. He drank from his jar of beer and shook his head. He glanced across the store again to where Mariah Matilda, her back to them now, silently sorted through boxes of ammunition. McGregor said in a softer voice, "Nothing seems to change much around here."

Damn them, Jack thought. *Damn the ones who killed Sallie, who took his boy, his girl.* He felt anger flare in him, white hot. Then it drifted down, sleeping again.

He finished his beer. "What about Sheridan?"

"Sheridan's mad. He made a vow to stop the Indians, but he's failed, plain and simple, according to the newspapers. The whole country's demanding an end to the fighting. They say it's all politics now with Sherman in charge. Sheridan's in a hurry now. The Indians're running out of control again, the government wants them stopped. Sherman wants them stopped. He's pushing Sheridan. Now there's talk of gold up in Colorado, Montana. Hunting grounds for the Cheyenne, Sioux." McGregor smiled cynically. "But there's gold.

You can't stop settlers with gold fever and Sheridan can't catch up to all the tribes. They just fade away, gone---." McGregor poured himself more beer and drank. "The Cheyenne talk peace at Fort Cobb but they break out, they're all getting set to raid again. Sheridan's got to do something."

"Yep. He's got to make a fight," Jack said.

"He won't catch them before winter snow," McGregor paused, thinking. He looked long at Jack as though pondering his next words.

"Tell him," Mariah Matilda said. Her random sorting had stopped. She came across the room to Jack. She handed him two boxes of assorted rifle shells, a strange gift. She stared at Jack. "Tell him what you heard," she said to McGregor.

McGregor drew a long breath. "There's word of a white boy up in Black Kettle's village."

Ely smiled later that day. "Well damn," he said. He seated the ax he was using to split wood into an elm log, not far from his rifle, and hobbled across the yard as Jack dismounted. He wore moccasins stuffed with sheep's wool and his head, when he took his straw hat off, showed a heavy scar that parted his hair.

"Looking good," Jack said to him, shading the truth a little.

Ely laughed. "Can't do no jump roping."

Jack looked around, thinking about McGregor's news.

---*a white boy in Black Kettle's village.*

Maybe just another damn rumor. So many.

He saw the corrals had grown bigger, big enough now to hold maybe a hundred yearlings, the hay barn was full for winter feed from the last cut. A second corral with its worn snubbing post for gentling wild mustangs, held a tall bay pony snubbed and fighting the halter. Half trained mustangs and saddle horses were mixed in to calm the mustangs, all milling around and curious, gathered at the fence rails to watch the events in the yard.

"That boy's taking his time learning his manners," Ely said of the tall bay gelding. "We got a new contract with the military for twenty mounts, all fifteen hands, healthy. Good price. Got a month more to finish 'em." Ely shook his head. "Shit, horses sure scarce now."

Jack nodded. He stood a moment, taking time to look down to the creek, the autumn gold of the old cottonwood trees, gold leaves blowing. The elms, the brambles. He studied the iron fence he'd built around the graves near Jeth's two old apple trees, both in need of a pruning soon. He saw the fresh black paint on the iron grilling

Sallie.

Three years, coming on four, he marveled, with a jolt of memory.

A lifetime---

It was hard to look away, to get on with the urgency he had begun to feel.

Ely rode well enough now without heavy boots, just moccasins, like any Comanche buck, Jack thought. He had the skill of adapting, but he'd never go on another trail drive. He did everything else. He hired wranglers when it came to chasing after Longhorn mavericks through the mesquite out on the free range to increase the MR brand stock, rode everywhere, brought in the hay, branded mavericks with the MR brand, cut the wild yearling bulls for steers, broke mustangs.

Painted grave fences.

The big gate stood open. Open as the day the bird man's wagon jammed it open with the mule down in the traces, riddled and dying from a dozen arrows.

Couldn't get in, Jack thought as he had hundreds of times in the past three years. *Couldn't keep the Indians out.*

Elizabeth's laundry line flapped in the breeze not far from the rock house. A kitchen garden lay behind the brush fence, going dormant with winter. A few pumpkins lay scattered over the tilled ground.

Two black children, one hardly more than a baby, sat on the stone steps by the doorway, playing some sort of simple hand game.

There's word of a white boy in Black Kettle's village.

The Cheyenne, Chief Black Kettle---.

"You come to bring Elizabeth that molasses? She want needles too. She making me new britches." Ely laughed. "She's telling me not to cuss so much. Me, cuss?"

Jack untied his saddle strings, gathering up two packages.

"You come to work? Chase some cows?" Ely asked wryly, a look of studied doubt on his cinnamon face. He took off his hat and wiped his forehead. Then he looked more closely at Jack's expression. "I guess not."

"Here," Jack said. "Take this one to Elizabeth." He led his horse to the corral fence as Ely pulled open the second package and found hard-soled winter moccasins and a bottle of rye whiskey.

"Keep your mind easy and your feet warm," Jack said.

Ely nodded. "Elizabeth don't like whiskey much, but she like my warm feet."

Jack glanced up at the house, at the playing children. He felt the kick of urgency.

There was going to be a fight, Sheridan's fight, it had to be soon because winter was near, even on this bright October day.

Sheridan's getting mad.

He pulled his saddle and blanket off. "Now catch me the best damn horse you got. I'm in a hurry."

Jack crouched on the ridge and looked down at the Lodge Pole River, the river some called the Washita River. More than a foot of winter snow covered the ground. Below, the Cheyenne village slept on.

They think they're safe here, he thought.

Chief Black Kettle's village lay peacefully silent under the white mantle of snow. A few night footprints had almost filled up, war ponies stood staked outside the lodges, heads down, enduring the cold. Thin wisps of smoke drifted above the lodges from banked fires inside.

The Cheyenne thought winter protected them. They believed the white chief at Fort Cobb, as they'd been promised. They were on the

Reservation here along the Washita River, and as an added precaution Chief Black Kettle had tied a scrap of white cloth to a lodge pole.

A few Arapaho and Comanche visitors slept in the lodges of their friends among the Cheyenne. They thought the blizzard had covered their broad trail leading down from the north, where they'd raided along the Santa Fe Trail, killing, looting, taking captives. They had all scoffed at the idea of a no-treaty white chief. They'd scoffed at the idea of a winter war.

Jack bent his head and rubbed his stubbled jaw. His hands shook a little as he waited. Around him in the dawn darkness he heard the soft preparations of the troopers as they tightened their horses' cinches and looked to their weapons. Four troops of the Seventh Cavalry made ready from this point, while Elliot and Thompson and Myers, with seven more troops, waited, hidden quietly in a perimeter around the sleeping village. Jack knew exactly why he and the others were here, after a hard march through the blizzard to this ridge. He'd heard at Fort Cobb, Sherman wanted a war against all the tribes for their continued depredations, maybe women and children spared if possible but generally no quarter given.

No quarter. The plan was to give the Indians a damn good lesson in real warfare. So, Sheridan assembled stores of supplies, wagon after wagon, at key points for the ambush invasion of Indian Territory. Custer was mostly just hot for the fight.

The troopers generally hated Colonel George Custer. They called him Hardbacksides. Jack had listened todays of muttering and gossip, but the troopers knew Custer was a good, tough fighter. His record in the War made him a star, but Sheridan had pulled him from a year of military suspension after serving ten months, where he'd been held for desertion and mistreatment of his own troopers. Now he was here, he was a hell of a hard fighter. He was here to obey orders and ready to salvage his damaged reputation.

The minutes passed. Cold came up through Jack's thick winter moccasins, through his body and floated out on the frost of his breath as he stared down at the village. He heard the troopers mount at a whispered command. His stomach hollowed in anticipation.

Shit, they're still asleep---.

"They don't have no wolves out watching," California Joe muttered, squatting beside Jack. "No damn camp guards at all."

He was a rough, red-haired buffalo hunter with eyes that crossed, a scruffy red beard, and known for his constant scratching. He was one of a number of tough buffalo hunters who called themselves scouts, but they were all along mostly for the fight, and for scouting new buffalo hunting grounds, and campsites with good sweet water. He scratched at his chest, at his crotch. "Where the Hell're them guards?"

Jack knew the Cheyenne, like the Comanches, hated to turn out early on a winter morning after a blizzard. They stayed in their robes with their lodge fires banked through the night. Below, in Black Kettle's village, Jack counted fifty-one lodges with smoke flaps turned to point out of the wind.

"Look at that one," Jack said softly. "It's a white flag."

Fitzpatrick studied the village as the light grew. "It's a white flag, by Ganny," he agreed. "What the hell?"

"Big pony herd's south of here---," California Joe muttered.

Mists lifted off the iced river as the dawn light increased. Jack could smell the fires now and see the spidery gray tangle of willows and brush along the creek. He could make out Black Kettle's lodge by its black markings, huddled near the protection of a stand of lodgepole pines. He listened for sound, for any kind of alarm, but all he heard was the wail of a baby rising eerily in the vast silence.

Not even a dog anywhere. Where are the dogs?

He wondered how many Kiowas, how many Arapaho and Comanches, had stopped here feasting and visiting after their raids along the Santa Fe Trail. He arose at last and turned away from the ridge.

Captives here.

No one knew for sure, maybe rumors again.

But he'd signed on as a civilian scout anyway, along with the buffalo hunters and the Osage and Delaware guides. He'd never mentioned his search to the military because it didn't matter here.

He slogged through the snow past California Joe's mule to his mount, a tall bay from the Seventh's *remuda,* and stood waiting where other scouts waited. He looked into the dark face of the Delaware scout who had sometimes been friendly, but the man just shook his head. The troopers waited, cold, tired and anxious from a hard, sleepless night. Some cursed softly, excitedly.

There was something not right about the dawn. He could feel it in his bones. He lifted his head, searching his mind and his senses for the transient warning.

"You got it too?" Ben Clark asked, coming up beside him.

"Got what," Fitzpatrick grunted. He yanked his fur hat down and started to light his cob pipe, then stopped and reached for his chewing tobacco and swore softly. No smoking, only quiet talking here. He shrugged out of his old army overcoat and dropped it in the snow, as the troopers had discarded their overcoats and haversacks for the quiet advance on the ridge.

"Why the hell didn't he send scouts down the river," Jack muttered.

"Easy," Ben Clark said. He was a grizzled older man of vast experience with military scouting, married to a squaw woman, well liked and friendly, and one of the three who knew why Jack was here staring down at the Cheyenne village. "I told old Hardbacksides there're more Cheyenne and Kiowas, a big damn camp around the lower bend of the river----."

Jack looked over toward the Osage scouts. He could feel their uneasiness, their excitement, but their faces were carefully empty. From the moment they'd smelled the first smoke and seen the steam rising down the river from where the Cheyenne's vast pony herd grazed unguarded, they'd had this look of trouble.

"They're looking to get some of them ponies after the fight," Ben Clark said softly.

California Joe gulped twice from his bottle of whiskey, dropped the empty bottle in the snow and scratched his neck. "I'm going after them ponies myself after the fight. Sell 'em in Texas easy---."

"Those boys're scattered all around the village," Fitzgerald said of the troopers, and then added of Custer and of the Indians below, "He wants 'em all dead---."

"Take it easy," Ben Clark said again, softly.

Jack checked the load in his rifle again. He checked that his revolver was free in its holster and the big knife secure at his belt.

Everyone knew the Indians killed captives to keep them from falling into the hands of the white soldiers and agents again.

"Maybe he ain't down there, Jack," Ben Clark said.

"He wouldn't look white now," Jack said. "He'd look like one of them." He kept his face stony calm even as his heart raced. "I think the girl's gone." He saw a flash of Rosebud's little face, her blue, blue eyes, her wisps of golden hair. He swallowed hard at the sadness, at the anger.

Fitzpatrick's jaws worked rhythmically at a cut of tobacco. "Supposed to be a white woman too. Bastards." He started to spit, hesitated, then let the juice go, murmured wryly, "Reckon they'll know we been here anyhow."

Below in the village, one of the lodge door flaps opened and a woman stepped out into the snow. A brindle camp dog came around the lodge from the back and stopped at a distance, its tail wagging tentatively. The woman stood for a moment in thick winter moccasins, wrapped in a blanket, looking around, listening.

Then Jack heard the sudden yell of the command, the piercing peel of a bugle blaring out the charge, mixed with wild notes of music, regimental music tearing into the nerves of every man with excitement, urging them forward with sabers drawn, to terrify the sleeping Cheyenne in the village below.

A scatter of fire came from Cook's sharpshooters on the ridge. The horses surged forward, the bugle notes twisted off into chaos as the music faltered and froze, and from every quarter in the dawn light above the Washita River, the Seventh Cavalry charged down on the sleeping village below.

The troopers swept down the ridge and rode among the screaming, shocked Indians who poured from their lodges and fled across the snow. They couldn't distinguish men from women in the poor light, but that didn't matter to the troopers, who followed orders. The Cheyenne men struggled with weapons, trying to fire and reload, to send arrows before the troopers rode over them hacking at heads and fleeing bodies. Women cried out and fell. Children ran wildly, stumbling, running in terror toward the Washita River and the scant protection of its banks and brush. Indian men tried to mount frantic war ponies tethered near their lodges, but the troopers shot them down and rode over them, sweeping through the village and out, almost before the last notes of the charge had died.

In the chaos Jack saw Chief Black Kettle, and his woman, mounted on the back of a war pony, at the edge of the Washita, where the Cheyenne, women and children, ran to escape the fight. He watched Chief Black Kettle topple slowly down the side of his pony, falling into the icy river, and a moment later the woman fell, and the pony bolted free along the bank where other Cheyenne men crouched in hollows of desperate resistance; while their women and children struggled against the ice to reach the other side.

Jack spurred toward the river, searching among the fleeing women and children, yelling a name lost in the chaos.

South of the camp, troopers turned back the Indians who fled toward the snow-covered sand dunes. From every quarter troopers closed off their escape and drove them back into the village. Some of the troopers waved the woman back, and those who did not obey fled east along the Washita River, some falling in the scattered fire of the troopers and of their own people.

Jack's horse served wildly to avoid the body of a Cheyenne man who lay naked except for his breechclout, bleeding heavily into the snow. He tried to get up and then went down again, and a blue-coated trooper with the shocked face of a farm boy fell beside him, an arrow in his side.

Jack dodged a lance thrust and turned his mount, shooting an Indian already bleeding from a chest wound. Everywhere the wounded dragged themselves across the snow toward the protection of the river, leaving red trails of blood behind.

"Jack!" Ben Clark yelled across the fight. He spurred away from Custer's side, waving wildly and Jack turned in his saddle, his heart thudding as he saw an Indian woman dart from a lodge, dragging a boy behind her. He saw a boy with a pale skin, a white face.

She was yards away from them across the camp. Between, troopers fought, men and women twisted in the bloody snow. She turned frantically, searching for escape. She started toward the river, but Meyer's troop cut her off; she turned again, trapped. The Osage scouts made for her with wild war screams.

Jack lifted his rifle. The child dragged back from the woman. He tried to pull free, but his child's strength was futile against the woman's power. Then the Indian woman snatched out a knife and drove it into his body an instant before Ben Clark's bullet killed her.

Jack flung himself down in the snow beside the boy and the woman. He drove the Osages back with a yell, and they rushed on by him, battle-mad for trophy scalps and enemy heads.

Ben Clark pulled his mount to a stop over Jack and the dead boy.

"No," Jack said. "Not Jeth."

Ben Clark spurred his horse around and raced east after the fleeing Cheyenne.

Jack tried to brush the filth away from the boy's white face, but his hands shook with rage. He stood. He lifted his rifle and turned back to the fighting, looking for an enemy. He saw a trooper running toward an Indian sprawled on the ground, bloody and dead. The trooper bent over him and grabbed for the Indian's bow, grabbing for a war prize.

"No!" Jack yelled, but he was too late as the Indian rose up and drove his knife into the trooper's neck. Jack shot, and the Indian died again, a Comanche by the pattern of his moccasins. The trooper thrashed as blood spouted from his neck, then lay calmly still.

Jack swung around to the nearest lodge and ran toward it. The Osage scouts came out, dragging a woman by the feet. Her head left a red scar in the snow. A riderless horse nearly knocked Jack over. He staggered aside and ran on to the next lodge. He heard someone, Custer shouting an order from the center of the village, and somewhere a woman screamed piercingly.

The lodge was empty and rank with the stench of old smoke and grease and the animal smells of furs and buffalo robes. A painted bull-hide war shield lay near the entrance, its feather decorations charred and smoking. He stumbled over a scatter of cooking pots strewn around the center fire pit. An album of faded daguerreotypes from some settler's plundered homestead lay flung against a willow-wand back rest at the rear of the lodge. Over his head a Cheyenne medicine bundle wrapped in beaver fur hung from a lodge pole. Rawhide parfleches stuffed with dried buffalo meat and corn, dried berries from the summer's harvest, skin bags of pemmican, wild roots and herbs, were packed down against the inside winter lining of the lodge against cold drafts seeping in.

Jack kicked embers from the fire onto the fur couches. He tore down the medicine bundle and broke it open, destroying the gods, scattering good fortune. He turned to leave and then a faint noise, a soft mewing sound, came from somewhere; a noise he could hardly hear in the wild sounds from outside. But the lodge was empty. Nothing moved. The buffalo robes began to smolder, sending up twists of rank smoke. He walked to the back couch, softly, his rifle ready. He drew his big knife and kicked the robes aside.

An old woman lay there, curled like an infant with knees drawn up and thin arms clutched across her chest. Her hair lay long, tangled, grayed by her years. She wore a soft doeskin sleeping tunic without any adornment. She looked shrunken, too weak, too frail with age to run away, with only the strength to cower and burn with the lodge. Her face was a tapestry of lines in the weathered brown skin, her eyes like little black stones sunk deep in folds. When Jack reached down to her she twisted away, slippery with skin oils, her teeth weasel-sharp as she scratched and bit. He grabbed at her again and missed as she fought him. She lunged away, legs crippled, struggling to escape across the lodge, finally hobbling, dragging herself upright at the door flaps. Jack missed her again, trying to pull her back from the fray but she threw herself out into the fighting. When Jack got to the door flaps she lay only a few feet beyond and already sprawled in the snow, her head smashed by a passing trooper's rifle butt.

Jack caught up a panicked Cheyenne pony and mounted, grabbing for the reins. Dogs raced through the village, howling and barking, adding to the din of screams and cries. He saw an Osage scout bent over a fallen Indian youth, busily cutting off his head.

He heard a yell, he thought it was an order and then a nearby officer's yell, something about a brevit or a coffin, a senseless yell to Jack as Elliot took twenty men of the Seventh down the valley after a group of escaping Indians.

In the south the other scouts were rounding up the huge Cheyenne pony herd, driving it toward the bend in the Washita River. The scouts had been ordered there but Jack raced his horse after Elliot and the fleeing Cheyenne.

Where? Jack thought, frantic in his search.

Cook's sharpshooters began to pick off pockets of resistance among the gullies behind the logs and brush along the Washita River. Dead and wounded Indians lay sprawled, half submerged in the frigid water, others struggled to cross against the razor edge of the ice.

Meyers and Thompson chased after another group of fleeing Cheyenne women and children, led by three men. They bobbed along the bank, running wildly. The snow all around them puffed up in little spouts as bullets struck. One of the Cheyenne men fell back to fire war arrows at two troopers who charged with raised sabers, and Jack shot the man before he could draw his bowstring back.

He'd lost Elliot in the confusion. He thought Elliot had gone east chasing after a band of escaping Indians. Jack found himself suddenly alone, beyond Meyers and Thompson and not yet up with Elliot's dash. A mile ahead lay timber where the Indians could take cover. But here in the trampled snow nothing moved. He reined in his pony for a moment's uneasy appraisal. He stared around, catching his breath, listening. Cautiously he pushed ahead to the top of a low brushy rise.

Twenty feet to the left he suddenly saw the cluster of Indians, all crouched down in the brush like rabbits. Mostly women. But one man stood over a woman's body. He was broad in his chest, heavy shouldered, with a round head and long braids of graying black hair. He stood with his bowstring drawn, an arrow ready. Jack got a shot off that missed an instant before his pony reared back with an arrow piercing deep into its flank. The horse began to buck and kick. It uttered an animal scream and fell backwards. Jack's rifle jolted free from his grasp, his hat flew off as his back hit the snow and he scrambled to avoid the thrashing hoofs. He heard the Indian man's wild, triumphant cry. He heard the whining rip of another arrow passing above him. A third arrow struck into the snow by his head. He saw the body of the man hurtling down on him.

He raised his arms and caught the bone-cracking blow of a war club across the underside of his raised left forearm. The club fell again, glancing from his head. Jack rolled away, his left arm numbing, his right-hand groping back, down for the big knife sheathed at his waist: groping, fingers grabbing snow, then leather. He felt his head, his brain, begin to shift, to glide away from him, a surge of engulfing pain begins to take him away. He struggled with the knife, dragging it up, with the blade free over his belly. He lifted his broken left arm, a useless shield as he watched the Indian man with the raised war club hurl himself down over him again.

He couldn't stop retching. On hands and knees in the snow, his belly convulsed, then finally stopped. He gasped for air like any damaged creature. He wanted to groan with all the pain. But his head, his struggling brain, had begun to steady with now and then the waves of sickness fading away.

The Indian man lay nearby, bleeding fountains from his belly, the big knife deep in his gut. He lay immobile, with his eyes open. His lips moved in the faint sounds of his death song.

Jack's left forearm pulsed with blows of pain. He wiped at his face to clear the blood from his eyes. He knew the Indian women would come for him with their knives if they saw his weakness. He swayed to his feet and moved his head slowly, searching for his rifle and revolver, found only his rifle in the snow near his hat. He almost fell as he bent over, his left arm hard against his body, holding the pain away. He managed to stay upright as he stood, swaying again. He was far from ready to fight again but he slowly understood that it didn't matter. Three troopers rode up in a dash, boys in blue, pulling in their mounts to hard stop, almost with a flourish. They looked down at him. They looked at his dead horse, and spoke, but Jack didn't know what they were saying. They looked at the dying Indian, the knife. One of the troopers lifted his rifle and shot the Indian man in the head.

The first fight of the battle at the Washita River had suddenly ended. Jack stood, looking around. The three troopers, with whoops and yells, rounded up the Cheyenne women hiding terrified in the brush and herded them back across the camp to the other Cheyenne women and children prisoners. No male Indian over the age of ten, or wounded, was left alive. Other troopers busily looted for blankets and food and anything of useful interest or information, on orders, the spoils of their hard fighting. They burned every lodge in the village until the air was heavy and dark with smoke.

Then some of the troopers began to take up defensive positions around the burning village. Maybe Custer and his officers had begun to understand that the Washita fight wasn't over yet.

Where's Elliot?

Jack pulled his big knife from the dead Indian's belly and cleaned it with snow. He stood listening as he heard other random shots, executions of the wounded enemies. Cheyenne fighters gathered on hilltops shooting down. The Osage scouts had ridden off to shoot the huge Cheyenne pony herd, Custer's orders, except for a few ponies reserved for carrying the captive women and children, and those they managed to steal for themselves.

Jack started forward with the thought of searching among the dead, looking for any captives, looking for Jeth, but it was too soon. Scores of riders swarmed up from the Cheyenne campsites on the lower Washita, all in fighting paint, screaming and whipping their ponies. Ben Clark rode up to Jack leading a big Seventh Cavalry horse with an empty saddle. The horse stood nervously shaking while Jack fumbled to mount and grab for the reins.

Ben Clark spurred ahead, yelling. "---ten damn miles of Indian camps down the river! Must be---." They raced away toward where the troopers were running from the field and others were herding the Cheyenne women and children captives together. Custer shouted the order and the troopers fell in around the captives, surrounding them.

The screaming band of Indians slowed, then stopped, yelling insults, waving weapons, lances and rifles, in their rage. Now they could not fire at the troopers without killing their own women and children.

Another band came from the upper Washita where the river ran in a bow. Custer held. Now there were hundreds of Indians in the woods and brush around him. In mid-afternoon, so short of ammunition that the withdrawal with empty guns would soon turn into a rout, and in fear of the Cheyenne attacking his supply wagon train, Custer began to march toward the Indians. The startled Indians, with their women and children held as hostages, retreated. At nightfall Custer turned around and marched his men back to his ammunition wagons and his supply train.

Where was Elliot?

The next day at the surgeon's tent, the surgeon, a busy, tired military man who wore rimless glasses and a bloodstained apron, looked first at Jack's arm, felt for the positions of the bones, then gave his arm a good pull to set the bones straight.

"---Shit!" Jack gasped

"Laudanum's gone, so's morphine---," the surgeon muttered. He waved a hand. "Ran out last night. You are number twenty-four here. Not counting the squaws and kids." He fitted a rough wooden cast to the arm and wound it with lengths of woven cotton cloth tied firmly. "Six weeks. Don't get it wet. Hold it up." He examined Jack's eyes, waved a finger, watched his reaction. He cleaned the blood away from the tear on Jack's head left by the war club and dressed it with carbolic and a patch of bandage.

"Tough head. Good for the military, but you're no damn use to them now."

He paused, then smiled almost reluctantly. "You'll look even more like a damn raccoon tomorrow. Boil up some willow tea, it'll help the pain."

"You look like a damned raccoon!" Ben Clark laughed later in spite of the grim evidence of the fight all around them at Camp Supply.

"Almost made it to the happy hunting ground," Jack muttered. He pointed at the snowy ground. "---where the shaggies always run." His lips grimaced in something short of a smile.

No, no White Dogs down there.

His damned Indian thinking. But he didn't care.

His stomach wobbled now and then. His head worked well enough so that he remembered more of the fight in brief flashes, but it still hurt like hell, and all around his eyes blood from the blow of the war club had settled under the skin and given him two big black eyes.

He made a sling from a spare bandanna in his kit, using his right hand and his teeth. "Said they don't need me anymore. Scouting days're over," he added wryly.

He felt dirty, disheveled, shaken, with a week's beard on his jaws. He felt bone tired. He'd wandered the battlefield for hours the afternoon of the second day, turning over bodies, searching, just to be certain, and watched Indian women from the lower river campsites gathering the bodies of their dead to give them respectful burial on lofty platforms made of poles. Some of the dead had their weapons still with them; bows with no more arrows, old rifles, lances, knives, all they could find after the troopers' foraging, to make their dead comfortable on their long road of death. Now their dead rested up in the hills, in the pines, and Jack felt lost, in the sense that while he'd found no body, thankfully no Jeth dead in the snow, he'd found no word either, and no sign. Even the captive Cheyenne women seemed reconciled, indifferent to their fate in captivity, enduring the facts of survival after centuries of tribal wars. They gave him nothing when he went among them asking, searching, after the officers had claimed the fairest of the young Cheyenne girls, and Custer had taken the daughter of a chief to his tent.

"They found two more, a girl and a woman," Ben Clark told him, without details.

"Where?"

"Up in the trees."

"The girl---."

"Maybe half grown. Dressed like a squaw."

The military claimed they'd found no captives, they claimed there were no records of white captives in Chief Black Kettle's camp even as they carried the body of the dead white boy from the battlefield at the Washita River, along with twenty-one dead officers and men of the Seventh.

Now there were two more.

When the Cheyenne and the Kiowas and the Arapahoe and the Comanches all gathered earlier in the month around Fort Cobb for talks of peace, their thousands of horses grazed the last grass under the snow. Then the tribes moved away to find new grazing and safety in the Territory, and good winter camps along the Washita River.

After the Washita fight he had listened to the Osages' gunshot killing six hundred or more of Chief Black Kettle's ponies in the great horse killing.

Sheridan's orders.

It was all a grim puzzle to Jack, as it was to some of the other men around him who limped, who swore and bore wounds, who mourned dead comrades.

Jack started to think that the battle had been for nothing in just about every way.

"I believe I'll head back now," he told Ben Clark on the third day after the fight. "I'm going to find me a hole and crawl into it for a spell."

Ben Clark looked around the camp, at the general military sort of planned chaos, troopers walking, limping, busy on orders, supply wagons, other wagons full of plunder from the battlefield, Osage and Delaware scouts making reports, horses and riders everywhere, officer's tents where they were still arguing over the enemy dead count and the story of the fight and sending off official dispatches to General Sheridan.

"Heard we killed 150 Cheyenne warriors. Some Kiowas and Comanches. Sounds high. Crazy."

Jack just looked at Ben Clark. "Makes a good story. Big victory."

By now everyone knew that Elliot had separated from his three companies in the fight and dashed off, with a detachment, after a group of Cheyenne and Kiowa warriors racing up the river to join the fight at Black Kettle's encampment. With yells of derision, in a single fierce charge Elliot and his detachment of twenty men all died.

Shit, Custer didn't wait to find Elliot and his men.

Ben Clark sighed and scratched is beard. "Old Hardbacksides wants another fight."

"They got their Indian war going now---invade the Territory, kill 'em all," Jack said, squinting with the throbbing pain in his head.

Ben Clark studied Jack. "There's all them settlers they killed."

Jack nodded. "Yep, they did," he said tiredly

Carter sighed. "I'm going home." He looked over the camp. "Take you a month to get your horse sorted out from the military, sign all the damn papers."

Jack smiled grimly. "I know where to find horses."

That night, lugging his saddle and gear, on his way to find one of the Osages' stolen Cheyenne pony herds hiding in one of the drawn nearby, Jack passed a man sitting on a stump at the edge of the encampment. The man was short and broad in the belly. He wore a city suit, new boots and a derby hat and a thick scarf around his neck. He didn't notice Jack's passing, he just seemed to be studying the night before his eyes. Snow had started to fall again.

The man was vaguely familiar to Jack, he'd been around the camp, with others like him, following like camp followers, quizzing the troopers, quizzing the officers, getting the official story, such as it was.

He remembered the journalists from his time in El Paso. Did they ever get it right?

Jack turned back and stopped in front of the man on the stump.

"You a journalist? You write stories?" He lowered his saddle and gear to the ground and stood waiting for an answer.

The man stared. He frowned at something he didn't quite understand. He hadn't noticed the falling snow.

"Yes sir," he finally answered. "Harper's Weekly. Mostly just a hack." He waved a notebook with a half-finished drawing of the battle. He shook his head.

Jack glanced at the drawing. "Then you'll write about it."

The man took a full minute to answer. "How?"

"Just write it."

Jack picked up his saddle and gear, one-armed and awkward, got it settled, and turned to walk into the wall of falling snow.

December. Cold, but no snow now. Had to leave the Osage pony back in the hills, carried a rancher's brand. Shit.

He'd used his catch rope and circled one of the Osages' stolen pony herds in the darkness and just kept circling quietly until the herd grew used to him, then he'd found the horse he wanted, gone in and roped him. The pony stood with the rope over his neck, Comanche trained after it had been stolen. He had a split left ear, and had the look of a tough saddle pony, once a rancher's mount with a clear brand on his rump.

Stolen once. Now again.

He slipped the halter over its head and saddled the pony. He took it past a sleeping Osage guard, hesitated, considered killing the guard and taking his head in the Osage custom with enemies, then smiled grimly and rode away.

Oklahoma

Caught a ride with a wagon train carrying supplies to the agency. I am tired, tired.

He'd slept for most of three days, half awake, wandering in the dark and aching, then woke up on a cot in an empty room with log walls and a tent top, and generations of mice foraging on the dirt floor. His saddle and his gear lay nearby in a heap where he'd left it, his rifle leaned against a wall. Cold and hungry, he chased the mice away from his gear and walked out in the cold to find the privy and the agent.

He found the agent and offered the words of thanks, but he didn't even remember how he came to the room with the cot, or when. He paused as his head began to pound again.

"Three nights. You better, Jack?" the agent asked, frowning. "You got some bruises there."

Startled at his name, he stared at the agent and understood that he knew this man; that he had been here before, in the Territory at this agency run by a Quaker missionary. He'd carried posters about lost children, searching. But now his head ached again, and he couldn't remember a name.

He was a man in mid-life, a busy man with a nicely trimmed black beard and thoughtful eyes. Jack saw that he counted boxes and bundles of old used donated clothes and leather shoes, tins of flour and corn and food in cans, all collected for the reservation Indians.

He was dressed well, is simple black clothing and he spoke often, and with passion about peace and good will.

Peace?

"Lost my pony back in the hills." Jack lied, then wondered why he bothered, no one had asked and probably no one cared, not even this Quaker man.

"You come from the fight?" the agent asked. He shook his head. "All the tribes are in a panic, what with Sherman's edict."

Jack drew a deep breath. "I'm looking for a white boy. Just a kid, a white captive---."

"Sure," the agent said. "I remember." He rummaged through all his goods, muttering, taking time away from his work.

"Look in here," he thrust out an old ledger with dog-eared dirty pages and a list of names. "What tribe was that?"

"Comanche."

There were a few new names, a few captives found, restored to their families. Jeth and Rose Rainie were on this list of captives, as well as Jack could make out with his aching head. They were listed as "Unrecovered"

Unrecovered.

"Then go find old Hard Bone," the agent said. "He's camping off east somewhere. He's assigned a house, but he won't use it. He's registered here in the Territory. One of the old reserve bands. He might know something."

Jack recognized this man, from long ago, a passing face from a visiting band somewhere in the Comancheria. His face now looked back at Jack, empty, withholding trust or recognition. The fire cast deep shadows around his painted buffalo hide lodge, the lodge of a once important man. A woman soothed a fussing child over in the darkness near a structure that looked like a large wooden box with steps, a door and one window.

This man was once a strong hunter, respected, well liked. A man who rode on horse raids and buffalo hunts, a successful man of his people who protected his people and fed his family well.

From the paintings on the lodge, and from the fine soft buffalo hide and pots of paint at his side, Jack guessed that this man, as he aged, had become the historian for his band, as Owl Stands had been the historian of his people, a man who told their story in beautifully drawn pictures on buffalo hides or rocks, so that the People would know who they were, where they had been, what they had done.

The end of day had turned cold again, but not as cold as the banks of the Washita River had been. Jack felt the cold through his heavy coat and wished he had a blanket to pull around him. He felt awkward with the cast on his arm, awkward with his head aching. As he approached, with ritual greeting, with respect, this old man put aside his pots of paint and his fine hair brushes. He rubbed his eyes, for the firelight had given him only dark light for his task. He looked up at Jack, his eyes squinting, searching. All the seasons of smoke from thousands of fires, from poor light, day or night, as he painted, gave him the eyes of a man almost blind at last. He gestured for Jack to take a place on the buffalo robe as a respected visitor. He was curious, but he was too polite to ask a question. He waited as Jack found the pouch of tobacco he'd brought as a gift.

This man's name was Hard Bone, only one of several names. He bent over the fire, sitting with his legs crossed, his body speaking to Jack of age and sickness, or perhaps only speaking of a vast weariness. His hair fell long and well-tended by his women, his clothes old but once fine. His face showed the lines of the years, the pain of wounds and perhaps the wounds of great disappointments. The pain of loss.

Jack offered his tobacco and they smoked thin brown-paper *cigarillos*. They began to talk

"Grandfather, I am searching," Jack said.

The old man looked into Jack's face, at the bruises around his eyes, a careful examination that seemed to search for some sort of answer.

Jack spoke with care. "I have come from the big fight up at the Lodgepole River. I am searching for a boy, but he was not there."

Hard Bone's squinting eyes went on with their search. He paused at the wound on Jack's head, again at the darkness around Jack's eyes.

"There was a girl," Jack said. "Small, only a baby. But she was too young. I think she has gone."

Hard Bone bent his head, smoking, listening.

"I am searching for this boy, her brother. One boy. And for the people who have taken him away."

Hard Bone puffed on his *cigarillo*. Soon he would need more tobacco, for Comanches relished good tobacco.

"Maybe just one person who has taken him away."

Hard Bone waited as Jack offered more tobacco. Carefully the old man rolled his brown-paper *cigarillo*.

"One person," he said. "There are others."

"One person, others. Anyone."

"Yes, I have seen such people." The old man puffed. "Maybe such a person."

A person, one person. Jack stared, the surprise narrowing his eyes.

"This person. He is one of the People?"

"He is like no one, maybe he lives at the edge of camps now."

"Is he alone?"

The old man shrugged. "Sometimes."

"But there are captives?"

"Sometimes. From Mexico sometimes. He trades with the Apaches. They want soldier guns. They always have captives."

"There are *Tejano* captives?"

The old man shrugged again. "Maybe there are *Tejano* captives."

On the second night of his words with Hard Bone, Jack said, "I have brought you three pack horses carrying goods for your family." The Quaker agent had taken Jack's Green River knife in trade and a promise for the horses and the rest of the supplies. "Pipe tobacco, good food and blankets. Sugar and corn. Coffee. Much more. It is all good from the agency, nothing spoiled, no worms, all clean."

What could this old man give in return for this generous gift, as was the custom? Something of even greater worth?

But Hard Bone asked, "Maybe you are one of the those people? The Sugar Eaters?" His voice carried a thread of scorn, for these were bad people, old-day mission Comanches who were used as slaves to build the first Spanish missions, then came to walk the bad medicine road, the one-god road with the white *padres*. They were lazy, they had abandoned the Comanche way and they bred with bad Spanish foreigners until now many were blue-eyed and had wavy white man's hair.

"I am Texian only."

If Hard Bone believed him he would accept the gifts, the offered tobacco, enough for a pipe, for further talk.

"You speak our own words," Hard Bone said, with a trace of approval because no Comanche bothered to learn another language.

"I speak good words. I lived with the People."

Hard Bone considered.

"You come here from the big fight?" Hard Bone gestured vaguely at Jack's arm in the sling, at his face.

"Yes," Jack said. "Yes." He thought the talk might end here, in the midst of all the fears, the anger after the big fight, of his own conflict about the fight, but he could say no more.

"Everyone is afraid now. We are afraid of the soldiers. But we talked to the soldiers about peace, long time back. They moved us around, we were in the reserve, safe there, but the White Dogs outside wanted to kill us."

"Long time back," Jack said.

"Now it is again," Hard Bone said. "Some of our own People outside fight along with the soldiers."

"Grandfather, tell me about this person. This one who has captives. Are there others?"

"Maybe there are others. The soldiers take the captives away from the People. I still see this one."

He waited as the old man thought in silence, maybe he knew more, maybe he was only thinking how he would repay this generous gift, all the good food, and then he just took the tobacco Jack had brought, filled his pipe and lit it with an ember. He pulled the smoke through the pipe stem and then he offered the ritual smoke to the Supernaturals.

Jack took the pipe and made his own respectful offering. "This man," he asked, "what is his name?"

"He has many names and also none. He is a shadow. A shadow, I think. Sometimes he is more than one, he walks in another skin."

"Who are his people?"

"The Antelopes maybe. One of the old Buffalo Eaters? He says many things."

"He is just a trader?"

The old man looked at Jack without answering.

"He trades captives?"

The old man smoked silently.

Jack backed away from his own intensity. "Grandfather, does he go among the People here?"

"He goes following something, they say. "

"But you see him here? With his captives? "

The old man looked at Jack sadly. "He takes them over the mountains, to the Mexican *Anglos*. Those traders."

Jack stared at Hard Bone. His heart sank at this information. "The faraway slave traders," Jack said, almost in disbelief.

Hard Bone nodded. "They pay him. He only wants guns and crazy water. He makes big talk."

Jack heard the old man's words as though they came from a great distance.

The faraway slave traders. Over the mountains. Maybe Santa Fe.

Unrecovered. Forever unrecovered---.

"Now everyone is afraid. We have heard the bad story of the fight. Maybe he won't come here again."

On the third night Jack came with only tobacco. They smoked the pipe again as friends and Jack listened, almost without hope.

Gone, he thought. *Too late.*

"There is a story." The old man said. He rubbed his eyes. He sighed. A young girl, a grandchild perhaps, dressed in calico and bright red trader strouding, with trash trinkets and faded ribbons tied in her hair, brought the old man a drink of water sweetened with honey. She offered Jack a drink. The old man watched her with a look of sadness on his face.

"We walk on the white man's one-god path now," he said in a tired voice. "We hoe the corn."

"The story?" Jack prompted after a moment.

"Yes, a story. I have heard of someone who is known sometimes as Man Who Walks Away."

Jack looked into the night. "There are many stories."

Hard Bone drank his sweetened water. "This one did a bad thing and then he went away. The great man said, I gave him food, I taught him the way of the People, but he walked away. My good son loved him, but this man did a bad thing. He was ungrateful. He was a bad *Tejano* man."

Jack sat with his head bent, listening to the truth.

"The great man said, I am looking for him now. I think all my sons are looking for him now, even the one who walks the long road. There is no honor."

Yes. No honor.

"Where did you find this story?"

"It was an old story about a white Comanche, that's all." The old man shrugged his silent answer as he looked at Jack, but his look held a certain shrewdness. "Well, I know nothing about such things. I speak of history on buffalo robes, but the buffalo have gone. I was a hunter for my family. There is nothing to hunt. Sometimes we have beef. We don't like beef. We are hungry. That's all."

Jack waited, for such quiet stories often took a long time, with courteous pauses. But his heart was heavy.

"We came to the Territory peacefully, but the young boys go out, they leave the reservations," Hard Bone went on. "It is too empty here, too unlucky. They want to raid and steal horses in the old way. They want to follow good medicine, not the White Dog's road. They want the honors. They want the praise of the People. They have nothing else to do."

Jack heard the words and knew they were true.

"They say work, here. What is work? They gave us honeytalk. We stayed away from this place. We did not want to hoe corn." The old man drew a deep breath. "They took us from the reserve, we thought we were safe there. But then we had to come here to the white man's place they call Territory. The agency. Yes. We came for food. The agent knew me, sometime maybe I signed a paper. All my people signed a paper. They called it a roll."

"There was a man who said he was from the Hungry band. I don't think so. He wanted food, but the agent didn't know him. He wouldn't sign the roll. No one knew him. There was no paper. Then the soldiers asked him questions. There were two boys and a girl. The man said these were his. No, I don't think so. He went away then."

"When did you see this man with the two boys and the girl?"

"Maybe just before the first frost."

October---he wouldn't go over the mountains in the snow.

Jack felt a rise of hope.

"But he heard the bad rumors. We all heard."

Jack drew on the pipe. Then passed it back to this man who was a keeper of history.

---But he wouldn't go over the mountains in the winter---.

He waited.

"There was the time when the soldiers wanted all the captives back. They still want the captives back." Hard Bone made a sound like mocking laughter. "Many times, they wanted the captives back but only a few brought captives. Some chiefs brought captives back. But this man just passed among the People."

"He had these captives?"

The old man nodded. "Others."

"More than three?"

The old man nodded again. "You have fingers on your hands. As many."

"How ---?" Jack stopped. He knew the People saw no reason not to lie or exaggerate in telling such stories if it served their purpose. He said only, "So many."

"Well, captives were important to the People then. Long time. Mexican women had many babies for the People. They learned how to be one of the People. They fought when we fought. We traded them for maize and pemmican when we were hungry, or for whatever we wanted. Now they are not important except to the soldiers. And to this person. He wants the old ways. I think he gets whites and Mexicans from the Mescalero and the Jicarillo Apaches, he trades them to Comancheros when they come but they don't come much anymore. He gets guns and carries them to the far-away People hiding in the mountains who have no new soldier guns. He trades crazy water. He gets more captives, mostly Mexicans. Long time."

Hard Bone drew on the pipe, considering how to continue.

"Good slaves, but now everything has changed. Now we just trade them if we have any, maybe for meat, that's all. We are here in the Territory now. We hoe corn now."

"You say from Mexico, from the Apaches?"

"Some come from the Jicarillas, some come from the Arapaho in the north. Even the Kiowa people I think. The agent said he had many of these White Dog and Mexican captives to find, many names on a list, when we signed that paper."

"This man," Jack prompted.

Over the mountains far away, maybe Santa Fe---but the winter snow---

"The People were afraid of him. Some People say he is like a hungry dog. Like a bad spirit. He had an old man with him. This old man wore a chief's eagle feather. He led a paint packhorse. The

People said there were only bones in the pack, death bones, they were afraid."

Bones. Few Comanche ever wanted to be near the dead for fear of all the evil spirits lingering nearby.

"Once the old man-made pictures as I do. They said he made pictures on rocks"

"I have seen pictures on rocks," Jack said. Everywhere in Texas and New Mexico, pictures telling stories, leaving messages over the centuries.

Bones, Jack puzzled

"He was admired for his wisdom. The old people knew of him. They respected his parfleche medicine bundle because they knew it was big medicine. But the other. He is unlucky. He brings a packhorse carrying bones---." The old man moved slightly, in a subtle shudder. "No one wanted that man around."

Jack struggled for patience in this slowly unfolding story. He listened to the soft sounds of the camp, women talking to sleepy children, men talking, moving through the lodges, through the shelters and the wooden boxes the agents called houses, quietly visiting. But the night sounds were different from his memory, for the people here did not have their wealth of horses, they had few dogs and no important weapons except knives.

No strong weapons, without the white chief's permission. Their voices were subdued as they talked.

"One day we came for the food again. Everyone came. It was a bad time, no rain, everything dry. The agent said he would give us each a steer and coffee and good flour without worms. I saw a man talking to the soldiers. He was tall, he wore Comanche moccasins, but he wore a hat, so I knew he was another Texian, maybe a *Tejano.* Maybe you. A boy was watching you. One of his trade boys. That man saw. He brought me a box of cigars and a small knife with a bone handle and a steel blade for skinning. He spoke to me respectfully." He drank again, then puffed on the pipe and passed it back to Jack.

Hard Bone thought about his story for a time. "Well, he asked me if I knew this White Dog person. I said no, no." He shook his head. "He believed what he wanted. He said he wanted to sell the boys."

"The girl?"

"No girl then. Gone. He knew the soldiers wanted all the captives, even the ones who wanted to stay with the People. He said many of his captives were like that."

"Not so many," Jack said quietly.

"He wanted more than the soldiers would pay in trade. They wouldn't trade him guns. But he thought the soldiers wanted to hurt him. They didn't like him, they would catch him and put him in a cage because he kept away, he didn't sign the paper. Maybe they wanted him for killing people, you know, White Dog settlers, those people. We didn't know. Well, no one wanted to be around that man. I never got much food, it was the right day for the food allotment the agent promised. There were many of the People there for food, but the cattle didn't come. They were late. We were all hungry then."

"Where could this man be now?"

"He goes anywhere, I think." The old man coughed and took a drink. Jack thought the talk was over.

"He's always looking. He's looking for a woman but none of the women want to go with him. They said he killed his first wife when she ran away from him." Hard Bone pondered this gossip story. "Well, it was his right by custom, but he wants Badger's first daughter now. He looks sometimes for horses because so many died in the soldier war. But he wants the new soldier guns, he whispers to us about the new guns. He likes the crazy water. These things are forbidden here. But he is greedy, sometimes I think he is a foolish person, sometimes I think he is just like a bad Kiowa. But even fools are dangerous."

Jack listened to the old man's word and felt the first scratching of fear.

On the fourth night Jack came back to Hard Bone. His head pained him often, but he had grown more adept with his damaged arm.

He sat on the buffalo robe with Hard Bone, rubbing the stiffness in his hand, and offered tobacco.

"I must find this man you speak of." He felt a chill run down his spine even as he said this.

Again, he could hardly believe his own hard edge of probing suspicion.

Maybe the Supernaturals just wanted a great laugh. A great terrible laugh!

Jack reached to his belt where he wore the big knife with the fringed scabbard, Owl Stands' great knife. He spoke softly, "Grandfather, this gift is for you." He held the knife out to the old man.

The old man looked at the great knife, its adornments. Its fringed sheath. He held it carefully, as though it had a power, a life all its own.

Hard Bone sighed. He nodded, without words. He pondered for several minutes, holding the great medicine knife. Then he said, "The big fight, everyone is afraid now. But I believe he will come again, he is always hungry for trading. And he wants the woman."

"The woman?"

"He wants Badger's first daughter, but she says no to him many times. He offers two or three horses but she's worth more. She used to go on raids with her brothers. Once she was famous."

"Tell him when he comes that I will buy these boy captives."

Hard Bone looked at Jack quizzically.

"Yes," Jack said. "I will meet him at the place where the big painted rock stands above a spring. The hidden place. It is in the Comancheria. The rock has many pictures, many messages. I will pay him what he wants. Crates with many new soldier rifles, many jugs and bottles with crazy water."

Hard Bone looked thoughtfully into the darkness. He believed he knew this old place, one of many in the Comancheria but none so known among the old people for its ancient pictures and its sweet water, for he had painted there too, but not for countless seasons. He was a traditional man in every way but now he could not go there again. Never. He could not leave the Territory-prison place and go so far without a paper of permission.

And they both knew, without any words, the big White Dog soldier crime of selling repeater rifles, any weapons and any whiskey to the hostiles. Such acts were forbidden and harshly punished with the soldiers' iron cages and ropes that hanged such criminals, certainly why the trader made himself a shadow, now that the white man's war had ended, and the soldiers were back for the big Indian War.

Jack persisted. "Tell him I will meet him with many soldier guns."

"Far away."

"Or closer, or anywhere. Speak to him, let him choose a place. How else will I find this boy I search for?"

Hard Bone smoked in silence.

"Grandfather, show me a better way."

Hard Bone pondered. "How will this person know you?"

"I will know him," Jack said. "This place is easier than going over the big mountains in the snow with captives. The Santa Fe traders won't pay much, they'll be asleep in their *jacals,* hiding. There are more soldiers now. This way is safer, no soldier post. It is almost a forgotten place. But I think he knows it. You know it. Tell him I will pay well for those two boys, but they must be undamaged. I will make it easy for him."

Hard Bone held the knife reverently. "Maybe he is too afraid now. He has no manners, everyone says this. Maybe he will just laugh."

"Let him. If he is greedy, as you say, he'll come. He'll sniff the guns and the whiskey. Tell him I will come alone. I won't hurt him." Jack smiled at his lie. "I will pay very well, Grandfather. Tell him to come at the sixth fullness of the moon from now."

"So long."

"Long enough for him to hear of this offer when he comes to the Territory again after a woman, Grandfather. Time for him to go there. If he is greedy enough, if he is such a man."

They sat in silence. The old man pondered. He would grant this favor, carry this message, since there was a debt. But he looked thoughtfully at Jack. "I think maybe you have another gift for him."

Jack hesitated. "This old gift will make his heart good and his spirit soar like the eagles. But maybe not. Maybe not."

Hard Bone shook his head. "I know nothing of such things, only that he wants soldier guns and crazy water."

"Grandfather, he wants more."

I think this person always wants more.

Hard bone said, "You are going on a long journey."

Jack considered the many meanings of such a journey, but he only answered, "Yes."

The snow began to fall again in soft flakes. It was time to end the talks, time to find safe shelter from the cold. To think about Bexar, to think about Luzita.

Time to think about the shadow trader, and the laughter of the Supernaturals.

His mind flashed back over the years to the wagon camp in Santa Fe. The Comanche traders and the scatter of townsmen watching the rape of the Mexican girl captive, the man who stood in the firelight at the edge of the watchers, staring only at Jack.

Time to think about the sixth moon. June

Three days later he left the agency by stage and made his way to Elm Creek and the ranch, picked up his California gold from Sallie's root cellar hiding place under the floor and spoke what news he could to Ely and Elizabeth, which was little enough except that he had been in a fight.

"That one at the Washita River?" Ely asked. "Shit, we heard." He examined Jack carefully. "Stay over," he said.

"Just fetch me my horse," Jack answered, and softened his voice for Ely's concern. "I'm heading back to Bexar."

At McGregor's store he gave them the news of Sheridan's Indian War.

"But no Jeth," Mariah Matilda said. She bent her head. "No little Rose." Her voice sank into sadness. "I believe they are gone."

"No ma'am," he told her again. "No. If they'd been there at the Cheyenne camp they'd be dead by now, the Indians would've killed them when the fight started, but we didn't find---." He drew a deep breath. "We found some. But we didn't find ours."

Back in San Antonio de Bexar, he was thinner but hardier as the weeks passed. His arm healed finally, came free of the cast and he could hold his new .45 Colt revolver nearly as well as his right hand could, but his arm remained slow and sometimes awkward. His head, with a three-inch scar, felt almost normal again.

But there was a difference. And he had come to believe that he would not find anyone at the big history rock in June.

Too damn long. Anything can happen---too far---.

Crazy.

There was talk of the big fight even months later, talk of other fights, Sheridan's campaign, rampaging Indians, talk of the weather, tornados over east, floods and the general weather misery Texas went through on a daily basis on the frontier.

He watched and listened to travelers passing through, occasionally sat with one of the gamblers for an hour of poker at LUCKY'S until he got bored, drank whiskey or beer with regulars and militia bands getting ready for another fight after horse thieves along the border.

But Jack stepped away when they made talk of him joining up with a militia.

He sat at a table scarred with rings from hundreds of wet beer glasses. He watched the *mestizo* wait girl as she dodged reaching hands and brought new rounds to the tables. She looked like she had some black blood mixed with all the rest, maybe Louisiana Indian and white, and she looked young and tired and not entirely clean. All the regular prostitutes abided elsewhere in their own fancy cribs where many stray girls ended up. Or they just ambled the streets and dance halls, careful to make no trouble for the random law. This girl just looked like she worked long and hard in the tavern. Not ready for the cribs yet.

Good luck, Jack thought. You'll need it

"Shit, this hits the spot," Moses Jones said as he drank from a jar of beer he'd snatched from the wait girl's tray. "Sit, boy," he said to his companion.

The men sat themselves down at the table with Jack. The older of the two heaved a heavy sigh. "Jack, how you been?"

"Good enough," Jack shrugged. "You?"

"Just got back from a dust storm so bad the crows was flyin' backwards," Moses Jones said. "Looks like you got marked up some. How's the other feller?" Moses Jones smiled at his own wit.

"Mostly gone," Jack answered. He nodded toward the mark on Moses Jones's neck.

"Yep. Another fight at the border. Dust up, damn horse thieves. Never did get this one." He drank and said, "Heard about the big fight up north. You think Sheridan's right or maybe just got his head up his ass?"

"He has got his Indian War."

"He has that."

"You after another bad bunch?" Jack asked.

"Yep. Bad enough."

"Where to this time?"

Moses Jones shook his head. "Getting worse. Everywhere. More than a thousand horses run off this time. Their *compadres* just waiting for them over the border."

Moses Jones, a rider with the Minuteman, and once a Texas Ranger who had ridden with Jack Hayes, had a face that twisted for an instant then settled back. Sometimes called Captain, he was years older than Jack, with long lines of wear and weather in his face. Like most old Texians, he'd worn the gray during the Conflict, but he'd come home because he hated Indians and the new gangs of Mexican horse thieves running stolen horses over the Rio Grande. He was wire thin and hard as dirt, Jack thought. He wore an elaborate gray mustache, a black city coat and vest with a sagging neck scarf, a battered old hat, and he'd been fighting Indians and outlaws ever since he was a boy back in Austin's days in the old Mexican times.

The younger of the two said, "I come a long ways to fight them fucking Indians you got here."

"Which ones?" Jack asked with a straight face.

"Any of them," the boy said. He frowned. "All of them."

"How about the horse thieves? The *bandidos*?"

"Them too, sure." He stared at Jack, suspicious of mockery.

He was a little drunk, a little surly and full of himself. He wore well-worn clothes, a vest, a new neck scarf and a low-slung holster and weapon on his right hip. He had a narrow face and prominent blue eyes that stared here and there, as though looking for something, maybe just a random fight to prove his worth.

"Ned here comes from Tennessee, wore the gray, fought with everybody, wore the hood until he got caught. It's a plain wonder them fellers didn't shoot him then and there." Moses Jones shrugged. "But the Unionists made him swallow the dog, swear to join up with the U. S. of A. again." Moses Jones shook his head and smiled. "So, he comes here to try Texas."

Ned glared, but he knew better than to challenge Moses Jones' wry amusement.

"Indians gone there, he says."

"Killed off or hiding in them swamps," Ned said with satisfaction. "Them black folks too, just trash." He spoke now with an affected drawl. Jack felt his face get hot, he wondered who this kid was trying to be, maybe just a fool badass hard case with a ready gun.

He thought of the fight in the snow along the Washita, the white flag, the cold, the screams.

Killed off. He felt a surge of anger.

"Shit, we still need good men same as ever, Jack," Moses Jones said. "Pay's gotten up to $25.00 a month."

Jack gave himself time to let his anger drain away into idle talk. "Some of those outfits don't pay anything, Cap. Cattle drives paying thirty dollars a month now," Jack said, watching Ned. "Some outfits paying two dollars a day."

Moses Jones said, Hell, you ain't no cowhand, its miser'ble hard work and eating dust for 300, 400 miles. Ask them boys going up Chisholm's road. When the railroads come through there won't be no more long drives, you ask me. Indians breaking out now and then but mostly it's getting to be rustlers and shooters. Tribes fighting the soldiers up on the border, blood feuds killing the shooters off, town folks making new laws. Shit, everybody's a judge nowadays. Set up court out under the trees, pistols or knives, whoever wins." Moses Jones gulped at his beer to wash down his long speech. He barked a rough laugh. "We got our choice of trouble for damn sure. All you got to do is bring a fast horse and your own gear and you'll get all the fighting you want. Do some good, get rid of them two-legged vermin. Maybe three months then you come on home again." He lifted his beer and drank again. "Some of the boys're going east, there's news of a Comanche fuss and some crazy Wichita's teaming up and hitting the settlements again. I expect they were drunk. Where's the damn military control?" Moses Jones scratched his head. "They're just running off the reservations every which way. Shit!"

"You like a good fight, Cap."

"Well I been doing it long enough. Quaker agents talking about peace. What peace?" Moses Jones scoffed. "Gotta make them Indians civilized, like us. Now the Mexicans're running off our horses. Come along, Jack. Do you good."

Jack shook his head. "Someday, Cap."

"My boys're ready, cold or not. Tomorrow, we're leaving before daylight. You got cause, and my boys want a fight."

"I got the other business," Jack said.

"Just walking away from a fight?" young Ned drawled in a challenge, his blue eyes watching Jack.

Jack studied him. He watched the boy's right hand as it inched across the table toward his side, his weapon below.

You are not going to last long, boy, he thought. "I expect there's more than one kind of Texian," he answered mildly.

Moses Jones barked another laugh. "Pay attention, boy."

But Ned arose just then, his eyes on the mulatto wait girl. He stomped away through the scattered groups of men.

"That boy ain't going to last long out here," Moses Jones muttered. "Or he'll end up a damn shooter himself, or just dead bait for the crows."

Jack laughed at the echo of his own thoughts.

"Going off to get hisself drunk," Moses Jones said. "Wants to ride with me. Just a fool kid with that outlaw pistol he wears."

Jack looked across the smoky room, his thoughts drifting. He watched a boy fourteen, maybe fifteen, sweeping, cleaning up after the sloppy drunks. His clothes were old, just hung on him, he was rail thin. Now and then he paused and coughed.

Farm boys. Run off from home, working for food.

Seemed like they were everywhere since the war.

Moses Jones drank, slow, easy. "What's going on, Jack."

A minute passed before Jack answered. "Heard about a Comanche trader who trades in captives. Won't turn 'em in. Mostly kids. Trades 'em around."

"Kids."

"It's a mean business with him. Mexican and white kids. Maybe some Ute kids I heard."

Moses Jones tilted back in his chair. Another minute passed. "He got a name? We know about him?"

"He's alone."

"Used to be a fucking damn buck never lasted long alone out there without his people backing him up, save his bacon, enemies everywhere, whatever. They just kill each other." Moses Jones made a vague gesture that encompassed all tribal lands, all Indians.

"Now everyone's scared, Cap."

"Sheridan---kill all the fucking Indians, by Ganny," Moses Jones said

They sat in silence for a moment. Jack shook his head. "He's like a damn Comanche shadow now."

"What's he want?"

"Repeater rifles and whiskey."

"Shit."

"Yep."

"He won't take horses?"

"One, maybe two boys with him, last I heard. No horses. Mexican horse thieves and rustlers've got all the horses now."

"Mostly those bastards wanted horses, food, trading around, it was easy."

Jack nodded. "He wants repeater rifles, make a big name for himself with the wild tribes or down in Mexico with the big *rancheros*, I expect."

"Never see 'em again," Moses Jones said.

"Yep."

"How you going to find him? Who knows about him?"

"Nobody knows much about him."

"Military?"

"Nothing. But---." Jack stopped.

Moses Jones waited.

Finally, Jack said, "Maybe I know him. From a long time ago. Maybe there's a meeting," Jack smiled grimly, "--- if he comes in and takes my invite."

"How you going to pay him?"

"Pay him?" Jacked asked. "No idea yet."

Moses Jones's chair legs hit the floor with a thump as he sat forward. "When?"

"June."

"Where?"

Jack shook his head.

"Damn it, Jack!"

"We're talking rifles and whiskey."

Moses Jones made an angry gesture, "So?"

Jack drank some of his beer. "Can't see you hanging from a rope in a stockade, Cap. Military don't much like riding against drunk Indians with repeater rifles."

Another minute passed. Moses Jones persisted, "You looking for company?"

"I'm looking for horses, pack horses. Supplies."

"Shit!"

"Sure. Military's watching everybody, the scouts, the militias. It's their necks. They listen to rumors, you know that."

"Horses and pack animals."

"Told him I'd be alone, I'd find him."

"Told him?"

Jack laughed. "Smoke signals."

Moses Jones finished his beer. He wiped his mouth on the scarf at his neck and stood. "You are one hell of a hard ass, but I wish you luck."

Jack said. "They generally kill captives if they get scared. Riders following too close. Throw 'em away. Comanches, Apaches, Cheyenne, all of them. You know that too."

Moses Jones studied Jack. Finally, he said, almost reluctantly, "You sure he's still alive? You heard anything?"

Jack shook his head.

"Maybe they tied the boy to the cactus a long time ago, Jack."

Jack frowned, the vision of this favored Apache death torture shaking him for a moment.

"He was eight, eight years old."

Moses heaved a sigh. "Yeah, they probably kept him. Turn him into a Comanche buck. Jesus." He looked around the tavern, the people. "I need a new saddle. That Don Ernesto still putting out good tack?"

"The best. Anything you want."

"Shit. Now where's that fool boy gone? Probably going to get himself dog drunk and shoot up the place---."

The next day Jack rode up to Fredericksburg again, the little German town where Indians sometimes came to camp and trade. The German folks and the hostile Indians had come to some kind of truce in the past that Jack didn't understand, but the Indians and the Germans got along and kept to their truce. A year past, the Indians brought a half-grown white boy for ransom, and left him with a German family and everyone watched to see what happened because so many believed it was too late for the boy, and shortly the boy began wandering the town at night, stealing, harassing younger boys, fighting and now he was just another frontier problem added to the many. But the Indians had brought no child captives recently, and no news.

June, Jack thought. *Will he come?*

He wandered often into San Antonio's *cantinas,* dance halls, stores, any distraction. He found one of the new Stetson hats in a dry goods store and chose a dark one, dark as his heart felt at night when he couldn't sleep. He found a double-barreled pocket-sized spyglass, used but useful, another steel-bladed Green River knife with a good buckhorn handle and a leather sheath, a second replacement for the one he'd left with the Quaker agent. He paged through a book with woodcut pictures, tall ships, sailors, words, vast endless seas, men lost at sea.

He took his weapon into the gunsmiths for repair and found a new Sharp's .52 caliber repeater rifle, the fine new Union rifle that shot faster than the Rebs' old single shot weapons.

North had the money from all them factories, the gunsmith grumbled bitterly, a familiar complaint all over Texas after the Conflict. *South had corn and hogs.*

He lived in the rooming house, bathed in the bath house and drank in saloons. He avoided the woman, the girl with the luminous eyes. *Luzita.*

Something was wrong.

I have to go for June. I have to go.

He listened to the tavern talk, the gossip, and slept fitfully, sometimes going back in his dreams.

The woman in the half-finished cabin long ago had said *Remember. Remember.*

Now and then he saw her, a woman's blurred face, the cotton dress she favored, and then she faded into a distant shadow.

He remembered back to his first moments as a boy, before the Comanches came, when he discovered the terrible mysteries of the prairies as they travelled in a good wagon, with the cow following, to their new free homestead land with all its promised sweet spring water, rich soil for sweet corn rows and game everywhere.

He remembered the scatter of human bones---*who's? And why?*

Another place, where so many buffalo had died beneath a cliff long ago, and grass growing tall and green there, *when?* The big round cave in the ground where bats swarmed up at night, the mud brick shelters melting in the rain in a lost canyon cliff. The man who drove their wagon away and never came back.

Something was wrong.

He woke at night, hearing the soft jangle of his friend's singing moccasins walking through the grass. He remembered his friend's flute, playing love songs.

He dreamed of the sleeping camp by the Washita, the snow, the white flag.

He heard someone yell,

 He woke hearing music, bugles, yells, gunfire. Screams.

Custer's music.

He dreamed of the big rock with the spring at its base.

I have to go---.

He rode through the cold winter streets, by the stage station, the post office, the old Catholic cathedral showing the scars of renovation, like the places where captive Comanche slaves had built the first old Spanish missions long ago and later, where Mexican slaves sometimes ended their Indian captivity. He rode past the old adobe house with the blue door, strongly built in the old style, but empty, abandoned under leafless winter cottonwood trees.

Not far from Luzita.

But he had to stay away from her now, away from her luminous eyes that sometimes saw too much, the questions he knew were on her lips. Her bright, wise laughter. Her spirit. Maybe even her anger. He didn't know why.

Because I have to go there for June---.

No news. No word.

With his new Sharp's, a leather case of ammunition, grain for his horse and his kit and blanket roll, he hunted through dreary days of snow flurries, gone for days at a time, maybe looking for game, maybe just gone.

Damn him, he thought, going over it again, again.

The white flag was flying.

He startled a flock of wild turkeys and watched their heavy flight as they flew through the pines and oaks looking for new roosts.

Getting colder.

He listened to the wilderness silence. He heard Custer's music again.

Damn him, he thought, far away in his memory.

He came to an old trace road in a stand of trees at the edge of a wide clearing bordered by low rolling hills, following deer tracks, not caring. He saw other tracks, deep Indian travois drag marks under the scatter of snow, and some newer shod horse tracks over unshod tracks, three ponies chasing after the travois, scuffing up the trail days before.

He sat his horse, staring at nothing, seeing the fight at the river again. The white flag.

Then he saw the clearing spread wide and open before him, gently rolling land, low hills rising on either side, dotted here and there with snow covered berry thickets and brush, long since bare and tangled, and scattered oaks. He listened to the silence and heard nothing that broke it, he saw only the pure, quiet deer tracks like a delicate signature in the snow. He saw the doe and her half-grown fawn poised and motionless in the distance.

The land went on forever, wide and inviting, as far as he could see. He drew a deep breath at the wideness, the wild beauty of it.

The remains of an old wood post sprawled at the edge of the trace, and near the post a warped board sign. He dismounted and pulled the sign up from where it lay half buried in a tangle of snow and dead grass.

This wild empty land, this wide, open clearing with its rolling hills and meadows, maybe less than a day's ride from San Antonio, had once been owned.

Owned?

Thousands of wild acres before him.

How can you own this land?

His Indian thinking.

He looked along the trace road, hardly more than a path as it cut along the edge of the trees. He looked at the wooden sign and saw the words burnt with an iron into the wood.

He began to laugh. Then the anger rose through him, the hot white rage at all he had seen, all he had lost.

What am I doing here? What the hell am I doing here?

Then he saw the deer start and bolt away in high leaps, their white tails raised and waving in panic.

He pulled his Sharp's from its saddle scabbard and raised it. Wolves, or a panther, but slowly, as he looked down the sights, something human crawled from the thicket, something small and human.

He lowered the Sharp's, watching, as startled as the deer. The small human shape rose to its feet with care, clutching at its clothes, hugging everything tightly, looking around, looking after the deer. It just stood there as though it could not move.

He saw it must be a child, bundled, muffled, its face lost in the layers of clothing, its head uncovered except for wild hanks of black Indian hair.

Jack stared, letting himself comprehend what he saw. What this meant.

Thinking, realizing what it had to mean for him, suddenly.

Now. Here.

Shit!

He remounted and started across the clearing, slowly, watching his horse's ears, watching for other alarms. But the child just stood, hardly noticing as Jack approached. When he was close the child suddenly began a wild, awkward scrambling back toward the thicket, the shelter, the hiding place, and Jack dismounted quickly and caught the child and held it hard against him.

He saw by her ragged clothing that this was a girl child, of four years or so. Her face was round, Indian, probably Comanche, but her face was drawn and streaked with dirt, her small body almost weightless, her struggles weak, her limbs stiff from the cold. She wore rabbit fur and a doeskin tunic and clung to a length of dirty woven trade fabric. Her moccasins were shredded but she had tried to wrap bits of torn fabric around her feet. Dead leaves and small clumps of snow and debris fell from her clothing as she struggled; she had buried herself under leaves, under anything that would give her a little cover, a little warmth. The snow had given her moisture but had made her colder whenever she swallowed. He knew she had had no strong food, no heat. From her weakness he knew she would soon die.

"*Basta!*" he said in Spanish, stern with her as she struggled, and then in Comanche, "*Taoyocha,* Child, enough!"

She hardly seemed to notice his voice or his words that broke the profound wilderness quiet with the harsh bark of sound, his anger, his impatience. She just grew weaker in her struggles. He held her until she grew still and then he remounted and carried her back across the snow to the shelter of the trees by the old trace road.

Damn!

With a fire and warmed water laced with small dollops of whiskey, he held a cup to her lips.

"*Hebeto.* Drink!"

He pushed the cup against her mouth. She opened her lips for the warm water, then wanted more.

What would Smith do? That doctor of everything?

Where the hell are you?

But Cicero Smith was years late.

Slowly he fed her more water and small bites of corn cake. She shivered, closed her lips, resisting, but then she began to revive, though her lips barely moved. He bundled her roughly in his own blanket and fed her from his cache of food, careful slow bites of dried apples, more corn cake. Careful swallows of whiskey and water.

Shit! Now this!

This weak child---.

He stayed by the fire through the night, holding the child with his back against a tree and building the fire's heat with whatever dry wood he could find. His horse fed on the last of the grain from his pack. He melted more snow water and ate more of his jerky and drank the last of his whiskey. The child just shivered and finally he had to hold her against his body with the blanket pulled tight around both of them. Once her eyes opened. They were empty of expression, just dark and enduring. Small enduring animal eyes. Her stiff lips moved in a whisper and he bent down to hear.

Ida ha.

Cold.

Little sister girl, you're safe, he told her, but she had fallen asleep.

When the first gray light came through the trees and the child had stopped shivering, he knew exactly what he had to do next.

The following afternoon he sat his horse and waited. The group of men before him, two in rough, heavy wool jackets and hats, two in clerical dress hugging shawls, stood talking, gesturing, looking up at the old San Antonio de Bexar cathedral showing the careful damage of renovation.

He lost patience and rode forward and stopped before the oldest man. He looked down at the man who hugged his shawl against the weak sunlight after the snow.

"Take her." He held the child toward the man who had not moved at Jack's sudden approach.

The *padre* stared up. His old, mottled hands tightened on his shawl. His face stared in an ancient mask of surprise.

"Take her now!"

The *padre* started to speak in words Jack scarcely heard. Church words. "My son---."

"I am not your son." Jack said, refusing the commonplace words. "Take her!"

"But my son---."

"No."

The others gathered closer, staring up with concern.

Jack dismounted and held the child out. The old man lifted his arms for the child. He seemed confused and astonished at her frailty.

"Now listen," Jack said. "You are a man of your one God, but you are not always right. You are not always good."

The old man frowned, still surprised. He seemed to be searching for a stern response.

"You people, you are not always the best way to---!" Jack drew a deep breath. "Listen to me. Take care of her. Find a good woman. Don't make her a slave or one of your servants here in your church or anywhere---."

"But---."

"Listen to me. She's a wild thing. They lost her. If her people come looking someday, or send someone, if they want to make honeytalk with you, if they are just---," he stumbled, looking for words. "Let her go. She's a wild thing."

Listen to me! They love their children!

"Listen to me!"

The expression on the old man's face began to change.

"She doesn't talk" Jack said. "She's lost. Left behind. She's starved. Find a woman to help her. Help her!"

The old man's face grew calm, enlightened. He was listening to some sort of puzzling confession, but for what?

"Her name is---?" He began a calm inquiry.

Jack interrupted with a wave of his arm, dismissing. "Nothing. She has no name. Write her in your record books. Call her Maria, or Carmen or---like all the rest."

He remounted and looked down at the old man, his voice quiet, "Do this. I will come back. I will watch."

He stopped by the land office, then went to the agent, finding the words painted on a dirty window.

"The land office sent me here."

The man's face was florid, his eyes small and blue. He was portly and officious and spoke with an Eastern twang, the sound and accent Cicero Smith might have called *New York.*

His name was Earl Bertram Bloom, by the newly painted sign in the window. He had associates. The sign mentioned a bank in San Antonio, other affiliations.

Just another carpetbagger.

"Ah yes, I am familiar with this fine property. Three thousand twenty-six acres, sir," he told Jack. He smiled, "not all that big by your Texas standards! Over West, they're talking hundreds of thousands of---."

"Big enough," Jack said. "For now."

"Well. It's got a good strong title," Earl Bertram Bloom went on. "Family head rights, no swamp or bog, two small springs. Good water, sir. Never been overgrazed. Good woodlots, mostly open rolling land---."

"You've been there?"

The realtor nodded, then cleared his throat. "Well, near there in my buckboard, sir. It's a bit rough, you know---."

"Sure. Indians. Comanches." Jack's mouth moved slightly, close to a smile.

Earl Bertram Bloom sighed. "Well, perhaps."

Nothing surprised Jack in this conversation.

"What price?"

"When the owner left, he specified that he wanted ninety cents an acre, I've got his signed paperwork right here---."

"Why's he selling?"

"I'm told he went off to the Conflict and sadly did not return. Now his widow says she has had enough of the frontier life, she's going back to Massachusetts and she's waiting for the disposal of the property---."

"You weren't here then."

"Ah, no. But I must mention there are others interested in the property, there's water, not like that cheap government land out west where the cattle men are buying up millions of dry acres for a few cents---."

"They can have it." He picked up the old board sign he'd shown Earl Bertram Bloom.

Carpetbaggers, the scourge of the damaged South. He just wanted to get this finished.

"I will offer seventy cents an acre for this property. Surveyed."

"Sir, if you ask around---."

"I have."

"Well." The man fussed with papers on his desk. "It is a low offer, but I must submit it nevertheless. Given more time---."

"Now. It's a fair price," Jack answered. "Half in gold."

The realtor stared at him, counting silently, and Jack smiled.

Next, he knocked on a faded blue door, but had no answer. The paint had peeled from the door and left raw wood, but it was still a proud old door. The house seemed to huddle under the old cottonwood trees as though age had hidden it, but it was a strongly built big old adobe, larger than most, not far from the river or the plaza. Its walls needed patching with new adobe plaster, its windows needed replacing but he saw no serious damage. He saw an old overhead thatch arbor not far from the front door, a place to sit in hot summer shade. He saw two old outdoor ovens at the back, other outbuildings, a well, a corral for sheep or goats, a small barn for storing hay, a low wall, and more trees, bare with winter.

He saw a place that reminded him of Estebanico, the santero.

He went to *LA LUZ*, empty handed, like a stranger. He thought Luz might turn from him because he had stayed away.

Because something was wrong.

But when she filled his plate and looked up, he said. "Come away. Let me show you."

"Show me what?" She had not seen him for weeks but her beautiful eyes were calm, just searching, although he thought he saw a quick flash of fire and then a moment of concern as she saw the scar on his head, and then maybe relief, gladness.

"Just come." He waited.

An older woman wearing a colorfully embroidered blouse, with her thick black braid of hair wrapped around her head, just watched him from the back where she worked measuring cones of brown sugar. Her aunt, maybe her cousin. Then without a word she came to the counter to take Luz's place.

They walked past a few side streets, not far from the drifting fragrances of apple pies.

I'll tell her about the land, he thought, voicing in his mind for the first time, finding the words.

About orchards.

He turned, guiding her to stand at the gateway of the low wall that surrounded the house with the blue door.

"The old *Tejanos* left here to live with their family in San Jacinto. Been a long time. I asked around. They might come back---or maybe not."

He waited, looking toward the house, its trees, their welcoming promise of summer shade.

"I'll rent it now," he said. "Fix it up, for them, for us."

Luz just looked, and looked, hugging her shawl closer against the cold.

"Come live here, with me," he said.

The words seemed to linger in a lonely but determined silence.

Come live with me.

She looked for long moments at the old house, the bare cottonwood trees. Then she turned to look up at him.

"Remember. I am my grandmother's child," she said.

He smiled with a great sense of relief. He knew the price he must pay.

"Yes ma'am, you are!"

"Then you must say the words. You must marry me," she said, her voice firm, but he knew that firmness was a great part of her woman's heart. Luz's lips moved just a little, longing to smile, to be certain, but wary.

He saw there the strength, the loving challenges he relished.

This Luzita.

He heard echoes too, words from long ago, a different woman,

Sallie, Sallie.

But now these were Luzita's words, and his.

"Yes ma'am," he answered. "I must marry you. I damn well want to marry you." He drew her close and felt no resistance, just her offered softness, her resilience. "Tell your grandfather and your brothers and your uncle and all the others that I have all the words they want."

Her eyes searched his face. They studied the scar on his head. "You have been fighting. I heard."

"Yes ma'am."

Her fingers touched his short beard, his brush of mustache.

"I'll shave it off," he said with a smile.

Her smile answered his. "No. But there's something else," she said.

"Yes ma'am. There's land now. For an orchard. Apples. Maybe pecans---."

She thought for a moment.

"But the fighting," she said.

He fell silent and wondered if he heard Custer's music again in the distance. But the day was only cold and quiet.

"All the fighting. You have been away. With the fighting."

He could only shake his head. He could only remember old Hard Bone, what he had done there at the Washita, and then not remember.

At last she said, "But you found nothing. You will always search."

He couldn't tell her yet about the shadow man who sold children.

"Yes ma'am, I will always search."

In March of '69, when the snows had left Bexar cool and the air freshened with the spring ahead, he made this woman his bride with all the bans and rituals the family expected. Their headstrong girl-widow now was safely married. They celebrated at a modest *fandango*, where everyone toasted this dubious union and rejoiced as best they could.

In time he sat at a table and drank tequila and ate black beans and chili with her grandfather and her brothers and her cousins. He listened to their polite stories and shared some of his own. They spoke as men unwilling to speak, yet, of personal thoughts and events with this stranger, this *Anglo* Texian, and Jack told them how the Indians taught a mustang never to step on a lead, how a good war pony always stood by his master even under enemy fire; the difference between hunting arrows and war arrows, how to snare wild turkeys in the woods, and follow bees to find the best honey trees. He told them how to catch eagles, and about a boy living among the Comanches. He told them about walking away, fighting, California, thieves, and how the apple orchards thrived in California valleys. How the *santeros* of Taos carved wooden *santos* in the old way for their church.

Finally, one dawn morning when the redbirds began to move through the trees along the river, he opened the door of their *casita* and found a blue roan gelding tied to the hitching post, a fine strong muscular horse, not one of the high-stepping town horses Luz's grandfather Don Ernesto and her people were famous for, but a fast, hardy Spanish horse, as hardy tough as a wild mustang, and ready to run.

In April Jack knew he had to go back, to find Hard Bone again up in the Territory.

Had the shadow trader come back, carrying his captives, looking for trade? The *Ki-Was Man*. Hard Bone had given him the Comanche name - the Bad Kiowa Man.

"He asked me what man wants to buy his property," Hard Bone told him as they smoked the good tobacco Jack had brought as a gift. "He has four now, another girl. Just a Ute girl maybe. I don't know where he got her, no."

Jack sat on the same robe as he had in the snow days after the Washita when they had first talked. Now Hard Bone had started to paint a new calendar robe on elk-hide cured to an elegant whiteness.

Hard Bone rubbed his old eyes. The fire burned low, mostly embers. A pot of meat and root vegetables bubbled on the coals.

"Well I had no name to give him. What do I know of such things? But I said I remembered about that big rock. I said I had been there, maybe some time I go back there. He said he saw picture rocks everywhere. He said maybe this one was too far."

The old man smoked in silence for a time. "That one has no manners. Every time he comes here he wants Badger's daughter, the one who fought the Apaches and got hurt in a big fall before the last snow, but she won't go with him. He says she is not worth much now."

Jack waited, listening to Hard Bone's gossip. He was a story teller, a lover of events.

"The Ki-Was Man said he had buyers over the mountain, good buyers." Hard Bone went on. "They hide from the soldiers. Now they have fewer captives to work for the New Mexico *rancheros* or in the mines in Mexico. Children are scarce, even Ute children. But he wants soldier guns. He said maybe he would go to the big rock, yes. No horses. He wants crazy water and soldier guns."

"I will go," Jack said to Luzita when he returned to her. He kissed her and drew her closer in the darkness of their *casita.*

"When*?"* She knew why, the knowledge lived like a pending wound in her heart. But of course, he would go.

"End of May."

"Where?"

"A place I know, a place I think he knows."

"Where?"

He shook his head.

"I will not try to rescue you," she assured him with a teasing smile. He smiled in return.

"No. But---."

"I will not." She drew a long sighing breath. She understood the hard realities of her world.

Her father, her uncles and brothers and cousins---.

The night silence surrounded them. They listened and heard an owl's soft voice in the old cottonwood trees out by the corral.

"That owl," Luz said, a nervous complaint. "I will go with you then."

Jack breathed for a moment, slow careful breaths.

"No one goes with me. He will kill the captives if I am not alone. It is their custom. My promise."

They listened to the owl's soft voice.

"What do you need?"

"Five good pack horses---I'll get them at the Tradedays coming up---."

"My grandfather---."

"He has offered. Your brothers have offered."

"What will you trade?"

Jack thought for a moment, listening to the silence of the night, then answered, "What I have."

PART IV

WHAT YOU'VE DONE

ॐॐ

He came to the great picture rock eleven days after leaving San Antonio de Bexar, following the old road, the water holes and springs to El Paso he remembered well enough, until he found the faint Comanche trace that branched off toward the great rock. He left behind the occasional traffic of freight wagons to and from El Paso and Conestoga wagons trailing milch cows and children and found the Comanche trace overgrown and almost lost to *chamisa* and clumps of *chollo* cactus.

He came early, before the sixth full moon, traveling in easy stages. He led a string of five pack horses carrying boxes and crates.

He sat Blue, staring upward. High above, the rock stood against the sky as he remembered, and below the deep pool of the spring water rippled in sunlight and shadow, with a scatter of green brush along the edges and a few doves and jays moving lazily through the branches. On the face of the great rock, he saw that little had changed, except some of the many pictures, the many stories, had faded. Some were made with paint, ocher, black, green, red, the Comanche colors, eloquent pictures of antelope, of ancient sheep with great curled horns, stick drawings of horses and riders, buffalo, some pierced by arrows, a man's painted hand, and others of the drawings were picked into the rock, hammered with rock hammers long ago. He saw scenes of battles, fallen enemies and jubilant hunters, an arrow with three sets of buffalo horns that bragged of a fight and three fallen foes. And he saw scrolling words as he would write them, dates as he would write them, from the old Spanish days far in the past, a different story, a different people passing by. He remembered, as a boy, marveling at how high the pictures extended above the spring up to the sky; until he remembered watching Owl Stands crawling up a ladder made of rawhide and strong sticks, to record new stories of the People into the face of the history rock.

The rock stood in a broad canyon made by the action of the spring water over the centuries. Once the Old People followed their own trace road to this place, even as far back as the Dog Days when the Old People walked. Over time others made the road but it was always a hidden place, lost, long ago fading away among the scattering of pines and stunted junipers and plains scrub above. He had spent a day searching for signs of the old trace path, so faint had this trail become. Here in this hidden canyon the cottonwood trees were in full leaf, bright green and fluttering with any breeze. Pine trees and junipers scattered in the canyon and on the rim. The canyon wandered for miles, almost invisible from the plain above, until the water disappeared under the sand.

He found the signs of the old path down, leading his string of horses to the water, sweet and cold even in the heat.

Still good water---.

He saw his reflection in the water, the short beard he'd grown, other changes.

He looked around, looking for changes in the canyon.

And he knew exactly why he felt the lurking anger, had known for weeks.

Maybe this trader is not Ki-Was Man.

Maybe I've lost Jeth again---.

Maybe I'm too late---.

Then he watered the ponies, removed their packs and hobbled them up on the plain to graze the summer grasses still fresh from the last rain. He turned back to ride Blue down the canyon slowly, searching, finding familiar places, mostly sand beaches, grassy openings, tangles of brush, cutbanks and shallow caves. Owl Stands' people, in their random visits over the seasons to this favored place, had camped at the old sites under the trees along the creek, their big pony herd grazing the plain above under watchful eyes, while the women gossiped and Owl Stands painted his ritual stories and news on the great rock. Even though the canyon was on the Comancheria, travelers from other tribes sometimes passed secretly through and went on their way. But the shallow canyon showed no signs of recent tribal visits. Every opening where sunlight penetrated, every ancient campsite lay overgrown, lost. Here at the head of the canyon he saw no pony tracks, no *travois* drag marks, no recent Comanche fire pits. No dangling ropes hung from the old cottonwoods where the children made their swings.

Thinking back, he remembered more. ---They banished him up on the plain twice. He wanted to go fight somewhere, chase the White Dogs. Didn't want to guard the herd---contrary, persistent, always trouble---the women laughed at him---.

Now sand and leaves and time had taken everything, and old men such as Owl Stands no longer climbed the great rock.

He searched, looking for the places where Comanche boys hunted adventure, trying to remember where. He found deer tracks, coyote tracks, lizard scratching in the sand, other animals coming to the water. He found middens of ancient trash where the ancestor people had lived and cooked in fire pits with burning stones of granite. Finally, he found the cave.

Now it was hidden, the entrance covered with the branches of grown trees and brush. He saw no trail, no sign of grasses broken by footprints. The cave was smaller than he remembered but it went far back, and its entrance opened broadly above the canyon floor. Once it had been a secret hiding place, a boys' lookout, a place to hide and tell brave stories, but when the bats circled from the cave at twilight, more each summer, and the boys found the old bones of strange small human beings at the back of the cave, human skulls, and the bear scat everywhere, the boys abandoned such a fearful and unlucky place.

He remembered there were at least two main paths into the canyon, the one in the distance where the walls of the canyon fell lower and the water pooled and sank into the sand, and the steeper trail down from the plain, at the great rock and the shadowed spring. There were other, newer earth slides tumbling down to the sand from past storms.

He saw now one thing he could do, from how he had pondered and planned in his mind for months, searching among the many ways he could prepare for the meeting with the one who held the boy captive.

He settled in to make his camp on the rim among the scrub pines and junipers. This was an old campsite with a few pines trimmed up long ago, an old fire pit, a place where the boys guarding the herds could lounge and watch the herds and tell each other bragging stories.

Days passed, and he watched the moon at night and thought this surely was a fool's effort. A solitary fool, who couldn't believe the search was finally over.

He remembered again how casually the Comanche threw captives away, weak captives, young children who bothered them, and he sometimes dreamed of burned bodies and snarling dogs.

The Quaker agent's ledger had held name after name of captives who had never been found.

Unrecovered---.

But he wants the guns, if he is the Ki-Was Man I know, he'll come after the guns, Jack thought, *he was always like the antelope you could lure to the bow with a whistle or a waving feather---hungry, always hungry, curious.*

His five pack horses grazed up on the plain, hobbled and foraging by day, but he kept Blue grazing close by. He led the horses to water at the end of the canyon every day and checked them for random bumps and injuries and gave each a handful of oats. At night he staked them close to his camp. He made no effort to hide his presence or the smoke from his campfires.

I'm here.

He climbed the great rock and found the old signs of ancient habitation, a few long dried crumbled mud bricks, low walls melted by the rains, silent ruins built long ago for safety from all the dangers on the plains below. He remembered as a boy, climbing up the narrow, crumbling trail to the top, more eroded now by the rains of the years. Little had changed here from that long-ago time, but now, for Jack, it was a lookout, a way to search the low rolling plain to the horizon.

He wrote in his journal, wondering how the meeting would go with the man who held the boy.

The greedy man. He knew it could go well or end badly, all by chance no matter what his fierce intent.

We'll see. We'll see if he comes at all. He carries the shame---if he recognizes me, he'll try to kill me. Jeth too. If it's Jeth. We'll see, even fools are dangerous.

He tended his camp, where he'd unloaded all the crates and all his gear and set up a small shelter against occasional rain. He never slept in his camp, always finding a different place. He brewed Luzita's coffee, savoring, wondering what changes to expect in this man old Hard Bone called Hungry Dog, the Bad Kiowa Man.

He puzzled again and again what would happen if Dohat recognized him.

---He has the right by their custom---he'll try. But not unless he has an advantage. He is a Comanche---.

I've kept this beard, let it grow---maybe he won't even recognize me---if he comes.

He found some reeds in the canyon and attempted to make a courting flute to take back to Luzita, thinking of her, wanting her. He paged through the almanacs he'd brought, studying whatever caught his attention. Orchards. The year's weather. Agricultural lore expanding through Texas with the settlers. White Dog civilization, words. Anything. He listened to coyotes howling and yipping at night. Every evening he watched the bats circling up from the big cave in the canyon and every morning he watched the hawks and falcons fly among them, snagging bats on the wing as the bats flew back to sleep the day away in the cave.

More bats now, he wrote in his journal. Random notes, worries.

---all that matters is getting Jeth free---.

---maybe I should talk to the Supernaturals---sure.

---shit, I'm no good at making flutes ---.

Every few days, he rode in a wide circle around the canyon, looking for sign of unshod hoof prints, but found only antelope and deer sign and scat. He foraged on snared rabbits, followed coyote prints and circling ravens to the bones of a dead fawn. He left his own sign, Blue's shod hoof prints.

I'm here.

From the top of the rock he scanned any movement, far away and nearer. Twice with his spy glass he saw a handful of antelope running north, the coyotes or wolves chasing after, probably just following.

Never catch 'em. Just playing, won't wear 'em down.

Another time he watched a band of mustangs, wild and wary, led by a paint stallion pushing his mares to water at the far end of the canyon.

He'd brought no mares for the wild stallions to steal. And no mules to bray.

And another time he saw a cluster of riders far away, heading south, hurrying. Even at the distance under the hot June sky he saw they wore no hats. He watched to see if they circled toward the lower canyon for water, but they kept riding south toward Mexico, where there were hidden springs and rainwater tanks worn into rock along the way.

The land above the canyon rim grew darker each night as the moon waned.

*If he doesn't come---*he wrote in his journal, but he could never finish the words. He just found a great emptiness within himself.

He thought about the man he sometimes called in his mind, the Child-Taker.

If he comes, he'll never leave. He will never leave.

Sometimes he wondered. He knew himself to be as hard and as practical as the most traditional Comanche,

---*had to stay alive*---.

His Indian thinking, that great fierce reserve buried deeply in his mind, even that useful cruelty of the wild people which they had taught him, was still there, still ready, a dark reality always held in check. He remembered of the fight at the Washita River. The blood, the killing. But he wondered. He'd never yet tortured and killed an unarmed enemy, nor raped a woman, nor thrown a crying child away.

But he'd pondered now, like any Comanche, how he would kill the Ki-Was Man, the Child-Taker. Then he wondered if he had become too much of a White Dog man---.

Enough, he told himself in disgust. *Whatever happens*---.

Then one morning, at the end of the old moon, as he scanned the land now moving under cloud shadows, he saw a flicker of movement quickly lost to shadow and sunlight again, then gone. He saw movement repeated, now and then disappearing as the land dipped and the sage and brush hid any sight of movement. There again, just the slight persistent passage, inching through the scrub juniper toward the head of the canyon. He moved around the camp quickly, gathering more wood for the fire, wary but excited and wondering. He pulled his shirt loose to hide his .45 tucked into his belt at his back, his knife sheathed there, hidden. He leaned his Sharps against a pine trunk, so he would appear traditionally weaponless for the trading, saw to Blue's stakeout, threw aside his moccasins and pulled on his boots, and brewed a pot of Luzita's coffee. Then he waited.

He's looking around, looking for sign.

Two hours passed, dragged, as he waited.

He's looking for hard sign. Troopers. Ambush. He's wary.

Then they came, through the shadowy midday quiet. Two ravens flew up with harsh alarm voices half a mile away, then closer, a doe bolted up from her midday bedding and raced across the sage to the east.

Jack poured himself a cup of fresh coffee and stood waiting.

Then they were there, emerging carefully to stop at the edge of Jack's camp clearing, with nothing more than the rustle of branches and the soft pad of the horses' hoofs.

The leader, the man Dohat---.

The Ki-Was Man.

Jack felt the surge of anger that was almost joy.

Dohat sat the back of a strong appaloosa stallion that worked a big Spanish bit in his mouth. He was the showy, high tempered kind of mount Dohat had always favored over Owl Stands' herd of paints and bays and roans. The appaloosa had a full tail, not like the rat tails of most appaloosas, and distinct black spots on his rump. Dohat led a tired paint pony. An old man sat on its back, hunched as though asleep, but one of his hands clutched a rawhide rope fastened to the halter of another paint pony that appeared so worn and thin that it came to a stop at Jack's camp with its head lowered. Occasionally it gave a shiver of pain. The parfleche pack on its back shifted as though alive, then settled. It appeared to have no weight.

Then came two boys on the back of a tough gray mustang, riding bareback.

The boy. The older boy.

Jack stared, then looked quickly away. He felt his heart race suddenly, pounding, then the pain of his long anxiety rushing away, his joy surging as he looked again at the older boy.

Then he grew calm again. He dared not show his recognition.

The last to come was a woman, a squaw leading a dun pack horse. She rode a sorrel mustang, a tired gelding with a bobbing head and a long white blaze face. The woman sat stiffly upright, her face without expression, her long black hair braided on either side of her face. She was dressed in simple doe skins. A colorful blue agency bandanna lay tied at her neck.

The old man who had once had the name of Owl Stands, sat his thin pony on an old wooden saddle cinched on padding of soft old hides and saddle blankets. An ancient musket rode in the saddle holster near his leg. His back was hunched, and his head bent, his hand caught in the folds of the blanket wrapped around his body. He did not seem to notice the trees, the high rock, the spring with its stream in the canyon, he did not notice Jack Rainie.

The reins of his pony fell to the dust, discarded by Dohat. The old man did not notice this either. With his head bent Jack could see the eagle feathers in his braided scalp lock, showing a chief's importance, but they were ragged, drooping. His blanket looked clean, almost new, his Comanche moccasins scarcely worn. The bit of his shirt showing at his neck was decorated with pretty beads and quills, finely worked but faded, soiled. He wore a single stone necklace. For Owl Stands, once an honored chief with many names, it was enough.

Jack saw that the old man's face had become a withered effigy, all power now wandering in canyons of dark, dried flesh. He was thin, somehow shaken by time. The seasons had truly taken him away. His hair fell in black strings from where the parting had been colored with red ocher. His ear lobes dragged down with heavy stone ear plugs, his strong nose had become thin and twisted, his mouth nothing more than the cut of a knife blade. His eyes were only dark pebbles, hazed over, empty, wandering. Lost. After a time, they settled on Jack.

Then Jack stared at the leader of the group, taking his time. He stared at the man Dohat, and his heart surged again, with anger, with the urge to kill him where he sat his restive appaloosa horse. He saw that Dohat had filled out, not with fat but with power, he appeared more muscular, harder, but his head looked round, large, heavy. He had made his solitary nest, his cave of identity, his secret habitation in how he dressed, in a conglomerate of the old ways of his people, but much more from among the new white people, those he professed to hate, as old Hard Bone had spoken, but those he always used to his own ends. The White Dog's clothes hung from Dohat's body in dirty calico shreds. He had adorned himself with dried human fingers, the tatter of a scalp with long pale hair, and with white man's peace medals, crosses, rings scavenged from captives and stolen from reservations, from anywhere, all useless junk he thought held strong medicine, intimidating power, showing his own arrogant importance and speaking of his many violent deeds.

---*he searches for something*, Hard Bone had spoken.

Now this hybrid man, in scorn of the new White Dog military, had made himself into a shadow trader known among the tribes but never mentioned in fear of White Dog anger, known for his collections of children and other captives ripe for sales to the few Comancheros who were left after the soldiers had scattered them. The Comancheros would take the captives south to sell to the silver mines in Chihuahua, or the salt mines, or west over the mountains on the slave trail to the *hidalgo rancheros* in New Mexico and California where they would labor in their houses and their fields.

Clearly Dohat thought of himself as more than a traditional warrior, in spirit and in deed, a great man stubbornly from the ancient days, and one who never lacked Comanche pride and courage. He gave the outward appearance of an admirable man, both clever and powerful, a man to be spoken to with courtesy and caution. But he carried a whispered stigma.

He had colored the part in his hair with red ocher, but Jack saw no eagle feathers in his braided scalp lock. He wore old hammered silver *conchos* in his braided hair, relics from his past, which made his head look larger. He had painted his face with bright bands of blue and red and black which almost covered the rash of tiny gunpowder pits in his face. Perhaps the streaks of paint were some sort of meaningless gesture for this meeting with a White Dog trader, perhaps for intimidation, or a reminder to the Supernaturals of his great worthiness. He wore a knife and an old *pistole* at his belt, maybe the same old Spanish weapon with its silver and gold scrolls and decorations Jack remembered. He held a horse whip, the looped handle wrapped around his wrist, and carried a powder horn and a lance decorated with feathers and strips of calico and a bit of human hair. A rifle rested in front of him across his saddle, a small painted shield fit over his hand.

Jack shook his head, he marveled at the sum of what he saw, what he remembered of this man. What he had become.

The older boy stood by the old man's thin pony, waiting, looking up. The old man sat unmoving, as though he had forgotten what to do, how to do it. The boy touched the old man's dangling leg, prompting. The old man leaned sideways slowly, with effort. The boy caught him and lowered him to a robe on the ground.

The boy's hair, the color of wet river sand, stood in a wild brush on his head, carelessly knife-hacked, longer and shorter. He was taller than Jack's shoulder, bone thin, his clothes simple rags of discarded deer hide, his eyes a startling pale gray in a face brown from the sun and the scattered freckles across his cheeks. He had not been disfigured with knife cuts as other captives often were because, by practical custom, he was surely thought to be useful in some way, a prize, though scorned as a White Dog. But he was unblemished, made docile by years of slavery, obedient. Clearly, he had value to his owners, whoever they might be in his past. He looked at Jack, then his eyes looked away at anything else.

When Jack looked at this boy now, so much taller than he remembered, it was as though he stared into an old, dim looking glass. His heart sank. The resemblance was clear, too clear.

The boy had scars and blue bruises across his forearms, some with half healed scabs.

Jack heard Dohat's sudden bark of anger.

Dohat leaned down from his saddle. The boy stood for a single hard blow from Dohat's horsewhip. His forearms took the whip.

No damage! The sharp words yelled in Jack's throat, but he made no sound.

Not yet, not yet.

The boy stood without moving, then he continued, fetching water from a water skin for the old man to bathe his face and hands, helping him drink from a gourd cup the old man tried to hold in his own shaking fingers, offering scraps of corn cakes and other soft food from the pack for the old man's weary mouth. The old man reached out his arms toward his weapon on his saddle, the boy brought it to him. The younger boy, small, chunky, with dusky skin and big wary brown eyes, stood nearby, a frown on his round face. He looked to be a Mexican boy of five seasons or so, with straight black hair falling in a tangle over his forehead. He too showed dark bruises across his shoulders. His frown spoke of confusion and watchful fear.

Dohat dismounted and stood in the camp clearing, holding the reins to the appaloosa stallion, just looking around, searching. He laid his weapons on the ground for the ritual of trading, except for his old showy Spanish *pistole* and his knife. The big horse suddenly tried to pull away but Dohat jerked at the reins.

"No pony soldiers here," Jack said in the People's language, a taunt that seemed to surprise Dohat. "You're late. I am going away soon."

Dohat's eyes narrowed at the Comanche words. He stared at Jack, at the crates that held his new soldier weapons and ammunition and everything he expected for this trade, all that Hard Bone's words had promised. He examined everything he could find. He saw how the pack horses were staked out, scattered back in the trees around the campsite, but one was closer and held cinched saddle blankets. He saw the blue roan horse saddled and staked nearby. He looked at Jack's gear, at the coffee pot on the fire, at every object in the camp. He sniffed the air, the good aroma of the coffee. He did not move, nor hurry as he finally examined Jack.

They looked at each other as distant strangers.

Dohat's eyes lost their intense focus, became almost dull, without interest. Maybe just his trader's face, or a Comanche warrior looking for advantage.

He showed no recognition.

There were no customary polite greetings, no friendly ritual words, no offered sharing of food or tobacco, no pipe to smoke. They only acknowledged each other with slight nods.

I will kill him when I find him---.

The words screamed silently into Jack's mind again as he looked at this man, his vow from long ago, his anger rising again like a blinding wall of hate.

---*he doesn't know me.*

Jeth first, then---.

The boys were still only trade goods now, only random captives with value but without identities.

Then Jack drank from his tin cup, savoring the coffee. He tossed the cup aside without offering any coffee to Dohat. He walked across the clearing in easy strides. He turned his back to Dohat, showing his scorn.

"Maybe you favor sore-backed horses." An old taunt, but now he bit back the words, the old anger, that might bring back the face of his youth.

He lifted the parfleche pack from the paint pony the old man had led, stirring up a soft murmur of dry old bones. Under the wooden pack saddle he found a scrap of padding and under that he saw the old pony's back scarred with healed and open sores and smelling of rot.

He set the parfleche pack gently on the ground. He paused, and again he heard the bones speaking softly.

His friend, whom he had loved, and killed.

Dohat frowned, surprised again at the lack of respect he found at this camp when he was clearly a man of importance, a clever man, even a dangerous man. His eyes sharpened as he examined Jack. Clearly this would not be traditional trading here with this rude White Dog, who might not yield to Dohat's general intent to intimidate such a worthless human being. He watched Jack, heard his discourtesy with flashes of anger and confusion in his face.

"I come here for the trade," Jack said, and shrugged. "You're late." Rudely, he didn't bother to look at Dohat as he unsaddled Owl Stands' saddle horse and caught up the reins of the boys' gray pony and the old pack horse. He heard Dohat's hissing breath of anger at Jack's high-handed way with Dohat's horses, at being rudely ignored.

"That old chief told me you come alone here," Dohat said loudly. His words had the harsh rasp of a hard-used older voice.

"I come alone," Jack answered. "It is enough. Plenty."

Dohat's broad mouth moved, almost a smile of scorn, a look Jack remembered. "So. How many soldier guns?"

"Enough." Jack started down toward the spring, leading the ponies to water. "The trade. Maybe we talk."

"Have I come so far for this talk only?" Dohat demanded.

Jack shrugged again. He wanted to look at Jeth. He kept on, down to the spring in the canyon.

"Maybe you don't want these woman-hearted boys," Dohat said angrily.

Jack looked briefly back at the boy and saw he had learned to let insults pass over him like the wind, there and then gone. He had learned to take blows without inviting more.

Woman-hearted. Had Dohat, in his cleverness, forgotten that women had the hearts of lions?

"I take these boys. You bring only two boys," Jack said. He made his voice even, not too eager, just business. "Three crates of soldier guns. Crazy water."

Dohat counted the five crates. "All," he said. "All I see there."

Jack turned away into the canyon. He freed the ponies to drink and graze the green grass of the canyon and came back up to his camp in the scrub pines and junipers.

"Jeth," he said. A Texian word.

The boy stared, his face still as stone.

"Jeth," Jack said again.

"No White Dog talk!" The Ki-Was Man said loudly.

He gestured to the woman, a sharp swing of his hand. With a face that seemed to be carved from bitter wood in its stillness, the woman dismounted and came to Dohat. She limped, favoring a badly bone-twisted foot. She gathered his lance and his small shield, everything but his knife, his *pistole*, and his rifle on the ground, to carry back to her place under the trees where she began to pull the saddle from her pony.

Dohat spoke again. The woman turned and walked further under the trees.

Dohat looked at Jack, taking a long time, enjoying his arrogance.

"Powder. Shells for the new soldier rifles," he said.

"Powder for that old *pistole*," Jack said, and stopped himself again. But maybe even such a slip could not get by Dohat's walls of arrogance.

Dohat stared at Jack, waiting, his expression now loose and empty.

"Yes. Powder, shells," Jack said.

"Crazy water."

"Yes."

Dohat's appaloosa began to dance and throw his head, fussing to get to the water down in the canyon.

"I saw mustang tracks," Dohat said idly, just a distraction.

"A few."

Dohat said, "Many horses. Many horses."

Jack shrugged.

"Maybe I get horses too."

"Get them." Jack shrugged again.

But what Dohat wanted from this distraction was what he saw as he looked around the camp, at the crates, at everything.

Jack waited.

"All," Dohat demanded.

"Three," Jack said. "For these woman-hearted boys."

Dohat lifted his chin in another arrogant gesture. "They are good. Good trade. Trained. White Dogs always want them." His voice hardened, just business. "You get silver maybe. Mexican men give silver. Mexican men want boys."

Jack felt his face flush with new anger. Finally, he repeated, "Three crates."

Dohat looked around, eyes narrowed, as though searching for pony soldiers or hiding White Dog Texians. Again, he took his time and found his own hatred as he looked at Jack.

Dohat pointed. "Show me."

Jack went to one of the crates he had opened earlier and pulled out a new Spencer repeating rifle packed in straw and two jugs of crazy water, undiluted hard whiskey, not the usual weak trade whiskey, but no boxes of ammunition and no powder. He left two new rifles in the crate, with two more jugs of whiskey. He laid the treasures on the ground and watched Dohat's eyes examine them carefully, a new rifle well-greased, never fired, in fine condition, and jugs of whiskey. Then Dohat dismounted holding on to the appaloosa's reins, dragging the big horse with him as he stepped across the clearing. He went to these treasures. He picked up the new rifle, saw that it was unloaded, worked the smooth, effortless mechanism, spread his lips in a smile, aimed the empty rifle, played with it, then laid it back down near where he had left his own rifle.

"No ammunition," Dohat said with a frown, a man always suspicious of White Dog trickery. "No powder. Where?"

"In another crate," Jack said, and wondered, *powder?*

Dohat took up one of the whiskey jugs, tore at the cork with his teeth and then drank deeply. Then drank again and sighed.

"Jeth," Jack said.

Dohat scratched his belly, pleased with the undiluted whiskey. He looked around the camp, at the crates of rifles, at the horses. "More White Dog talk I hear---."

"Who is this old man you bring to the trade?" Jack interrupted, speaking his own diversion, but he watched for signs of recognition, any slight sign.

Dohat ignored the question, rude in his own way. He had clearly decided to abandon any traditional Comanche trading ruse. He looked off across the canyon. He looked up at the big rock. Small Mexican Boy came across the camp in careful steps, ready to take Dohat's big horse away to water and grass in the canyon, maybe a familiar but somehow dangerous task. He stopped, waiting. The appaloosa snorted and shook its head, smelling the water and grass, annoyed by his restraint.

Dohat drank from the whiskey jug again. He looked off across the canyon again. He looked at the big rock again, at the sky, where distant dark clouds had grown heavier with night rain.

Jack thought, *once we came here---*.

But Dohat only said in his rough voice. "What does such an old man want? He fell off his horse, he has no tongue. It is over for him. *Tebitze,* it's true," he said, speaking to the quiet.

"I have heard old bones speaking, I have heard these stories," Jack interrupted. "What Comanche man carries death with him when he travels with such a pack?"

Dohat turned slowly to stare at Jack, then over at the old man, a look of hard impatience crawling across his lines of face paint, quickly replaced by a look of anger, even fear, for rumor, for his long, storied association with death and the witchy power of the Supernaturals, for old bones riding in the parfleche pack.

For just a moment his expression said that he would leave this old man by the side of the trail soon, by intent, maybe by a whim. Let the wolves and the foxes have him, let the ravens quarrel. His importance had long since left him, his honor had become only a whispered memory.

"The trade," Jack interrupted, making his voice short, impatient, sounding bored with such rambling talk which, as a common stranger, a White Dog trader, he should not understand.

Dohat just stared at Jack again, as though weighing, taking the measure of this ignorant White Dog trader, pondering this man who spoke strange knowledge. Cautiously, feeling his way with more words, he said, "This old man is already taking the long road, sure enough."

The woman, the squaw, turned away from her tasks in the trees and stood in the shadows, watching.

Jack looked over at Owl Stands and felt the brush of memories again, thinking how he had survived those years among the People, how this man had punished him for every mistake and doled out rare moments of acceptance, how he'd come to believe, finally, that Jack had attained the deeds and the attributes to become one of the People, trusted, a true brother to his good son, and another son to him.

He remembered how this Ki-Was Man had tried to kill him with breaking bones, secret arrows, with clubs and lies.

He remembered how the old man had loved his good son.

His good son.

And how his friend with the singing moccasins had died. Now bones. He looked over at the parfleche pack.

"All," Dohat said again. His voice rose with a new anger. "All!"

Jack took his time to answer, in the traditional way, making him wait for his words. He thought of how, in the long ago, Dohat had craved fame and respect among his people, the goal of every Comanche boy. As he grew older, he had often laced his words with deception and misdirection and taken pride in this Indian power that often fooled the White Dogs, with their scraps of paper and their honeytalk, when the People met with the Comancheros and other traders, and no one faulted him for this. But Jack remembered how Dohat had been proud of his cunning, even when it brought him frowns and silence from the People and anger from his father. He had always been a brave fighter, always ready to take any advantage, always weighing his chances to win as any true Comanche, but he had not always been a wise one. And he carried the great shame, a family duty the People would talk about in stories and never forget. Only a coward failed to avenge the murder of a relative.

But Jack believed this person, this Ki-Was Man standing in front of him was now more a clever fool who's every youthful flaw had grown into arrogance, who knew nothing of the White Dogs' ways except to scorn them and mimic them and take advantage. His own people shunned him. He did not know the true way of his own people, he had never known the way.

"Jeth," Jack said, again in English. "We're going home."

A great question flared suddenly in Dohat's eyes, and vanished just as quickly, scoffed away, covered with deeper caution. Maybe the sudden caution came from a remembered look on Jack's face, an inflection in his voice. Dohat didn't understand the words, he had no White Dogs' words, but he looked from Jack to Jeth, once, then twice.

"The trade, now," Jack said, interrupting Dohat's scrambling thoughts with more discourtesy. "Four boxes, I take the boys now. You take your soldier guns. We are finished here."

"All the soldier guns." Dohat stared hard at Jack, but he was still confused, frowning. He took a step forward.

Now. Jack thought. *Now.*

He turned his back on Dohat again, taking the risk, and stepped casually toward the tree where his carbine leaned. When he turned back to glance at Dohat he settled his carbine in the crook of his left arm and began to search through his pockets until he found his tobacco pouch. He filled a brown cigarette paper, offering none to Dohat. He bent to the fire for an ember to light the cigarette. When he straightened, his rifle was trained on Dohat's belly.

Dohat's appaloosa stallion, impatient, shook his head and squealed suddenly. He began to crow hop, creating a chaos of dust and noise in the camp clearing. His ears flattened back, and his jaws snapped at the air. Dohat jerked the reins hard to control him, dragging at the big Spanish bit.

Small Mexican Boy stepped carefully closer, hesitant, trying to take the reins of the big horse. Jeth stood across the clearing, behind them.

Suddenly Dohat said. "Now I see you!" He yelled the words again. "Now I see you!"

"What do you see?" Jack taunted.

Maybe he was just a little drunk already on the hard whiskey, but Dohat spoke in a slow, husky, voice. His eyes held the glitter of his sudden, fierce comprehension, his growing rage.

"You. That one. That one!"

At that moment Jack saw that everything had changed. "Jeth, go, get away! Go now!"

The boy stared at him.

Jack felt a kind of huge, grim relief sweep over him now, a wonderful reckless indulgence, years in the making, and he had no fear for himself, no matter how this ended for him with this ugly, violent Ki-Was man. But he had to get the boys away before they became hostages, victims of the long-ago enmity and no longer just woman-hearted trade goods.

To Dohat, Jack said, "Stand away. The boys go now. With me."

"With you!" Dohat's glare fell on the rifle in Jack's hands. He looked around, stunned at what he now knew, his brain struggling. He looked at the crates of soldier guns, all the ammunition, all the horses, everything in the camp. Everything.

His expression hardened to hide his moment of amazed comprehension, but something had blazed up in his heart. His hands shook.

Then he seemed to remember the second jug of crazy water and stumbled as he turned, maybe just a drunken fumble. He pulled at the appaloosa's reins, dragging at the big bloody bit. He picked up the jug, but he couldn't pry the top off. He drew his old Spanish *pistola* from his belt and angrily smashed at the cork top with the heavy butt.

Small Mexican Boy flinched back in alarm. Dohat dropped the jug when the appaloosa pulled back again fighting the drag at his mouth.

To Jeth, Jack called in English. "Go! He'll kill you!"

"You," Dohat said again, his words slurring slightly, but he was calm now, clever. "My father's ugly White Dog slave. That one."

He began to laugh at the great joke, his laugh a humorless rumbling sound. "Maybe you made this woman-hearted boy. You! I see it now. I know you!" His laughter grew. Now he made his own taunt. "Maybe there is a boy here called Woman's Heart. Maybe---."

Jack drew a deep breath and spoke. "The People give you another name. They call you KI-Was Man. Bad Kiowa Man."

"Uh, uh," Dohat said with another big laugh, liking the name, careless, already knowing the name. He began shuffling his feet. He turned, looking for Jeth as though looking for a target.

"Where is the great Comanche Kiowa warrior?" Jack said scornfully to draw him away from Jeth.

Maybe Dohat was a little drunk, just waving the old *pistole* and pulling distractedly at the appaloosa to control it.

"The one who bragged of his deeds to the women at the dances?" Jack stopped, searching for half-forgotten Comanche words. He watched Dohat wave the old *pistole* like some magical prize of battle, his rifle still laying on the ground.

Jack went on, relishing the words as he found them. "The women just laughed at him. Has this person been driven from the People with shame? Shame? Is he finally an outcast? Is he nothing more than the waste from the Territory's latrines? Nothing more? Has he learned to hoe corn?"

Jack shifted his carbine, just enough as he made it ready. He watched Dohat, his eyes never leaving the ugly face. Now he spoke quietly to Jeth, in Texian. "Take a horse. In the canyon. Go now." But he wasn't sure the boy understood any of his Texian words.

"Then what?" Jack almost smiled at the Ki-Was Man, making his angry challenge, goading. "Will we fight like Dog Soldiers?" He laughed suddenly, feeling a new rush of anticipation. "Yes! Will we fight in the old way till one of us dies? I am ready. Are you looking for death?"

But Jack knew that Dohat might not take the ancient Dog Soldier challenge, unless he was sure of a winning advantage in spite of the taunt in the old warrior brag.

Dohat stared across the clearing at Jeth.

"Go. Now," Jack called to the boy more urgently. "He'll kill you!"

The boy frowned, he looked hard at Jack, at Dohat.

Dohat turned away from Jeth. He turned back to Jack. Something had awakened in his brain, some resolve, something old and ugly. The appaloosa kept pulling away, its mouth bloody with foam. Dohat kept jerking at the reins, jerking. He waved the old *pistole*, turning it here and there, aiming it skyward. Jack raised his Sharps, but now the appaloosa danced and plunged between Jack and Dohat.

The big appaloosa stallion reared again, squealing, screaming like a woman. Dohat threw the reins away from him and grabbed at the small Mexican boy, he grabbed the boy's hair and dragged him up, he dug his fingers into the boy's chest and stopped his breathing, he held him hard against his body. The boy began to struggle and gasp for breath.

Jack sighted his rifle, aimed for Dohat's head in the seconds of chaos. He heard a sudden rising Comanche yell. He looked toward Jeth, thought he saw the old man reach feebly toward his saddle. He looked back to Dohat's big round head, the Mexican boy, he aimed and squeezed the trigger on his carbine. But he was late.

Dohat's useless old *pistole* exploded toward Jack with a thunderous roar and a puff of black powder, one shot, lifting a flurry of birds into wild flight from the canyon cottonwood trees.

The slug from the old *pistole* hit Jack and knocked him backwards.

An instant of stark silence filled the clearing.

Jeth dropped the water skin, scrambled, fell in his haste, then bolted toward the thickets down into the canyon.

Jack slammed into the duff of pine needles and leaves, hard on his back, astonished. He heard another sudden barrage of rifle shots as he thrashed through the leaves, trying to rise, then wild shots all around him, and one of the pack horses tethered behind him in the trees began to scream and thrash. The big appaloosa stallion bolted away across the clearing, head up, trailing his reins, down to the canyon trail and the water below.

Jack got to his feet in slow stages and held on to one of the trees for balance. He searched around for his rifle, but it was gone, knocked away. The top of his left arm had a slash of red, a spot of blood leaked from a cut on the side of his jaw. He reached to the back of his belt with his good arm, searching, but now slow, slow. The .45 came away into his hand. He watched as Dohat, his rifle already grabbed up from the ground and fired in a first wild barrage, now slowly, carefully it,came up. He aimed and shot again.

Jack fell again. As he struggled to rise he felt something strike him across his shoulder. He heard the Comanche battle scream, Dohat striking, counting coup on a living enemy.

Jack got to his feet a second time, more slowly, with more deliberation, the surprise still pounding in his head. He found the tree again and straightened as best he could. His colt had gone, fumbled from his hand into the leaves and growing darkness when his leg gave way to the rifle shot and he'd sprawled backward the second time.

He looked across the camp clearing. The shock of the moment took him a single hard instant to fully comprehend.

But Jeth was gone. Away. Free.

He didn't see the small boy anywhere. Gone.

Jack stared at Dohat, who stood with a glaring grin on his face, wiping away blood where Jack's bullet had grazed his cheek, the Sharps head-shot gone awry by an inch.

Jack leaned against the tree again, carefully, numb with anger, with shock.

He felt where the big slug had taken him in the left shoulder, rummaging around inside without exiting in his back. He wasn't sure if the slug had found bone. His left arm hung at his side, useless. Once broken in the Washita fight, now damaged again.

He saw that his right leg seeped blood above his knee from the rifle shot. But not in spurts of arterial blood.

He shook his head, feeling the shock, the anger, the sudden hard surges of pain. "Shit."

But the boy had gotten away. The boy was free.

Dohat stood still, watching Jack. He searched Jack with prying eyes, like searching fingers probing and searching for any other weapon, any pistol, any magic White Dog weapon, any new danger to him. But his expression quickly began to change as he saw only this White Dog man, at last his victim standing before him, his hands empty, red with his own blood. He saw this man who had shamed him so many seasons in the long ago and every season since.

Then he began to howl with hoarse laughter, he threw back his head and shouted the Comanche cry again, that scream that always curdled the blood of enemies before they died.

Jack waited for the afternoon silence to come back. This was no ordinary Comanche man, he understood, finally. This was no Comanche fighter whose cruelty had tribal purpose, even pride.

He wiped his mouth with the back of his right hand.

"The other boy," he asked.

Dohat waved the words away, only the words of a dead man. He made a gesture to the darkening sky, a celebration, as though thanking the Supernaturals for the great gifts they had given him, almost by whimsy, by diabolical accident because they loved such jokes. And by his own cunning distractions with the appaloosa horse and the Mexican boy. He laughed to embrace his own power, he laughed again to celebrate the death of his old enemy and his lifetime of shame.

"You!" he said scornfully, ready to brag after so many years. "Now I have you. I have carried this old man's son---."

"The bones of his good son," Jack said.

Dohat's face seemed to swell again with fury. He raised his rifle to shoot.

"You are the Ki-Was brother who hated the good son---."

Dohat aimed.

"Not yet," Jack said

Dohat scowled. He seemed startled by Jack's words.

"Not yet?" He laughed again, angrily. "Murdering White Dog--- now I send you on the long road---."

I don't think so---.

Jack smiled in spite of the pain that had begun to pound hard in his brain. "Go ahead, open the boxes," he said. "Go ahead. See what I brought you."

Minutes later, Dohat glared at Jack in a new fury. He stood in the litter of the crates, all hacked apart, splintered, open, nothing but rocks in the straw, nothing but trash.

"Where are the guns?" Dohat said, his voice dropping low, husky, the gravel sounds of outrage at this White Dog, this trickster. "Where?"

"Where you will never find them," Jack answered.

"Where are the soldier guns?" Dohat rough voice grew louder; he was stunned by what he had not found, stunned by such White Dog trickery.

Jack listened to the groaning of his dying pack pony back in the trees. He winced at the pain in his shoulder. He prodded gently. The pain took his breath.

"You've just shot a horse," Jack taunted finally. "Big Ki-Was Man. You've lost the boys, you have no guns. You are nothing."

Dohat walked toward Jack, furious, quietly drunk, waving his rifle.

"Careful," Jack said. " If you kill me now you will never find the guns."

"Where? Where are the soldier guns?"

"In a hidden place." Jack lifted his head at the scramble in the twilight sky. "You've brought out the bats."

The bats swarmed in a spiral, rising in the dusk. The first puff of wind from the edge of the coming storm touched Jack's cheek, a soft message of the rainy night ahead.

The Ki-Was man shrank from the swirling bats overhead. He glared at Jack, remembering everything now. "Where? Where is the hidden place?"

"You will not find it."

"Maybe you lie, like all White Dogs."

"Yes."

"There are no soldier guns!"

"Maybe the bats will tell you. Maybe they have them in their cave---."

"There are no soldier guns!" Dohat screamed at Jack.

"Maybe not. Maybe there are guns. Many guns. Waiting."

Dohat stared. "Maybe I will build a fire on your White Dog belly and listen to your screaming---."

No. You will not. Not yet. You love the guns and the crazy water. Everything I have. You want everything.

"Be quick. The rain puts out fires," Jack said with a short laugh, but now it was all getting harder, he'd lost enough blood to make his knees feel like water and he decided it was time to sit down, he'd just slide down keeping his back carefully against the tree. Let the rain come. He was getting tired, shaking, he was suddenly thirsty.

"Tomorrow," he said.

Fool. Fool, how will you brag of this day? Who will believe? What lies will you tell? Will you take my head as proof, like the Osage warriors take heads? Who will respect you? Who will care?

Jack sighed. He worked his bandanna loose one-handed and bunched it against his shoulder to slow the seeping blood. He couldn't stop the shaking.

"Tomorrow," he said again. "I'll lead you to the guns. Now I'm finished talking."

The boys are free.

He woke from a painful doze and heard Dohat and the woman arguing back in the trees across the camp, where they had spread a shelter for the old man against the rain. He made out the appaloosa stallion, half wild by nature but maybe just from grazing loco weed or maybe just from Dohat's beatings, but he'd been Dohat's crazy advantage, his commonplace easy ruse with all the wild confusion he'd needed. Just a moment's distraction.

---that damned old Spanish pistole---.

He didn't understand.

He couldn't begin to count the mistakes he'd made.

But the boys are free.

So, he watched Blue, the other horses brought up from the canyon by the woman and tied under the trees, the squaw's two horses led down, then up again. He knew Dohat would never go down to the canyon and the bat cave in the darkness, he remembered all the bad medicine he feared from the bats.

---long ago---.

The night was pitch-dark, with only a low glow from Ki-Was Man's campfire. He heard thunder rumbling nearby. He felt the sudden rain spatter against his face, cooling him as the fever heat began from his wounds.

----tomorrow---.

He licked his lips, thirsty, taking in the water.

---powder---for that old flintlock pistole---I should have figured---.
---that useless shitty old pistole---.

"Shit," he said again but he wasn't sure he'd spoken aloud, if he'd said the word that seemed to say it all.

The rain swept through in sudden hard spatters and then stopped, but the storm still hovered. He moved carefully to remain sitting, get his back closer to the tree. Then he found that his wrists and legs were tied together in loops of old rawhide rope.

The woman. She'd probably gone through his pockets for what she could steal, but maybe she hadn't gotten everything. Angry at Dohat and his orders, she hadn't bothered to draw the ropes on his hands hard and tight, but just tight enough to hold him. He watched as she came out into the open night and began to tend the fire where strips of charred horse meat hooked on green branches arched over the embers. She put more wood on the fire and sat for a moment, her blanket held around her shoulders. Thunder rumbled almost overhead with explosions of sound and hard flashes of lightning. The smell of the meat cooking, the fat dripping and sputtering into the embers, woke Jack with hunger and nausea and thirst. A dozen thoughts scattered through his mind, but only one mattered.

He tested the wound in his shoulder, but he got a jolt of pain in his left arm when he raised both hands because they were tied together in front of him now. But he found only a little seepage through his bunched neck scarf. His leg was stiff, painful.

---tomorrow---think about tomorrow---.

He rested with his back to the tree and watched Dohat and the woman hunch over the fire, tearing at the half-cooked horse meat with their teeth and knives. In the darkness they were like black shadows, demons from an ugly dream, with only occasional flashes of firelight flaring on their busy hands and faces.

They began to argue again, Dohat's voice rambling angrily. They had found Jack's shattered carbine and thrown it aside. They had found his Colt lost back under the pines, a precious find. Probably the woman found it in her search for other booty until the darkness and the rain stopped her. Occasionally Dohat lifted the revolver, twice he shot at the sky and laughed. Occasionally he lifted a jug of crazy water and drank. The woman argued, an adversary to his orders, but she was easily overwhelmed by his strength, his hard power over her, and then Jack saw Dohat lean toward her and swing his hand at the woman's face.

She took a glancing blow as she ducked away, but Dohat gave her a growl of laughter and seemed satisfied with his discipline. He drank again and rubbed his belly, then looked across the camp and stared at Jack. He got to his feet and walked slowly toward Jack, his gait unsteady, but with a concentrated purpose. He stopped and suddenly began a little victory dance, head down, crying out his brave deeds, his coup against his enemy, his cleverness. He lifted his head and gave the Comanche scream, then danced to Jack's side and stopped. He stood over him in the darkness, smiling. He drew his left foot back and kicked hard, then kicked again.

Jack gasped as the pulses of pain slowly subsided. His leg had begun to bleed again. As his breathing steadied he suddenly had a flash of memory back, back to a day when, as a boy he'd watched Dohat kick a dog over and over until he broke its spine, just a practical solution because the dog stole food or got in his way.

"You will never see the soldier guns if you keep this up," Jack finally said the truth to Dohat. "You will have no soldier guns and no slave boys to trade. You will have nothing." He wanted to smile again but his lips were too dry.

Dohat stared down at Jack, thought for a moment.

"No guns, you lie. Honeytalk. White Dogs lie. Now I will tell the People what I have done. You---."

"Tell them what?" Jack interrupted. "Empty words?" He watched as Dohat stood over him.

"White Dog," Dohat muttered, again, Indian-drunk and now mostly boastful and thick headed and filled with his own power. This man, his enemy, the source of his seasons of shame and disregard among his own people, would die tomorrow or the next day at his hand, after he'd found the soldier guns. Maybe the belly fire, maybe he could think of something worse. He imagined the cries and screams of his enemy. He aimed the Colt at Jack, he kicked again, harder, then he walked away into the darkness at the edge of the clearing to relieve himself. When he returned to the fire he pointed at Jack and spoke to the woman, his voice a harsh growl of orders as they argued again.

But Jack wasn't listening. He made himself think about the boys, trying to override the pulses of pain.

The boys. A hard trade, hard, but without regret. Always possible, always this ugly chance. But they were free.

But mostly he felt flat out anger at his own mistakes, this hard outcome.

---that shitty old single shot pistole---.

How far could the boys go before daylight? Would rain cover their sign if the Ki-Was Man went after them?

---when he goes after them---.

Time---they need time---how long will tomorrow last--?

Did they take horses?

But the woman had already gone down into the canyon after his horses. Dohat had Blue. Would Jeth remember the old stories, the old lore he'd pestered to hear as they'd hunted along the creek back in the rock house days?

He thought about how to stay alive tomorrow.

---*long enough*---.

Maybe lead Dohat back up the old road toward Bexar with the promise of the hidden guns---.

---*fool, fool.*

---*but he wants those guns*---.

He thought about what had happened here, where anything could happen, and had.

He puzzled over Dohat's old single shot rusty Spanish *pistole*, he remembered it never shot at all, just blew a cloud of gunpowder years ago, useless, useless. But Dohat's miracle, his hidden prize---.

He'd forgotten about Dohat's manic persistence, the big medicine of the Supernaturals in that old *pistole.*

Now he had Jack's Colt.

---*those soldier guns,* he thought.

And he thought about what was left to him, about how to do what he'd come to do; the simplest way to kill the Ki-Was Man in the morning. He thought about how to use one of the Comanches' favorite tricks, always clever, always treacherous, always taught to Comanche boys.

He wondered if he could do it, get his hand free, if he got the chance to goad him close---.

---*chance*---.

He fell into a doze again, wondering.

When he roused later he felt the nudging, the insistent small pushing against his side, and saw it was still black night, windy but without rain. Bats circled above. He looked up at a patch of open clouds with stars overhead. He heard a human hissing sound and turned his head to look into the woman's face.

In the darkness he studied her round, sullen face, saw only a glimpse of her eyes as she quickly looked away from him. She had a plain face, without beauty but firm, even hard. A good Comanche face. She held her thin lips compressed, holding some angry thought. Her tunic appeared simple and unadorned as much as he could see of it in the darkness, but she'd stained it with blood from butchering the dead pack horse. She smelled of wood smoke and cigarette smoke, probably his tobacco. She pushed a gourd cup of water at Jack's mouth insistently.

The Ki-Was Man wanted him alive long enough to find the soldier guns. Tomorrow. He drank deeply.

He nodded his thanks. He started to speak but now he noticed the sheathed knife thrust under her tunic belt.

His knife.

She'd found his knife, hidden by the tree at his back.

His words fell away in dismay, his voice sounded rough, worn. Lightning flashed as the woman hurried away. Rain spattered down again.

He tested the bindings on his wrists with careful pulls, testing the pain for as much as he could handle, trying to get his right hand free. Then rested against the tree, tired, waiting to try again.

But he had nothing now, without the knife he'd hidden at his back.

He roused later and saw the sky was clear and dark again, but thunder still rumbled and wandered overhead, and lightning flashed in the distance. The rain had left only a light covering in the dust.

Dohat and the woman huddled at the fire, gorging on the half raw horsemeat again, in the Comanche way of filling their bellies against the time when food grew scarce. Dohat wore Jack's hat, pulled down with the brim flattened. Jack watched them with interest, working slowly to get his right hand free. They were like the diabolical black shadows he'd seen earlier, maybe worse now, to Jack, after his hours of pain. They were humped primordial shapes with occasional grunting sounds of satisfaction. Then the larger of the two figures stood.

The Ki-Was Man wiped the grease from his mouth and belched his satisfaction. He had found one of Jack's shirts in his rummaging through the camp and wore it now like another trophy. He waved the Colt again, at the woman, at the sky, and spoke a word Jack couldn't hear. Then he grabbed up his blanket and stepped back to leave the fire, but part way across the clearing to the trees he lost his balance and fell sideways, the hat flying off. He lay there for a moment. He didn't move, as though pondering what had happened. Then he pulled his blanket around him in a haphazard way and lay still. The woman watched him, holding a piece of meat before her mouth. She looked up at the sky, looking for more rain. She watched Dohat as though she expected him to rise up and walk away like a ghost. When he began to make snoring sounds, she took the meat and ate again.

Jack waited to be sure Dohat slept, like drunken Indians often slept where they fell by the doors and gates of trading posts.

Minutes ticked by. He felt the heat throbbing in his shoulder, spreading. He worked at the bindings on his right wrist. Then he spoke softly.

"*Nerphther*---sister." His voice was so rough he wasn't sure she heard. "Sister."

The woman stopped eating and looked around the clearing.

"Here. Come here."

She looked toward him, hesitating. Maybe this person sitting all bound up under the tree was too much trouble, even tied up and waiting to be killed, but still too much bad luck. Better to stay away. She looked over at Dohat and spoke an angry word. He didn't move. Then she filled the gourd cup with water and started toward Jack.

"*Boisapah*," Jack said. "Crazy water."

He heard her grumbling voice as she turned to spill the spring water out of the cup. She rummaged around the fire and found the third whiskey jug where Dohat had left it, half empty. She limped over and sat a little distance away from him, warned away by his silence, his bad look. Too much blood. This one would not last very long tomorrow, and she didn't care. He was not unlike the enemies she had bloodied and fought against, herself, enemies of her people. He still had his hair but Dohat would take it later and brag on it. Maybe take his head to prove his identity, this long ago enemy. She frowned and looked off into the darkness, going away in her thoughts.

"I see you are Badger's first daughter," Jack said finally.

The woman started, then turned her head, slowly, as though she hadn't heard what she'd heard. The sullenness gradually fell from her face like a veil falling away. She looked astonished, suspicious.

"You were a famous fighter, you and your brothers," he said.

She stared at him, still without words.

"You fought many Apaches. You took many horses. Many horses. You were so rich with horses you gave many of them away."

The woman let her breath go in a long sigh.

"Now you are here."

Here.

As rough as it was, he kept his voice low, watching her carefully.

She just stared.

"Give me the knife," he said, using soft friendly words. "Sister, he has a bad heart."

She didn't move, only searched his face, looking for something.

"Now you are here," he said again, reminding her.

She turned her face away, staring into the darkness.

"Give me the knife, and I will send him on the long road in the morning."

He waited, then said, "Sister, I will kill him tomorrow."

Her breathing grew deeper, more rapid. She stared into the darkness.

He waited again. His words came softly. "You must go from here. Go before daylight."

He held his tied hands out for the jug. He poured the whiskey over the wound in his shoulder, over his arm. The bullet wound in his leg was bigger that he'd thought, ugly, gaping. He poured whiskey into the wound, flinching, trying not to make any White Dog sound at the shock of pain, but at least the alcohol might keep infection in check for a day, maybe long enough. Maybe a chance. For him, for the boys.

He lifted the jug to his mouth and drank and drank again. He offered the jug to the woman.

"Everyone praised you," he said to her. "All the tribes. You were known everywhere, you were honored."

The woman took the jug and drank. She moved her twisted foot for more comfort. She glanced over at Dohat, she breathed heavily for a moment more, as though wandering through memories. Then she whispered, "They are all gone away."

By this he knew she had no relatives left to protect her. No father, no brothers, no uncles. She was crippled, no longer a valuable fighter in the old ways. She was alone.

They are all gone away.

"Now you are here," he said again.

She studied the bindings on his right wrist. She let the minutes pass before she answered. She took the new blue agency bandanna from where she'd tied it at her neck, her only adornment. She held it out to Jack. He folded it and pressed it against his shoulder.

---tired, tired---.

"Take what you want from that man. Leave the knife here. Leave the crazy water here with me. He'll come looking. Go before daylight. Leave us."

She stared at him, judging his body, his strength. She stared a question.

But clearly, she knew.

He shook his head. "*Mea*," he answered. "Go. Leave us."

He watched her slink away into the trees across the campground, just a dark stealthy shadow. She moved silently, favoring her twisted foot. He heard a few soft sounds from the trees, a wicker from the appaloosa stallion, other horse sounds that faded away into silence. The Ki-Was-Man slept on wrapped in his blanket. Jack worked his right hand free of the twists of bindings. He flexed his fingers to get the stiffness out. He rested for a long moment.

Now.

He leaned forward from the tree at his back in slow, careful stages. Sweat filmed his face at the effort. He searched around with his right hand, fumbling through the pine needles and leaves, for a moment he thought she'd taken the knife with her but then he felt its hard shape hidden in the leaves. With his teeth and his right hand, he got his knife free of the leather scabbard that he'd hidden wedged at his back, where the tree had kept it until the woman found it. He closed his eyes, waiting, until he breathed more easily.

He'll see the crazy water jug, he'll come close---.

Chance.

He cut the bindings on his legs and then pushed the knife into the duff of pine needles and leaves under his leg, hiding it near his right hand.

---come close---let me kill you---.

It was almost a prayer.

An hour before daylight the sky darkened again. Thunder rolled overhead, pounding, rolling on toward the north. Far away the lightning flickered. The trees thrashed, and another spatter of rain fell. Jack licked the rainwater and stared across the campground. The Ki-Was Man moved in his blanket, finding more comfort, undisturbed by the light rain. He grunted and then lay still again. Soon he would rouse from sleep as the light came. The Ki-Was Man would begin the terrible day ahead.

Jack waited for daylight.

He blinked wide awake at the last rumble of thunder that wasn't thunder. He watched the bats circle and disappear down toward the cave in the canyon. But something was different. Across the campground he saw movement, subtle, silent, faint noise, then stillness came again, and the light slowly grew. He watched, mesmerized, frowning as the gray light crept over the trees, over the great rock, over the sleeping mound, the comfortable, blanketed body of the great Ki-Was Man. The light crept over a figure sitting nearby, sitting cross legged, quiet. Motionless. Looking toward him.

He stared as the light grew, trying to comprehend.

He saw Jeth.

Jeth lifted one hand. He held something. Then he let it drop. He waited another moment, then got to his feet and walked toward Jack. He walked slowly, cautiously. He squatted down by Jack, his gray eyes searching Jack's face. His look became wary, uncertain. Two thin lines, bright in the growing light, trailed down his face. Then the uncertainty left his face, his lips moved, he almost smiled. He sighed deeply. He reached out and took the shaking hand held out to him in the old familiar greeting.

They left the Ki-Was Man wrapped in his blanket, shot dead in the last clap of thunder and soon to be forgotten. Only trash. They piled no rocks over him to protect him and honor him but sent him on his way along that terrible death road where the Supernatural demons and jokers, always waiting, would torment him forever, a man without honor who deserved no better, one who had no value to his People, one who had never known the way.

The small Mexican boy watched from a distance, hovering, his eyes darting from Jeth to the dead Ki-Was Man, and back again. He clutched a scrap of damp blanket around his shoulders.

Jack held his knife out to Jeth. After a moment Jeth took the knife. He and his father shared the moment of understanding. This was the hidden steel blade with which Jack would kill the Ki-Was Man, but now it had another use.

Jeth handed Jack a cup of trade whiskey he found left in the jug, then a cup of water and a handful of corn cakes and pemmican. A scrap of torn calico washed away the blood. Jack watched as Jeth turned the knife blade in the campfire embers, adding wood until the steel blade glowed. Jeth cleaned the hot blade as best he could and came to Jack without hesitation, pulled his shirt back and laid the blade quickly against Jack's shoulder where the bullet wound seeped, then repeated the burning at Jack's thigh. Always a boy of few words, much like his father, and now a youth with the cruel world he had known for years hovering in his eyes, he watched his father carefully. But he had learned the practical lifesaving here-and-now habits of the

Comanches and he set about looking around for bandage material. He found an old shirt under the trees, discarded in the Ki Was Man's angry assault on the camp the day before, and tore it into a firm bandage binding Jack's arm to his body.

"Better," Jack muttered. He drew a long breath of relief as the burning faded and ate the corn cakes slowly.

"You were supposed to be fifty miles---," Jack said slowly, "the hell and gone by now---free." His voice was rough, unsteady after the long, hard night, but there was no rancor or accusation. His eyes held a look of wonder. "But you're here."

He couldn't stop looking at the boy, at his sun-dark, freckled face, his eyes, so familiar, small changes, everything, as though he was some sort of outlandish and amazing miracle.

Jeth tried to speak but his words were only sounds.

Finally, struggling with the words, he said, "bad kid."

His words were like awkward, hoarded sounds he'd saved over the years. A moment of memory. A moment echoing from the past. His sounds were accented, not clear, just bastard Comanche English, but Jack understood.

Jack's laugh came as a tired echo, remembering: Sallie Rainie's freshly baked sweets cooling in the rock house window. Years ago.

"Real bad." He said. "Real bad---." He reached for breath, slowly savoring the huge sense of relief, the wonder.

Jeth was free and the Ki-Was Man, the ugly Child-Taker, was dead. Finally, dead. They both smiled.

"Long---." Jeth struggled with the word and worked at the binding without saying more. In the early light Jack saw the three scars on the back of Jeth's left hand and knew they meant Jeth had been traded over the years, three times, among the tribes.

---*later for the stories,* Jack thought tiredly. *Later.*

Suddenly he wanted to weep but it was just a rush of huge anger, huge relief. He drew another long breath. Rambling a little, he said "Tired."

Jeth groped for more hoarded words in English again, then just repeated, "Tired."

The rabble of ravens came in the gray mid-morning, making a fuss in the pines above the dead pack horse back in the trees. Soon the four-legged scavengers would follow the puffs of tainted carrion wind and come for the dead horse, for the Ki-Was Man.

Jeth gestured, searching for a word.

"Go," Jeth said at last. He stirred up a tin of medicine tea from simmered willow bark he'd harvested from the canyon. He'd packed willow leaves and spider webs against Jack's wounds. They would open again, and the suppuration would drain away some of the infection over the days ahead. He had a little of the trade whiskey left to pour over the wounds, but he had found no other healing herbs. He handed the tea to Jack. He watched Small Mexican Boy searching around the ground, wandering back into the trees, among the empty crates. He carried his loot to Jeth, then cautiously approached the Ki-Was Man, fearful of all the dead spirits around him, and found Jack's Colt .45 and Dohat's old single shot Spanish big medicine *pistole* and carried them to Jeth with a look of pride. He picked up Jack's almanacs, ripped apart, a comb, an empty bottle of carbolic, Jack's hat, the last of Luzita's coffee, scraps of food, a tin plate.

He found one of his moccasins lost during the fight and sat to put it on. He found a thin blue book with some of the pages half torn, Jack's journal.

---*that bastard*---.

But the words were weak, not enough in speaking of the Child-Taker; there would never be enough.

Jeth stood up suddenly, took up a water skin and walked across the camp clearing to where Owl Stands had slept the night away dreaming an old man's dreams. He fed the old man, dressed him for travel, cinched the old pads and saddle to his paint horse and helped him mount. He greased the sores on the back of Owl Stands' pack pony and resettled the parfleche pack of bones carefully.

The old man's good son.

The bones were quiet now. The long wandering trail had ended at last.

An hour later the horses stood watered and tied into a string for travel, some packed and the others bareback. The big appaloosa stallion stood restive, shaking his head at the lingering smell of blood and ready to bring chaos to the moment again. Blue, saddled and waiting, looked over at Jack, his busy ears flicking back and forth. The boys' gray mustang stood nearby watchfully.

Owl Stands sat his old paint pony, looking off into the distance over the canyon. He looked at the great history rock for a long time. The ravens suddenly set up a wild scolding in the pine trees, maybe one of the four-leggeds, a coyote or a wolf, had arrived like a shadow at the dead pack horse.

One big black ruffian raven flew into the clearing and landed on the dead Ki-Was Man. He ruffled his sooty feathers and then bobbed up and down making his harsh cry of possession.

But Owl Stands didn't seem to notice. Maybe he no longer cared. Maybe the only buried scrap of memory in his damaged brain told him it was time

Time. His paint pony started to move away, the two old horses walked slowly, back the way they had come.

Jeth started forward, but Jack touched his arm. "Let him go."

Jeth hesitated, then watched quietly.

Jack stood now beside Jeth, an effort that left him lightheaded and weak. He set his right hand on Jeth's shoulder for support as he watched the old man and his little caravan disappear into the junipers and pines. He knew the old horses would wander on, the pack horse just following without a lead, just habit. They would go without guidance. Habit. They would stop now and then to snatch at any grazing, they'd wander through the pines and junipers, out into the open sage; on, stopping at storm water caught in stone tanks along the way, on through the day and the night, and sometime later, when the old man fell and lay as still as the rocks and trees, they would stop and wait for a while, then they would go on until the old pony with the parfleche pack of bones dropped wearily.

They left the camp in the scrub pines and junipers slowly, carrying what they needed for the journey back to San Antonio de Bexar.

Home, his father had said. So far. Not the home Jeth sometimes remembered, but now to be his home. He led the string of horses and followed his father, watching how he fared on Blue ahead, how he rode favoring his wounds. How he survived.

I am going on a long journey, he'd said. But Jeth wasn't sure what that meant, except for the long way ahead.

Only Jeth looked back once at the canyon with its solitude, its hidden spring of sweet water and the towering rock with its centuries of history and pictures that spoke to the People of who they were and what they had done.

They rode into the outskirts of San Antonio de Bexar nine days after they left the camp by the big rock. They had traveled at night, finding water holes and springs and grazing for the horses, avoiding the heat of the July days and the random travelers on the road. Jeth did not know how to trust the random travelers, if they were friendly. If they were his people. But who were his people? Once he followed a freighter carrying blocks of salt from the salt flats near El Paso and snatched what he could in the darkness. When they'd eaten the last of the horsemeat he snared rabbits and gave Jack what he would eat; the white meat of rattlesnakes, doves, whatever he could find. But their story had already begun, started by a freighter hauling kegs of wine from the El Paso vineyards to Bexar, who had come upon them at dusk one day as they neared Bexar and offered jerky, liniment and a half-filled bottle of wine. Offered help, but Jeth just shook his head. They were alone, they had come so far, and they were almost home. At the edge of town children followed, curious about the two dusty riders, the small Mexican boy, whose eyes were big with apprehension, perched on the back of a thin, plodding pack pony, one of a string, with one thin appaloosa stallion. Others watched from a distance, wondering. But news was often ugly, unbelievable and often just curious, and traveled quickly. They were used to strange sights. By the time the riders reached *LA LUZ* and stopped in front of the little *jacal*, Luzita waited outside, with all her sisters and cousins hovering in the doorway. Her curls of russet hair blew in a warm breeze. Her luminous eyes watched eagerly, watched Jack approach on Blue, and Jack rubbed his eyes and thought she was surely more beautiful than he could possibly remember. Then her face grew lined with sudden dismay. He stopped Blue in front of her and straightened his shoulders a little and winced. She drew a deep breath.

"Back," Jack said.

Luzita nodded.

He'd thought of speeches to say to her, brave words. But he couldn't find those words now.

"Just another battered damn Texian," Jack said slowly.

"Yes," she answered. She understood the true words.

"Jeth," he said.

"I see." She had a quick look, a smile for Jeth. To Jack she said firmly, "Yes, I see. You are back."

Yep," he said.

She waited.

"It's done---."

"Yes. Now we will go."

"Go," he repeated. He saw her resolution, a quality in her he had always admired. But now he had no will to question or resist and didn't much care.

"You will go with me." She walked to Blue and took his bridle, gently stroking the tired horse's muzzle. She drew another deep breath. She looked up at Jack. She whispered words that only he could hear. Soft words, resolute words.

The rigidity of his long efforts to endure drained from his face. Now maybe he could just let go a little. Just let go.

She took him to a doorway, four streets up from the *jacal* and just off the plaza, with Jeth following.

JOHNSON LEE, M.D. ~ MEDICAL SURGEON, SAWBONES AT LARGE

The sign looked new, bold, with a kind of reckless attitude about it, clearly not subtle or discreet in this bitter Southern town. The big sign had no other adornment except for a small Union flag painted in one corner. She knocked on the door, then pounded until the door opened. A tall red-haired man wearing rimless glasses stood there, looked at Luz, at Jack, then moved out into the twilight to catch Jack as he slipped from Blue's back.

Six days later Jack heard the mumbling words. His own wandering words, a commotion of voices beyond somewhere, beyond where he lay. He heard his own voice. Then someone far away spoke, repeated, answered.

---damn useless pistole---.

When Jack didn't answer, the far away voice went on more clearly, words he could finally understand.

"---Well, you are one hell of a tough son of a bitch," Johnson Lee said as Jack came back from the darkness of festering gunshot wounds, fevers and exhaustion. He looked around the small room, the high window, the shelves full of bottles and general medical odds and ends, at the long wooden case like the one Cicero Smith had carried for his knives and clamps and saws. He looked at the man sprawled in the only chair, a covered basket and a jug on the floor beside him.

The man spoke, "I will add lucky, damn lucky. Only nicked the bone, took off a little, didn't get the joint. Slug just settled there. Festered there. You can thank modern medicine, sir. We know a lot more about gunshot wounds from the recent conflict." The man paused. "Mostly cannon, shrapnel wounds and sawing off arms and legs. But more about sepsis. Just plain puss." He smiled after sharing his graphic opinion. "How you feeling now, sir?"

The man had stiff red hair and a long rough face that he kept immobile as he watched Jack. He was clearly tall, with long legs and big feet in cavalry boots. He looked awkward even as he sat, maybe just a little uncoordinated but no less confident of his presence and his abilities.

He folded his large hands across his belly as he waited for Jack's answer.

Jack fell asleep before he could reply, drifting away again. He awoke a day later and frowned.

"Like hell," he answered the red-haired doctor's distant question.

The red-haired man still sprawled in his chair, wearing a different rumpled shirt and rimless glasses. Clearly time had passed. The covered basket and a jug rested on the floor near his feet. He laughed. "Like hell, no shit there. Where did he get that salt? The boy? Looks like he tried damn near everything---."

Salt. Jack hardly listened. He explored in his mind and found all his limbs intact, only a dull, deep pain in his shoulder and leg that felt familiar now, as though it would never leave him, and a vast general exhaustion. He wasn't sure yet if he was going to survive or just linger until it was over. Still a dark question. He cleared his throat. "But better I reckon. Some better."

Johnson Lee nodded. "You got a ways to go yet. Takes time. Maybe six months, a year, maybe more. Get rid of the fever. The wound's still draining. Mess, real mess, full of garbage, old flintlock ball black as tar. All twisted up. Hope I got it all, but I've treated worse. Usually horses." Johnson Lee smiled again, enjoying his own heavy-handed wit.

Jack frowned, searching. "Don't remember much." But he was surprised to be alive at all, and he remembered Luz, and coming back to her, He remembered her beautiful face, her eyes, her look of dismay.

"Tell her I'm good." Almost a lie but with possibilities.

Johnson Lee nodded.

"Just tired." Jack thought about Jeth. "The boy?"

"Comes with the lady every day. Maybe saved your life, tried everything, might have killed you too. Hell, something saved you.

Texas tough, like they say." Johnson Lee smiled. "Likely just rumors."

"The boy," Jack asked again.

"Watched me when I dug out all the old slug fragments and trash. Skittish, never says a word."

Sallie, Jack thought, a frequent drifting dream. *We got him back--- we got him.*

Jack winced as he tried to sit up on the cot unsteadily, fell back, weak, then finally made it. His head spun and knotted his stomach. He felt the fever humming in his blood like a dark song. He felt bone thin, he saw his own thin arms, the bandage on one. He waited as the spinning in his head subsided.

"Sherriff came by. Looking to see you."

Jack stared his confusion.

"Sheriff," Johnson Lee confirmed. "Looked more like one of the new deputies, new shirt, shiny new belly gun. Wanted to fine you for breaking the peace. Three Yankee dollars---."

"Breaking the peace---?" Jack mumbled.

"I'd say he's new at this business---."

"What business?"

"All that crowd outside, the newspaper folks. The lookers. You're famous, sir. In all the newspapers. Wanted to see you. I told them they couldn't get in without a ticket." Johnson Lee laughed.

Famous.

"Shit."

"A few still hang around to see if you're going to die. Want to be the first to carry the news---."

"News. Tell 'em to go look at the damn camels---."

Johnson Lee blinked three times, as though his patient had suddenly relapsed into delirium. "Camels?"

Jack scowled. He started to answer, then stopped, surprised at this rambling unimportant trivia from the chaos of fever dreams.

---ugly damn camels, ravens, a dancing wild man, the screams, the rain---.

He mumbled another curse and just shook his head.

"What the hell happened out there?" Johnson Lee asked slowly, carefully, his curiosity finally getting the better of him. "You're famous. Those fools outside want to know, they'll pester---."

"No." Jack had no story for Johnson Lee, or the newspaper people.

He looked around the room, he looked at the familiar basket on the floor by Johnson Lee. He drew a deep breath, savoring the basket's aroma. His stomach growled with hunger. He cleared his throat again. "I expect that's food there---."

Johnson Lee laughed again, relieved. "There is. Miss Luz. The lady brings it fresh every day. Damn good victuals." He patted his belly then paused thoughtfully. "The lady never fusses. Swear to God, she never dithers. She watches me, never misses a damn thing." Johnson Lee opened his eyes wide in mock fear. "A real caution, I'd say."

Fierce. Her grandmother's child, Jack heard her voice saying the words. Years past.

"---I believe I'll catch hell with her if you don't continue to thrive."

Thrive.

Luzita.

Jack smiled.

After he'd drunk two deep swallows of water and slowly eaten some of the wonders of Luzita's basket, he felt the first stirring of clarity, of genuine optimism for survival ahead. He reached for the jar of water again.

"Hold up," Johnson Lee said. He took the jug up from the floor. "It's as good a tonic as any you'll find. Drink up. Got everything in it. Made it myself."

Jack drank, then lowered the jug suddenly, almost dropping it, and stared at Johnson Lee. "ELIXIR."

"Yes sir---." Johnson Lee's eyes widened. He peered through his rimless glasses. He stared at Jack, as though thinking sudden amazing thoughts, seeing amazing sights, then he began to laugh again. "By God, you're Jack! Of course! Jack! Hell yes, you must be young Jack!"

---calls himself a sawbones, that's the sign he put up, Jack wrote in his journal six weeks later. *Got him stirred up talking about camels, he said. Don't remember. Told him nothing about Jeth.*

He studied the handwriting, frowned at the crawly look of it, so unlike his usual scrawl, once bold. But improving. Not fast enough.

Just takes time. He said six months, maybe a year to heal up, another spell to just be mean-sore, but good enough to raise some hell---.

Jack managed a distant smile in the jumble of memories.

"Well, you got that son of a bitch," Moses Jones told him with satisfaction on his second visit days later. He brought with him a bottle of rye whiskey and the look and feel of a busy rough world, hot and in a hurry, where the wind blew, and the fall sun beamed down beyond the house with the blue door.

"Yep."

Jack never said more than that, never the truth about Jeth, about how everything happened. Let Jeth tell his own stories someday.

"Shit, with no guns to trade," Moses Jones said, a hint of wry amusement in his voice. "Hell of a story---."

"Three Spencers. We brought 'em all back. Drank the whiskey," Jack went on with his work. The story had spread widely, had been repeated over and over and written about in the dusty days of late summer, but it was old now and he was tired of it, even of the little he'd spoken about it to Luzita, to the military at the fort, to the *alcalde*, to the new law, to Don Ernesto.

Moses Jones laughed. His voice trailed off as he studied Jack working to get the stiffness from his arm.

The doc had told Jack the arm and shoulder might be useless, never quite right. He kept working, rubbing at the pain.

"I made a fool mistake," Jack said finally.

Moses Jones offered Jack his flask of whiskey, then took a deep swig himself. He waited.

"That damned old rusty *pistole*." Jack shook his head, holding back his irritation, his anger. "He never could figure out how to get a spark, no slugs, just gunpowder, how to load it. Nothing to load it with---burned himself with gunpowder when he did get a spark. How can you be dumb as a post but still shit cunning?"

But maybe the Ki-Was Man wasn't dumb as a post; Jack's greatest mistake all these years, whenever he thought back.

Maybe everyone's mistake about the raging bitter hostiles.

Maybe the Ki-Was Man was just a cruel exaggeration of his own people, those bitter dying nomads who would never hoe corn.

Moses Jones waited again. His eyes were sharp as he watched Jack, sharp and thoughtful. Something nagged at him, something about the fight at the great rock, the little he'd heard, about that useless *pistole*. Then he wiped the sweat on his face with his neck scarf and rambled on with the news.

"Military knew something about him, heard he carried captives, wouldn't turn 'em in or sign into a reservation, called him Crazy Dog, old time mean Comanche---."

---*old time mean Comanche,* Jack thought. *Worse, much worse.*

"---Military thought he was gunrunning to the Apaches over in the mountains. Disappeared for months at a time, then showed up at a reservation stirring up trouble, then gone again. Had two, three different names---."

"I kept asking. Military never told me a damn thing---."

"They just never caught up with him. Too many *banditos* to chase." Moses Jones stretched out, uncomfortable in the heat and the hide chair under the arbor, watching as Jack began to work the horsehair strands of the new *mecate* he was weaving for Don Ernesto.

Busy work---work that took him away from hard thoughts and back to his time with the old saint-maker in Santa Fe.

Jack listened to Moses Jones talk on with his news, not much interested because he knew Moses Jones was just plain set on recruiting him for his riders and he was just as set on finding his own way back.

Back to what?

But the long days had begun to wear on him.

He went on working the strands, working the stiffness and nerve damage out of his arm and hand.

"You remember that kid, name of Ned. Kid from Tennessee. Heard he got himself killed up north, Oklahoma." Moses Jones took out his cob pipe, rapped it clean of ash and stuffed it with tobacco. He lit up and puffed thoughtfully. "That boy had a mouth on him, shit for brains. Fought with some old hide hunters and skinners looking for more shaggies and all liquored up. Thought he was a bad Texian *hombre*. Not near as bad as them old boys." Moses Jones shook his head, "Hard damn country."

"Those boys signed up to scout for the Lodge Pole fight." Jack frowned. Now, somehow, it seemed easier to talk about that fight. The Washita fight. "Mostly went along looking for new buffalo camps and new buffalo killing fields, good water---."

"Heard tell they'd shoot five hundred shaggies in an hour. From one stand. That'll starve the Indians quick enough."

"Some were good men." Jack paused in his work, letting his concentration drift away as he thought back, thought about the shaggies, the huge killing fields littered with the bodies of rotting bison.

"Shaggies getting scarce," Moses Jones commented, as he had many times in the past. "Fellow told me he come across sixty, seventy cows up north hiding out in prairie draws."

Everyone knew Sheridan wanted the wild Indians hungry, even starving.

---long time yet, Jack thought, *long road ahead.*

The fever had almost left him, but sometimes crept back, stealthy aches and pains---his leg, his shoulder. As the slow days passed, the mystery of the salt that Johnson Lee had wondered about, finally came back to him.

"Salt," Jack said aloud, following his memory. "Wagon went by, oxen carrying a load of salt from the salt flats down near El Paso."

"Salt?" Moses Jones said.

Jack thought for a moment, "Jeth followed the wagon and hid in the brush, took what he wanted as the wagon went by, then came back in the dark. Wagon never stopped."

"Jeth wanted the salt. Comanches crave salt. Food, tanning, treating wounds---." Jack thought for a moment, "He followed the wagon and hid in the brush, took what he wanted as the wagon went by, then came back in the dark. Wagon never stopped."

Moses Jones smiled. He scratched the stubble on his jaw. "Heals up wounds. By Ganny, them Comanches know that." He waited for details, then asked, "I heard about that slug you took." .

"Which one?"

Moses Jones puffed on his pips. "Hell, the stampede."

"The stampede," Jack said. His lips quirked in a hard smile. "Sure enough. Doc said the slug was soft, he polished the black away, didn't look like lead. Damn thing came up bright silver. I believe he got himself a surprise."

"Silver! Hell yes, a surprise. Every Texian's still out there, still digging for that Spanish silver and them gold doubloons the Spanish hid when they were running from the Mexicans back in the war. Hid 'em everywhere---."

"Raw metal just out of the hillside. Dohat found it like the Apaches did, just dug it out." He'd never talked about this to Moses Jones, or to anybody else. Now he wandered back, remembering the Child-Taker's grand habits, his lofty beliefs, his magical boasts.

Moses Jones waited, letting the silence fill the moment.

"We were kids, learning to hunt. No guns. Trying to catch an eagle for the feathers, catch whatever we could. He ran with the Apaches one summer---." Jack held up his hand for Moses Jones's whiskey bottle, drank deeply, then handed it back. "They all wore metal belts and hair ornaments, big silver *conchos*. They made 'em just using charcoal and pounding the hell out of that heavy dirt."

"Apaches no friends of them Comanches."

"His mother and cousins were Kiowa Apaches. But he did whatever the hell he wanted," Jack paused then laughed and shook his head. "Bragged he could make magic with that old Spanish pistole. Magic fire, rusty firing pin, no flint, no lead for slugs. Thought it was big medicine, like the old stories. Wouldn't let anyone touch it. His protection, the Supernaturals. He waved it around like a club---."

The fool, the bad Ki-Was Man---.

But he'd figured it out, maybe a long time ago. Not Jack's first mistake with the Ki-Was Man, but his last. He thought about the dead Ki-Was Man, now lost, an eerie spirit wandering the dark winds of the Supernaturals, his magic weapon belching fire and death.

His Indian thinking again, creeping back.

"You still got that there pistol around here somewhere? Bring it back with you?" Moses Jones asked.

"Never saw it again, just got left behind." Jack shrugged.

Moses Jones idly watched blue jays squabbling with a crow in the cottonwood trees, making a testy racket on a quiet day. "Had a run in with some rustler's last scout." He drew a deep breath, a tired breath of resolve and memory. "Damn rustlers. Shot one of my boys--- Sandoval. Called him Sandy. Good kid, they shot him in the belly, died hard three days later. I believe he wanted help from us, get it over with---you know---."

Jack looked at Moses Jones, hearing, just nodding.

"Well shit." Moses Jones fell silent for a time, thinking back. "We caught up with them damn rustlers after we took care of Sandy. They were pushing cattle, slowed 'em down. Just plain fools. We left three of 'em hanging from an oak tree, didn't even know their names. Didn't care. Left a shovel on the ground under the tree."

Jack heard the tiredness in his voice, saw it in his pale eyes. Old man's eyes.

"Shovels getting scarce these days," Moses Jones reflected.

Jack looked back toward the corral under the cottonwoods, where Jeth rubbed down his mustang after a ride. He saw how Jeth's shoulders pulled at the back of his shirt as he worked.

He's growing, likes Luzita's sweets---.

"Boy doing good?" Moses Jones asked.

"Good enough. He works at it. Doesn't talk much." Jack paused in his work, reflecting. "He's remembering. Comes all at once sometimes."

"He don't talk about going off, chasing Indians, raising some hell?"

Jack bent his head over the *mecate* he was working on, without answering.

"Recall I got tired of bone soup when I was about his age," Moses Jones said. "Just run off. Never went back."

Jack finally asked, "Where to next?"

"Going on a scout, maybe a month. Break up more of them horse stealing camps along the border, catch 'em before they cross the Rio. Got to keep going now that the Rangers're gone."

Jack stared at Moses Jones. "They'll be back."

Moses Jones' eyebrows lifted in doubt. "Well hell, the U.S. of A. *Federales* plumb ran out of money---."

"We're Federals now, Cap. The Rangers broke up because of taking different sides in the fight."

But Moses Jones had to finish his rant. "Them politicians can't count, think civil law's all we need here." He got to his feet with a sigh, stamped his boots, loosened his shoulders. "Might get the Vigilantes back, or the Militias. Oh hell, the Rangers'll be back even when they're always in the wrong place when we need 'em." He worked his shoulders again. "Getting too damn old. Too many nights sleeping on the ground. One of these days I'm going to give it up and just sit in a chair on my gallery, drink Shine till I'm dog drunk and telling crazy stories." He spat tobacco juice and wiped his mouth. He squinted at Jack, "I'm holding a place for you with my boys. Get yourself ready. It ain't over."

When the old man had left, Jack stood abruptly. Moses Jones's words echoed like a sudden drumbeat in his mind.

It ain't over.

What the hell am I doing here?

A question he'd asked himself before. But now it was different.

Inside, he sat at the table he'd built for Luzita. He lit the lantern as the light faded. He found the stash of newspapers he'd set aside, old ones and new ones, something to do later. He found the articles about the Rangers, just the information and, here and there an editorial, but nothing new.

He pushed the papers aside.

He picked up the big metal fragment, a distorted echo of a round shape that had lodged in his shoulder for days until Johnson Lee dug it out. It was only a jagged metal shape, but bright silver, and Luzita saved it in the little clay dish. Maybe important to her but the fragment held no importance to him anymore.

He picked up his pen and began writing in his journal.

Doc's a stranger here, had to talk about that slug, said it was a wonder, didn't know he'd start a silver stampede, all those gullible greenhorns chasing silver everywhere. But he's a good man. No relation to Robert E. He painted the Union flag on his sign. I told him he'd starve here if he wore the blue. Said he'd been starving here till I came along. Claims he came from the rebellion but he doesn't talk about it much. Watches his back at night when he's on the street, mostly Reb soldiers, drunk, hanging on to the gray. Says they're going lawless, looking for Jayhawkers, tells them he doesn't care who he treats, blue or gray.

"Ran into a Reb last week. Not much older than your boy," Johnson Lee said on one of his frequent visits. "Started cussing at me. Claimed he wore the hood back in Mississippi, had no use for Jayhawkers---or 'them black bastards, thinking they can vote'---his words. He had a limp. He wanted to shoot me for some reason." Mocking, Johnson Lee rounded his eyes, his rimless eyeglasses shifting on his nose. "I told him I'd take his leg clean off, no charge, just to show my goodwill, him wearing the gray and all. Damned if he didn't decline."

Johnson Lee pushed his glasses up on his nose and began poking at Jack. "This hurt?"

"Yep."

Johnson Lee looked at Jack's arm. "This clearing up yet?"

"Not much."

Jonson Lee examined Jack's leg. "This better?"

"Not yet."

When Johnson Lee reached for Jack's shoulder, Jack dodged his rough interest with a laugh and a grimace, "Not yet---."

"Well you're getting some weight back, looking better. Just takes time." He smiled. "I've seen more flesh on skeletons."

Johnson Lee and his casual, gruff manner always lifted Jack's spirits, yet he saw the dead serious, no nonsense inquisition deep in the doctor's eyes, behind his glasses and his easy manner, as he examined Jack.

Not yet.

Just takes time.

"Well hell, then It's time for a drink. Here. I made up a new batch. Smith said it was a secret. Came in handy when the troopers were burning all the dead horses after a fight. Awful stink. ELIXIR helped when we ran out of opium and morphine. Smith's a touchy son of a gun about that formula."

"Formula?" Jack scoffed.

"Reminds me. He said when he first caught up to you, you were a half wild white Comanche with an arrow in you and a whole tribe of Comanches chasing after you. Just figured you must've done something right. Said he saved your bacon in Santa Fe."

"He talks a lot," Jack answered but he didn't mind, smiled, remembering Cicero Smith's flamboyant ways and his frequently shady exaggerations.

"Said he turned you into a regular ornery badass white man---."

"I reckon he told you about the time he got himself buckshot out in California?"

"He mentioned that in passing, a minor event---."

"Yep," Jack said, and laughed.

"Now drink up. It'll do you good. Both of us." Johnson Lee thrust a jug of ELIXIR at Jack. "Then I've got to get back, the surgery'll be full by now."

They drank and savored the quiet moment. Johnson Lee sighed. "There was a brawl at LUCKY'S last night. Two gamblers dead, three drovers gunshot. A kid swamping the saloon got in the way. Scatter guns. Wasted lives. God help me, it's hard to treat just plain brawling fools when I think of those fields of soldiers up in Pennsylvania. I hope to God I never see anything like that again,"

Jack dipped his pen and went on in his journal.

Doc says he and Smith wore the blue together, met up in a surgeon's tent in Pennsylvania. Bad fight. Every farm house and building taken for a hospital, still not enough. They teamed up after the war. Doc came on to Bexar after Smith found the old posters about Jeth and Rosebud I put out. Doc figured Bexar was as good a place as any, just plain tired of the war, and Smith went on to Santa Fe, coming back this way with his wagon. Taking his time. I expect he'll stop along the road to visit with the ladies.

Jack put his journal aside and took up his ledger, counting again the number of bare root apple plants due from California by mail coach for the coming winter's planting. They were all grafted to strong varieties suited for the Texas climate, according to his almanacs and all the books and the tracts he could find. His cache of California gold had shrunk but remained substantial in these Reconstruction days, where gold and silver sent greenhorns and carpetbaggers scrambling after old Spanish doubloons and Apache silver. He thought about Cicero Smith, that good flimflam man, about big California valleys and orchards. He thought about his Texas land, just waiting.

He took up his journal again.

The almanacs and Don Ernesto, Luzita's granddad---that old jefe has grit. He rousts his sons and grandsons to get the land cleared. He drinks his tequila and never raises his voice. Fifty acres right off, he says. Stumps out, land ready, springs cleared. Hector and his brothers made a good start, Don Ernesto says there's more land nearby. Just waiting for California gold. Maybe. Good soil, water. He's pleased with the appaloosa stud in his remuda now. He's taken a liking to Jeth.

But it ain't over. Moses Jones's words.

Because Sheridan had his war, in what the journalists claimed is the last long resistance of the hostile tribes.

Fight the hostiles the way they fight the troopers, the only way to win against them.

His shoulder ached again, nagging. He felt battered sometimes, mostly from the long road back to Bexar from the picture rock, other times. But just about every Texian man had Indian scrapes and wounds and such stories to tell; brave fights, noble causes, gators over in the swamps, panthers, outlaws, runaway slaves, witches in the woods.

But that old man long ago under the Comanche stars had been wise in his words and sometimes kind in his deeds.

Only men died who were willing to die.

Maybe so, maybe not.

But his youth had slipped away, and he'd hardly noticed. Most times he'd made his way from day to day like everyone else and just felt baffled by the old mysteries. He paged back in his journal, back to November 28, of '68. He looked at the entry he'd made the day after the Washita fight, sitting on the ground by the surgeon's tent waiting his turn, cold and hurting.

He paged forward and began to write.

The white flag.

Black Kettle and his village, what happened? Military told him his people were safe inside the Territory.

Major Elliot---the troopers said Custer hated him.

No quarter. Custer's orders?

The women and children, what happened to them?

He was no journalist, they had pestered him after he and Jeth came back from the picture rock, but he never gave them the lurid story they wanted and Jeth remained silent.

How much will he remember? How much will he forget? He had finally allowed Luzita to trim the rough thatch of his hair to his shoulders, his face had faded from the burned and freckled look of his captivity. The scars on his arms had faded too and might soon be ignored and not act as a reminder.

When the McGregors came down from Elm Creek, he just walked up to Mariah Matilda and let her hug him in one of her long bony hugs, and McGregor kept wiping his face with his big white handkerchief. Jeth told them that the Comanche man who caught him just wanted the black mare. He recognized the mare, she was a famous Arikara race horse. Every Indian wanted the mare. All the Comanche men gambled for her whenever they could. Any man who owned her would brag about her, win bets and have a big name among the tribes.

So the Comanche who caught Jeth traded him to an Apache at the mountain agency when he'd gone to get food. He was afraid the agent would cheat him and put him in a cage and make him eat swine if he tried to sell the White Dog boy to the agent.

That was all he'd said in his halting words.

Jack found a school for Jeth, not one of the padres' schools, but one with a single room and soon to grow larger as the population of Bexar grew with Baptists and Lutherans and Methodists. Jeth held back from the school, wary. He seldom spoke. He often roamed the town at night, gone for hours, looking, searching.

Jeth couldn't name what he was searching for, but he knew he was damaged somehow. He listened to his father's steady words telling of the rock house days, the creek. Or he followed his father out to his land, the orchard without trees, and listened when Jack told him of the orchards in California. But there were gaps in his father's words, where his memory couldn't go. His mind searched on his wandering night rides for what was missing, and what was still lingering in his guarded memory.

A house with whitewashed walls. A big empty bed.

Moments of the past unfolded slowly over the weeks. His hoard of Texian words grew, echoed back and were seized for their scraps of information.

One day he decided to call his father's woman Miss Luz, maybe because others often called her by that name. She was not his mother. That memory still hid from him, somehow promising pain. But he saw how this woman meant no harm and treated him and his father well. She walked to her *Jacal*, and back every day, bringing good food, good sweets, wonderful spicy aromas. She didn't use harsh words of complaint. She knew how to make everything good in the house with the blue door, even when Jeth sometimes went outside to sleep under the stars. He wanted to like her, he knew he would like her, but he would let time reassure him in this.

He began to understand white man's work again, familiar to him sometimes, although no Comanche man would bother with such trivial tasks. He went to *LA LUZ*, just to watch, and when they offered him some small busy job, he felt as though he had stepped across a threshold into a different world, where Small Mexican Boy, without a single word to anyone, had been swallowed up by the women, who wanted to nurture him and keep him. On the military lists of Indian captives, his father told Jeth that his name had been moved to the "Recovered" list. But there was no name and no description for Small Mexican Boy.

On the Tradedays in Bexar, Jeth wandered the streets, leading his mustang and staring at the booths and venders selling tools, old tack, sheep's wool, old clothes, bolts of fabric, goat hides, handmade knives with horn handles, books. He came to a kiosk where a woman with smooth dark skin and long black braid sold herbs tied in bundles, flowers, pecan nuts, sweets with pine nuts. Jeth offered a coin for one of her cakes, one of three coins his father had given him, but the woman looked into his face, as though it was familiar, then she gave him the sweet and waved him on.

He stopped at a clearing one day, where horses and mules milled in a rope corral and men called out prices. Further along, plumes of dust rose in the air as men and boys raced their horses around a track and other men called out bets. He saw a big black mare waiting to run, a boy on her back.

Racer.

But this black mare had a white star on her forehead.

"Where?" Jeth asked weeks later, when he saw his father saddle Blue and tighten the cinch.

"Going to New Braunfels." Jack answered, his voice quiet, matter of fact. He hesitated only a moment. "Looking for Rose."

The old cottonwood leaves in back of the house with the blue door rustled softly in a breeze, then fell quiet. But neither Jack nor Jeth heard the silence.

"Rosebud," Jeth said abruptly.

Rosebud

"Yep." Jack gave Jeth time, watching the revelation take him, fill him, as though he suddenly saw a child with little blue shoes.

Jack watched, then said, "Come along then."

But they didn't find Rosebud at the little village of New Braunfels where the Comanches and the people had traded peacefully for decades.

"Well hell, no Rangers anymore," Moses Jones declared on a visit to check on Jack's general fitness. "Now it's getting worse up along the border. Missouri. Kansas. Shooters, lynch mobs. Shit, I don't reckon it'll get much better. Not in this old dog's life, by Ganny." He puffed on his pipe, made a face at the taste, a tired frown settling on his face. "That Jack Hayes, I ever tell you about him? I rode scout with him and the Rangers back in the '40s, Then he went off in '49, led them Forty-Niners over that wagon road to California, thought of going myself. Shit---that Flaco---smartest damn Apache I ever did run into." He drank from his bottle wiped his mouth and handed the whiskey to Jack, rambling on. "---Then we got Rip Ford and his boys. That Chief Placido and all his Tonk scouts. They killed all them Comanches and ate 'em. Plain killed 'em and ate 'em and Rip and his boys just stood there and watched. Ask me, the Tonks scared them Comanches to death, spooked 'em with them new heavy five shot Colt Walkers---."

Jack remembered the stories; Tonkawa scouts, Tonkawa fighters, man-eaters who ate the hated Comanches they killed.

"I expect all of Texas remembers the Rangers standing by."

Ugly stories, familiar to Jack but he listened to all of them because the stories seemed like treasured memories to Moses Jones, the old days when everything was both worse and better.

"---Now we got them outlaws shooting up towns in Kansas and them Klan fools back in Tennessee---," Moses Jones' voice trailed off.

Doc says it sometimes feels like the North won the war but the South sure as hell's winning the Reconstruction.

Moses Jones roused and grumbled, "Shit, that blue nag of yours is getting fat, Jack. We still got fighting to do, nothing much changes, by Ganny---."

But Moses Jones was wrong. Everything was changing. Who was it long ago who had told him about the chaos of change?

One day Jack took up his tools and decided to enlarge the school and repair the stove chimney against the coming winter. Something to do, start slowly, day by day, do what he could to build his strength. But the old church nearby took his attention, until he went there, walking through the rubble of renovation until he found a padre and asked.

"Little Sister Girl. A Comanche, a little kid. She was cold and hungry. Got lost. I left her with you people."

But no one knew, or remembered. He heard the vague words, the dull words, with anger stirring in his belly, familiar anger. Little Sister Girl had faded away. Maybe she had died from her cold days hidden in the brush, from her hunger, or maybe she had been recovered. Or maybe she was just lost in the dim archives of the old church.

Finally Jeth followed his father to the school and watched as he fitted a new window, adjusted the sagging door with new iron strap hinges, spoke of plans to re-plaster the adobe walls. Then Jeth decided. He walked into the school room, looked around, then sat in the back, for no reason other than that was where the taller boys sat. At first they were curious, then they attempted to tease with words because he was different, but he let the words flow over him like a breath of wind in the way he had learned among the Comanches. When they grew rougher, they quickly found themselves lying in the dirt. He never bothered to tell Jack or the woman of these little scrapes, they were unimportant. But Jack knew, he remembered his own return to the white world and he figured Jeth, like other captives, faced the same thing.

But Jeth had learned to smile sometimes, even laugh now and then, a gift in his blood from Sallie Rainie. Laughter was like a moment from the past, a slow, cautious discovery. A liberation.

Maybe at last, Jeth had found the memory of his mother, and held it close to himself.

He never spoke of little Rose. He had no knowledge, no information about captives for the military authorities or the agents or his father. Even now another of the lost children from the Elm Creek raid had not been found.

And more often as the months passed, Jack knew Rosebud, not yet three, had been too young to survive the hard aftermath of the Elm Creek raid.

Where are you Rosebud?

I should have gone after them, I should have tried---.

Then came the chance moment at Hard Bone's lodge five years later that led Jack to finding the Ki-Was Man and Jeth.

Jack looked out through the blue door of his casita across the narrow street to the plaza. He saw the drovers and stockmen hurrying toward *LA LUZ* to line up, waiting for food; a good hot meal of black beans and chili with freshly baked *sopas* and apple pie.

Jeth wandered in, rummaged around in the tin for one of Luzita's sweet buns she kept there, then joined Jack carrying his books, and a batch of newly printed posters he'd picked up at the printers.

Little Rosebud again.

Jeth looked hard at his father.

"He was here. That one."

"Old Moses?"

Jeth nodded. "You going off with him?"

Jack hedged. He took his time answering. "I'm carrying a load of goods to McGregor tomorrow, bolts of calico, school supplies, she's starting her school. McGregor wants new plows, tools, shovels, spades, lime. Hector helped load, wagon's ready to roll barring the weather, maybe a storm coming."

Jeth waited.

"Time I checked on Ely, get the news." Jack studied his son. "See how he's doing with all the work, the branding. Prices are getting better, he sent word maybe three hundred and twenty yearling so far."

But Jeth shook his head.

Not yet, Jack thought. He's not ready to go back to the rock house.

"Rangers," Jeth said.

Jack studied the boy again, thoughtfully. "They're not here,"

Jeth waited.

"You know about them?"

"Some."

"What?"

Jeth's eyes narrowed. "They fight."

"Yep," Jack felt a ripple go down his spine, he wasn't sure why. "They got disbanded. It's the civil law here now."

"What's that mean?"

"Texas law. Town law. Sheriffs, deputies."

"Like the ones come here talking to you?"

Jack thought about the civil law. About the word LAW that had once given him such fear when he was a green kid and knew nothing of the white man's world.

"Yep."

"They want you?"

"They're trying. But they got to wait a while if they want me."

Two men had stopped at the house with the blue door a week before. They sat in the shade under the arbor and drank beer, just casual, easy. They spoke to Jack with a certain deference that brought a wry smile to his face.

I'm famous.

The two men talked on about the weather, maybe a fall storm on the horizon. They swapped a few stories, told some jokes and talked about the new laws. They wore hard-used coats and vests, dusters and black string ties. Their boots were worn but polished. Their Stetsons were new and they were careful to set their hats down crown first when they wiped the sweat from their faces. Their badges were shiny and obvious, their hand weapons hanging in holsters belted around their waists. They mentioned the weather again, just making talk.

"Looking around, I expect. Nothing here for them." Then Jack spoke what was just about certain in his mind, what he saw in the faces of Bexar people. "The Rangers'll be back. We sure as hell need 'em."

"When?"

"A year, maybe more. When there's money to pay them."

"How d' you know?" Jeth frowned.

"They'll be back when things commence to go to hell and the Feds get the funding for them, or the local politicians get them the money."

"I'm going."

"Off with Moses? He won't take you yet. You're not old enough. He's a good man but he's getting tired. He'll be finished with the Minutemen pretty quick. He knows it."

"Going with you."

Jack looked down at his journal, hearing from Jeth the conviction, his own certainty that he had never really spoken, never fully acknowledged. But Jeth knew.

"Maybe they don't come back," Jeth said.

"I expect it'll get worse. Doc patches up the hard cases at LUCKY's but they got a good start already."

Jeth took a bite of his sweet bun. He looked at his father thoughtfully. "When?"

"Maybe when you're sixteen, seventeen. Older. Depends---."

Jeth took another bite of Luzita's sweet bun. "Not here now."

Jack studied his son again. He saw the streak of what-the-hell in Jeth; the hard-headed determination once he'd made up his mind. It was something Jack recognized, here and there, in other hard men, and in himself. And there was a mystery in Jeth as well, a vast unknowable silent place where he had lived for five years, more, but Jack figured something had kept him alive and toughened him. Now he saw something else he recognized in himself.

Jeth munched on the sweet bun, watching his father, always with that look, probing, wondering, in his eyes.

"Long time," Jeth said.

Here was the kind of friendly, guarded stand-off he and his father often came to. Both felt the challenge of wills, both felt the iron of determination, their two minds tested by hardships. They both knew about cruelty, casual killing, little children thrown away, fear of pain, death, terror, being lost and alone in the emptiness of a huge, silent land.

But they never spoke of it. They kept their silence. They both felt this hard acceptance, as quiet as the land itself that allowed them to go on, to survive. And they both felt how it twisted their minds, their hearts, how they saw their world, how they struggled to understand, to endure.

"I'm going with you," Jeth said again.

"Sixteen, seventeen, not so long." Idle words, but Jack remembered exactly how long the years were to him long ago, to any boy, to Jeth. Jack sat back in his chair. "Boys your age, gone off after the war, left home. Maybe there was no home left. Boys like you end up swamping saloons, hungry. No money, stealing. Getting jailed. Or they sign up for trail drives, eating dust, getting shot up, dying out on the prairie." Jack paused, fragments of his own memory jarring him for a moment. "Well, too damn long for Moses, he couldn't wait to go off. Your age, he told me he got tired of bone soup at home so he quit and never went back."

Jeth smiled, then laughed. "Bone soup." He swallowed, savoring the last of the sweet bun.

Then he moved around the table, he sat across from Jack with deliberation. His eyebrows came together, not in a frown but in a moment of serious concentration, serious concern. Jack saw struggle in his eyes, heard it in his voice

"I saw you," he said at last.

"You saw me?"

"At that place---."

"What place?"

"At that place where white men come, they have soldiers---." Jeth's words stumbled, "Where they have food for Indians, steers, just take them---."

Jack stared. "An agency?"

Jeth nodded. "That."

"You---," Jack's voice faltered. "When---?"

Jeth stretched his arm out, showing his height, showing his father when, "This."

"You saw me?" Jack's voice went suddenly dry.

Years ago.

Jeth nodded again.

Jack stared, his mind scrambling in confusion, remembering in a kind of shock, all those agencies, where? All the searching, all the questions, all the fear that he would never find the boy. An agency, just one of the many, then Hard Bones' idle words, searching, the years---.

"But why---?"

"You were wearing a hat---big damn White Dog hat." Jeth made a sound like a laugh, maybe at his own words, but it was a bitter sound. "I couldn't get no closer."

They sat in silence.

"You," Jeth said. He nodded, as though in further confirmation.

Jack sat numb, speechless with confirmation.

"Apples," Jeth said. "I left some in a camp. One time, after. Them little apples, no good---."

Little wild apples.

"---maybe you find. On a stump---."

Jeth's spoke in broken words, awkward words now and then. He finally sighed. He watched his father intently. He'd been talking to his father for years, saving words from the past, messages, trying to reach him, trying to be found.

The silence stretched on and on.

Finally Jack spoke, so quietly, so internally shocked that he wasn't sure what he said, or if Jeth heard him.

"Shit."

"Yep," Jeth said.

The lights of San Antonia de Bexar blinked on slowly until the village, now a city, held a peaceful glow. A Mexican cart with old noisy wheels passed by in the plaza. They heard drunken laughter, far away a voice yelled a question that was never answered.

"Rain's coming," Jack said, distracted.

"Yep."

Jack stared out the open doorway. He wiped his eyes and sighed. He turned his head to study Jeth.

"The Rangers then."

"With you. Maybe long time."

"It's not over," Jack said, because he knew that the chaos of Reconstruction, the slow end of the wild tribes were not over yet. "But we've got time."

He couldn't stop the sudden sorrow that swept over him. *Lost. I never saw him there, anywhere---.*

And then the lifting of the great weight of the years the rise of sudden, profound thankfulness that this boy was back, here, safe.

Found.

"We've got time." Jack said again. He drew a long breath "Time."

Jeth waited.

"We'll plant the orchard this winter."

"Yep."

"Land's ready."

Jeth nodded.

Plenty of water. Springs're cleared up."

Jeth nodded again.

"We'll begin."

"Yep," Jeth said.

Early winter bore down as Jack sat at the table with his journal, Night winds started to bluster, he smelled the rain coming from the storm that had hovered on the horizon for a week. He arose and limped to close the door. He crossed to the corner fireplace to build heat in the three rooms of the house with the blue door. He stared into the fire for a time, thinking of all Jeth had told him, and all the words hidden behind his simple words.

Someday, Jack thought.

The rain fell in a momentary torrent, then eased to a steady blowing shower. He heard the rumble of thunder far away.

She'll be wet, he thought, but Luzita never bothered with nature's whims on her daily journeys back and forth to *LA LUZ*. They were more a challenge to her than a trial, and just a part of her life.

She came through the door with rain and wind following her, a wet shawl over her head and wrapped tight around her shoulders, but her arms were so full, holding baskets of hot food and *sopas*, fruits and pecans and fresh sweets, that the shawl fell away. With all the rain and bluster of the storm, she brought with her the scent of damp cotton, her own body fragrance and all the wonderful aromas from her little *jacal*. She dropped the baskets and bundles down on the floor, on the hearth, on the little counter where they kept pitchers of water. She turned to Jack and stood wet and bedraggled, laughing.

"Now we will have our food, but first I will be dry!"

"He means it," Luzita said later. "Is he sleeping?"

"Back in his room buried under a quilt."

"He is almost a man but he is still a boy," Luzita said. "All my good food. His belly is full and he can't go out riding around tonight, *verdad?*" She wrapped her own quilt around her shoulders but the old adobe walls held the fire's heat and she was comfortably warm.

They listened to the dripping of the rain, the whinny of Blue, sheltered in their small hay barn.

He saw me.

He finally told her the whole story, everything he had held back, the fight at the picture rock, all that happened, his mistakes, the Comanche woman, what Jeth had done.

But before he finished he saw the look in her eyes and realized that she knew already. Knew something.

"How'd you know?"

She touched his shoulder. They sat in the big bed they shared. "The talk about that old pistol. So much talk, so much silence. But you found him, you brought him back."

"No ma'am." Jack shook his head, emphatic. "More like he brought me back---."

"You found him," Luzita said. "You, only you." She searched for words. "All those years." Her eyes held a moment of shine, almost tears, insistence. "You found him. But there was so much mystery. Something happened. *Si*, I knew. He was silent. He never said. You never said."

"He didn't tell you?" He persisted.

Luzita lifted her chin to look deeply at Jack. "He has the great silence." She spoke with certainty, about a way, a silence she understood.

After a moment Jack said, "He wants the Rangers. With me."

"*Si*," she answered.

"Maybe two, three years, when he's old enough---."

She almost laughed. "So long for a boy. He is his father's son, do you forget? He is eager. He is hard in his mind, his heart---."

Had to survive. Had to---.

"---So much determination, so much---." Luzita's voice trailed away as though she couldn't find more to say. Her lips moved in soft Castilian words. Finally she smiled and began to rub Jack's shoulder, his arm, in a ritual they had come to enjoy.

"We'll start," Jack said finally.

"*Si*. Then you will both go. He will go with you. With the Rangers when they come back. You say nothing, but I know. You are like my brothers and my uncles and the others. My father. So many. You will go."

He studied her beautiful face, her wise, watchful eyes still with their shine. This was the reality she understood, the stories, the sacrifices her sisters and all the mothers and cousins knew, always remembered, this woman who was so much herself and so much her grandmother's child.

"I'll sign up if they'll take me then," he said. "Hell, they'll take me if the civil law's already waiting on me."

"And that old one, that *viejo* who smokes the pipe?"

"The Rangers."

"*Si*," she said again, "they will take you---and I will be so busy making all those hungry *hombres* fat with chili and apple pies at *LA LUZ*."

He smiled. "We'll have time before he's old enough and the Rangers come back."

She laid his shirt back and massaged his shoulder with her strong hands. "You will go. You will both go."

"Yes ma'am." He drew himself up, wincing a little.

He grinned for her. "Doc says I'll be ready to hunt gators with a switch by then, by Ganny."

She paused, considering how to answer.

"Yep," Luzita said, and smiled again.

Jack looked down at his journal later, with lantern light lying softly across his pages. He listened to the steady rain, a quiet sound. Luzita and the boy slept and he was alone.

Soon he would need another journal, new pages for new words.

He thought back to the great picture rock standing alone in the solitary wilderness of the Comancheria, he thought of the hundreds of painted rocks telling their stories all across the wild land, some hidden away in caves, everywhere, lost in the tangles of trees and rocks and shade, with all their secrets and silence. He thought of that great rock where he had drunk the cool sweet water as a boy. He thought of all that had happened there. He saw in his mind all the brave pictures, all the history. All the ancient pride.

He saw the boy and himself, searching, finding each other.

He thought about little Rosebud, and his Sallie. Others.

He looked down at his journal, his storytelling. He drew a long breath. He dipped his pen and frowned.

I expect the old Comanches would call me easop. Liar or storyteller. Which? It means the same thing.

He knew what was ahead for him, for the boy. He paused for a moment, thinking about it.

He wrote the next words.

But it is good to know who you are, where you've been.

He paused again, then wrote slowly.

What you've done.

➮ The End ➭

EPILOGUE

THE LAST ENEMY is generally a work of fiction except for the known historical events such as the Elm Creek Raid and the Battle of the Washita River, also known as the Lodge Pole River. Both have been subject to disagreement among the experts, not surprising considering the statements of known participants who suffered losses during these events and the eye witnesses who observed and passed on stories that often became questionable facts.

We do know that George Armstrong Custer almost lost that significant battle because he failed to send scouts to report the strength of the enemy, winter camped down the river, numbering in the thousands, including visiting hostile tribes. The military reported that there were no captives seen among the tribes. Others swore they had been seen, hidden or killed.

And we know that little Millie Durgan, a young girl, was among the captives in the Elm Creek Raid, and was not recovered nor heard of in spite of Britt Johnson's recovery efforts, for which he eventually paid with his life.

The practice of taking captives after battles has existed from the beginning of human civilization, certainly long before the Europeans came to the Americas. Slavery was already here as the tribal people fought each other for dominance and spoils.

On a personal note, back in the day I remember standing in an ancient and very beautiful Spanish cathedral glittering with emeralds and precious metals while my host describes the joy of the native converts in New Spain as they struggled and dug and died for the jewels and the silver and gold displayed in that cathedral and in many others in Europe and elsewhere in New Spain.

In North America the tribes were generally not interested in gold and jewels, except as curiosities. But slavery was a useful and practical way to enrich tribal numbers after battles over hunting grounds, through increased birthrates with captive women and girls, to strengthen bloodlines against incest and through the training of young boys into their culture of heraldry and warfare. Of the rare captives who survived, many became devoted tribal members, a few who were recovered were never accepted back into the white man's world. Others were permanently damaged. There are no records of the huge numbers lost.

Little Millie Durgan, lost for decades after the Elm Creek Raid, appeared again in later life. She had been raised by a loving Kiowa family, married and had children. When she was an old woman her children urged her to go back to her white world and, reluctantly, she returned. She learned to speak a little English and finally died in a comfortable White Dog house.

Cynthia Ann Parker was taken captive as a young girl. She lived among the Comanches, married and had children. One son later became a famous Comanche chief who was ultimately scorned by his own people for adopting the white man's road. When Cynthia Ann Parker was forced back to the white world against her will, she struggled to return to her Comanche family, escaped and was later captured again and taken back to the white world. Eventually she starved herself and chose to die.

The settlers, surely with burning grief and anger, had to acknowledge and accept this sad reality of death, of enemy capture and slavery as the price of their own boldness and courage as they spread across the Comancheria and other tribal lands. Jack Rainie, who thought of himself as an ordinary man born into a world of ordinary chaos and hardship, never accepted this reality. He, and others like him, chose to prevail.

www.ingramcontent.com/pod-product-compliance
Lightning Source LLC
Chambersburg PA
CBHW030546180626
46816CB00005B/1420